Sword Art Online Alternative
GUN GALE ONLINE IX
4th Squad Jam: Finish

Keiichi Sigsawa

ILLUSTRATION BY
Kouhaku Kuroboshi

SUPERVISED BY
Reki Kawahara

NEW YORK

SWORD ART ONLINE Alternative Gun Gale Online, Vol. 9
KEIICHI SIGSAWA

Translation by Stephen Paul
Cover art by Kouhaku Kuroboshi

Edited by Dengeki Bunko
First published in Japan in 2018 by KADOKAWA CORPORATION, Tokyo.
English translation rights arranged with KADOKAWA CORPORATION, Tokyo, through TUTTLE-MORI AGENCY, INC., Tokyo.

Yen On
150 West 30th Street, 19th Floor
New York, NY 10001

Visit us at yenpress.com
facebook.com/yenpress
twitter.com/yenpress
yenpress.tumblr.com
instagram.com/yenpress

First Yen On Edition: June 2021

Library of Congress Cataloging-in-Publication Data
Names: Sigsawa, Keiichi, 1972– author. | Kuroboshi, Kouhaku, illustrator. | Kawahara, Reki, supervisor. | Paul, Stephen (Translator), translator.
Title: 4th Squad Jam: Finish / Keiichi Sigsawa ; illustration by Kouhaku Kuroboshi ; supervised by Reki Kawahara ; translation by Stephen Paul ; cover art by Kouhaku Kuroboshi.
Description: First Yen On edition. | New York : Yen On, 2018– | Series: Sword art online alternative gun gale online ; Volume 9
Identifiers: LCCN 2018009303 | ISBN 9781975327521 (v. 1 : pbk.) | ISBN 9781975353841 (v. 2 : pbk.) | ISBN 9781975353858 (v. 3 : pbk.) | ISBN 9781975353865 (v. 4 : pbk.) | ISBN 9781975353872 (v. 5 : pbk.) | ISBN 9781975353889 (v. 6 : pbk.) | ISBN 9781975315320 (v. 7 : pbk.) | ISBN 9781975315979 (v. 8 : pbk.) | ISBN 9781975315993 (v. 9 : pbk.)
Subjects: | CYAC: Fantasy games—Fiction. | Virtual reality—Fiction. | Role playing—Fiction. | BISAC: FICTION / Science Fiction / Adventure.
Classification: LCC PZ7.1.S537 Sq 2018 | DDC [Fic]—dc23
LC record available at https://lccn.loc.gov/2018009303

ISBNs: 978-1-9753-1599-3 (paperback)
978-1-9753-1600-6 (ebook)

10 9 8 7 6 5 4 3 2 1

LSC-C

Printed in the United States of America

THE 4th SQUAD JAM FIELD MAP

AREA 1 : Airport

AREA 2 : Town / Mall

AREA 3 : Swampland / River

AREA 4 : Forest

AREA 5 : Ruins

AREA 6 : Lake

AREA 7 : Craters

AREA 8 : Highway

Sword Art Online Alternative

GUN GALE ONLINE

Playback of SQUAD JAM

SYNOPSIS OF PARTS I AND II

SHINC started SJ4 atop the airport runway.

They fell victim to a monster-summoning trap, but managed to survive and found a set of wheels. To avoid a battle with dangerous rival team MMTM, they left their truck behind with a time bomb attached.

Sadly, MMTM was too clever to fall for the ploy, but it created an opportunity for SHINC to move south in search of a battle against LPFM.

That's when three members of SHINC got sniped, putting them in terrible danger. They were ultimately saved by the big alliance, led by Fire—the very man scheming to marry Llenn.

Fire invited the remaining members of SHINC to the frozen lake, where the alliance was situated. There, he offered SHINC the chance to take on Llenn's team, as long as they temporarily joined his coalition first.

With no apparent reason to decline, SHINC took him up on the offer. Naturally, Llenn was unaware of this development.

Shirley and Clarence escaped from LPFM. The two roaming members didn't show up on the scan. Thus they stealthily waited for their chance to take out Pitohui.

Unfortunately, it didn't go well for the two. Just when it seemed they had their shot, Pitohui slipped away on a vehicle, leaving Shirley and Clarence behind.

Llenn's team found some three-wheeled motorcycles called trikes and used them in a fight on the airport runways that covered the northeast quadrant of the map. Their opponents, MMTM, were on trikes of their own.

It was a high-speed group skirmish in wide-open surroundings. LPFM dealt some major blows to MMTM, but Pitohui also suffered a terrible injury. It was looking bad until Shirley stepped in with some skillful sniping, claiming that only *she* could be allowed to kill Pitohui. LPFM remained ignorant of that little bit, however.

From there, Llenn's squad headed toward the ruined city in the northwest. SHINC was awaiting them there, ready to do battle.

Llenn charged in, delighted at the opportunity. At long last, she'd finally have the duel to the death with her friends she wanted.

Unfortunately, Fire's alliance chose that moment to make their move.

In the face of an overwhelming assault, Llenn's and SHINC's fates remain uncertain…

CHAPTER 12
To Prevent Disaster

CHAPTER 12
To Prevent Disaster

"Run away, Pito! I think another enemy's coming up from the south!" Llenn warned. But there was no response.

She peered out from a side street sandwiched between two ruined buildings. Unfortunately, Pitohui's smoke grenade had left a thick haze over her surroundings, and she couldn't tell what was happening beyond the fog.

If the hit point gauges Llenn noticed out of the corner of her eye were any indication, however, Pitohui and M were on the ropes.

Llenn could hear a vibrating sound, endlessly repeating, like a buzzer. Pitohui had shown her a video once that depicted the source of this sound: an ultra-high-speed weapon called the M134 Minigun.

Pitohui was also on the video, begging the man who owned it, Behemoth, to sell it to her. "I'll pay you whatever you ask!" she insisted, but he brushed her off.

When Llenn saw how fast their hit points were dropping, she braced herself for the worst.

Is this…an insta-kill…?

Pitohui and M had undoubtedly taken some hits from the Minigun. Its rate of fire surpassed several dozen bullets per second; it was tearing them apart.

Next to Llenn, Tanya was talking to someone, probably Boss,

but Llenn couldn't hear her. Actually, she *could*; she just wasn't processing the conversation.

As her teammates' hit points continued to drop lower than even Fukaziroh's 20 percent, Llenn found herself unable to do anything but pray.

"Help…God of *Gun Gale*!"

Suddenly, she heard Pitohui say, "Armored Humvees! Forget us; go to the west!"

Pitohui's and M's hit points finally stopped dropping, but each had only a tenth of their life left.

"Boss! Llenn says enemies are coming!"

Boss heard Tanya's report while watching the Minigun on the Humvee destroy Pitohui and M. Then the turret atop the vehicle slowly rotated so the gun was pointing toward them. A bullet line extended right toward Boss's chest.

"Yeah…I know…"

The muzzle blazed to life.

Certain she was going to die, Boss gave her final message.

"If you survive, run for safety! Don't wait around for the rest of us!"

She wasn't sure she was going to get all of it out before she perished—but thankfully, she did.

Much to her surprise, she actually suffered no damage.

"Huh?"

There was a wall in front of her, a concrete one.

Sophie, the strongest member of the squad, had used every last ounce of her strength to lift a collapsed portion of a nearby building's wall, propping the slab up with her back.

The concrete was about six feet to a side and only two inches thick, but it had deflected the bullets upward because it was at an angle.

All the fury of that hail of lead bounced upward into the sky. After every few bullets, a tracer flashed. Little red lights repeatedly streaked off into the distance. It was a pretty sight, like fireworks.

"Boss! Inside!" urged Sophie. Boss leaped into a building on the right side of the street, carrying the PTRD-41.

She moved more nimbly than her large size would suggest, but the Minigun's shots chased after her like a streak of fire. She only just barely managed to make it out of the way. Both of her pigtails had been struck, shortening them a bit. The braids came loose, and her hair fell onto her back when she leaped into the building.

With her hair undone and draped over both sides of her face, Boss looked like the classic image of a fallen samurai warrior who'd lost his liege lord. Sophie let go of the concrete wall and lunged through next to her.

"You all right, Boss? Take the others and run!" Sophie said.

Boss confirmed that the other four hadn't lost any hit points yet. While she and Sophie had attracted the attention of the Minigun, the rest had fled into the buildings on the other side of the street.

"What will you do?" Boss asked Sophie, who was busy healing, though her hit points hadn't risen above 20 percent.

"I'll back you up as you retreat! I'm talking about the Humvee and Minigun! If you try to run without help, they'll wipe you out!"

Boss understood the implication in Sophie's words—she was going to sacrifice herself here to protect the rest of the squad.

Boss knew that she would do the same if she were in that situation—just like what had happened back at the airport.

So Boss didn't insult Sophie's honor by contradicting her. Instead, she gave the other girl three words: "Do your best."

When the smoke cleared, the battlefield was suddenly quiet.

The Humvee was still sitting smack in the middle of the street. The Minigun on the roof turret was circling around, hungry for a new target, but no such prey appeared.

"Well?" asked an armored man in a mask and sunglasses

from the driver's seat as he peered through the bulletproof windshield.

His teammate standing in the turret space behind him, dressed in the same uniform, glared down the street and answered, "I can't find them. I'm sure I hit the two from LPFM, but they got blasted into the building, and I can't get a visual anymore."

"You shot the hell out of them. They can't still be alive," remarked the driver.

Moments ago, after Pitohui and M fell out of sight, the one manning the Minigun had continued to pepper the building with bullets. The first floor of the dilapidated structure was riddled with holes. Surely, anything inside had been torn to ribbons.

"I'd agree, but I don't see any death tags. Those two are real tough; we can't make assumptions. Most likely, SHINC got away without much injury, too. I'll keep an eye out; you handle the reporting," said the vigilant turret gunner, his thumb on the trigger. If anyone jumped out into the open, he would unload on them instantly from the safety of his bulletproof shielding.

Despite the overwhelming advantage he possessed, he refused to get cocky or lazy. The driver put the Humvee in reverse to ensure that he could immediately back away if someone attacked.

"This is Car Two," called the driver to his distant teammates. "LPFM's grenadier spotted us, and we engaged. We'll wipe them and SHINC out, as discussed. Requesting backup in this area."

"What does this mean?" Llenn asked Tanya, who was running alongside her to the left.

It was a broad and simple question, but Tanya knew what she meant. They were supposed to be enjoying their duel, so why had other squads interrupted? Who were they? How had things gotten to this point?

In short, Llenn wanted to know what SHINC had been up to in SJ4.

Just as Boss and Pitohui had instructed, the two were running off to safety on their own. They were the fastest players on their respective teams, and they covered lots of ground.

No matter what they did, they didn't stand a chance against the monstrous armored Humvee with a Minigun. Even approaching it seemed ill-advised. What's more, they had no idea if the enemy had reinforcements lurking behind it.

Given that situation, Llenn and Tanya's best bet was to escape to somewhere they couldn't be picked off. At worst, if the rest of their teams died, the two of them would still be safe.

"We joined their alliance because we were about to get killed by a different team! They showed up and saved us. We were in the middle of their formation on the frozen lake, where a weird tall guy in a tracksuit promised to help us get our duel with you. That's why Boss agreed to go along with it all."

Stupid Fire, Llenn thought, gritting her teeth.

"So I can assume the Humvee is part of the alliance?"

"Yup. I mean, they drove us here like a taxi service. We had no idea they had a Minigun, though! A hidden, secret weapon! Very clever!"

"If they'd stayed put and let us wear ourselves down, they could have swooped in and wiped both our squads out."

"Pretty much."

"Why did they start attacking us before then?"

"No idea! But they broke their promise! I'm gonna tell the teacher on them!"

Okay, so…that was definitely my fault…, thought Fukaziroh.

She was creeping down the staircase as silently as she could to avoid drawing attention to herself. She could hear Llenn's voice through the comm, but she wasn't going to say anything herself.

She'd been busy bombarding the enemy with grenades when she just so happened to spot the Humvee. On a lark, she thought about attacking it from the roof of her ten-story perch, just for something fun to do.

Unfortunately, they'd spotted her before she could. Fire's henchmen sure were canny!

Fukaziroh's grenade attack had tipped them off; they'd spotted the bullet line before she fired. So they shot her first, sending a lead present right into her chest.

The attack hit the weak seam in the protective plate armor covering Fukaziroh's chest and back, tearing a diagonal hole through her. It was a very long-distance sniper shot, one that could have only been accomplished with excellent aim.

By some stroke of luck, it missed Fukaziroh's heart, and she only lost half of her hit points. Fukaziroh was very hardy thanks to all her time playing *ALO*. Llenn probably would have died twice over from the same shot.

However, Fukaziroh had quickly discovered she wasn't out of the woods yet. Something had flown toward her from a distance and exploded on the roof.

The explosion had tossed Fukaziroh's body across the roof to slam down next to the staircase that had taken her up there in the first place. Shrapnel had bitten into her body, dealing more damage. Barely 20 percent of her health remained.

If only that was the worst of it.

Fukaziroh was missing her MGL-140s. After the shock of the blast, Rightony and Leftania had left Fukaziroh behind and gone on a journey. They'd flown off the top of the building and landed on some lower floor.

Their weapon icons were still visible in the lower right corner of Fukaziroh's vision, so they hadn't been destroyed, but they were likely buried in the rubble below. Fukaziroh didn't know if she'd have time to go down and search, or if she'd even find them if she tried.

As she descended the steps, she thought, *If I hadn't tried to attack the Humvee at that moment...maybe LPFM vs. SHINC would still be on, and win or lose, at least Llenn could have gotten her fight. This is my fault.*

Thus Fukaziroh decided to play dumb for all she was worth and told Llenn, "Geez, so not only do they collude, but they also like to betray people?! What do they think this is, SJ3? What a bunch of jerks! Cutting ties with them was the right idea!"

"Fuka! You okay?"

Llenn hadn't heard Fukaziroh's voice in quite a while. She leaped up onto the side of the rubble and stopped there. Tanya followed her lead.

They'd moved a few hundred yards to the west of the street where they'd fought earlier. The road was littered with chunks of concrete, which would keep the Humvee away.

However, there was always the danger of a sniper, so they kept low.

"I'm alive. This isn't some zombie game. You can see my HP. Time for my injection," came Fukaziroh's reply. The force her voice usually carried was noticeably absent; she was trying to keep quiet.

Llenn glanced to the top left and saw Fukaziroh's hit points slowly increasing from 20 percent. Two med kits would get her back to eight-tenths of her life, but the process would take six minutes.

Below Fukaziroh's HP bar, Pitohui and M hadn't budged from 10 percent.

For whatever reason, they weren't using their emergency med kits. They also weren't moving or contacting anyone over the comms.

Llenn prayed for their safety but kept her focus on Fukaziroh.

"You aren't pinned down beneath anything or trapped by the enemy, right?"

"No, I'm fine. I got hit on the rooftop where I was earlier, but it's not worse than a cat scratch."

"How so?! Wait, what are you doing?"

"I'm slowly making my way down the stairs. I don't know where the enemy might be hiding. If I just pop out, I could get shot. It's not SHINC that's doing it, right?"

"They're Fire's buddies! I don't know what they've got aside from the Minigun! Or how many there are!"

"What's a Minigun? Is it cute and mini?"

"It's horrifying! It has a super-high rate of fire, so if they catch you with it, they'll turn you to dust in an instant!"

"Dust… Hey, Llenn, do you know about dust explosions?"

"Is this really the time for that?"

"Just wondering if I could explode after I get turned to dust."

"No."

"Oh, I'm almost on the first floor. Talk to you later. Who were you chatting with earlier, your imaginary friend? Or was it Tanya?"

"The latter."

"Then you two get along and scamper off. That's what Pito said earlier. Survive. Or in Spanish, *sobrevivir.*"

"But…"

"I'll be fine. I'll hide as much as I can and skitter around like a cockroach. From this point on, we're each responsible for our own safety. If we're lucky, we'll be able to regroup! I'm gonna switch off my comm so I can listen for the enemy."

With that, Llenn's communication with Fukaziroh came to an abrupt end.

"……"

Llenn was left speechless. Next to her, Tanya exclaimed, "Ah!"

She turned at the sound and saw the silver-haired woman looking ready to cry.

"Sophie's dead."

* * *

"Do your best."

A few minutes earlier, Boss was giving Sophie her final message while considering how best to survive while preserving as much of the team's strength as possible.

The five aside from Tanya were on either side of the major street, hiding in buildings.

Boss and Sophie were on the right side. Anna, Rosa, and Tohma were on the left.

Boss could hear Tanya speaking, but it was clear that she was in conversation with Llenn. They were probably far away by now. She'd be okay for the time being.

Boss switched off her communication with Tanya for the moment. Then she addressed the rest of her squad.

"We're going to survive this, one way or another! Then we're all going to bury our boots deep in Fire's ass!"

The words came effortlessly, but they weren't the type of thing one should go around spouting.

"Yeah!"

"Got it!"

"*Khorosho!*" roared Anna and the rest. Boss's trusty companions put a smile on her face. It looked very creepy.

Despite their enthusiasm, Boss couldn't think of a way to break free from this predicament without substantial casualties. There was no exit on the backside of the five-story building and no connection to the adjacent structures. She could use a plasma grenade to bust open the wall, but that would probably make the building collapse onto their heads.

They'd have to go back out into the street. And that would mean exposing themselves to the assault of the Humvee's Minigun.

If Sophie played the decoy, it might create an opening for the remaining members to escape.

No, Boss decided. That wasn't going to happen.

It was about thirty meters from their hiding place to the intersection where they could find safe cover again. Fortunately, there were no obstacles in the street, so once they were out in the open, they'd need only a few seconds until they could round the corner to safety.

However, those few seconds would be a significant challenge.

Regular guns were one thing. But there was no way to escape the Minigun.

It was the kind of weapon that could literally kill a person in an instant. In five seconds, it could flood the street with bullets. None of them would escape its wrath. They would all die.

So what was the plan, then? A direct attack on the Humvee, over three hundred meters away? It would require sneaking from building to building until they could hurl grenades.

That seemed even less likely to succeed. Boss and her squad would be picked off before they got close to the Humvee, and even if everything else somehow actually worked out, the driver had the option of simply backing the vehicle away.

Boss was thinking so hard for an answer to their predicament that she didn't even notice that Sophie had circled her and started rebraiding her hair. It was something that Kana often did for Saki in real life.

"There, that's better."

"Huh? Oh, Kana—I mean, Sophie, thank you."

"Let's do this! Make sure you don't trip, everyone!"

"Wait, do you have a plan?" Boss asked her.

"What Llenn's team just did, remember?" Sophie grinned as she extended a hand to Boss.

"Timing is crucial! No mistakes. Everyone, stow your weapons in your inventory for now. I'll carry the Degtyaryov!" Boss ordered her teammates.

She put away her silenced Vintorez sniper rifle and her backpack, then cradled the antitank rifle like a laundry drying rod. It was very heavy, so holding it gave her an encumbrance penalty, meaning that her usual agility was no longer at her disposal.

But there was no other option. The Degtyaryov was going to be crucial against the armored Humvee, and it could come in handy further down the line, too.

"Is everyone ready?" Sophie asked. "I'll match your timing. Don't worry; this isn't as nerve-racking as a competition meet!"

Sophie had a thin length of rope clutched in her hand. It was made of a tough nylon material called paracord. Tied to the end of it was a round object resembling a watermelon.

Sophie stood right next to the broken window and shouted, "Here goes! Yah!"

She spun the end of the rope clockwise and hurled it into the street like a shot put.

"Four! Three! Two! One!"

Zero! Boss and the other three leaped out.

Suddenly, the large plasma grenade attached to the end of the rope exploded. It was a present from Boss.

A hemisphere sixty-five feet across exploded outward with azure brilliance in the middle of the street.

"Shit! They got us!"

The Minigun shooter did not fire.

The burst that covered the width of the street either destroyed or deflected all bullets that tried to pass through it. SHINC was almost certainly running for safety behind that blast.

"Very clever!" praised the driver. "But..."

All he had to do was wait three seconds.

The gunner let the delayed sound of the blast and the accompanying rush of air pass over him. His hands tightened around the handles of the Minigun. His thumb hovered near the red firing trigger as he waited.

The surging explosion of the plasma grenade ended after about three seconds. If he fired at just the right time and swept across the width of the street, he should still be able to catch SHINC as they hurried along it.

One more second.

The gunner's thumb slipped over the trigger and squeezed down hard.

Right as the blue hemisphere faded away, another took its place.

It was the same type of burst, one that was only possible with a grand grenade. And this one was closer to the Humvee.

Again the thundering sound and rush of air washed over the Humvee.

Then came yet another.

This one was even nearer, about seventy meters from the Humvee.

"Someone's coming closer to us!" called the gunner, who had figured out the enemy's tactic. They weren't using the grand grenades as a shield to escape but were throwing each successive one closer so that they could approach.

"Got it! I'm amazed they can throw grand grenades that far, though!"

The actual perceived weight depended on the player's Strength stat, but still, they were weighty objects. The driver was skeptical, but the gunner was actually watching it happen.

An object—the grand grenade—soared over the thirty-foot-tall explosion of its predecessor. A six-foot rope was tied to it.

"Ahhh, it's got a cord tied to it to add more centrifugal force."

"Ohhh, I see!"

Though the blasts and dust concealed it, the men in the Humvee could guess at what was happening out of sight.

The moment one explosive was tossed, a SHINC member hit the MATERIALIZE button in an already-opened game window, producing another grand grenade tied to a rope. If you grabbed that, hit the activation switch, and spun it exactly one time via the cord before releasing, even one of those heavy objects would travel a fair distance. In other words, if a shot put throw was too difficult, you could use a hammer throw instead.

The men in the Humvee were left guessing who had come up with such an idea.

They thought that SHINC's players had to be skilled at tossing things in real life. But neither of them had any clue as to how they'd gotten their practice. With plates, when they got into shouting matches with their husbands, maybe?

The fourth blast was 160 meters away.

The gust of explosive force rattled the heavy Humvee's frame.

"Damn that replenishment—I still can't believe they're actually tossing those things out there," the driver muttered.

"But it's also what's enabled us to go ham on shooting. It's a wonderful rule."

"Agreed."

The Minigun's greatest strength—its incredible rate of fire—was also its weakness. It chewed through ammunition in the blink of an eye. A gun like that would not find nearly as much use in this situation without a helpful custom rule automatically restoring all ammo at regular intervals.

The fifth bomb landed 130 meters away. Each new burst instantly blasted clear the dust of the previous one but created a fresh cloud of its own, so there was no increase in visibility.

"They're close. And getting nearer. Should we back up?"

"No. Pulling away or approaching, it makes no difference. Plus, it would be rude to them not to engage here. Let's give it a try."

"Give what a try?"

"You'll see."

The fifth explosion began to fade, and the sixth grand grenade plummeted toward the ground—and it was within the gunner's line of sight.

"Yaaah!"

Vrrrt! The short bark of the Minigun was the sound of a swarm of 7.62 mm bullets that caught their grenade target.

The downside of plasma grenades in *GGO* was that they were easy to set off if shot. The large ball-like thing exploded in mid-air, forming a perfect sphere over the middle of the road.

It was a pale-blue orb, like a bright planet shining on the city street.

"It's beautiful," murmured the driver.

The shape's apex was quite high in the air, while its bottom-most point nearly made contact with the ground.

"Now they can't throw the next one over," the gunner explained, aiming lower. Once the light was gone, he'd sweep the street clean, like using a broom made of hot lead.

However, once the azure explosion began to wane—

"What?!"

The man at the turret couldn't believe his eyes. A woman came charging through *before* the blue light had vanished.

She was short and wide, as stocky as a fantasy dwarf. The gunner had overheard Boss call her Sophie.

"Nice aiming! Well done!"

Sophie had known that one of her lobs was bound to get hit.

The closer she got, the surer it was that the Minigun would hit the grand grenade and blow it up before it hit the ground.

That meant that when it did, she had to be ready to slip around it instead.

The pushback from the blast wouldn't make that easy, but it was her only chance to close in on the Humvee.

With shock waves buffeting her body, Sophie raced between a building and the blue sphere until she saw the armored Humvee.

It had been far off before, but now it was just a hundred meters away.

At this very moment, Sophie had the option of running into the building to hide. If she fled into the five-story building, the Humvee couldn't follow her, she'd be safe from grenades from above, and it would give her an avenue of escape.

However, that would also enable the Humvee to proceed down the street and attack her teammates from behind. She had to keep it where it was.

Once Sophie was thirty meters closer, she began to twirl around her last rope-tethered grenade.

"Take this!"

She hurled it with all the finesse she'd honed in real-world gymnastics and all the strength of her in-game avatar.

The gunner and the driver watched it happen but remained dubious.

"No way."

"She can't."

They didn't believe Sophie could hurl that heavy grand grenade the remaining seventy meters. They expected it to fall short and form another blue wall of an explosion.

"Don't move! I'll finish her!" ordered the gunner.

"Got it!" answered the driver.

All the man in the turret had to do was shoot Sophie before the grand grenade exploded between them.

His aim was true, and dozens of bullets hurtled at Sophie, instantly shattering her body into polygonal pieces. She burst as surely as if a bomb had hit her.

Sophie from SHINC was out of SJ4.

"Yes!" the driver exclaimed.

"Shit!" the gunner spat at the same time.

The grenade Sophie had given her life to toss made it those critical seventy meters that separated her from the Humvee. However, it didn't make it through the roof and inside the vehicle.

Instead, it landed just a few centimeters in front of the Humvee and exploded there.

The man at the Minigun saw that it wasn't a grand grenade this time, nor even a regular plasma grenade. It was an M67, a standard American issue.

In other words, it was just a plain old shrapnel explosive you could find in the real world, no bigger than a baseball. Hurling one of those seventy feet was far easier than throwing a watermelon-sized explosive.

It was set to explode five seconds after the pin was pulled, and it let loose in front of the vehicle. The Humvee was heavily armored, so an antipersonnel shrapnel grenade wasn't nearly enough to destroy it. The payload didn't pierce the body or glass; it only shook the chassis a bit.

However, the tires were a different story. They popped immediately.

Sophie could have aimed for the open top of the Humvee, but

that would have been much harder. Flattening the tires was a much easier task.

"She got us… Damn, what a woman," the gunner said, grinning behind his mask as he realized how perfectly Sophie had outwitted them.

"She was always after the tires! Damn, nice one!" remarked the driver as he checked his side mirrors and put the Humvee in reverse with its two flats.

The Humvee was a military vehicle, so it came equipped with special run-flat tires with an internal structure that enabled them to stay more intact than regular tires when running without air.

Even so, driving the thing was difficult. The Humvee wouldn't be able to keep charging ahead for long.

The driver chuckled as he gripped the shaking steering wheel. "Ha-ha-ha! That's a pretty smart opponent. I gotta say, this Squad Jam is really fun."

The gunner chimed in, "Yeah, they're good. We'll probably get scolded if we try to have all the fun for ourselves."

* * *

"Sophie's dead," Tanya said.

A moment later, Llenn heard Pitohui's voice in her ear. "Llenn, are you okay?"

She wasn't sure at first whom to respond to but decided to prioritize her teammate.

"I'm fine! What about you, Pito? What's happening?"

"I'm super-good. Ahhh, I can finally move again!"

"But you're almost dead!"

"Just took an emergency med kit."

Llenn noticed that Pitohui's and M's HP gauges were slowly refilling.

They were both at just around 10 percent. Pitohui had two med kits, so she'd be back at 70 percent in about six minutes.

M had all three of his items still, so he could get back to full health in nine minutes—assuming he didn't get shot.

"Is M there with you?"

"Yep. You alone?" Pitohui asked.

"I'm with Tanya!" Llenn admitted.

"Okay. You play nice now. Watch the scan and report in. We'll talk after."

Was it that time already? Llenn hastily pulled her Satellite Scanner out of her chest pocket. At her side, Tanya was already staring at her own screen.

Llenn checked and saw that it was already 1:40.

Only ten minutes had passed since she'd spotted SHINC and charged in after them. She'd been running and fighting virtually every second since then. It was almost too much.

The tenth Satellite Scan was already in progress. She hadn't noticed her wristwatch buzzing thirty seconds beforehand because she had been busy talking to Fukaziroh.

The scan had started from the south and was already about halfway up the map.

The leaders of the six allied teams were all still gathered on the lake. Their respective members were doubtlessly on the way over. They had cars, so Llenn couldn't forget that they'd be arriving much sooner than anyone on foot would.

MMTM was at the airport with only two members left.

ZEMAL hadn't budged from their spot in the crater area. Were they asleep now?

As the scan moved north, it showed Llenn's own location. That meant the enemy knew where to find her, but it also indicated to Llenn herself where she actually was.

She'd been running all over the ruined city, which was in the northwest part of the map. By shogi board rules, going west and then south from the northeast corner, it was Sector 7-1. SHINC's dot, belonging to Boss, was one square over, in 6-1. That was where Llenn had been fighting SHINC earlier.

Llenn looked around for more enemies and quickly found them.

The sci-fi soldier team, T-S, was on the western end of the ruined city, in Sector 10-2.

Seeing that Tanya was talking to Boss, Llenn told the part about T-S to Pitohui as the scan concluded. It sounded like Pitohui was running somewhere.

"What should I do?" Llenn asked.

"Stay there for now. They know your location, remember, so keep your eyes peeled for enemies. If you catch even a glimpse of them—"

"I know. Run full speed west."

"Exactly. We'll head there from the north. Of course, we're pretty beat up, so if we trip and fall and die as a result—sorry."

"Don't say that! Honestly, I'm amazed you're alive after the Minigun got you…"

"Yeah, I thought we were dead, too! But as it happens, luck was on our side."

"What'd you do?"

"It was M. He covered me up."

"Oh, with the shield plates on his back…," Llenn said, figuring it out instantly.

Even one of those plates would completely stop a 7.62 mm bullet. M must have used his considerable size to protect Pitohui.

But even if the plates stopped the bullet, the force of the impact would remain.

"You took damage from being pushed down?"

"Yep. That turret is scary. It can hit a single spot when it's spitting dozens of bullets per second. It smashed M and me against a concrete wall. In real life, we would have broken all our ribs."

"Yikes…"

Thank goodness this is just a game, Llenn thought. It was a sentiment she'd had about *GGO* many times over now.

She wondered if the person whose crotch she'd sliced vertically in SJ2 was still playing *GGO*.

"The Humvee was still right in front of us the whole time, so we couldn't leave the building until that short, squat girl from

SHINC did her thing. Once she popped the front tires, the Humvee backed away."

"Ahhh…"

Llenn didn't know the details, but she guessed that was how Sophie had died.

She'd have to thank her later. Or maybe feed her some snacks.

While Llenn was talking with Pitohui, Tanya was in communication with Boss, getting a report on the situation.

Thanks to Sophie's sacrifice, the other four were unhurt and running their way.

"Let's regroup!"

Boss replied, "Of course. We've got to get back at them for this— *Gfk!*"

"Boss?"

Tanya could see on the gauges that Boss's hit points had immediately gone down 30 percent. She was at 70.

"Sniper! On the left!"

Boss toppled over in the intersection.

It was the second major junction from the point where she'd escaped. There was no way across it without exposing herself to a potential enemy to the south.

Faced with no alternative, though, Boss had risked it to escape to the west.

Tohma, Anna, and Rosa had safely slipped through the hundred-foot danger zone already, but since Boss was carrying the heavy PTRD-41, her running speed was slow, and a bullet had caught her through the left thigh.

"Rrgh!"

Boss lost her balance. Her left leg could no longer support her weight, and she couldn't stop herself from falling.

However, if she fell onto her stomach, the sniper's next shot was sure to hit her.

"Daaa!"

Clutching the lengthy PTRD-41, Boss spun her body, using just the strength of her right leg. With the spear-like gun as an axle, she rolled over and over, evading two bullets that whizzed past.

Boss's movement seemed too swift for a body as large as hers. Such a maneuver wouldn't come naturally unless you had plenty of acrobatic experience.

"Sniper to the south! Boss is hit!"

Anna promptly threw a smoke grenade around the corner, creating a screen of gray between Boss and the sniper, who had to be somewhere to the south.

"Where are they?" wondered Rosa, who had her PKM machine gun at the ready behind Anna. She wanted to spray some covering fire through the smoke, even if there was little chance of hitting the enemy.

Anna could only answer, "I don't know!"

There had been no gunshot when Boss had been hit or on the following two misses. Anna hadn't spied a muzzle flash, either.

So the sniper was using a suppressor. It was merely a metal tube with a small chamber inside, and it was fairly easy to craft if you had the item blueprints and the technical skill. Nonetheless, a suppressor was a terror in the field, where it could make your location impossible to trace.

All SHINC's members could tell based on the short firing interval was that the gun was automatic and that the shooter was part of Fire's allied team—as well as one other fact.

"They're really coming after us now!"

"I bet!" Tohma agreed, pulling Boss, whose leg had gone numb, and forcing her to crawl out of the intersection.

Somehow, Boss managed to get there, but she'd had to drop the thirty-five-pound PTRD-41. While the smoke hid it for now, it was currently resting in the middle of the intersection.

Boss scowled and said, "I won't be able to run for a while. You guys go ahead!"

"But—!" protested Tohma.

"If you don't hurry, another sniper will take up a position at the next intersection!"

"Ugh!" Tohma couldn't argue with that logic.

Now that SHINC knew they were outnumbered, it was clear that they'd quickly be cornered unless they withdrew and regrouped.

"I'll catch up! Prioritize meeting up with Tanya!"

"Got it! Good luck!"

Anna, Rosa, and Tohma left Boss behind and ran off. As they went, she called, "You heard that, Tanya? You guys can still manage. Take point, like always. Flee to the west, bit by bit, making sure it's safe first."

"G-got it! But what about you, Boss?"

"When I can walk normally again, I'll try to recover the Degtyaryov."

"That's crazy!"

"Maybe."

Amid the heavy smoke, Boss massaged her thigh, trying to regain feeling.

If she jumped out into the intersection now, the enemy couldn't snipe her. And the shooter wasn't foolish enough to waste shots that wouldn't land. But Boss couldn't see the PTRD-41, either.

To give up on that gun or not?

Boss's leg was still numb, so she waited for the smoke to clear.

If she could see, and she thought there was a chance she might be able to retrieve it, she'd take the risk. If it really looked like there was no way, she'd give up.

She wasn't desperate enough to die for the gun, but she didn't want to leave it behind, either.

Before Boss could arrive at an answer, however, a gust of wind sent the smoke whipping away, exposing the scene.

"What are you doing here?!" Boss exclaimed despite herself.

Standing in the middle of the intersection was a large figure dressed in green camo.

M was aiming the PTRD-41.

CHAPTER 13
Retreat I

CHAPTER 13
Retreat I

Boss was looking at a large man in green fatigues carrying a backpack and M14 EBR on his back.

And he was lying on the ground, aiming her own team's gun, the PTRD-41.

The long barrel was extending from a fan-shaped shield constructed of three panels on each side.

"Why are you here?"

Without looking in her direction, M replied, "I'm borrowing this."

The next instant, a bullet struck his shield and bounced away.

The shot took a nasty angle right toward Boss, and she had to hit the ground flat. "Hya!"

However, that had given M what he wanted. "Over there, huh?"

The PTRD-41 roared.

A tremendous amount of propulsive gas burst from the front end of the muzzle and the brakes to the sides, along with a sound that resembled the detonation of a bomb. The force kicked up a cloud of dust around M.

A massive bullet, 14.5 mm in diameter, weighing two ounces, rocketed off at the stunning speed of Mach 3.

M was now using the very gun that SHINC had acquired to destroy his shield—from behind that shield, no less.

"……"

Boss could only watch, her cheek pressed against the ground.

"Tsk! That shield is cheating, man!" snapped a player dressed in bright-green camo with a mask and sunglasses. He pulled back from the window.

He was inside a building about four hundred meters away from M and Boss's location. He'd been sniping with his sound-suppressed M110A1, but now he scooped up the rifle and rolled to his left. That was the quickest way of moving since he aimed right-handed.

It was a quick and assured maneuver. In an instant, he was hiding behind a thick layer of concrete.

The bullet came rocketing toward him and gouged a huge hole in the building, chipping loose a chunk of it that struck the man directly on the head.

"Gah!"

The impact instantly caused him to lose 40 percent of his health. If he'd been a split second later in his dodge, the bullet would have broken through the wall and still had enough power to split his skull.

His outfit and mask were covered in dust now. "Tsk! That gun is cheating, too! Yeesh!"

Picking up his weapon, he bolted out of the room. As he ran down the hall, he stuck an emergency med kit against his skin and muttered, "He knew I was going to grab the rifle and pivot to the left… What a brilliant player. Gotta watch out for him."

Then he turned his attention to his comms and addressed his similarly dressed teammates. "I couldn't get the kill shot. Let's all meet up. You too, Leader. These guys aren't going to be as easy to beat as I thought. Tell the Humvee guys, too. We need to set up a perimeter and close in on them! This is getting fun!"

The booming sound echoed off the tall buildings. Once the dust had finally settled, M peered through his scope and muttered, "Looks like I let him get away."

There was a large hole in the concrete wall, but if the player behind it were dead, there would be a faintly visible DEAD tag floating in the air.

"Nyah-nyah, you suck!" taunted Pitohui.

Boss sat up and saw a woman dressed in black pressed against the corner on the other side of the intersection, holding a KTR-09 with a drum magazine in one hand and two sections of a shield in the other.

It was the very player Boss had been in a shoot-out with just minutes earlier.

Boss tinkered with her inventory and brought out the backpack and Vintorez, then said, "If you bring that gun over here, I promise not to turn it on you."

"You only want me to bring it to you?" M asked considerately. "If we carry it together, we can run at full speed."

"I can work with that, I guess!" replied Boss with a grin. It was more than she could have requested.

"Hey, you two, why don't you just get married already?" taunted Pitohui, like a kid in the schoolyard.

Boss did not hesitate to use her final emergency med kit. Her health would be back to full in another three minutes.

Pitohui crossed the intersection, using the shield to protect herself, and guarded M's position in the middle while he folded up his portable barrier sections.

During the smoke screen, M must have spread them out and scooped up the PTRD-41, then set it down and aimed it, all going by nothing but intuition.

Boss had been entirely unaware of their approach. They could have shot her dead without her ever knowing they were there.

That was lucky...

Now that she'd acknowledged her own mistake, Boss kept her Vintorez scope to her eye, watching the south until Pitohui and M made it over to her.

"Ya-ha! Things are getting pretty crazy!"

"No kidding!"

Pitohui, Boss, and M took off running to the west.

They split the weight of the PTRD-41 by having Boss carry the barrel end and M the stock. This way, they could at least move at M's maximum running speed.

Pitohui took up the rear position, lugging the shield in her left hand and running backward so she could watch for any enemies that might be in hot pursuit.

Through her comm, Boss told the rest of the team, "I'm with Pitohui and M. We're stuck in the same boat. Meet up with Tanya, then tell me your location."

The others chimed in, delighted to know that she was safe.

As they ran, Pitohui asked, "Is the leader of the allied team a tall, skinny guy named Fire?"

"You know him?" Boss wasn't particularly surprised. She figured that he was probably a reasonably well-known player. And he had a very distinctive look.

"So I was right. And who's in those six teams?"

There was zero chance of SHINC going back to that alliance, so Boss decided to spill the beans.

"There's Fire's team; they all wear tracksuits. There's one squad in bright-green camo; I've never seen them before. A third is equipped with tough-looking chest protectors. All three of those groups have masks and sunglasses. Of the remaining teams, one is RGB, the optical gun team. The other two are newcomers I don't know, unfortunately. Based on how things were at the lake, the latter three were likely recruited after the Squad Jam started."

"Mm-hmm. Who's driving the Humvee?"

"The team with the chest protectors."

"Uh-huh. Including the guy with the Minigun. That's a pain in the ass," remarked Pitohui.

Boss recalled how the two had looked earlier and decided to speak her mind to them. "I can't believe you took turret fire at that distance and survived… I thought it was instant death."

"Oh, I cut 'em all down with my lightsword."

"Well, that's incredible," said Boss flatly, not bothering to retort with a joke of her own. "Sophie died on our side to allow us to escape."

"And that helped us survive. When you talk to her later, make sure she knows we're grateful."

"Got it. Man, that combination of Minigun and Humvee really *was* a pain in the ass. And with a sharpshooting sniper, too. Plus, they outnumber us..."

They ran for their lives, knowing they might get shot at any moment.

"That's true. They're probably setting up a perimeter around us now. They'd only need half of their six teams to do it."

"What's your plan?"

"You feel like running with us?"

Boss thought about it for two seconds. "I can't see any other way. Once we've taken Fire out of the picture and we're the only two teams left, then we can finish this."

"Sounds good to me."

Eventually, Boss got the excited signal from the rest of her squadmates, who'd met up with Llenn.

"We see you! Over here!"

* * *

The entire stretch of action from the moment LPFM challenged SHINC until M stopped firing had been tremendous content for the audience in the pub. They cheered, screamed, jeered, and otherwise watched with great interest.

The direct combat was over for now, so the on-screen feed switched to a hazy aerial angle that could capture entire squads at once.

One of the big screens featured Fire's team sitting on the frozen lake. There wasn't a single member of the unusual camo or chest protector squads, making it clear that they had all shipped off to the ruined city, leaders included.

RGB continued plugging away at the never-ending swarm of monsters with their optical guns. They were shining in the spotlight.

The other large monitor displayed the ruins in the northwest sector.

Though it was hard to tell because of the rubble of all sizes littering the streets, LPFM and SHINC were bunched up together. A little pink blur stood out against the world of gray.

Thus began another famous Squad Jam bar round of predictions. They were like drunken dads at a baseball stadium yelling whatever came to mind for anyone to hear.

"Both the Amazons and Llenn's squad have taken a lot of damage. I don't think they can win."

"The allied team this time is just plain tough… Is that it? The favorite's just gonna win, no surprises?"

"Nah, that just tells you how crappy the previous united squads were. Of course, if I were in charge, they'd be doing even better by now!"

"Those masked guys are terrific, even on an individual level. And their hardware is impressive."

"Anyone can win if they get a Humvee with a Minigun on it!"

"Are you sure about that? Their front tires are flat."

"They've got spare tires in the back, right? Or they could switch them out with one of the other Humvees."

"Oh yeah, I guess that's true."

"Technicals reign supreme in urban combat. You can bet on it. The pink pip-squeak and her friends don't stand a chance."

The crowd's opinions were varied, but they all seemed to agree that the scales were heavily tilted.

Incidentally, a "technical" was a lighter vehicle equipped with weaponry, even something as simple as an unarmored pickup truck with a heavy machine gun in the bed. The mobility from the engine's power alone was a huge advantage. With armor that could deflect anything short of antitank rounds, plus the Minigun on top, the Humvee was nearly unstoppable.

"They're cheating! Cheat, cheater, cheatest!"

"You just want to accuse someone of cheating…"

"Yeah! I like saying that word."

"What's that supposed to mean? And *cheatest* isn't a word…"

A man who'd been watching since SJ1 said exhaustedly, "There are three Humvees in total, right? They can use those to chase their opponents around the city and pick off the rest with snipers. There's no escape from the northwest sector of the map. They're trapped. My poor Llenn—she's done for…"

A man with a shaved head clapped the dejected one on the shoulder. "I agree with you, man."

"You finally admit that she's *my* Llenn?"

"Not that part!"

* * *

It was 1:48.

Llenn's group was hiding in a corner of the ruined city.

They had changed positions once, to avoid spawning monsters that would appear if you were camped at a spot for five minutes, and were discussing their tactics in the meantime.

Those present were the remaining five members of SHINC after Sophie's death, Llenn, Pitohui, and M.

Fukaziroh had been unaccounted for since she switched off her comm. That was concerning, but her hit points were recovering without incident, so they knew she was still alive.

Hey, it's Fuka. She'll manage on her own.

Llenn wasn't worried at all.

Shirley and Clarence's situation was similar. They'd remained unharmed throughout; their hit points hadn't once dropped, wherever they were now.

Llenn's group was currently at a major intersection. It had two lanes going in each direction, so it was quite spacious, a good 150 feet to each side. There was plenty of sturdy protective cover, too, between building walls and toppled trucks.

There was also a tall structure that had fallen entirely onto its side. How it had wound up like that while still intact was a mystery best ignored. The important thing was that it was a big help to them.

The sides of the building formed a sixty-foot wall that protected them from the south and east. So only the west- and northbound roads of the intersection were open to movement and visibility.

This meant that Llenn and the others didn't have to worry about snipers from the east or south. That made it a good defensive position to take.

The group stayed low and kept their gazes on the perimeter. If any enemies approached, they would withdraw at full speed to the west, of course. Anna and Tohma kept their eyes to their Dragunov scopes, and Rosa had her PKM machine gun at the ready for support, too.

M set down the PTRD-41 so he could hold his M14 EBR while he kept to Tohma's side. The shield was all folded up in his backpack now. There was a large hole in the center of the thing through which you could see the plates.

Clouds covered the sky over the city, and the wind passed through the buildings, gusting and softening here and there.

"And that's the situation. We got chased out by Fire's allied group," Boss explained.

"Damn that man!" swore Llenn without thinking.

Nearby, Pitohui shouted, "Aw, crap!"

"Hmm?" asked Llenn, confused.

"You know him, too? What is this Fire guy's deal?" Boss pressed.

She figured that if both Pitohui and Llenn knew about him, he must be a pretty famous player, so she only asked in order to learn more about her opponent.

But Llenn got flustered and stammered, "Um! Well, uh… That is, you see…," causing Boss to sense that there was something more here. So did the others in SHINC.

Arrrgh!

Llenn regretted her slip of the tongue but came to realize that Pitohui's surprise had been intentionally exaggerated to draw attention.

Grrr, Llenn thought, grinding her teeth.

"Look, you might as well tell them, right? They know you in real life, after all," Pitohui stated breezily. Now Llenn had no reason to refuse.

Over the next twenty seconds, Pitohui explained about Llenn and Fire and how they'd staked a marriage on the outcome of SJ4.

The teenage girls playing SHINC launched screams of excitement, which were noticeably lower pitched than if this had been the real world.

The people watching this discussion from the aerial camera could only guess at what in the world they were talking about.

"I see. So you want to fight at full strength… Very well," Fire said into his comm.

He was standing on the frozen lake, surrounded by his teammates in dark-blue tracksuits as well as the gray camo squad, the one in desert camo, and RGB.

Like earlier, no one aside from RGB had their weapons out. They were, for the moment, unarmed. And none of the unique camo or sci-fi armored guys were around. All the Humvees were off in other places, too.

Fire was giving the twelve not at the lake their orders. His voice was devoid of pleasure, sadness, or delight.

"Sorry for placing all those restrictions on you before. Go ahead and enjoy the battle now. You may remove all of them from the game, including the little girl in pink."

"So you see, there's a lot of complicated stuff going on this time. But trust me when I say that Llenn was reeeeally looking forward to fighting you!" Pitohui concluded. She gave Boss and the others a wink that was so overdone that you could practically hear it.

"..."

At first, Boss didn't know what to say. The rest of SHINC was much the same.

However, she then broke into a sudden howl of "Lleeeeeeeenn!" and came hurtling over to squeeze Llenn's tiny hands in her giant mitts. Boss's grip was so hard that it could have shattered the pink-dressed girl's bones.

"Hyeep?"

"We'll keep you safe, Llenn! We'll make sure nothing ever happens to you!"

"Hwaeh?"

Apparently, some mental switch inside Boss—more specifically, inside her player, Saki—had been flipped, activating the part of her that read plenty of romance manga. The burly gorilla woman leaned in close, her eyes sparkling and wet.

"Don't you dare let yourself be locked into an unwanted marriage! You can't do that!"

"Well, nothing's been decided yet, so—"

"We'll do whatever it takes to protect you!"

"Um...but if anything happens, the best thing is for you to pretend you don't—"

"I'll lay down my life to protect youuuu! Think of me as your shieeeeeeld!"

Hang on a second. What about our fight? Our big duel!

Boss cast a ferocious glare at the rest of her team. "Hey! You prim little ladies heard that! From this point on, we'll fight and die to protect our princess from being forced into an unhappy marriage!"

What? Why is she convinced I'll get married?

"Raaaah!"

Why are they all shouting? That's scary! She's good at working them up.

"Oh my!"

And stop smirking gleefully over there, Pito. I see you.

Boss's newfound passion showed no signs of letting up. "Hey, M! Build a box with your shield! Then put Llenn inside, wrap it up with duct tape, and we'll carry it! If we get surrounded, we'll throw it far away so that Llenn can escape!"

What am I, some precious treasure? Let me fight! And don't hurl me! I'll die on impact! Someone get me out of this! Llenn thought, exasperated.

"Now, now, Evacchi. Calm yourself. Let's just chill. Coooool down," placated Pitohui, the very cause of this state of affairs. "First of all, we need to think about how we're going to survive. Even as we speak, the circle around us is shrinking."

"Yes. That's true," Boss remarked.

Even the way she snaps back to being normal is scary.

M interjected, "I hate to interrupt your excitement, but it's time for the scan. Everyone keep an eye out. Leaders, watch your screens."

Whoops, already that time.

Llenn had once again missed the vibration of her watch that was supposed to alert her thirty seconds before the scan. She rolled her sleeve up and looked at the inside of her left wrist again.

"Huh?"

There was no watch there.

At some point in the fighting, it had gotten knocked off her arm. Well, no wonder she hadn't felt anything.

Dang. I've been wearing it forever...

The watch itself was cheap, but Llenn couldn't help but feel saddened to lose something that had been with her through it all since the first Squad Jam. She hoped that this wasn't an omen of things to come.

1:50 PM.

The scan started from the east.

Llenn, Boss, Pitohui, and M watched their screens, keeping themselves low.

"MMTM's still at the edge of the airport. We've knocked them down to two," announced Llenn as the results rolled in.

"Got it! Good to know!" Boss replied.

Since it was just a pair who remained, Pitohui wondered aloud, "What if they're making a baby now?"

"No dirty jokes, Pito!"

The scan proceeded to the west.

"On the lake! Aha, only four teams now! WEEI, PORL, SATOH, and RGB!"

That told Llenn all she needed to know. All twelve members of the other two teams were probably nearby now.

"My suspicion," Boss began, "Is that WEEI is Fire's team. Based on the last scan, I feel like their dot was close to where he was sitting. That's just my guess, though."

"Got it! Good to know!" Llenn repeated.

The scan continued westward. ZEMAL was in the crater area, and they ignored that part. They were probably building their own home there—a house made of ammo magazines.

On went the scan. Llenn's group focused on their own location and that of the enemy.

"Aha! WNGL and V2HG!"

They *were* in the ruined city after all. Llenn memorized the names of the enemy teams that were moving in for the kill.

As usual, it was tough to say the abbreviated tags in Squad Jam. She decided on "Double-N" and "V-Two."

The two squads were in practically the same location. Going by shogi board rules, they would be near the northeast corner of Sector 8-2.

Next to appear was SHINC and LPFM's own location, making it clear to the other survivors that they were working together now.

They were in the north-central part of Sector 9-1. Barely more than half a mile from the enemy.

"They're close," Boss grunted. Once the scan was over, the enemy squads would come charging in, all in formation. But just as the process was about to finish, another dot lit up.

"Oh! That's close, too!" Llenn exclaimed. Yes, another group was still around. It was the champions of SJ2, the hardy armored soldiers T-S. They were in the lower right part of 10-1.

In other words, Llenn's group, the pair of enemy teams, and T-S all formed a neat little triangle on the map.

"Farther off than I expected, but that's all right," said Pitohui.

Boss figured out what she meant at once. "Aha, you want to drag them into this fight."

"Yep! We didn't have anywhere to run but west, so having one other team in that direction adds an uncertain variable to the enemy's calculations."

"But *they* could choose to attack us, too."

"Absolutely. But that, too," Pitohui said, straightening up with her KTR-09 in hand, "is part of the game, isn't it? C'mon, gang, let's enjoy this!"

Boss and Llenn traded their scanners for their guns.

"What's the plan, M?" asked Pitohui, kicking the large man's leg.

While they discussed, the pair of enemy squads, WNGL and V2HG, could either move in or stay put and conduct their own meeting. There was no way to know which they would do.

As usual, M aired his thoughts. "It's a passive strategy, but it wouldn't be bad to set up here for now. The Humvees are a pain to deal with, but they can only get to us from the west here, and they can't approach without us spotting them. T-S will see them as well. And there's rubble, so we can take cover from snipers."

Ah yes. That's not bad, Llenn thought. If it could protect them from the menacing Humvee, Minigun, and snipers on top of that, it was a good plan.

"However," M went on, "we might be able to hold this position for a long while, but we'll never win that way. What if they send more against us? T-S could flee or join the allied team, too. And monsters will pop up in five minutes. We could probably have Pito kill the scout with her photon sword."

Uh-huh. Good point, Llenn agreed silently.

"Makes sense," Boss appended. "We just need to make sure we don't shoot the first one." Like the squad leader she was, she had a plan of her own to suggest. "What if we keep everyone safe here and send Tanya west to scout? She can find out what T-S is doing and where the Humvee is."

"Not bad," admitted M.

Llenn was going to offer to go, too, but held herself back. Running point was a job that could be deadly. It was clear that Boss was volunteering her own scout to spare Llenn that danger.

"All right. In that case—"

M was about to say something like *Let's go with that.*

But he couldn't finish, because Pitohui shouted over him.

"Launcher!"

GGO players had fast verbal warnings for their teammates in various situations.

For example, "Sniper!" plus a direction, if it was known, was a quick one used when a long-range shooter was detected. Yes, even when a player got shot and died.

"Launcher!" was the call for a grenade launcher. It warned teammates to watch for a projectile coming in at an angle from above.

"Ah!"

Llenn and everyone else looked upward. They saw the bullet line.

Straddling the collapsed building to the east was a large, curved red line. It extended down to a spot on the ground about thirty-five meters from where they were holed up, and it grew shorter and shorter as it vanished from the top down. That was because the projectile was flying toward them.

They heard a faint *pomp* in the distance from the launcher being fired.

Boom!

The grenade exploded on the road just as they threw themselves flat.

Fortunately, it was just a regular grenade, not one of the expensive plasma variety. It sprayed shrapnel for five meters in every direction, but no one got hit.

That told them something. There was an enemy grenadier on the other side of the collapsed building firing at them.

Either this new opponent had been where the scanner had indicated, and they'd used the Humvee to zip over, or the grenadier had already been in place there as a precaution. Regardless, Llenn and the others were in the enemy's range.

"Split up! Watch for the next one!" Pitohui commanded, and the entire group did its best to scatter. If that had been a plasma grenade, they would all have died.

They went separate ways around the spacious intersection, keeping their eyes on the sky. But of course, that wasn't the only source of danger, so they had to constantly look back down and up again, back and forth.

"How were they able to fire so accurately at us…? How did they know we were still here?" Boss wondered out loud.

The scan only showed one's location to within a few dozen meters. And there was still the possibility that their whole group had kept moving to the west after the scan passed over them.

But that grenade had very clearly been a pinpoint attack on them.

"Next one!" shouted M. The line of the second grenade had a very different trajectory. A gust of wind had likely knocked the projectile off course.

Everyone froze, and there was an explosion over fifty meters to the west of the group—another normal grenade.

"If we had Fuka with us, we could shoot back," Pitohui said. She pulled her M870 Breacher off of her hip as a means of shooting down any projectiles that she might not be able to avoid.

Llenn, too, lamented Fukaziroh's absence. If she were here, she could calculate where the enemy was on the other side of the building, based on the angle of their lines, and fight back with her MGL-140 grenade launchers.

It might not be a surefire strategy since the enemy could avoid incoming fire, too, but it would have been better than being attacked in a completely one-sided manner.

"So are they shooting at us because they know we don't have a launcher…? Can they actually see who's here?" Boss pondered.

"A spotter?" Rosa muttered.

Blam!

Anna answered the question with a shot from her Dragunov.

She pointed the scope-attached sniper rifle to the sky south of them and began firing. After several rounds, she yelled, "Drone! To the south! Very high up!"

Of course! Llenn and the others realized.

Drones were a recent, rare, and expensive addition to the game. If M had one, there was no reason the enemy couldn't as well.

"Dammit, they had surveillance on us! No fair!" Pitohui moaned. She was probably kidding.

Anna and Tohma fired their rifles at the distant target, but after ten attempts between them, none had landed.

Rosa pointed her PKM machine gun in the same direction but decided against firing. The drone was a tiny speck of a target against a cloudy gray sky. It darted from side to side like a UFO. Shooting down something like that was impossible.

"Launcher!" warned Tanya when she spotted another line. Those in its vicinity scattered again. The grenade landed in nearly the center of the intersection. Rosa was only just quick enough to get out of the way in time.

"Hya!"

A split second longer to duck behind rubble, and she would have died. If she'd decided to shoot at the drone earlier, the explosive would have hit her before she could even move for cover.

It was a good thing the enemy's grenade launcher was a single-fire model. If it were a consecutive-shooting launcher like Fukaziroh's, and pumped six projectiles in their direction at once, half of the group could be dead by now.

Even so, Pitohui said, "This is bad. Should we retreat to the west?" and M had to answer in the affirmative. Staying here meant suffering through this bombardment.

"It's the only option. There are others aside from the launcher to the east."

"What if we hide in the fallen building?" asked Llenn. "At least there we're protected from attack."

"They're watching us right now. All it means is that they'll surround the place and trap us like rats," replied M.

"Hmmm..."

Llenn understood that running west also meant traveling on the road, where the Humvees had high mobility. They might run into T-S, too.

"In any case, if the drone's watching us, then it doesn't matter which way we go; they've got us purrfectly pinned!" said Tanya, whose cutesy choice of words seemed to suggest she was trying to soften the situation a bit. It was hard to tell if she was successful.

"Yeah... I'm guessing they're not overdoing the grenades because they want to keep us trapped here," guessed Boss.

Hrmm. Isn't there some other option, other option, other option...? wondered Llenn, unable to give up.

"That's it!" she blurted out. An idea had come to her. "What about M's drone? Can we use that to knock out the enemy drone?"

"You mean...collide with it?" he asked, just to be sure. The drones had no weapons.

"Yeah!" Llenn replied energetically.

Naturally, she hadn't forgotten that it had cost M 110,000 yen to purchase.

But M wasn't the kind of man who would quibble about waste. He waved his hand to bring up his inventory screen. Soon there was a lattice of lights taking form in physical space.

"Launcher!" Anna warned. Llenn and Pitohui were closest to the line, so they darted out of the way.

The grenade landed and exploded between the two of them. When the smoke cleared, M was there with his drone in hand. "The problem is, I don't know if I can get it to hit the other one..."

That was uncharacteristically unconfident for M, but it was based on an understanding of his own skill. He had practiced using the drone for reconnaissance, but he'd never tried engaging in an "aerial battle" by ramming it against another target.

Ding-ding.

Just then, a bicycle bell rang.

"Huh?"

Everyone thought it must have been their imagination. It wasn't the sort of sound you'd hear in the midst of battle.

And yet, when Llenn turned north, she saw a pretty blond girl riding on what was indeed a bicycle.

Ding-ding.

"An aerial drone battle, huh…? Would that be my role, then?" the girl said in a highly affected voice.

Llenn's face split into a huge smile. "Fuka!" she cried.

Fukaziroh lifted the edge of her helmet and smirked.

"Kept ya waitin', huh?"

CHAPTER 14
This Summer, Fukaziroh Leaps and Llenn Races

CHAPTER 14
This Summer, Fukaziroh Leaps and Llenn Races

"Kept ya waitin', huh?"

It was a very cool line to make her entrance on. But then a solid line came silently down over her head.

"Run awaaaay!" Llenn called.

"Huh? Hyaaaa!" Fukaziroh leaped off the bike and sprinted to one side. She dived behind a large mass of concrete at the same moment that the enemy's grenade landed.

Krshunk!

The handy-dandy bicycle that Tanya and Fukaziroh had used to such great effect was instantly reduced to scrap metal. Its pieces vanished shortly thereafter.

When Fukaziroh poked her head out from behind the rubble, bits of concrete rained down and pattered off her helmet.

"Aw, my sweet ride… Farewell, *Pretty Miyu…*," she lamented.

She gave it a name? Llenn was taken aback. More importantly, she was overjoyed. "I'm so glad you made it here safely!"

Fukaziroh had gotten down from that building without being spotted and busted past the eastern side, where the enemy was—or wait…maybe not? Were there no enemies?

"The bad guys are on the other side of the collapsed building! One Humvee and three dudes! I saw them in the distance!"

Aha! Yes, she is *awesome!* Llenn thought without reservation.

"I got the hell outta that place when they fired on me, but it got easier once I spotted the bike. I rode it as far out of the way north as I could, then found out where you all were during the scan and built up some speed to zoom past them while the guy was shooting the grenades at you from the Humvee! Bikes rule!" Fukaziroh explained all at once.

"Amazing! Wait, where are your guns?" Llenn inquired, realizing that she was holding neither Rightony nor Leftania. Fukaziroh never put her weapons away into virtual storage, but perhaps it was necessary when riding a bicycle.

"Oh, those… I was careless enough to loosen my grip on them, and they got blown away in the blast… I looked around but couldn't find them, so I set them free. They're probably running around wild in the pastures now. But I've still got my pistol, so no worries!" Fukaziroh answered smoothly.

"Wh-what…?" Llenn was stunned.

"Aw, man," lamented Pitohui, staring up at the sky.

The absence of those two grenade launchers meant more than being unable to return fire here. It was a major loss of team power in general.

Sitting around bemoaning their situation wouldn't help, though. Llenn returned to the first thing Fukaziroh had said upon her return. "What did you mean, 'my role'?"

"I'm glad you asked!" Fukaziroh exclaimed, trotting right over to M. "Here, get out the VR goggles and control stick."

"Huh? Are you going to fly the drone, Fuka?" Llenn asked over her shoulder.

Fukaziroh turned around and gave her a thumbs-up. "You bet!"

"……"

M hesitated, but after Pitohui came up and whispered something in his ear, he said, "All right. Go ahead. Crash it if you must; just bring that enemy drone down."

"Sounds good! But in the meantime, pick me up and keep me safe!"

* * *

What does that mean? Llenn wondered, a question mark over her head.

Fukaziroh took off her helmet and attached a set of VR goggles to her face. M handed her the controller with the flight stick, which she took in her left hand.

As Fukaziroh had commanded, M then picked up her tiny body and lifted it to his shoulders. This way, if a grenade launcher attack should come after them, he could ensure she didn't get hit.

Like Llenn, Team SHINC kept their eyes on the sky and the horizon, but they couldn't help but sneak curious glances at what was going on with their allies.

"Here we go!"

Fukaziroh pressed a button on the controller. The resting drone extended its arms and began to rotate the propellers on the ends.

Then it abruptly shot upward as if it were on a spring. Over the buzzing of its wings, Fukaziroh shouted, "Hya-haaa! Here we go! Fly, my pretty! Fly, *Charming Miyu*!"

If only she could come up with a better name, Llenn thought, watching the drone shrink into the distance. Hopefully, this would be the key to breaking their stalemate.

"We're all counting on you, Fuka!"

"Don't worry; I got this!" she answered cheerily.

Hey, Fukaziroh, when exactly did you learn…to pilot a drone? While Llenn thought up a haiku, she had forgotten something important.

No more than two hundred meters away from Fukaziroh and Llenn, there was a Humvee in wait.

Inside were three members of Team V2HG. They were the ones kitted out with sturdy chest protectors. All of them wore face masks and sunglasses.

Although only a short distance separated the two parties, a huge building was resting on its side between them. This left the opposite side invisible and unapproachable from here.

And that meant attacking from above was a practical option.

One of the men stuck his head out of the roof turret surrounded by bulletproof plating, holding an M79 grenade launcher.

It was a single-shot weapon that folded up in the middle. Americans had used such armaments in the Vietnam War. The wooden stock was angled on the top rather than the bottom, and the weapon resembled an ugly shotgun.

His M79 was painted with yellow highlights in a kind of tiger pattern. It had been done in imitation of a weapon that appeared in one of the classic Vietnam War films. He'd been popping off shots for the last few minutes over the building in front of them, but a man wearing VR goggles in the passenger seat delivered the bad news.

"They're still unharmed."

He was the drone pilot, of course, and held the control stick in his right hand.

The bombardier grumbled, "Damn. It just doesn't work like in the movies," and pulled the empty grenade cartridge out.

The one in the driver's seat said, "We don't wanna wipe 'em all out anyway. Let's have a more exciting battle."

He had the Humvee in gear, waiting with his foot on the brakes. If anything happened, they could move instantly. That meant the vehicle had been idling the whole time, but they still had over half a tank of gas.

Pomp!

The man with the launcher adjusted his angle and fired a grenade. It made a cute sound and launched a 40 mm bomb into the air.

A few seconds later, they heard a distant explosion. How had it gone? The drone operator gave them the answer.

"Dodged it. But they're not running away. I guess they want to hole themselves up there?"

"It's not a bad idea, but they're only going to make their situation worse over time," remarked the guy with the launcher as he loaded another grenade.

Just then, all three of them heard a voice speaking directly into their ears.

"This is Leader."

The comm they were using was a standard wireless item with which you had to press the switch to send your audio, rather than the simultaneous open-channel type. Many players preferred this style, since it involved less chatter, felt more realistic to them, or allowed them to grumble to themselves without anyone hearing it.

"Message to Car Three. Road spotted. Car Two heading out. T-S is no threat. Car Three, stop bombardment and remain on alert. Our guests will approach on foot from the south. Over."

The report had come from their distant companions in Car One.

The Minigun-toting monster was Car Two, and they had identified a route to put themselves on the western road. Team T-S, previously in the vicinity, had scampered off and was not a priority now. The camo squad, WNGL, a temporary part of the alliance, had stepped off Cars One and Two and were now looking for their own sniping positions among the city's ruins.

The driver responded for the rest of his group. He put his hand to his throat, where the switch was, and stated, "This is Car Three, I read you. We will remain on standby without further attack. Just leave some for us, huh, boys? Over."

"I dunno if we can promise that. Just tell us when you're bringing your drone back. We'll launch ours to take its place. Over."

The conversation was finished. The driver shrugged and asked the man sitting next to him, "How much longer will the batteries last?"

"About four minutes."

The man with the grenade launcher noted, "That's a fair amount. We might end up cleaning them out before the time's up, without any extra surprises."

But no sooner were the words out of his mouth than the drone operator exclaimed, "Aaooow!"

Llenn watched through Boss's binoculars as Fukaziroh's drone, the *Charming Miyu*, buzzed and soared high into the sky.

It rapidly circled around behind the enemy's surveillance drone, which was weaving from side to side regularly but maintaining a steady altitude.

Then it launched into a diagonal sweep, straight for a body blow to the other drone.

A simple collision would damage the drone's propeller, so she employed the one method that would avoid that kind of wear and tear—meaning she used the drone's flat body to hit the enemy's rear propellers. It was a brilliant maneuver, deftly twisting the flying craft's bearing just before it collided with its counterpart.

The enemy drone lost its right rear propeller, and with it all sense of balance. All four blades were required to maintain stability, so there was nothing it could do now. It dropped from the sky in a tailspin, like a kite that had lost its string.

It seemed like the process took a long time, but it was only five seconds before the enemy drone collided with the side of the fallen building and burst into little polygonal pieces that vanished.

Fukaziroh's drone did a little victory backflip. SHINC cheered at the feat, and Llenn murmured, "Amazing..."

On the other side of the fallen building, someone asked, "What happened?"

"I don't know! It just fell! We've lost the drone! Aw, dammit, that was expensive!" lamented the member of V2HG who'd bought the thing.

The man with the grenade launcher hit the switch on his radio and said, "This is Car Three. Drone down, drone down. Over."

"This is Leader. We'll send up ours immediately. What's the cause? Did you get shot down? Over."

"I don't know. It shouldn't have been the battery...but regardless, drone down. Over."

"You just want to say that phrase, huh? Over."

"Was it that obvious? Over."

"Enough with you and the Hollywood movies! We'll send up ours. Remain in position. Over."

* * *

"I knocked it down!" exclaimed Fukaziroh, who was still wearing the VR goggles. Then she switched to performing traditional reconnaissance duties. "Oops! Just spotted another Humvee! Yeah, I can see that cute little ass from above… This one doesn't have a Minigun on it! Just one person on board!"

"Where are they?" Pitohui asked.

"An intersection to the south of here. All I can tell is that it's a few hundred yards out—oh! Hang on, he's getting ready to launch another drone!"

"Rich bastard. You know what to do, Fuka?"

"Naturally!"

Pitohui opened up a screen that looked like a tablet and set it so that Llenn could see the information, too. It was a direct feed from the drone, so the image was constantly shifting and shaking, making for a disorienting watch.

"You're not going anywhere!"

The other drone, which was completely identical except that it had been painted brown, was closing in. Within moments, it completely filled the image on-screen.

"Number two!"

The man in the roof turret of the Humvee protected by bulletproof plates watched the drone he'd just hurled up into the sky go—and get smashed by another drone painted white.

"What?!"

His fell. The enemy one stayed aloft.

"……"

Although he understood what had happened, he couldn't understand how it was possible.

"Fuka? When did you practice piloting drones?" Llenn asked. She couldn't help it.

Without taking off the VR goggles, her friend replied, "Never. But it's not my first time flying!"

Oh! Llenn remembered at last.

Fukaziroh was here in *GGO* now, but most of the time, she was a fairy in *ALfheim Online.*

The biggest selling point of that game was that you could fly.

Of course! That's right!

Now Llenn recalled what she'd looked up before testing out *ALO*. Every character in that game had wings, so with some practice, you could learn to use voluntary flight by moving muscles that human beings did not typically have. How did people fly around before getting used to that? The answer was obvious—flight sticks.

Fukaziroh was used to swooping here and there in *ALO*, so piloting a drone using VR goggles for a first-person view was second nature to her.

From her perch on M's shoulders, she exclaimed in English, "Yahoo! I'm flyiiing!" But she didn't forget her mission, either. "Onward to distant skies! Well, I guess not. What next, Pito? Should I bop this guy on the head?"

A man inside the Humvee was looking up at her. While the mask and sunglasses hid his expression, he was unquestionably frustrated.

He was the only one in the Humvee. No sign of any other teams around. Once she'd checked and memorized the appearance of the buildings around her position, Pitohui said, "We're done. I know where he is. The Minigun should be to your west. Look for it."

"Roger!"

As the drone that stared him down flew off to the west, the leader of Team V2HG put a hand to his ear and tapped it a few times. "Hook up your comms, everyone!"

He said to his five teammates, "My drone is down, too. They knocked it out of the sky. The enemy one rammed it. They've got one hell of an acrobatic pilot over there. It went west."

"That's amazing!"

"Are you serious…?"

"Whew! Impressive!"

The members of V2HG were alternately stunned and intimidated.

The driver of the Humvee equipped with the Minigun asked, "West? That means it's coming this way. Should we shoot it down?"

The leader considered this briefly. The Minigun was an excellent piece of antiair weaponry and had a fair chance of hitting the drone. It was about to turn two o'clock, so they didn't have to worry about ammo, either.

However, they needed to keep the Humvee in place to block their opponent's escape route. If they moved, the enemy would have a chance to sneak off to the west.

V2HG's leader made his decision. "Stay where you are, but try to knock it out of the sky!"

They weren't just one team at the moment. They were in an alliance with a squad of experts, WNGL.

"We'll have to leave the rest of the heavy lifting to them."

The drone buzzed just past the side of the standing building and took a hard turn around the corner, bringing a target into Fukaziroh's sights.

"Spotted the minigunner!"

She headed west down the main road, nimbly zipping past the scattered debris in her way, before coming to an unexpected, screeching halt.

"Ugh!"

The turret protected by armor plating spun around to face her.

"Some sharp eyes on this one!"

Fukaziroh tilted the flight stick left, completely altering the bearing of her vision. A terrifying amount of light surged in from the right.

Fukaziroh lowered the drone's elevation.

* * *

Pitohui's screen showed lines of gunfire lancing forth from the Minigun toward the camera. Only Fukaziroh's exceptional control kept those bullets from striking the drone.

Suddenly, the Humvee was much larger in the video feed than it had been moments before. If Fukaziroh hadn't zoomed in the camera, that meant she'd flown much lower to the ground.

"Why? Why isn't she going higher to get away?" Llenn wondered.

Pitohui answered that for her. "It's the opposite. If she goes up, then the total angle of the drone's strafing ability is smaller, and the Minigun has to move less to adjust. It's better to stay low and close, darting around while watching the turret's maneuvers."

"Ohhh, I get it now… Very smart, Fuka…"

Llenn looked over at Fukaziroh, who was sitting on M's shoulders, her mouth twisted into a delighted grin. Her left hand was jerking the control stick back and forth wildly.

Llenn recalled when she'd gone over to Miyu's house and watched her kick ass at a shoot-'em-up game. It was in Llenn's first year of high school, right after they'd become friends.

Karen had hardly ever played a video game in all of her fifteen years of life, so seeing Miyu with all those game consoles in her own bedroom was a kind of culture shock.

Now it was five years later, and Karen was playing full-dive VR games.

"C'mon, sucker. If you're mad about it, why don't you hit me?" Fukaziroh taunted. She was only flying the drone and had no means of hitting the enemy. All she could do was weave through the enemy's hail of bullets.

However, Fukaziroh was occupying the powerful Minigun and Humvee, buying her squad valuable time.

"Pito, they're stuck in place! We can escape to the west now!"

"Mmm," Pitohui murmured noncommittally.

"I think that would be a good idea, too. What's wrong?" Boss asked.

Pitohui replied, "Did you forget that there's another squad?"

Crap, I did, Llenn thought.

"Ah, that's right," Boss replied. "But we have nine people here. If we come across a team of six, we can blast them back to kingdom come."

It was a bold statement, and not at all a bluff, but Pitohui just shook her head. She took one of her photon swords out of the pouch on her back and extended the pale blade. Then she swung it, severing the head of a monster that was popping up over the broken concrete.

That action, as casual as swatting at a mosquito, had just bought them another five minutes of peace from any monsters in this area.

Pito really is amazing, Llenn praised silently. She hadn't noticed the monster at all.

Pitohui stowed the photon sword and resumed talking. "That name, WNGL. I just figured it out. They're the Lancers."

"Ohhh, *them*," appended M, who was still carrying Fukaziroh on his shoulders. The girl's fingers and head were continually twitching back and forth.

"You know them?" Llenn asked.

M couldn't move his head very much with Fukaziroh on top of him, but he managed to indicate an affirmative answer. "They're a fairly well-known squadron. To be a member, you have to be a sniper capable of acting on your own. Very extreme group."

In real life, snipers worked in teams with a spotter; taking a position on your own made you too vulnerable, and it was frowned upon. Yet, plenty of people played *GGO* alone, so solo snipers weren't that rare.

Pitohui continued the explanation. "But there's a very severe test to join the squadron. *GGO*'s already packed with gun freaks, and WNGL are the snipers, so they're the freaks among the freaks. They've chosen to disregard everything except for pushing the limits of their sniping accuracy."

Wow, there really are all kinds in GGO, Llenn thought, and then she scolded herself. *Hey! This isn't the time for losing focus!*

"Then...they're tough?"

"In terms of individual sniping techniques, they're probably the best team in *GGO*. They're good at hiding behind cover and sneaking up on enemies, too. I don't think *all* of them can snipe without a bullet line, but they're all good at aiming from angles and positions where the target won't see the line anyway."

"Urgh..."

If the bullet line was out of your field of vision, it might as well not exist. No matter how fast Llenn was, she couldn't dodge a line on her back that she couldn't see.

"Now, you'll notice the squadron's tag suggests more than just the name Lancers..."

"Is it Long Lancers?"

"Close, but no cigar. See the W? It's Wrong Lancers. WNGL."

"Wrong Lancers..."

"That's the sort of twisted folks we're up against."

Boss considered the discussion and, without taking her eye off the surroundings, particularly to the west, opined, "If all of them are solo snipers, doesn't that give them terrible team balance?"

SHINC had more snipers than the average squad, but that was still only two people. If you included Boss's close-range Vintorez due to the silencer's muzzling effect, it brought the count to three.

"Yeah, it's not good. So they're really at a disadvantage in a team battle-royale event. I wouldn't expect a group like that to join a Squad Jam. They're all hard-core players, so I didn't think they'd be interested in a frivolous event like this," said Pitohui. "But..."

"Winning aside, if they're focusing on cooperation with the other squads under Fire's control, they can be a lot more effective," Boss remarked.

"Exactly! If they've been placed up ahead, it's not going to be an easy escape route." Pitohui gave her a thumbs-up. She seemed to be enjoying their perilous situation quite a lot.

Llenn, meanwhile, was furious.

Damn you, Fire! How much did you spend to hire these

cutthroats? If there was ever an opportunity to talk with him, that's what she wanted to ask.

"Crap! Quick little bugger!"

The battle of Fukaziroh vs. Minigun was currently tilted in the former's favor.

While the gun turret could be swiveled with electronic controls, its speed could not match the drone's sheer mobility. In addition to weaving left and right, Fukaziroh could do the occasional backflip and abruptly drop toward the ground to evade the enemy's aim.

"Forget it!" cried the gunner after several fruitless tries. Although he stopped firing the gun, he kept his eyes on the drone and his thumb near the trigger in case he needed to shoot.

Sensing that the gunner wasn't going to shoot her down, Fukaziroh began to circle around the Humvee at a height of ten meters.

"It kills me to admit, but it's too hard to hit that thing. Should we move?"

"No, stay in place. We'll run the drone out of battery."

Fukaziroh was too fast to be hit, but that didn't change the fact that she had no means of attack. A surprise kamikaze dive wasn't going to help if the drone didn't have lethal power. And barring some extraordinary stroke of luck, there was no way she could damage the Minigun.

"What do I do now? Wait like this until the power runs out?" she wondered. The battery readout on her headset and Pitohui's screen indicated that only a third of the charge remained. Flight time depended on what you were doing with the motors, but it was likely going to be in the air for only two to four more minutes.

"If you just wanted me to distract them for a bit, that's one thing, but this thing's expensive, right? Should I be flying it back here?" Fukaziroh inquired from atop M's shoulders.

"Hmmm..." M was faced with one of his most difficult decisions ever. His mind was working at a breakneck pace.

The fallen building and rubble protected their current location. It had good visibility and was reliably safe for now. However, the group couldn't set up permanent residence here. The longer they remained, the greater their disadvantage grew. If the enemy pressed with an all-out siege, it was only a matter of time until they clinched victory.

If they were going to run, now seemed the best time, as the Minigun wasn't active. Unfortunately, their only routes were to the south or west, and they didn't know where the Wrong Lancer snipers were hiding. It would be too dangerous to run down the spacious road as a group. Like Boss earlier, they could very quickly get shot and knocked out, perhaps without a chance of fighting back.

If they left, it was hell. If they stayed, it was hell.

Yet, M had another solution—attack.

Go on the offensive by staying put in this location and sending the speedy Llenn toward the Minigun.

Even skilled snipers would find it difficult to hit such a small and swift target. If she could approach the Humvee while it was distracted by the drone, she could toss a plasma grenade into it.

That was the best move in their current situation.

However, M didn't dare choose a plan with a reasonably high chance of killing Llenn when Karen's future hung in the balance.

In a previous Squad Jam, he would have employed the tactic without hesitation. He'd done it before.

Two seconds later, before M could recover from the paralysis of his indecision, Llenn cried, "That's it! If I just run over there as fast as I can, I can toss a grenade at the Minigun!"

*　*　*

It was 1:57, according to the clock in the bar, when Llenn leaped into the enemy.

"Oh! She's moving!" the audience cried.

The image on one monitor zoomed out as it followed her mad dash.

Another screen's shot followed over her shoulder in a close-up, keeping her centered in the frame. Because she was running so fast, the scenery around her was little more than a blur.

Llenn waved her left hand, bringing up her inventory. A gray camouflage poncho appeared and settled onto her body.

"Ooh, a transformation!"

She continued to race through the ruins of the city, dressed perfectly for blending in.

Barely a minute earlier…

"But that means you'll—," Boss protested.

"I know it's dangerous. But this is Squad Jam. I've got to make sure the team wins! I won't win if I'm the last one of us standing!"

"…"

"Thanks for the concern, Boss. But remember, I'm the lucky girl! I'm the champion of SJ1! I'm gonna tear it up just like I did before!"

"…All right. Best of luck!" Boss acquiesced.

Llenn took off as fast as she could. There was no fear of tripping and falling. The bulky poncho's air resistance would be a problem in real life, but *GGO* had no such hindrance.

She kept her P90 in place under the cloak, ready to shoot at anything that moved. If she got targeted by a sniper, however, it would be best to simply keep moving.

M's voice on the comms gave her directions. "Left at the next intersection. Then you'll be on a big, wide road. Be wary of snipers and run down the middle, zigzagging every two seconds."

"Got it!"

With the help of Fukaziroh's drone, now at a healthy altitude, and M's judgment with the map at his disposal, Llenn continued her sprint.

"We've got an incoming hostile," said a man in a mask and sunglasses quietly. He was wearing a vivid-green camo outfit in the distinct style of WNGL members. His voice was deep, calm, and smooth.

The man was in the city's tallest building, on a floor high enough to enable him to see over any other. He stayed hidden to the side of a broken window frame with a large pair of binoculars in his hand.

"Small target. Wearing a camo poncho. Has to be LPFM's speedster."

A hundred meters below him, the little figure ran in a jagged formation down the street.

He put down the binoculars and looked at his map. It was not a Satellite Scanner map but a piece of waterproof paper he'd quickly copied the device's map onto with a pen.

There were numbers listed on the chart's roads. On top of that, features were recorded for each intersection—a flipped-over truck, for example, or a big scar on the southeast-corner building's sign.

WNGL had been painstakingly copying down these details by zooming in on the map at maximum resolution while on standby atop the frozen lake throughout SJ4. Thanks to this, they had easily identifiable names for all points of the map.

"Target is running south down East Eighth Street in a zigzag pattern. She'll reach the intersection with South Fifth Street in forty seconds. She'll have to pause there for an instant to turn right," the Wrong Lancer explained to his team.

"First to bag the target wins the prize."

"Haven't been shot yet! So far, so good!" Llenn reported to M as she ran.

A minute and a half had passed since she jumped out of her hiding spot. She'd covered a great distance already, and the sniping squad hadn't shot at her yet. She didn't know if that was because they weren't nearby or because her zigzagging was keeping them from getting a bead on her.

"That's a good pace. When you come up on the big intersection ahead, go right. In another hundred feet, there will be an alley to your left. Take it three hundred feet, and you'll reach the street with the Humvee. It's about a hundred feet to the right of the intersection. I'll have Fuka keep it away, but be careful."

"Got it!"

Yes! I'm gonna do this! I can *do this!*

Once Llenn got into the alley, the Humvee with that damned Minigun would be a hundred feet to her right after a three-hundred-foot run.

With her speed, she could close that gap in an instant, pull two plasma grenades off her belt, and toss them right inside.

Happily playing out the scenario in her mind, Llenn hit the end of the street and charged into the intersection—only to trip over a chunk of concrete there, crashing spectacularly to the ground.

CHAPTER 15
A Rampaging Duo

CHAPTER 15
A Rampaging Duo

"Hya, aaah, aaah!"

Llenn tumbled over and over, her hands stuck inside her poncho and unable to help her stabilize. She rolled with great speed into the intersection, then bounced off the street one last time and crashed into the back of a yellow school bus without any tires.

"Bwehf!"

At last, she stopped.

"Durgh!"

And fell to the ground.

But Llenn had absolutely no idea that the instant she tripped and fell, a powerful .338 Lapua Magnum bullet passed right over her head.

It would have blasted open her skull if she hadn't fallen.

"Good luck...is the sign of a hero...," a man muttered, pulling the bolt handle of his weapon. It expelled an empty cartridge from the gun's right side and loaded the next round into the chamber.

The man was inside a toppled container truck four hundred meters to the east of where Llenn had fallen. It was dark inside the empty trailer with just one door open—the perfect place to hide.

He was resting on the floor with a Barrett Model 98B sniper rifle. It was a bolt-action antipersonnel weapon made by the American company Barrett, famous for its .50-caliber antimateriel rifles.

The 98B fired .338 Lapua Magnums, well regarded for their balance between strength and size against human targets. Like the .50-caliber antimateriel rifle, it could strike a target at 1,200 to 1,500 meters.

Since its bullets were so large, the Model 98B was about four feet long. A magazine held ten rounds. It was the kind of gun that would make Pitohui exclaim "Sell it to me!" as soon as she saw it.

This man, of course, was one of the Wrong Lancers. He wore that distinctive green camo, a mask, and sunglasses.

The back of Llenn's head was in the center of the crosshairs after she fell. He'd zeroed in at four hundred meters, meaning the scope was already focused at that distance. All he had to do was pull the trigger.

However, the man did not shoot—because his target had already been struck.

"Ouch!"

Llenn grimaced against the pain of the bullet in her shoulder, but she did what she needed to do to survive. Meaning she rolled herself under the body of the school bus to hide.

With her cheek right next to the ground, she could see more bullets pinging and scraping against the asphalt of the road. Two more shots would have gone right through her if she hadn't rolled away.

Llenn crawled toward the middle of the bus for safety.

"Dammit!"

"What's up?" M asked through the comm.

"I tripped in the intersection and got shot! Sniped!"

Although she couldn't have known this, if she hadn't faltered where she did, Llenn would already be dead. Her hit points were down to 70 percent, so she used one of her healing kits immediately. Now she had two left.

No more bullets flew at her under the bus.

"I'm hiding under a vehicle right now. I don't know where the enemy is! Am I safe to jump out?" Llenn asked, hoping her allies could send the drone to check.

"I don't know. Can't send the drone. Fuka's keeping the Minigun occupied right now."

"Aw..."

Llenn took off the poncho and crawled on hands and knees past the middle of the bus toward the west face. With the P90 in her right hand, she used the other to hurl the poncho out from under the bus and into the street.

Pshk!

A bullet immediately tore a hole in the cloak. That was frightful reaction speed and accuracy from the enemy sniper. She couldn't leave from under the bus now.

"I'm completely in their sights! I've gotta stay put!"

"Okay. Well, we've got bad news, too," admitted M.

"What's that?"

"The drone's battery has less than a minute left."

"Ugh!"

"Also, there are twenty seconds until the scan. They'll find out where you are."

"Gah!"

"But there's also good news."

"What's that?"

"We know they've got a number of snipers, so after the scan, we're popping up and moving west."

"Bravo!"

"We'll do everything we can. Good luck, Llenn."

"Got it!"

The only problem was, this didn't actually give Llenn any idea of what to do herself.

During Llenn and M's conversation, Pitohui watched the footage from the drone. She told the pilot, "Fuka, get as much altitude as you can!"

From atop M's shoulders, Fuka replied, "Got it! I'll fly it so close to the sun that it melts! Fly, phoenix, fly!"

That was definitely not the correct mythological figure,

but regardless, Fukaziroh sent the drone into a rapid vertical ascent.

Pitohui watched the scenery expand on her screen, paying careful attention to the west. She spotted a pair of metal tracks running straight across the scene at an angle—and resting atop them, a diesel locomotive. With nimble fingers, she zoomed in on it.

And smirked.

The tattoos on her cheeks bunched up.

The clock hands pointed to 2:00.

The SJ4 battle had reached the two-hour mark. That was a new record; SJ3 had lasted for an hour and fifty-nine minutes. And this record was likely to grow even larger.

The audience in the bar knocked back drinks and snacked on their favorite foods, enjoying the action.

When they saw that Llenn was stuck under the bus, they shouted and jeered.

"Oh no, Llenn's really done for this time! Gweh-heh-heh."

"Why do you sound so pleased about that?"

"Oh, no reason. Just thinking of how I can console her when she comes back heartbroken after losing."

"Gross!"

Meanwhile, SHINC and Pitohui's team leaped out of their hiding spots as soon as the scan was finished.

Tanya was in the lead, followed by the rest of SHINC, then M with Fukaziroh on his shoulders for some reason. Pitohui took up the rear position.

"Here we go… Do those two squads have any chance of winning?"

"Probably not. They're trapped in the northwest corner like rats."

"There's still six teams in that big alliance."

The crowd's view of their chances was grim.

* * *

"Eugh, I think I'm going to be sick," said Fukaziroh, shaking back and forth on M's shoulders as he stomped along. She had her right arm clamped around his head.

When there was no word for at least thirty seconds, she yelled, "Llenn! Are you still stuck?"

"Yes! They're shooting at me, and I can't even hear it!"

"We're almost out of batteries."

"It's okay! Go back!"

"You idiot! We can't just leave you behind!"

"Fuka…"

"What I mean is that we don't even have the juice left to fly it back."

"Are you kidding me?!"

Dammit…

At this point, Llenn was just a pink ornament brightening up the underside of the bus.

She'd retreated back to the middle to protect against a lucky deflection off the road surface, but that was all she could do. In the meantime, enemy snipers could be advancing on her, so she turned around, worried that she'd see approaching feet.

The only silver lining was knowing that her teammates were escaping to the west because she had attracted the attention of at least two Wrong Lancers.

Does that mean I'll stay here and be a sacrifice for the rest of the group, like a true leader? Llenn wondered, rolling onto her back and staring at the long drive shaft on the bottom of the bus.

Then the intro to Mendelssohn's "Wedding March" started to play in her mind, *Pa-pa-pa-paaaa, pa-pa-pa-paaaa*, accompanied by the image of a priest in a tracksuit.

"No!" Llenn shrieked, and she tried to leap to her feet, only to smack her forehead on the drive shaft. "Ulgh!"

"Where shall we 'drop' the drone, M?" asked Fukaziroh. It was a rather cruel question to put to the owner of the device.

The battery was nearly gone. Sadly, the supply regeneration that had taken place at two o'clock hadn't extended to the charge of a drone already in flight.

Still, they didn't need to drop it on anything. If it crash-landed somewhere with dead batteries and stayed there, they might be lucky enough to get it back at the end of SJ4. Of course, Fukaziroh had no intention of relying on a plan so dull.

"I'll just buy another one!" Pitohui said. That was all the permission needed.

"Okay, drop it wherever you want," M stated.

"That's what I like to hear!"

The man from V2HG behind the Minigun watched the pestering drone shoot straight upward, high out of sight, and wondered, "What the hell is it doing…?"

He hadn't been able to shoot it down, and it had gone off somewhere, but it had come back into view just moments ago. The next chance he had, he was going to blast it out of the sky.

"Hmm?"

Suddenly, the little speck of the drone was getting much larger.

"Mmmm?"

Now it was big enough that he could accurately make out its shape.

"Dwah!"

It landed on his face.

"What's up? Did you get shot?" asked the driver in a panic.

"Owww! Dammit, no, the drone just slammed into me!" exclaimed the gunner, pressing a hand to his face. It had struck him on the eyes and nose, so he lost about 3 percent of his hit points, but that was nothing.

However, it did hurt like hell. The sunglasses he wore to match the rest of the team got knocked off.

"Dammit! Huh…?"

The drone was stuck on the exterior of the Humvee's bulletproof plating. Of course, the propellers were damaged and would have to be replaced for it to work again, but the thing hadn't been completely destroyed yet.

Peeved that both of their own drones had been knocked out and loath to let the enemy recover this one so that they could use it again, the man said, "I'm gonna bust this thing."

He leaned out over the side of the vehicle's armor and lifted up the drone. The man saw his eyes reflected in the camera on the underside of the device.

"You won't be needing this anymore," he said, and he threw it down onto the street surface.

The drone's body cracked and burst into 3D graphical shards.

Then the man's head exploded.

"You won't be needing this anymore."

On the street, about five hundred meters to the south, Shirley lay in the shadow of a car. In her arms, of course, was the R93 Tactical 2.

She'd made good use of her one opportunity to snipe when it arrived. Her bolt went back, expelling the empty cartridge, then forward again to load the next explosive round.

On the other side of the car, Clarence peered through binoculars. "Another hit on the first try! What are you, some kind of sniping angel?!"

"Shut up."

Through her lens, each girl saw the driver turn around. When he witnessed his headless teammate toppled over inside the car, he froze.

"Let's get the driver next!" said Clarence.

"No, that glass is bulletproof… Even my explosive rounds won't work."

"Then I'll approach and get into the vehicle!"

"Are you serious?"

"Of course!"

Shirley stared blankly at Clarence's confident grin.

"Fine. Do whatever you want."

"Whoo-hoo!"

The pair stood up and went around to the "vehicle" they'd parked behind the car. The one that had silently brought them here.

"They got Grant! Headshot! Enemy location unknown!" the driver of the Humvee reported, staring at the corpse of his former teammate with the head blown clean off.

He went ahead and offered the best guess he had. "It was a sniper. Probably to the south. You don't think it's *them*, do you?"

"We'll check, just to be sure. Come back over here."

"Got it."

The driver put the Humvee into gear, circled through the intersection, and headed east. It slowly made its way toward the primary vehicle—where his leader waited.

At the same time that Shirley was taking out her target, Llenn got caught in someone else's scope.

It was one of the Wrong Lancers, equipped with a Model 98B. He'd been hiding in the bed of a truck earlier, but now he was resting on top of it. That gave him a bit of height and just the right angle to aim under the distant school bus.

The gap underneath the broken-down bus was little more than a narrow line when viewed from four hundred meters away. However, the man got his aim right on that spot, put his finger to the trigger, and pulled.

His bullet rocketed forth and disappeared beneath the body of the bus as though sucked into it.

Bsh-gank!

The sudden burst of sound caused Llenn to jump with shock.

"Hya!"

Once again, she smacked her head on the underside of the vehicle.

I'm being shot at! They've got a bead on me!

Llenn understood what had happened. The bullet had gone

under the bus, bounced off the concrete, then bounced off the bus, creating a tremendous racket.

There was a bit of smoke coming off some part that was dangerously close to the fuel tank.

Oh no, oh no, bad, bad, bad.

Llenn rolled, moving toward the front of the large vehicle, trying to get behind the front wheels so she could use them as shields.

"Found her. She's back in pink. I can hit her."

The man with the Model 98B had Llenn dead to rights.

Rushing closer to the front wheels had put her right in the man's sights. The bus's wheel wasn't big enough to completely hide her body, small as it was.

She was rustling and doing something, but her lower half was exposed.

"Sorry, gang. This one's mine," the Wrong Lancer stated, steadying his aim.

From this angle, the target wouldn't see his line. He placed his finger on the trigger, waiting for the bullet circle to appear.

With his sniping ability and powerful gun, the bullet circle was tiny. Even at its largest, when his heart beat, it still remained full on Llenn's lower half.

It didn't matter how he pulled the trigger, the bullet would find purchase. He couldn't miss.

All he needed to do was move his finger a millimeter.

"Everyone, listen up. The Humvee's been sniped. The guy on the Minigun is dead," said his team leader.

The man stopped, pulling his finger away. The bullet circle vanished.

"They think it was our mistake. I very much doubt that, but we need to be sure. Did any one of us accidentally shoot him? I won't be mad; just be honest and admit it if it was you."

The man laughed and heard his teammates laughing as well.

"Okay. I didn't think so. I'll pass on the message. That means there's an enemy in our midst. Be careful out there," the leader cautioned one last time.

The man put his finger back on the trigger. Once he'd made his shot, it was time to get up and escape to more secure ground.

Just when he was about to pull the trigger for good this time, the bus exploded.

But shortly before that…

Staying here would be bad. Like bad-bad, not good-bad.

Even as she hid behind the wheel of the yellow school bus, Llenn was aware that it didn't change her predicament much. There was no guarantee the next bullet wouldn't hit her. Even if it didn't, there was the possibility it could strike the fuel tank.

She had to get away, and she hadn't a moment, no, an instant to lose. Getting indoors was the only thing that could save her.

Is there any way, is there any way, any way, any way…?

Llenn's mind buzzed and rotated at ferocious speeds.

It landed upon a quote she'd read once, though she couldn't recall where: "When people see their life flash before their eyes before death, it's nothing other than the mind desperately seeking a way to avoid dying amid sudden peril."

Now was that moment—although Llenn had already experienced as much several times in *GGO* and the Squad Jams.

Stuck in a place where she couldn't move, bullets bearing down outside? That had happened in the very first Squad Jam. In the midst of her battle with SHINC, in fact.

That time, Llenn had been hiding behind a boulder when she came under powerful machine-gun fire. If she left her spot, she'd get hit, but if she stayed right there, they would get her anyway.

A plasma grenade had saved her. And it just so happened that Llenn had a few of those with her now. Previously, she'd used the explosion as a shield and escaped in the opposite direction.

Can I do this? Will it work?

It felt like her panicked flashback had given her the answer.

No, wait. It won't work...

Back during that battle with SHINC, Llenn had known where the shooter was and which way to flee. Plus, she'd been on her feet.

This was different.

Llenn could see a building ahead of the bus, but she was practically in the center of the intersection, so it was at least thirty-five meters to the structure. With a sniper already training on her, she didn't think she could make it over safely.

So much for that! My pre-death recollections must be out of ammo or something! Llenn lamented. Suddenly, she remembered something from SJ3, during the first battle on the cruise ship.

The image of Tanya, blasting through the air like a cannonball.

All the Wrong Lancer snipers in position to aim at Llenn, including the man with the Model 98B, saw what happened next—a plasma grenade blast lifting the bus.

The hefty vehicle floated upward, rear-first. The thing's underside was swallowed and crushed by a surge of pale blue five meters across, but the blast was strong enough to lift the entire back end of the body. It almost looked like someone had attached an invisible rope to the rear bumper and hoisted it.

Next, the fuel tank ignited. The yellow school bus was immediately wreathed in a crimson explosion.

"What the...? She blew herself up...," muttered the man with the Model 98B as he got down from the truck bed.

"Wait, no! She got away!" called a voice in his ear. It was a teammate positioned high above on a building.

"Oh? How?"

"The blast! She used the explosion she caused to hurl herself away!"

Llenn was inside the burned-out building, covered in dust and glowing red from the scrapes all over her body.

"It…worked…"

She crawled farther back into the darkness, away from the light of the bus's fire, keeping herself safe from sniping for the moment.

It had been a very reckless bit of inspiration.

The plasma grenade went off at the back of the bus, about five meters away from her. The force of the explosion burst through the undercarriage, pushing her away from the vehicle.

And she went ahead with it, having no idea how much damage it would cause her.

Her entire body was covered in fine scratches. The med kit she'd used earlier was still going; by the time its effect was complete, she'd have about 80 percent of her health left. She'd sacrificed about 20 in that little stunt.

But it's better than dying! I can keep going now!

Den-de-de-dehhh, duh, den-de-de-dehhh, duh, den-de-de-dehhh, duh, den-de-de-dehhh.

Mendelssohn's "Wedding March" gave way to Wagner's gallant "Ride of the Valkyries" in Llenn's head.

"What's up, Llenn? You okay?"

"Yep! I got away from the snipers, and I'm inside now!"

"Nice job, partner. We're all on the run and unharmed for the moment! Ah!"

"Fuka?"

"Correction. Anna got shot. That's pretty bad," Fukaziroh replied, her voice overlapped by the low sounds of weapon discharge. Probably Rosa's PKM.

The noise abruptly stopped.

"Ah, Tanya's hit, too. I hope she's not dead…"

"Arrgh…"

"Don't worry about us. Just focus on surviving and getting out of there!"

"Awww…"

"This extra info is only going to complicate things for you. I'll shut off the comm until we're safe."

"All right…"

Llenn pressed her finger to her own ear to turn off the radio, and the world was suddenly quiet.

The only sound was the eerie burning of the bus, echoing through the building.

When the sound of Llenn's explosion reached Car Two, now without its gunner, the driver stopped the vehicle.

Using his side mirrors, he checked to see if he was being attacked. But there were no enemies on the road running east to west, and all he could see around him were buildings and rubble blocking the way.

"Good."

He stepped on the gas again, moving the Humvee east to rejoin his comrades.

Something was galloping along after him.

"The hell is that horselike thing?"

"A horse."

Someone in the audience did not come off as very intelligent.

One of the screens displayed a Humvee busily weaving its way around obstacles as it traveled down the street while a horse gave pursuit.

The steed had come from a side alley to the south. Two women were riding on its back.

"Huh? Is that seriously a horse?"

"You just start playin' *GGO*?"

"Uh, yeah. About three months ago."

"Can't blame ya for not knowing, then. I don't mean to be patronizing, but I'll clue you in. That's called a robot horse. It's a mechanical mount, but not a monster; it's an item a player can ride."

"Ohhh. You can ride them?"

"No."

"What?"

"Normal players can't. You'll get thrown off. Happened to me. And there's no skill you can pick up that just magically gives you control."

"But they're riding it."

"You gotta be able to do it in real life."

"This is wild, Shirley! Is there anything you *can't* do?!" Clarence whooped, clinging to Shirley's back as she bounced on the racing steed's back.

From this position, she was screaming directly into Shirley's ear, so the other woman grimaced and replied, "I wish it was enough to shut you up!"

"Heh... You can't kill me."

"That's not what I meant. Oh, wait, that's a good idea."

"Aw, c'mon. Aren't we teammates?"

"Just cram it, before you bite off your tongue!"

Shirley had the R93 Tactical 2 slung in front of her body, her hands busy clutching metal-wire reins.

The helpful mount that allowed them to move quickly without making much noise was a metal horse about the size of a thoroughbred.

It had all started nearly an hour earlier.

After failing to snipe Pitohui on the highway, the duo had searched for a convenient vehicle so they could get around quickly. This was the best they had located.

There'd been a large SUV parked diagonally across the highway. A trailer had been hitched to it, and inside was the steed.

The trailer was on its side, so Shirley and Clarence had thought the horse broken at first, but when they approached, the metal horse's eyes lit up in response. Slightly awkwardly, it kicked its legs until it could stand up, then rotated its neck toward the door to look at Shirley and Clarence.

"There, there. Hey, you wanna go for a ride?" Shirley asked

the steed gently, but the robotic thing just shivered and shook its head.

"It's saying no," said Clarence, who was carrying the backpack full of explosives.

"C'mon, come on out," coaxed Shirley, pulling the horse out of the trailer. "There you go. Your legs are just fine. You've got a very nice body."

Softly and kindly, Shirly stroked the silvery beast's forelegs, then its back ones. The robot steed was easily over seven feet from head to ground.

"A-aren't you frightened?" asked Clarence, trembling at a distance of twenty feet or so. She looked ready to point her AR-57 at the creature at a moment's notice.

"Don't stand right behind it. It'll kick you to death," Shirley threatened with a rare smile.

"Eep!" Clarence moved back to twenty-five feet.

As Shirley adjusted the saddle and stirrups to proper positions, she explained, "It's fine. *GGO* horses and real horses are the same: If you act gentlemanly, they'll respond in kind."

"But we're ladies."

"I don't mean literal gentlemen. Also, would you really call us ladies?"

"That's up for debate. So can you ride it? I've heard it's tough."

"That's correct, which is why I practiced horseback riding a lot in the game. Lots of the people in my squadron are into equestrian stuff."

"Are you serious? What are you people even doing in *GGO*?"

Shirley was still technically a member of the Kita no Kuni Hunter's Club, the team that had entered SJ2 with the tag KKHC.

The squadron consisted of Mai Kirishima (Shirley) and some fellow hunters licensed in Hokkaido. Their actual sharpshooting and tracking capabilities were quite considerable.

In addition to shooting real ammo and dismantling prey, they could do backcountry skiing, use snowshoes, and drive snowplows and snowmobiles. Some of them could also ride horses.

Mai was especially enamored with horses; when she'd lived in Tokyo as a girl, she had traveled quite a long way to visit a country club. As a college student in the outdoors club, she had ridden as often as she could.

Even now, making a living as a nature guide in Hokkaido, she borrowed horses from a nearby ranch for the occasional ride. Her guide activities involved riding tours and trail riding at that very ranch.

When KKHC learned that there were (mechanical) horses in *GGO*, they'd started practicing.

Robot horses were extreme, high-performance mounts, in ways both good and bad. It was like riding a top-class racing Thoroughbred, with maximum marks in both speed and surly disposition.

Walking and trotting weren't so bad, but moving at full gallop took everything Shirley had.

She and the other members of KKHC had fallen many times, sometimes landing on their heads and dying before a respawn—a valuable experience that a rider could only have once in real life. Thankfully, it had all paid off in the end.

However, it had never come in handy during a PvP battle until today.

The horse charged onward.

It was in a full-on sprint, at a speed it hadn't exhibited until now.

The target was the Humvee ahead, short one passenger after their recent sniping.

"You're so cool, Shirley! Dammit, I wish I knew how to ride a horse!"

"I can teach you sometime!" Shirley replied with uncharacteristic excitement.

"What? No, it's too scary," Clarence shot back. Shirley's glee turned to dejection. "Anyway, what now? Shouldn't we be going after Pitohui?"

"These guys are preventing us from doing that. So we'll take this one out first."

"How?"

"We'll...we'll..."

Shirley hadn't thought of anything.

"Oh boy, you really are hopeless, huh? Then leave it to me! I've got a *great* plan in mind!" stated Clarence with no shortage of confidence. She waved her hand to bring up her inventory and stowed not just the backpack full of explosives but also the AR-57 that was her primary weapon, its magazine pouches, and even the thigh holster for her Five-Seven sidearm.

"Huh? What are you doing?" asked Shirley, glancing back at her.

"Bring us up alongside! I'm gonna do an action flick move!" answered Clarence, now lightly outfitted in just her black combat fatigues and boots.

"If you fall off, I'm not going back for you!"

"Aw, that's so mean."

"What about your weapons?"

"Right here."

"Huh?"

Shirley turned back to look at Clarence again and saw that she was pressing a hand to her chest.

"What?"

"Hey! Humvee! Behind you! They're right behind you!" shouted the spectators in the bar, not that anyone could hear them.

"Aaah!" yelped the V2HG driver of the Humvee. "What the hell...?"

He had noticed his bizarre pursuer. Looking closer at his side mirror, he muttered, "A horse?"

It was indeed.

He spied two players on top of it, and it was clear at a glance that they were not his friends.

"You're kidding me. I'm not dealing with bandits on horseback."

Deciding that this was not the time to be fighting while on his own, he stomped down on the gas pedal, then on the brakes again, as he wove left and right around the rubble, then the gas once more.

"Awww, crap!"

He drove as fast as possible back down the street he'd just taken so much care to pass through.

"Yah!"

Shirley kicked with spur-less boots, nevertheless urging on her robot mount and charging headfirst toward the rubble. That left the horse with two options: speed up and leap over the wreckage or stop and throw off its two riders.

"Jump! You can do it!" Shirley urged sincerely. The robot horse responded in kind.

"Hyaaaa!" Clarence screamed as the horse bounded effortlessly over a pile as tall as a human being.

Before leaving the ground, Shirley made sure to hover forward over the saddle, lifting Clarence with her, so that she could smoothly return to her seat after landing.

"That's it! Good girl! You did it! Wasn't that fun?"

"Hell no! I felt like I was going to die!" yelled Clarence.

"I wasn't talking to you!"

The robot horse's hooves, clad in shoes of an unidentified metal, clacked loudly on the asphalt as it gained on the nearby Humvee.

"We're almost there! What did you want me to do?"

"Line up on its left side!"

"If you're sure," Shirley responded, pressing her heels into the horse's flanks and tugging the reins a bit to the left. "It's your funeral!"

The mount sped up a bit more and came up level with the Humvee's flank.

"Yaaaaah!" Clarence shouted. Now it was her turn to jump.

She soared awesomely through the air and landed horrendously on her stomach against the bulletproof armor plating.

"Gurgh! Ghoof!"

The stunt proved fairly damaging, sapping 20 percent of her total HP. She could have ruptured an internal organ doing that in real life.

"Owww!" Clarence winced. She crouched on the rear portion of the vehicle's roof, outside the armored turret, then waved her hand. It brought up her player window, where she hit just one button.

Then she jumped down inside the Humvee.

Thump! The driver heard someone land inside the vehicle.

In the center of the Humvee was a pantograph-style standing platform for the gunner. It was pretty noisy when someone was stomping around in it.

Obviously, the dead body wasn't going to be making footsteps, so the sound had to be from an enemy—one who had boarded the Humvee.

The driver slammed on the brake pedal and swung to his right, reaching with his left arm for the HK433 assault rifle he'd placed between the front seats.

He straightened out the rifle's folded stock with a smooth and practiced motion, disengaged the safety, pointed the barrel behind him, and stopped.

"Huh?"

A woman was standing in her underwear.

In the place where his headless teammate had previously been, there was now a woman showing a shocking amount of skin.

She was a willowy creature with short black hair and pointed facial features.

Her figure was slender, without much shapeliness to it.

The only things hiding her blindingly white skin were a few patches of black cloth.

The top was a sports bra.

The bottom was a short thong with a tantalizing triangle

between the flesh of her thighs. However, because of how she was standing, it was hidden by her curves so that it looked like she wasn't wearing anything at all.

Below her bewitching smile, the lines of her neck met the deep crease of her smooth collarbone, followed by the slight slope of her upper chest, the subtle swell of her breasts beneath the bra, the faint outline of ribs along her sides, the narrow tuck above her waist, the bulge of her thighs, her slender fingers, her delicate ankles, her…

All these details instantly seared themselves into the man's mind, frying his brain. Hot blood pumped through his entire body. Let's not talk about where it was going.

He could sense it. There was a wonderful scent inside the Humvee.

The woman grinned at him and leaned over, putting her face and chest closer to the driver's seat.

"Hey…you wanna touch my boobs?"

"Huh? Uh, yes," the man replied with a knee-jerk reflex. He put the gun down and reached out toward the black fabric over her chest.

She took his hand gently with her own.

"Ooh!"

"Right here…"

She guided it toward her breast. Meanwhile, her other hand moved behind the driver's seat.

The man's hand was getting closer and closer to her.

Gulp.

Just a few more inches, and he'd make contact. He'd know what it was like.

And it was in this dreamlike haze that the woman's left hand snuck around the back of the seat and fired a Five-Seven pistol at his face.

From less than an inch away, the muzzle spat out a bullet that passed through his forehead and out the back of his skull.

Despite the hole in his head, the man's body continued to twist, reaching even farther. It was his last vestiges of life, clinging to one purpose.

Tits!

His fingers just barely brushed the surface of the black material.

"Aaah…"

The man's hit points ran out, and he died.

Between the mask and the sunglasses, his expression remained a mystery.

Shirley spun the robot horse around.

"Here you go!"

From the roof of the Humvee, which had plunged directly into a pile of rubble, Clarence tossed out a man's body with a DEAD tag floating overhead, as casually as if hurling a sandbag.

She was in the furthest possible state of undress for an avatar to be—in her underwear.

"And another!"

There went the second body, soaring through the air with ease.

Shirley offered her honest opinion on the matter: "You're pretty strong."

"Eeeek! Don't look at me, Shirley! You perv!" playfully shrieked Clarence.

"You don't have to run through the clichés with me. I can see exactly how you did it. Not that I could do the same."

"Huh? Yes you can. Just hit UNEQUIP ALL GEAR AND CLOTHING."

"It's not an issue of knowing *how* you did it."

"But you got bigger tits than me."

"That's not the problem, either."

"You gotta use every weapon at your disposal."

"I think we need to sit down and have an honest talk later," Shirley stated. She glanced around and pushed the robot horse forward. From her high vantage point, she could see down into the Humvee.

In the turret space surrounded by armored plating was the

impressive six-barrel Gatling-style machine gun, the M134 Minigun. It puzzled her.

"What is this part for? Is it a water hose?"

"What?! You play *GGO*, and you don't even know what a Minigun is? You're so behind the times!"

"Sorry. Is it powerful?"

"The *most* powerful!"

"The most powerful gun is the one I have."

"Yeah, yeah, we all think that. Hey, that horse is scary. Keep its face away from me!"

"Good grief," said Shirley.

If she hadn't pulled back on the reins at that moment, the bullet would have gone through her thigh.

Instead, the sniper's shot hit a joint of the robot horse's front left leg, gouging out a chunk of its mechanical body.

The startled creature reared back. Shirley immediately slipped her feet out of the stirrups, let go of the reins, and leaped off the horse to the right.

It was standing upright on its back legs. If Shirley hadn't jumped, it probably would have fallen backward and crushed her underneath.

Instead, when its front hooves landed on the ground again, the instability in its damaged left leg caused it to lose its balance. In the meantime, another bullet passed over Shirley's head.

"Shit!" She tried to bring her R93 Tactical 2 around to aim.

"Just get inside! This car's armored! You know how to drive, right?" said Clarence, throwing open the driver-side door from inside the Humvee. The bulletproof metal and glass protected Shirley.

"Why should I—? Shit!" Shirley swore. She tossed the long rifle inside to Clarence, then hopped into the driver's seat. As she did so, a bullet struck the neck of the fallen robot horse to put it out of its misery.

It was something Mai had done many times to deer she'd hunted.

"I'm sorry!"

The horse's head fell limp as Shirley shut the car door.

"Oh, it's cool! No worries!" said Clarence.

Shirley settled into the driver's seat and said, "Not you—the horse. Say a quick prayer in thanks. And put on some damn clothes!"

"You got it!"

Clarence brought up her inventory, then pressed the EQUIP ALL button. Black combat fatigues wrapped around her body, magazine pouches popped over her limbs, and lastly, an AR-57 appeared in front of her. It was like a magical girl transformation.

Clarence tossed the backpack filled with explosives into the back as soon as it took shape. Thankfully, that weak impact wasn't enough to set the contents off.

The Humvee's roof was low for such a large vehicle, which made the space feel a little cramped. Especially with the Minigun's bag full of batteries, the ammo feeding rail, and the boxes containing thousands of rounds of ammo taking up two full seats in the back.

Glank!

A bullet hit the windshield, leaving just the tiniest gray mark. If not for the reinforced glass, the bullet would have hit Shirley. She'd only seen the bullet line for the briefest moment.

It wasn't lineless sniping like Shirley and M could do, but it was precise aiming done on the circle's very first contraction. That said a lot about the shooter's skill. Under ordinary battle conditions, it would be nearly impossible to avoid such shots.

"Very sharp," praised Shirley, reaching into her waist pouch for the binoculars so she could peer ahead.

About five hundred meters away, there was another car of the same sort pointed toward them, with a man inside the turret holding a sniper rifle behind a shield of bulletproof glass. He looked ready to kill.

"Oh, I bet he's mad. Sorry we killed your friends."

"Hey, Shirley! What happened to your noble goal of killing Pitohui?"

"I haven't forgotten. C'mon, let's get out of here…"

Shirley put the Humvee into reverse and hit the gas pedal.

* * *

"Shit! It didn't work..."

The leader of V2HG realized that it was pointless to shoot at another Humvee just as protected as his own. He pulled back inside the roof. "Lucky bastards," he swore.

He set down the L129A1 he'd been using and got back into the driver's seat. The gun was an automatic sniper rifle that fired 7.62 × 51 mm NATO rounds. Like the Heckler & Koch HK417 and Knight's Armament SR-25, it was an ArmaLite AR-10 derivative developed after the patent expired. Therefore, all three of those guns looked alike. Anyone not well versed in firearms would have difficulty telling them apart.

The L129A1 was the name given to the weapon when the British military adopted it. The official model was the Lewis Machine and Tool (LMT) LW308MWS.

Gun names could be tricky because a gun possessed a product name given by the manufacturer and an official name assigned by the military force that purchased it.

This man, the team leader, was the very player who'd shot Boss and the other members of SHINC in succession on the south side of the airport. Naturally, his teammate had been lying when he'd said, "We took care of the DOOM sniper who shot you guys." Just a little acting to smooth things over with SHINC and get them into the alliance.

However, even a sharpshooting sniper with an excellent rifle stood no chance against an armored Humvee. The leader of V2HG thought that was unfair. Maybe he'd forgotten that he was also in such a vehicle.

"This is Car One. I've got bad news and bad news. What do you want first?"

"I know Johann's already down! I'm on my way! Let's get revenge!" answered the man who'd been shooting the grenade launcher earlier. Despite losing his teammates, it sounded like he was enjoying himself even more than before. This was what people who played *GGO* were like.

"Okay, bad news it is, then. Two ambush troops from an unknown team took over Car Two and the Minigun."

"Fu—"

That one knocked the grenadier for a loop. But he recovered quickly. "All right, fine! Forget about cornering LPFM and SHINC; let's take it back!"

"No. We're abandoning Car Two. We'll head west a different way."

"I'll follow your orders, Leader, but I want to know why."

"Even with a Minigun, we'd have difficulty breaking through that armor to get to them, especially if they're on the move. And those snipers have to be pretty tough to survive this long. Like the original plan, we'll push the target northwest and surround them. Once we've eliminated LPFM, our contract with Fire is over. Then we can do whatever we want."

"Got it… This is just a side comment, but what reason does Fire have to want to wipe out LPFM so badly?"

"This is my own side comment—I don't know, either. I made sure not to ask. But as long as he's hiring us, I intend to give this job everything I've got, to the point of death."

"To continue the side comments, how much did he pay you for this? I'm really curious."

"Ah-ha-ha-ha! When this is all over, or at the last possible moment, I will reveal all. You guys'll be shocked, I bet. Oops, that's a side comment, too."

* * *

Gagonk!

The Humvee smashed into a block of concrete.

"Uagh!" Clarence's body rocked from side to side, her right shoulder smacking hard against the door. "Ouch! So you can do everything, but your driving sucks! Does this really count as knowing how to handle a car?!"

"Shut up! No comments! Just watch!" Shirley snapped, her

hands on the wheel. She took her right hand off to move the gearshift and put the Humvee into reverse.

Grunch! She pushed it too hard, and the right rear corner of the vehicle smashed into a junked car behind them.

"Oh, come on! This isn't how you're supposed to play *GGO*!"

"Ugh! Shit!"

Mai Kirishima had a standard driver's license, a necessity in the relatively spacious Hokkaido region. However, while she loved and had mastered riding motorcycles and horses, her appreciation of four-wheel vehicles did not carry over into skill.

Her usual set of wheels was a 4WD car she'd bought for cheap from a coworker. And she tended to drive slowly and carefully.

Not long after she first got her license, Mai bumped another car in a parking lot. It wasn't a lot of damage, but the owner was furious, and her insurance had to cover the repair bill. From that point on, she tried not to drive whenever possible. Since you *had* to use a car to be a working adult in Hokkaido, she did it anyway. There was little other choice, especially in winter.

"This thing is too big! It's like a giant truck!" Shirley ranted, smacking the steering wheel.

At over seven feet wide and nearly sixteen feet long, the Humvee was huge. The average city car in Japan was under five feet wide, and a compact vehicle was under six. Even a full-size SUV was barely more than six feet wide. So the Humvee was massive in that sense.

Mai had never driven anything this big. And she wasn't used to the wheel being on the left side, with the shifter over on her right. There were also armor plating and bulletproof glass on the side windows, which really stifled her peripheral vision. She couldn't see anything behind her.

The Humvee scraped rubble on the right side but managed to get free of the tight space, only to proceed toward another obstacle in the road.

Shirley sighed. "I guess that guy was a really good driver…"

"Maybe we shouldn't have killed him. But if we wanted to make him our slave, you needed to get in on the action, too, Shirley."

The pair headed back west down the road they'd taken with the robot horse, but the going was very slow. At least the other Humvee that had shot at them had decided they weren't worth pursuing, giving them one less thing to worry about.

"It's this road's fault. Let's look for a better one and go west. That's where Pitohui's group is. We'll push them into the northwest corner and attack!"

"Seriously, Shirley? You're just going to run them over?" Clarence asked.

"Huh? I don't know… I'd rather not," answered Shirley, suddenly feeling a surge of her real-life fear of driving.

"No, you should! You're not honor bound to only play as a sniper!" urged Clarence, helpfully misunderstanding the other woman's hesitation.

Shirley drove on a bit, then turned right at the next opportunity, moving into a narrow alley. The path was only sixteen feet across, but fortunately, there was almost no debris in the way. The course continued straight north.

Shirley pressed down on the gas to accelerate. At last, she could drive normally.

About a hundred yards ahead, there was another intersection with a wide-looking street.

"That's it! That's the victory road of triumph that we were promised!" howled Clarence, pointing.

"Let's hope. Also, *victory* and *triumph* is redundant."

"So we'll turn left! The direction you hold your teacup!"

"Good thing I'm right-handed. We're coming for you, Pitohui!" snarled Shirley. Her hatred for Pitohui got the best of her, and she plunged into the left turn without applying the brakes first.

"Hyaaaa!" Clarence shrieked from the other seat as the vehicle headed for the building on the opposite corner of the intersection, unable to complete its turn at this speed.

"Ah! Crap, crap, crap…"

Shirley slammed on the brakes as hard as she could, closed her eyes, and prayed. The tires screeched and skidded, sending the vehicle sliding sideways until the right rear side of the Humvee crashed against the building.

Grchank!

"Gaah!"

"Daa!"

Clarence and Shirley were jolted by the impact.

The side of Clarence's head slammed against the frame of the bulletproof window, leaving a glowing damage mark on her skin. She'd lost 5 percent of her hit points. Shirley had clutched the steering wheel and had managed not to get hurt.

Clarence pressed on the new welt on her temple and turned to complain. "I told you, it's not that kind of game! Should I drive instead?"

"Sorry… I'll be more careful."

"Sheesh. C'mon, let's get going!"

"Fine, fine…"

Shirley carefully pressed on the accelerator, and the Humvee crunched and scraped as the dented corner came loose from the building.

As the vehicle drove away, it left behind a dead body that had been crushed in the impact. Next to the man with the DEAD tag floating over his body was a Barrett Model 98B rifle.

The Wrong Lancers' first casualty had been from a car accident.

CHAPTER 16
Retreat II

SECT.16

CHAPTER 16
Retreat II

Llenn's grenade blast gust thrust up the bus and busted her buns. Try saying that three times fast.

But it hasn't really changed the situation that much!

She was still stuck in one place. The only difference was that it was in a burned-out building rather than under a school bus. The structure seemed like it had once been an electronics store. The interior was eerily quiet, with all the cracked and broken TV screens around.

Llenn searched for a staircase. A floor or two of height would at least give her a better view of her surroundings.

Unfortunately, there was no upward route to be found on the inside. Apparently, it was a rental space because, to deter theft, there were no side exits, either. The only way in or out was the north face adjacent to the street.

Llenn huddled in the back of the darkened interior, watching the brighter windowed side intently. If anyone came along, she was going to give them a bellyful of P90 lead on full auto.

How long after two o'clock was it? She'd lost her wristwatch, so only the Satellite Scanner would tell her, and she didn't dare bring that out in case the illumination helped a sniper find her.

If she waited around for at least five minutes, would a monster appear inside? She couldn't help but worry. What if she failed to kill it with her knife?

Aw…I feel so alone…

Being a lone warrior sounded cool and all, but *lone* was simply short for *lonely.*

Llenn considered just darting out into the street and testing her luck, but the thought of a silent sniper scared her out of taking the plunge. Unlike the recent playtest, Squad Jam was a one-and-done deal. If Llenn died, something terrible would happen.

"What should I do, P-chan?" she thought, asking the gun slung around her chest, but there was no answer.

"What should I do, Kni-chan?" she thought, asking the knife behind her back, but there was no answer.

"What should I do, Pla-chan?" she thought, reaching to rub a plasma grenade, but she wisely stopped herself.

Zbwoaa! There was a tremendous roar from the street, like a wild animal snoring.

A Humvee!

Llenn remembered that distinct sound from SJ2, having heard it many times. It was the engine of a military Humvee, a water-cooled V-8 turbo diesel with 6,500 cubic centimeters in displacement.

The noise was echoing between the buildings and getting louder. That meant the Humvee was approaching from the east, Llenn's right side.

Based on the sound, there was just one of the vehicles. More than that, and it would have been a cacophony.

Ugh! What should I do? Llenn wondered.

What if that was the Humvee with the Minigun? That one should have been on the other street a hundred yards to the south. If it was the same one, she really wanted to throw a plasma grenade at it. That was why she'd left her group in the first place.

As long as the enemy didn't know she was here, she could hurl a bomb under the car as it passed. The little bit of fortune that had brought the enemy to her would, at last, allow her to fulfill her mission.

Yet, Llenn also had another idea. *What if I could jump inside when it passes?*

While the roof was surrounded by armor plating, the turret itself was open. Llenn knew that because she'd ridden in one during SJ2. So she'd pop out, run straight for it, and leap up and into the Humvee. In SJ2, she'd jumped *over* a Humvee pursuing her, so the timing shouldn't be too hard.

A more reliable strategy would be to set off the plasma grenade in front of the Humvee to make it stop. It might even momentarily blind any snipers waiting with sights trained on the road.

Once Llenn jumped inside the car, the Humvee's armor would protect her from any snipers in wait. However many people were inside the Humvee, she'd just have to give them hell.

She'd spray and pray with P-chan, and when her ammo ran out, she'd swing her knife. There was no risk of killing one of her own teammates. It was the perfect situation for the same kind of fighting she'd employed in the domed jungle of SJ2.

I can do it… I can… I will! Llenn swore.

She couldn't deny that there was an element of recklessness to the idea, but it was still far preferable to being trapped here by snipers and left behind by her friends, just to wait for them to get wiped out.

I'll do it!

Llenn felt like she could hear the blood vessels in her brain boiling.

Suddenly, the engine's roar got much louder. It was very close. Llenn adjusted the timer on a plasma grenade with her left hand, extending it from three seconds to four.

She was going to press the switch and coordinate it so that when she tossed it out into the middle of the street, it would explode right on contact.

The sounds of the Humvee grew even nearer.

C'mon, c'mon…

Llenn rushed up to the wall and pressed the switch on the grenade.

* * *

There was a sudden flash of light up ahead.

"What?!"

The Humvee driver slammed on the brake pedal, and the lumbering vehicle just barely came to a stop in front of the blue orb. If it had passed through the plasma explosion, the energy would have chewed the front half of the car to shreds.

The blast shook the heavy vehicle, sending dust in through the open roof.

Something else came in through the aperture, too.

"Taaa!" shrieked a small pink person who hurtled inside and landed butt-first on the metal plate in the back of the Humvee. "Yeow!"

She twisted around, baring her fangs, and pointed a P90 submachine gun at—

"Huh?"

She only noticed just before she pulled the trigger.

The people turning back to look at her from the driver's and passenger's seats were technically her teammates.

Unfortunately, her understanding was slower than her reflexes.

The P90 fired a single bullet into the center console.

"Hyaaaa!" "Daaaaa!" Clarence and Shirley screamed together.

"I'm sorryyyy!" Llenn added to the mix. "But why?!" she cried, just as startled as the other two.

She'd put together this mad stunt, half expecting to die doing it, and had come face-to-face with none other than the teammates she'd split off from over an hour earlier.

"What are you doing?" Llenn demanded, still holding the P90.

"Don't point that at us!" Shirley snapped.

"We'll pay you back for the motorcycle we stole!" Clarence wailed.

Llenn lowered the P90 and glanced to her sides, noticing the metal ammo railing connected to the Minigun. "I'm not going to shoot you! Wait, did you steal the Humvee *with* the Minigun? That's amazing!"

"Yep!" Clarence boasted. Technically, it was her lingerie performance that had done the trick, so she'd earned the right to be proud.

"Give me a ride, then! Everyone's running west—let's go help them!"

"Uh-huh. And is Pitohui with them?" Shirley asked, her eyes sharp.

"Ooh—!" Llenn gasped. The hand holding the P90 twitched. If Shirley happened to spot Pitohui, she might seriously drive over her with the Humvee.

Wait a second, are they really on our side? Should I be thinking of them as enemies instead?

"Should we go at it, then?" Shirley asked, glaring at Llenn. But her gun was resting sideways on her lap, not ready to fire.

"Hey, Llenn, are you good at driving?" Clarence asked for some reason.

"Huh?"

"You can go right ahead and shoot Shirley if you take the wheel. And then we can be good friends!"

"Okay, I get it. So that's how it's gonna be, then…," grumbled Shirley.

"I can't…," Llenn admitted.

"Neither can I. So if you shoot Shirley, this big old hunk of metal is useless."

"Got it… Setting aside the stuff about Pito, just drive! There's a sniper around! That's why I couldn't escape until you showed up!" Llenn explained. Shirley did not seem particularly happy about the answer.

Gank! Gank! Sparks showered down on them through the roof from a pair of shots. That made the decision a bit more pressing. Llenn nearly caught one bullet through her foot.

"Hya! H-hurry!"

"Dammit! Fine!"

The engine roared to life again, and the Humvee carrying three members of LPFM rolled over the hole left by the plasma grenade, the tires passing around the edges. More shots collided with the vehicle, creating no small amount of noise inside.

"What time is it?" Llenn asked Clarence.

"Um...2:08!"

* * *

Roughly ten minutes had passed since they'd watched Llenn leave just before two o'clock.

Pitohui, M, Fukaziroh, and the five members of SHINC couldn't even count the number of times they'd thought they'd die in the intervening time.

When they determined that Llenn had successfully held off the Wrong Lancers, they'd decided to leave their intersection base and move west. In some respects, it had been the right answer, and in others, it had been a terrible, terrible choice.

At that point, a trio of Wrong Lancers, including the leader, were heading toward Llenn. The remaining three were waiting calmly in place.

A few minutes later, though they'd spotted two squads moving together, they'd held their fire. It was only three snipers to the eight fleeing targets. The Wrong Lancers knew from experience that if they started firing, they'd only be able to take out two or three opponents at best.

Instead, they let Pitohui's group head west. Perhaps, after a while, they'd feel like the coast was clear and indulge in a bit of rest. That would be the Lancers' chance to strike.

Then the snipers left their building perch and followed on foot. They made liberal use of cover, careful not to let the rear guard spot their pursuit. The tactic was one that the Wrong Lancers employed often.

The sniping started around 2:05.

There were three of them, all wearing green camo, masks, and sunglasses, but there were two kinds of sniper rifles between them.

One had an RPR. That stood for Ruger Precision Rifle. It was a bolt-action sniper rifle made by Sturm, Ruger and Co. in America, using .308 Winchester cartridges belonging to the 7.62 × 51 mm NATO standard.

The straight-angled stock and pistol grip gave it the countenance of an assault rifle. The RPR wasn't necessarily used in great numbers by any military, but it was popular among civilians for being very cheap for such a quality armament. It was also reasonably priced in *GGO* and gave a sniper everything they could want.

This man's RPR was painted the same color as his camo, which made it hard to tell where the shooter ended and the gun began.

There were only two kinds of weapons between the three of them because the other two used the same sort of gun. Each had an Mk 12 SPR automatic sniper rifle. SPR stood for Special Purpose Rifle.

The SPR launched 5.56 × 45 NATO rounds, the same caliber as the M16 and Type 89 rifles. The firearm itself was a custom M16 model, so it looked similar. But the barrel had been tinkered with to make it capable of high-precision sniping, and it used special bullets. There was also a suppressor.

It had an effective range of about seven hundred meters, which was shorter than that of larger-caliber sniper rifles, but it had the advantages of precision and lighter weight. Even better, because it was based on the M16 assault rifle, it could fire semi-auto if needed.

There was another benefit to having two of the exact same gun set up the same way (scope, bipod, other accessories) on top of that.

The clone jutsu.

Not that they were ninjas. There was no in-game skill or item in *GGO* that made that possible.

But when you had two avatars with the same height and figure, both with their faces hidden, it was impossible to tell them apart.

Within the squadron, the guys liked to joke that these two were the "Wrong Lancer Brothers," but they were absolutely not related and were from totally different parts of Japan. They were just a pair of gun nuts who had met in *GGO* and found that they got along.

As such, they always dressed themselves up the same way. Here in SJ4, they wore camo and used Mk 12 SPRs. They worked as a two-person team, but at a distance.

When the situation called for it, one would reveal himself and attack while the other remained in hiding. When the first one took fire from the enemy, he would simply turn and run without putting up a fight. Once the enemy chased after him, the other one would pop out of hiding and attack.

To the opponent who got shot, it would seem like one player had warped or used a clone technique to create a double.

These tactics made the two of them the best antipersonnel soldiers on the Wrong Lancers. They were at their most useful when the squadron was under attack by PKer hunters, as well as during moments like this.

The next member of SHINC to fall after Sophie was Anna.

She became the first target of the man with the RPR.

"Hrgh!"

He shot her through the left flank from behind, where she couldn't see the bullet line.

The powerful rifle's projectile took 80 percent of her hit points all at once, dropping Anna to the ground. The fact that it wasn't an instant kill meant that she had time to warn her teammates.

"I'll hold them back! Keep going!" she shouted to her friends. Then she threw herself behind some debris and took position with her Dragunov. She'd keep the enemy here until she died.

Everyone understood that it was the best possible move. "Damn… Everyone run!" Boss ordered.

"Shit!" swore Rosa, pulling back after giving some covering fire with her PKM. She took off running, watching Anna grow smaller and smaller.

"That's right! Just go!" repeated Anna. She had her Dragunov at the ready, lying on the ground behind the rubble to wait for the next attack by herself. Through her 4× scope, she caught a glimpse of a moving bit of camo. "There you are!"

However, before she could take proper aim, a bullet hit her head from a different direction.

"Damn…"

She was sent back to the waiting area.

When Boss learned of Anna's death, she gave the order to her three remaining squadmates and her other comrades.

"Next person to get shot, don't stop! Everybody run!"

"Follow them."

"Roger that."

"Roger that."

Three Wrong Lancers entered pursuit.

After they took out the sniper, the other seven enemies had stopped fighting back and focused on escape. It was easier for the Lancers to shoot them when they stopped, so it was a wise tactical decision—but it pushed the pursuers to get serious.

As a general rule, snipers did not like to sprint. The last thing you wanted to do was spike your heart rate.

However, the Wrong Lancers went to extreme lengths to eliminate their own weaknesses, which meant they practiced like Olympic biathletes, running four-hundred-meter dashes before testing their sharpshooting.

Through this grueling training, they learned how to aim and shoot with the proper timing to minimize the bullet circle even when their pulses were racing.

The man with the RPR wove his way through the rubble, then climbed up onto a flipped-over truck and aimed at the figure running at the head of the fleeing group, four hundred meters away—an avatar with silver hair.

"Gyahuh!"

The bullet from the RPR hit Tanya in the shoulder and spun her around. It was only her excellent sense of balance that kept her from falling to the ground.

"Dammit! I hate snipers!"

"You were lucky! Keep running!" urged Boss, who was delighted that it hadn't been an insta-kill. Internally, she was considering leaving Pitohui's squad behind.

M was the slowest out of all of them, so he was holding the group back as a whole. And if SHINC used their athletic ability to the fullest extent, they could take cover in a nearby building—leaving only Pitohui's people as targets for the snipers.

Pitohui was fixated on running to the west. She had decided they should keep going, even under fire, but Boss had no idea why.

What to do...?

A bullet flew at her head as she pondered.

It was Pitohui who ensured that Boss tumbled over and out of the way; she'd run up alongside her at some point. When Pitohui noticed the bullet line, she threw out her foot and tripped Boss.

Boss fell to the ground in a defensive position, saw the bullet line over her head, and heard the scream of the projectile as it raced by.

"Get up! Almost there!" encouraged Pitohui, pulling Boss up and toward the shelter of a large pile of rubble.

"Okay!"

Boss gave up on her idea. At the same time, she had another thought.

Karen knows Pitohui's player in real life. She's got extreme destructive urges but is also a very serious and earnest person...

It made her want to know what Pitohui was like in real life, too.

The person who did the most during this retreating battle was the one typically equipped with a pair of grenade launchers and a 9 mm M&P—Fukaziroh.

Being the smallest person there, she was the most challenging target, and she scurried from one spot to the next like a little mouse.

"Here you go."

"All riiight!"

M gave her a grand grenade that she wrapped in a cloth that she used to fling it with all her might.

It was a simple concept. She draped one end of a long, thin piece of fabric around her wrist, then put the grand grenade in the center of the cloth, activated it, and wrapped the explosive up. Once she was holding the other end with her other hand, she was ready to throw.

At this point, she would wind up and spin her arms around, then let go at the right moment so that the heavy object hurtled out of the cloth. It was a primitive but effective method of throwing; Sophie used it sometimes, too.

The explosion wouldn't reach a distant sniper, but the azure blast would shield them from bullets and send up dust that worked like a weak smoke screen. Alas, it wasn't enough to topple buildings.

But while this might have slowed the Wrong Lancers' pursuit, it did not stop it outright.

"Ugh!"

They accurately read M's zigzag pattern, and he took a shot to the thigh. They knew that his backpack was holding the modular shield, so they'd aimed lower. M continued running on his numb leg.

Pitohui was hit, too. She spotted an enemy behind her and pointed the KTR-09 that way to put down a screen of fire. No sooner had she done so than a bullet struck her from the other side of the street.

"Ugh!"

She twisted the moment she saw the line, so it went through her left shoulder instead of her chest and heart.

"Wait, no… They're… That's it!"

Pitohui had deciphered the secret to the clone jutsu the enemy was using.

* * *

And now it was 2:08.

They'd taken more shots, to the point that every last one of them was glowing with damage somewhere and down to between 70 and 50 percent health.

"Found it! Over here, Pito!"

The seven survivors of the retreat battle had reached the locomotive.

The direct rail line that ran southeast along the map stood out among the city's crumbling remains. Resting atop the tracks was a massive metal object measuring seventy-two feet end to end. Its exterior was battered and ancient.

"Hide behind it! Don't get in yet! It's booby-trapped!" Pitohui instructed the other six. They picked up speed, hurrying to reach what was the perfect shelter from the snipers. "And pay your respects to the squatters who got here before us," she appended after a moment.

"Huh?" Tanya wondered aloud. She ran with her Bizon readied at her waist, reached the locomotive before anyone else, and swung around the back.

"Oh! Hey…! Long time no see!"

There she found the fully armored sci-fi team T-S, already hiding.

"This is Llenn! Where are you guys? Something crazy has happened over here!"

Llenn hooked her comm back up while in the passenger seat of the Humvee so she could get in touch with her squad.

The vehicle was slowly making its way down the street with Shirley behind the wheel. She was trying to avoid the debris and dead cars in the way, but very unsteadily. And in some cases, unsuccessfully.

Clarence stood in the turret, hands on the Minigun's grips, thumb at the trigger. She'd given it a brief test earlier, so they knew it still worked.

The incredible noise and rate of fire startled them, but the weapon was fixed to the Humvee, which made it more comfortable to use and aim than an ordinary gun. Clarence saw that the weapon's bullet circle was calm and steady.

Naturally, the enemy could see the bullet line like a searchlight, but she didn't care. If any enemies were ahead, she'd destroy them with her overwhelming firing speed.

"Yo, glad to hear you're all right. Let me tell you, it's been party time over here!" came Fukaziroh's voice in Llenn's ear.

She could see that Fukaziroh's HP was currently at 70 percent. It wasn't that long ago that she'd gotten blasted atop the building, so she had to be out of healing kits by now.

"Wh-what's the situation? How is SHINC?"

"Anna died, unfortunately. Hurts to lose a fellow blond… She's watching us from the great big waiting area in the sky now."

"Oh… But everyone else is all right?"

"Banged up but alive."

"Aw…"

"More importantly, what about you?"

"I'm in a Humvee," Llenn started to explain, but then Fukaziroh screamed "Hya!" and there was the sound of a grenade blast on the other end.

Around the locomotive, it was, as Fukaziroh had put it, *party time.*

Two Humvees arrived at a point on the road with a good view of the train just after M finally got behind cover. They loosed a tremendous hail of gunfire at the locomotive; if M had been four seconds later, he would have been dead on the tracks.

The two Humvees stopped about 350 meters away, one in front of the other, in the eleven o'clock direction from the train's nose. One came to a stop at an angle, exposing its right front side, and the other took the same angle slightly behind. That gave them sight lines while minimizing the amount of exposed armor.

The team leader started sniping with the L129A1 from the roof of Car One. From Car Three, which had a trio of passengers, two got out and used the vehicle's body as a shield. They added their HK433 assault rifle and M79 grenade launcher to the offensive barrage.

A grenade landed on the roof of the locomotive close to Fukaziroh, startling her while she was conversing with Llenn over the comms.

"Hya!"

The last group member set up an H&K MG5 7.62 mm machine gun behind the armor plating of the rear Humvee and fired bursts at intervals of three seconds.

"Hwaaa! Look out!" cried Pitohui with glee, shooting a descending grenade with her short shotgun, the M870 Breacher. The explosive had been on a direct course to land on them behind the engine. If she hadn't blown it up in midair, three members of SHINC would have died.

M hastily spread out his shield in front of the tracks. He stood about three meters from the engine to draw the gunfire to himself.

Sadly, the enemy was too smart. Rather than shooting M, they scattered their shots to the train's front and rear to keep the group from escaping.

"Hrmm..."

M fired back with his M14 EBR instead, but the bullets bounced harmlessly off the Humvees' armor. A bullet line shone right through the seam in his shield.

"Ah!" He tilted his head away from it, and an L129A1 bullet passed through. "Very nice aim."

Behind the engine, Fukaziroh asked Tohma, "Should I bring out the big guy?" referring to the PTRD-41 she had in her inventory.

"Yeah! We can use that on the Humvees—"

"Don't bother! They'll snipe you the moment you set it up!" Pitohui warned. The other two looked at each other and recognized the truth when they heard it.

"Fine...," replied Tohma, crestfallen.

However, Fukaziroh just patted her on the back. "Hey, I'll hold on to it a bit longer for ya. Don't worry, I won't shoot or sell it."

While that part of the group was putting up a good fight, Boss was busy getting in a yelling match with T-S.

"If you're going to shoot me, go ahead! But you're not going to last long after that!" she screamed. Her fury was so intense that it totally shut down T-S.

Ervin, who wore the number 002, touted an XM8. The others had their Steyr AUGs and SAR 21s pointed at the rest of Boss's ragtag party. If T-S pulled the triggers, they could wipe out the two squads in three seconds.

"Do you understand what's going on here? We're getting shot by crack snipers from the allied team!" she snapped as bullets panged and twanged nearby. The attackers were clearly going after the train itself, chipping away at the metal. Some of the rounds bounced beneath the locomotive, and one spiraled upward and hit one of the T-S soldiers. It did not do any actual damage.

"Th-then what should we do?" questioned Ervin, who always felt compelled to speak for the group.

"That's obvious!"

They'd fought on the same side in SJ3 and in the recent playtest, but now the two sides were enemies. Boss knew the reason they'd stayed out of trouble so far this game. T-S had figured out about the allied team after watching the Satellite Scan. The squad must have been hoping to run around and hide until they could pick off whoever survived, just like they had in SJ2.

Boss could hardly blame them for the tactic.

"In the current situation, do you really think you'll make it out of this without working with us? Just help—it doesn't have to be for long!"

Kaboom! The ground behind them shook with an explosion from an M79 grenade launcher. That seemed to make the difference for T-S.

"A-all right, I guess..."

* * *

The four members of V2HG watched as a soldier in battle armor emerged from the front of the locomotive.

"It's T-S!"

They'd studied videos of the previous Squad Jams, so they recognized that look at once. They focused their gunfire in that direction. Even if the bullets didn't go through the train, they only needed to knock the target over.

However, T-S was not quite the same as in previous battles.

"Launcher!" some of the V2HG squadmates yelled, a warning about the M320 grenade launcher their target was holding.

Pomp!

Number 003 from T-S shot a 40 mm grenade onto the hood of the front Humvee, where it exploded.

V2HG's leader had already descended below the line of plating on the roof, so he avoided harm. The windshield went cloudy with damage from many projectiles, and the hood itself was punctured and dented.

White smoke rose from the engine. The Humvee would not be going anywhere.

However, V2HG did not suffer any direct casualties and resumed firing. The leader aimed his L129A1 at the hands of 003, who was busy loading his next grenade, and pulled the trigger.

The bullet struck the M320 and knocked it out of 003's grip.

"Hey, idiot! Who leans out that far to shoot?! You've got a good weapon—use it properly!" Pitohui snapped at 003, who slogged back bashfully.

Apparently, he was so confident in his incredible defensive ability that he'd forgotten the golden rule of gunfights: Keep yourself as covered as possible when you shoot.

003 picked up the M320 and mumbled, "Aw..."

The thick barrel had a bullet embedded in it. Pulling it out wouldn't do much to get the weapon back to fighting form.

"That was expensive..."

"Then fix it!" Pitohui yelled as a grenade from the enemy M79 flew over. It hit 003 directly and knocked him three meters backward.

While his excellent armor was unharmed, it did not prevent the impact of the blast from ripping through him. 003 was killed instantly. He fell limply to the ground with a DEAD tag over his body.

"Dammit!"

"Those bastards!"

The rest of T-S were furious. Now their plan to swoop in and seize victory unharmed was totally ruined.

"Ahhh, rest in peace," said Pitohui. Fukaziroh prodded her in the side. "What is it, Fuka?"

Fukaziroh spoke to her in a quiet aside, acting like an elderly person with a frail voice so T-S wouldn't hear her.

"You wicked girl... I saw that... You could have easily shot down that grenade, eh...?"

"Oh? You think so?"

"You thought that a grenadier without a working launcher... held no use to us...and whose death might liven up the scene a little...eh...?"

"My goodness, how could you suggest such a thing?"

"By the way, have you forgotten something...?"

"What?"

"I might have lost Rightony and Leftania, but I've still got five plasma grenades strapped to my back."

Pitohui grinned devilishly.

"But I'm only using them if I have to," Fukaziroh muttered before slinking away.

Tanya was in the engineer's seat of the train engine. She opened the door and shouted, "I undid all the traps! There were a ton of them! Whoever set them was a real piece of work!"

Pitohui looked up with satisfaction and replied, "Nice job!

Okay, everybody, time for escape via train! All aboard! You too, M! You're the only one who can operate the controls!"

"All right! Coming!" M replied, putting his gun over his back and folding up the shield. He used it to block himself as he moved back to the locomotive.

"You too! Stay on the right side, and you won't get shot!" Boss instructed her teammates and T-S. There was a line forming at the ladder on the rear of the locomotive.

On either side of the train was a narrow catwalk from the rear up to the engine room. It was long enough that all of them could line up and not be exposed.

Even T-S climbed the stairs, awkwardly bonking their bulky armor here and there. The catwalk was a little narrow for them.

Boss was the last of her team to grab the ladder. As she did so, she thought back on a conversation she'd had with Pitohui while they were making their escape.

"It'll be fine, Eva. I can guarantee that the train there will work. So even if they trap us in the northwest, we can still get away."

"What makes you so confident?"

"Simple! First, the design team, including that idiot writer, put extra vehicles on the map this time. All of the pristine ones placed in visible locations are going to be usable. This corner of the map is where MMTM started. If they examined the train, they would have seen that it still functions. They didn't use it because it would have inconvenienced them."

"Huh? In that case, why wouldn't they just destroy it so no one else could ride it?"

"That'd be the normal choice. But Daveed's not like that. I knew he'd booby-trap it to take out players who rushed to utilize the train during the endgame. He left it here because *it still runs."*

I would never have read that far into it. I guess it's because I have less life experience. I'm still just a high schooler, thought Boss as she climbed up and off the ground.

* * *

M was inside the cab.

Unsurprisingly, the chamber at the front of the locomotive was not reinforced with bulletproof glass, so he stayed low to protect himself. First he went to the engineer's seat on the right side. He turned the main power on behind the chair.

The large lever thunked forward. With the electricity on, the lights—at least, those that were still working—lit up. The two monitors ahead of the seat did nothing.

Next, M pressed a black button with ENGINE START written on it in English. That was all it took for the huge turbine to begin shuddering to life. A deep rumbling issued from the rear of the train. The various tools and displays were all dead, but at the very least, the engine was working.

With luck, the force generated by the engine would run the motor.

When M had operated a similar, though smaller, vehicle in the past, that had been the case. He could only pray that the difficulty of running this train hadn't been increased because this was a special event.

M spotted two levers on the left side of the seat. One was the master controller that went forward and back—in other words, the gas. A similar switch to its left had to be pushed forward from the rear—the brakes. To the side were numbers going up to eight that indicated intensity.

"Okay, here we go! Everybody grab on to something!" M called out, still crouched over in the seat because the windows were vulnerable.

"He says we're about to move, everybody! This is great and all, M, but what about Llenn?" Fukaziroh asked once she'd warned everybody on the side of the train.

Pitohui glanced at her wristwatch. It was 2:12. The scan was already over.

She assumed that none of their group had possessed the wherewithal to watch for the next one, so she decided to reach out and ask directly.

"Yo, where you at?"

"Huh? No way!" Llenn exclaimed.

Shirley and Clarence had their comms turned off, so they asked her "What was that?" and "What's up?" in unison.

The Humvee was making its way west down the large street, weaving around junked cars and occasionally scraping them. The scan minutes earlier had informed Llenn and Clarence that they were about half a mile away from SHINC. They should be coming into view very soon.

Unfortunately, the driver was very slow—er, make that *safe*. Llenn thought she'd have reached her group by now if she were running, but she didn't mention that because Shirley was trying her best.

Instead, she reported, "Pito and SHINC—oh, and T-S, too!—are about to escape south on a train!"

"What?! To hell with that!" fumed Shirley.

She had a right to be angry. She'd rushed from the lower right corner of the map up to the top left. On motorcycle, foot, horseback, and even terrifying Humvee, she'd given chase, but now her target was about to zip out from under her nose. It felt like a blood vessel in her brain was going to burst.

"Pito! Wait a second!" Llenn shouted into the comm. "You won't believe what's going on over here! I'm riding in a Humvee!"

"Oh? How?"

"Shirley and Clarence! They stole the Humvee with the Minigun! We're heading your way!"

"What? You're in a car? How have you not caught up with us?" inquired Pitohui.

That was an excellent question.

"Well…it's slow for a car, and we're driving carefully!" Llenn explained.

"Oogh!" Shirley made a sound like someone had stabbed her in the heart. "Yeah, my driving sucks… All I do is hit other cars…"

Her green-haired head hung low as the trauma of her past flared up.

"Aaah! Eyes up!" Clarence screamed.

Grak-crunk! The Humvee scraped against an abandoned car sitting in the road.

"We're going to do whatever we can to get there, Pito! Just wait a bit longer!"

"Sorry, won't be in time. If anything, Llenn, why don't you just make a break for it in that Humvee instead? The scan will show you instead of us, but it's way better to stay in the car, as long as you've got gas."

That might be true... It's good to have company here...and we still have about a third of a tank, Llenn considered. She was on the verge of agreeing when she stopped and shook her head.

"No! Then we're not a team! And Squad Jam is about fighting as a group! We live together and die together! As much as we can, at least!" she insisted.

"..."

Shirley listened in silence. She was supremely annoyed at the way Clarence crouched, patted her shoulder, and said, "She's got a point, doesn't she?"

However, Llenn's words had given her an idea, and she decided to put it into action. "Fine, then—leave this one to me!"

Shirley stomped on the gas pedal, sending the Humvee ramming into the burned-out frame of what had once been another car in the road.

"I swear I'm going to kill Pitohui before the end of this Squad Jam!"

The Humvee picked up speed like an enraged bull, and soon it was going three times as fast as before. Shirley deftly spun the massive vehicle around a toppled bus.

"What are you doing there?! Die!" she yelled when she spotted a man in camo who had been lying in wait with a plasma grenade. He panicked at the Humvee's abrupt charge and tried to run away, but she smashed him from behind.

Clarence watched the man fly into the air, DEAD tag already floating above him, and exclaimed, "Whoo! That's the spirit, Shirley! That's the kind of game this is!"

There were four Wrong Lancers left.

"M, get the train moving!"

"You got it..."

M reached out with his left hand and pulled the controller back, all the way to the side notch that read *8*.

There was a deep, loud rumbling noise, and a beat or two later, the 180-ton, seventy-two-foot locomotive began to move.

On the right-side catwalk, SHINC and T-S raised a hearty cheer.

"Whoa, whoa, whoa! That thing works?!" shouted the members of V2HG in disbelief.

Their targets had stopped shooting back from the train, so they'd decided to stop wasting so much ammo and wait for their allies, the Wrong Lancers, to arrive. They hadn't expected this development.

The man with the M79 grenade launcher sighed. "Even in that state, it'll still run. They must have someone who knows how to run it. What a sight. I wish *I* could drive it. Or ride on it."

"What are you whining about...?"

"Nothing. I got this!" he answered, firing the M79. The grenade exploded against the side of the train. "How d'ya like that?! Huh...?"

The locomotive was slowly but surely picking up speed. The 180-ton hunk of metal wasn't bothered in the least by an antipersonnel shrapnel grenade. Shooting it with a gun would do even less.

"We'll need an antitank cannon for this," commented the machine gunner. He asked the man next to him, "Why didn't you buy any plasma grenade rounds for that thing?"

"I've never seen those in any war movie."

"This is why I keep telling you to watch some sci-fi."

* * *

The locomotive leisurely but unquestionably gained speed. At the front of the right catwalk, Fukaziroh clung to the rail, feeling the breeze on her face, and cheered, "Whoo-hoo, I'm on a steam train escapade! How far will the rails take me?"

"..."

The members of T-S were silent, seeing off their dead comrade. Their faces were hidden behind their helmets, but they were probably looking grumpy.

Boss clung to the rear of the line with Rosa, paying close attention to possible enemies chasing after them.

"Humvee!"

There they were.

The armored car with the detestable Minigun came roaring toward them, screeching into a hard left turn to pursue the train.

"Rosa!"

"Got it!"

Boss let Rosa take her place. Even if they couldn't puncture the armor, they at least had to try to keep the enemy at bay.

Rosa rested the PKM against the railing.

"Raaaaah!"

Dun-dun-dun-dun-dun-dun. The bass of her gun augmented her battle scream.

The bullets hurtled toward the Humvee and produced a shower of sparks upon collision.

The attack prompted Llenn to cry out, "Stooooop! Don't shoooooot!"

Ultimately, the three girls were subjected to constant gunfire until Fukaziroh finally sent word down the crowded catwalk of who was in the Humvee.

V2HG piled into their one working Humvee to chase after the locomotive. That's when they saw the lost third Humvee already in pursuit.

"It's them! They did come!"

"Minigun thieves!"

"Let's get 'em!"

The rearmost of the two Humvees was the one that still ran. Three members of V2HG filled its seats while a gunner stood in the center turret space with an MG5.

Just then, a voice came over the comm. "This is the Wrong Lancers. We finally caught up. Let us on, if you can."

V2HG's team leader took his foot off the accelerator. A glance at his right-side mirror revealed four men in camo with rifles in hand, sprinting for all they were worth down the street. They were a hundred yards away.

He was impressed with their tenacity but hurriedly shouted, "No! Stop! Hit the dirt!"

From their angle, the Wrong Lancers could only see the train. The building in front blocked their view of the Minigun Humvee.

By the time they realized what was happening, it was too late; even diving to the ground wasn't enough to save them.

"Four hostiles on the left! Light 'em up, Clarence!" said Shirley, hands on the wheel.

"Got it!" Clarence rotated the turret forty-five degrees. There was a large flat button near the base that used a motor to turn the entire thing.

As the gun rotated, so did the bullet circle. Taking only a moment to adjust her arms on the Minigun's grips, Clarence started shooting even before the circle was trained on the four men.

"Let 'er rip!"

Vrrrrrrrrrrrrrrrrrrrr!

Fire and sound erupted from the rapidly rotating armament. Every bullet the Minigun loosed also expelled an empty cartridge and belt link from the bottom of the weapon; they spread throughout the Humvee's interior in no time. Like all debris of this kind in *GGO*, they rapidly turned into light and vanished. However, the constant source of momentary light gave the interior of the military vehicle an unearthly glow.

The barrels continued to spit fire, hurling dozens of 7.62 mm bullets every second toward the Wrong Lancers like a deadly whip of lead. All four snipers were instantly split in half.

"Aw, shit!"

The leader of V2HG and another member of his squad in the front passenger seat watched it all happen in the side mirrors.

The deadly Minigun, whose power they knew all too well, sent a stream of bullets, glowing red with tracer rounds, through the quartet of Wrong Lancers.

They'd already gotten reports of two of them dying in battle, so this spelled the official end of the Wrong Lancers in the fourth Squad Jam. The elite team of snipers, who'd done their best to carry out Fire's orders for the sake of victory, who had scored many kills and were second to none at sharpshooting, were gone.

"Shit!"

The man in the turret fired the MG5 machine gun. His aim was true, and the bullets struck the enemy Humvee, but of course, none of them punctured its thick skin.

Then he saw an undulating red light that resembled an aurora. It was the bullet lines of the Minigun. He was aware that when a gun with such a high rate of fire shot while moving, the lines overlapped so that they looked like a carpet of crimson in the air.

That cardinal blanket was now passing through *him.*

"Tch!"

The man willingly let go of his gun and kicked his legs up into the air, dropping his body down inside the car. The Minigun roared again, showering the Humvee with bullets. They chipped and scratched the car's armor plating, but it held firm. V2HG's leader shifted into reverse, so they were only exposed to incoming shots for a moment.

However, the man's machine gun was heavily buffeted and toppled back inside the Humvee from where it had been left atop the turret stand. He reached out and caught it in both hands. A quick check showed that it wasn't totally destroyed, but several marks were on the barrel, and it didn't look safe to use anymore.

"Aaah! Nooo!" the man lamented. Reluctantly, he stowed his gun back in his inventory.

From the back seat, the man with the M79 said, "Damn, that Minigun is strong!" with more than a little delight. He handed over his HK433 to the guy who'd lost his MG5, who accepted it gratefully.

"No kidding! I bet Grant must be pretty damn happy with it!"

The Minigun's owner was either in the waiting area or back in the bar by now. The members of V2HG were too busy at the moment to recall the satisfied smile on Grant's face when he'd first gotten the Minigun or the gleeful way he'd carried himself.

As the enemy Humvee crossed to their left nearly 350 meters ahead, the man who'd been in the turret smirked to himself and muttered, "Still, they aren't unstoppable."

CHAPTER 17
Fire on Ice

SECT.17

CHAPTER 17
Fire on Ice

It was two fifteen.

The train rode on the tracks straight through the ruined city, belching black smoke and shaking the ground.

Behind it was a Humvee. Its engine was also very loud, but nothing like the train's.

Inside the car, Llenn excitedly exclaimed, "Pito! We got four of them!"

Clarence's skill had played a part, but the bullet circle and incredible firing rate of the Minigun had done most of the work—taking out more enemies in one fell swoop than they had all game so far.

"I saw that! Well done!"

"Heh-heh-heh. So what's the plan now? Should we just follow the train and go along with you guys?"

The locomotive was currently running at about forty-five miles per hour. There were no roads to the sides of the tracks, but the rails were on a flat embankment of gray gravel in keeping with the American-style scenery. It was about ten yards across, with no fences.

Shirley was driving over that surface at around fifty miles per hour. Whether this made for an easier time than taking the debris-ridden streets or she had simply gotten over her fears of handling such a large vehicle was unclear. Only about two hundred yards separated the locomotive and Humvee.

Llenn didn't know how far Pitohui intended to run, but she figured they could follow the surging train and help cover it when it stopped.

However, Pitohui replied, "That's probably not going to work."

"Huh? Why not?"

"Have you forgotten the map? This track goes over the lake up ahead. The ground's probably only as wide as the tracks there. I don't know if the Humvee's tire span will fit that. Can you really make it over? I'm not going to stop you!"

"Ugh, that's right… Oh, but we can still drive on the lake! It's frozen! I mean, Boss's team already—"

"That's right. But the highway cuts across there. The railway goes over the top, so we're fine, but you guys…"

"Oh…"

In any case, it wasn't going to be possible for the Humvee to accompany the train.

"So is our only option to switch rides?"

"Pretty much. That's why I said we should work separately. Why don't you just roll your way straight into Fire's camp?"

"But we're a team! Plus…"

Llenn couldn't deny the appeal of attacking Fire with the heavy vehicle. She wouldn't refute that the idea of planting a fat tire tread on his smug face had a certain charm.

"But he's surrounded by his elite team, right? I don't know if we can pull it off for sure. I'd rather follow your plan, Pito. You're taking off on the train because you have an idea in mind, right?"

"All right, got it. Then think of how to catch up and get on board."

"Okay. Stop the train."

"Can't do that."

"Why not?"

"Have you not looked behind you?"

Behind? Llenn glanced at the rearview mirror on the right. There was a second Humvee in pursuit.

"Ack! They're chasing after us!"

The enemy was about three hundred yards back, in hot pursuit. Unlike Llenn's ride, this one was traveling to the left of the tracks.

However, no sooner did Llenn take stock of that than the hostile Humvee came over to the right side…and then back to the left. The maneuver caused the pursuers to fall behind a bit, but they sped up to close the distance again. It seemed to be an intentional slalom pattern.

"Very smart of them. They've been sticking behind us about a quarter of a mile away without getting too close. That puts them out of launcher range and lets them watch out for grand grenade traps. They're probably watching us so they can report everything to Fire. I bet they've been doing that this whole time."

"Urgh…"

Even worse than being persistent, they were good at their jobs.

"That's why we have to hurry. If Fire's group on the lake can cut us off to the bridge and plant plasma grenades on the supports, we're done for. Game over."

"Got it… You don't have to stop for us! We'll go and take care of those stalkers! *Then* we'll switch over to the train!"

"Okay, good luck. You don't have much time left."

"Clarence! We got a stalker chasing us! I need your help again!"

Clarence was sitting in the turret at the center of the vehicle, looking very relaxed, but when Llenn called her, she stood at attention. "Huh? Yeah! Where?"

She looked behind them and spotted the enemy Humvee. She pulled her head back into the car and shouted over the roar of the engine and the wind, "But I can't punch through it!"

"The tires, then! Aim as low as you can!"

"Oh yeah, maybe that'll work!"

Clarence grabbed the Minigun controls and hit the rotation switch with her foot to turn left. And when she was close to perpendicular to the vehicle, the turret stopped.

"Huh?"

It wouldn't move any farther.

"What's wrong?" Llenn asked.

Clarence admitted, "Uh, I think this is the kind that can't face backward."

"What?!" Llenn spun around and looked at the turret stand. "Oh…I get it…"

A picture was worth a thousand words. The Minigun's ammo was being fed into the weapon's right side with a metal rail. The huge ammo box connected to that rail was sitting atop the rear right seat. So, no matter how flexible that metal rail was, it could only spin so far. About ninety degrees left or right was the most it could manage.

"So there's no way for us to shoot backward…and they know that. No wonder they're so bold about following us," Llenn murmured.

Clarence added, "That makes sense. Otherwise, they wouldn't allow us to see them in the open. Forget it, then." She released the Minigun controls and sat down again.

"Let's just do this, then!" Shirley barked abruptly, and she slammed on the brakes.

"Hurbf!" Llenn's body collided against the passenger side of the dashboard.

"Aaah!" Clarence toppled into the space between the driver and passenger seats.

"Yaaaaah!" Shirley spun the wheel hard to the left, although they hadn't totally slowed down yet.

"Aieeee!" Clarence got thrown against Llenn this time.

"Brhrgh!" Llenn got smushed.

The Humvee crossed over the rails to the other side and continued until it had made a 180-degree turn.

"Warn us before you do that, driver!" Clarence complained, resting on her back atop Llenn.

"Get—off—me!" Llenn insisted while trying to wriggle free.

Shirley ignored them and hit the brakes to make the Humvee stop.

"Dwah!" Clarence had been standing up, and the sudden halt tossed her off her feet and back onto Llenn.

"Mrgh!"

Shirley grabbed the R93 Tactical 2 sitting on her lap, got out of the driver's seat, and climbed into the turret. There, she rested the R93 Tactical 2 on the vehicle's armor plating and peered through the scope. Her target was the Humvee straight ahead, at a distance of 250 meters.

The enemy had panicked and stopped when they saw the sudden U-turn. It was plain they were hurrying to shift into reverse.

"I don't think so," said Shirley, pulling the trigger.

The explosive round flew over the rails and hit the other Humvee's left front wheel, inside of which the projectile exploded.

The tires were tough and thick, but they weren't meant to withstand a burst from inside. The rubber's exterior split away and flew into the air, sputtering from the force, leaving only the rim.

Still, the Humvee squealed backward, its bare wheel digging into the gravel.

"Next!"

Shirley rapidly reloaded her rifle. While they were moving targets, there was no way she'd miss something as large as those tires within a range of 350 meters.

The right wheel ruptured just like the left, leaving only the rim. Without the tires to lift it up, the front of the Humvee noticeably dipped.

Yet, it still had enough power in the rear tires to drag it backward. It struggled like a wounded beast.

Shirley slid back into the driver's seat. Clarence had finally gotten back to her feet, although Llenn was still pinned under her.

"There, I've stopped them. Now finish the job!"

"They blew out the tires! They're coming after us!" cried the leader. He gave up on driving, understanding that fleeing was no longer an option.

Even the heavy-duty armor on the Humvee wasn't going to last forever if the Minigun started blasting it from close range. The choice was clear.

"Everyone, off! Fan out and run!"

The last thing they wanted was to make themselves easy targets for one sweep from the Minigun, like the Wrong Lancers. The heavy doors of the Humvee opened, and three people jumped out.

"Leader?"

However, the driver's door remained shut.

"Go! Just go! Hide among the ruins and run back to the lake as fast as you can! That's an order!" the leader commanded. He took his L129A1 sniper rifle and stood in the turret.

The others did not turn back to look again. They ran pell-mell for safety, trying to reach the buildings twenty meters away.

"They're running!"

"Shoot, shoot!" Shirley urged Clarence, who obliged with the Minigun.

The tracers followed the man who fled to the right side, but he was small and distant. With the rumbling from the car upsetting her aim, she was unable to hit him.

"Sorry; I let them get awa— *Ack!*"

Clarence's report turned into a scream at the end.

"!" Llenn swung around and saw that Clarence had toppled from her standing position. There was a glowing red light on her left cheek.

"Ohhh!"

The bullet must have shot right through the tiny gap between the armor plating and the Minigun itself. Clarence's hit points were dropping fast.

She was surprisingly tough, though, so it wasn't an insta-kill. It was severe nonetheless. The pain and numbness were likely akin to being slapped across the face.

It would be pointless to ask if she was okay, so Llenn didn't. Clarence's voice sounded tearful.

"Aaah, it hurts… How could you shoot a woman in the face?! Is this because I didn't show my boobs…?"

"What? Boobs?" Llenn asked, blinking.

"Forget about that!" Shirley snapped. "There's a sniper in their turret! Just shoot the big one, Llenn! You don't have to hit him!"

"Huh? Uh, okay!"

Llenn had never shot a Minigun before, but it was up to her now. She stood between Clarence's legs as the other girl went to lie down in the center of the Humvee.

Then Llenn came to a realization.

"Um…my face can't reach…"

With Llenn's height, no matter how hard she stretched, she couldn't see over the Minigun and armor plating.

"Daaaa! You tiny little freak!" Shirley snapped. She was always salty.

"Aw, come on, I'm not *that* small."

"Why do you sound happy?!"

"It's a long story. And I don't think this is the right setting to get into it…"

"You're *already* taking too long! We're almost there!"

They were only a hundred meters from the target now. He was blasting away from the roof, putting more and more holes in the windshield.

Shirley raged, "Arrrgh, maybe I should just ram him!"

"No! It's not that kind of game!" Llenn cried.

Suddenly, she was much taller. Clarence was lifting her up from below.

"Wheeee! Look how tall you are! Now shoot him, Llenn!"

"Thanks!"

She put her hands on the grips and pressed what she assumed was the trigger.

Vrrrrrrrrrrrrrr!

At first, Llenn thought a fire had broken out in front of her. Waves of virtual heat from the barrels of the gun washed over her face.

Do they really need to simulate all *of that?* she thought.

Initially, Llenn's aim was all over the place. But gradually, the red lights of the tracers and the stream of kicked-up dirt followed the bullet circle toward the Humvee.

There was a massive shower of sparks.

The enemy vehicle lit up yellow like a Catherine wheel. The red tracer rounds from the Minigun bounced off the target in all directions. The sound of deflected projectiles formed a chorus with the roar of the weapon. The force of the gunfire rocked the heavy vehicle and pushed it backward.

Through the sea of flames, Llenn watched the target get closer and closer. Eighty meters, seventy, sixty.

She didn't know how long she needed to keep firing, so she just held down the trigger.

Under the fire hose of bullets, the enemy Humvee's armor finally met its end. After dozens of rounds, the armor finally dented inward and began to let shots through.

"Hrgh!"

The projectiles tore into the vehicle's interior and bit into the driver's thighs. He ducked down inside the car, the bullets cutting more holes into the metal around him.

"I'm done in here!" he called to his teammates. "Don't worry about winning; just find a way to take them out! That's our mission! I'm counting on you! And by the way, our payment for this is—"

But he never got to finish that statement.

The damage reached the Humvee's gas tank and, true to *GGO*'s nature, promptly ignited it. The car exploded into a massive fireball, killing the man stuck inside.

"V2HG is down to three," informed a voice in Fire's ear.

He was sitting atop a vast, wide-open lake, white as could be, with his legs splayed out, gazing emptily at the sky.

Five of the people around him were wearing the same sort of tracksuit he was. On the distant horizon to the west was a collection of twelve tiny dots, specks of darkness running at full speed toward the bridge.

"I see. This little tournament event is lasting longer than I had anticipated," Fire admitted, still peering up at the gray above. "But I believe in you all. I'll wait here and trust in your hard work."

"Uh, Leader, you sure we don't need to move yet…?"

Kenta from MMTM was seated on the eastern end of the airport runway, his back resting against a trike.

Next to the vehicle was David, the team leader, completely flat on his back. The STM-556 he always used rested at his side. His hands were folded behind his head, and his eyes were closed. It looked like he was taking a nap.

"We're still fine. What time is it? How many minutes?" David inquired, not bothering to look at his own watch.

"Two eighteen. Still got two minutes," answered Kenta, going by *his* watch and giving David the time until the monsters appeared.

"Next, we can move to the highway, I suppose. We'll watch the two twenty scan there."

"Leader."

"Hmm?"

"I understand that you're not abandoning the competition, but it's kind of creepy to see you so indifferent about this."

"It's because there's nothing we can do. So we're taking a break until we head for the final confrontation. Never thought I'd be so relaxed in a Squad Jam."

"Ah, okay. Wait, does that mean you already have an idea of where it's going to be?" Kenta asked, turning to look at David.

"Yeah. A vague one," replied David.

"Damn, Leader. Or 'Damnlee' for short. Where is it?"

"Not yet. I don't want to look bad if I'm wrong."

"Tsk."

David cracked his eyelids, and the gray sky filled his vision.

"Don't die before then, Pitohui," he muttered. "Don't die before I can kill you myself."

* * *

The train raced onward.

The speedometer read 60, presumably meaning miles per hour. Given that they had the train on the highest setting, that was the fastest it could go.

For the people on the catwalk, that was plenty thrilling. Beyond the flimsy-looking railing, the ground and the ruined city swept by at a ferocious speed.

There was also a deck at the front end of the locomotive where a person could stand.

"Ha-ha-ha! I'm flying, Jack!" said Boss, who was living out one of her favorite movie scenes.

"Can we be done with this yet?" asked Rosa, who had been forced to play along.

M was in the driver's seat, properly seated, with his left hand on the brake lever.

Pitohui was on the left side of the cab, keeping an eye on the surroundings with binoculars.

At the speed they were going, they could cover a mile a minute. Pitohui gauged that they were in Sector 9-3, going by shogi board format. There wasn't much visibility with all the buildings around, but the frozen lake should be fast approaching on the train's left. The tracks would rise onto a bridge over the body of water.

By now, Fire's team had undoubtedly received a report that Pitohui's group was escaping via locomotive. They had to be on their way to destroy the bridge—the only question was if they'd already gotten there or not.

"Get us there in time, okay?"

"Pito, my girl, that might not be possible, eh? If only we were all as speedy as little Llenn," replied Fukaziroh, who'd heard Pitohui mutter under her breath. The catwalk was very cramped and crowded, so she was chilling in the engine room.

Fukaziroh did some quick calculations in her head. The train had been running for a little over two minutes. It was about a mile from the center of the lake to the bridge. It would take an ordinary character three minutes, if not more, to run that.

"They won't catch up. We'll get past. Llenn's car is another matter."

"Let's hope so. But what if the enemy has some other sets of wheels?"

"Huh? According to Boss, they're out of Humvees now."

"Let me amend that. What if they have something to ride left in their back pocket…?"

"Pardon?" asked Fukaziroh, looking skeptical.

Pitohui did not answer. She opened the door in the cab's center and called out to "Jack and Rose" on the front deck.

"Hey, you two! Romance time is over. Come back inside; we're approaching the lake. Watch out for attacks from the left!"

"Okay, fine," said Boss, who stopped cheering and squealing. "All members, keep an eye out! Watch that lake carefully! By the way…how's Llenn doing?"

"Don't leave me behind!" Llenn wailed.

The three-person group had succeeded at turning the enemy Humvee into scrap, but the train was far ahead of them.

No matter how hard Shirley flattened the pedal against the floor, it couldn't go faster than seventy-five miles per hour. That was the maximum possible speed for a Humvee in *GGO*—or perhaps just in this Squad Jam.

They drove and drove, but they couldn't seem to catch sight of the train.

"I wish someone would jump into our way. I wanna run 'em

over!" Shirley exclaimed, rather horrifyingly, holding on to the wheel with just one hand. Llenn ignored her.

The only hope was to get to the locomotive as soon as humanly possible.

Please, if there's anyone who can make this happen, make my wish come true.

The person who could make Llenn's wish come true was on the lake.

Six men stood at the center of that frozen body of water. If they were caught on the scan, it would make clear that they were PORL—one of the allied teams, which had been waiting on the lake for the entire Squad Jam.

The group was dressed in gray camo fatigues. It was a useful pattern in a city, but it did a decent job of blending in on the ice, too.

This group did not wear masks and sunglasses. Each of their faces—randomly created by the character generator—looked very excited.

They were six hundred meters from the bridge.

It was quite visible from here. The narrow concrete bridge, dull and gray, had several legs thrust into the lake, while the bridge itself was a flat, horizontal line. It grew closer and closer as they approached.

PORL was moving very swiftly indeed. They crossed the frozen lake much quicker than Llenn would have, even at a full sprint.

Each member was sporting an item on his feet. They'd kept them hidden in their inventories when SHINC had been around.

One of the men on Fire's team had found the tools in a boathouse on the lakeshore earlier: ice skates.

Five hundred meters from the bridge.

With powerful strides making the most of their Strength stats, PORL's members moved at a speed that would be record-breaking in the real world. And there was no muscle fatigue in VR, so they could continually move at maximum velocity.

Four hundred meters.

Now the tiny image of a train moving out of the ruined city was coming into view.

"That's enough! Let's do it!" commanded the man who was presumably PORL's leader, waving his left hand to bring up his item storage.

"Yeah!" the others responded. They stopped pushing forward, letting momentum continue to carry them. As they did, they drew their weapons from virtual space.

"Enemies on the left! Six on the ice!" called Fukaziroh, peering through binoculars from the cab.

Tall buildings no longer flanked the locomotive. The terrain was full of plants and the occasional one-story building. The track was rising steadily, leading to the narrow bridge that crossed the highway and lake. The structure was visible now, though still appearing no larger than a spiderweb.

"Tsk!" Pitohui spat.

"But how did they do it without vehicles?!" wondered Fukaziroh.

"Look at their feet."

"Huh?" Fukaziroh zoomed in with the binoculars and looked down. "Ohhhh! They're wearing ice skates! That's not fair, man!"

"I knew those things were near the lake," stated Pitohui, who seemed pleased that her guess had been right—and also upset that the situation was now worse because of it.

"You know, I really hate ice-skating. We had to do it so much in gym class. It gets you so tired out," remarked Fukaziroh, displaying her Hokkaido roots. The northern island was the kind of place where it got so cold that you could toss water onto the ground at school and make your own skating rink. Miyu and Karen had only ever known the kind of skating where you played until you got tired.

In Hokkaido, you never had those romantic mishaps where the girl grabbed the guy on their date and went, "Eek, I'm scared! *Oh!* We're so close now…"

"What now?" asked M, his hand resting on the train's brake lever.

Pitohui pressed the binoculars she'd snatched from Fukaziroh to her eyes and answered, "Why aren't they coming to the bridge? Do they not have a grand grenade…?"

If they didn't have one of the extra-large plasma grenades, they couldn't blow up the bridge. Or were they not going to make it in time?

Just then, as if to answer that question, the enemy pulled out their firearms.

When Pitohui saw the weapons take shape, she swore, stuck her head out of the cab, and screamed, "RPG incoming! Brace for impact!"

The approaching enemies were equipped with RPG-7s—Soviet-era rocket-propelled antitank armaments.

The RPG-7 was a very powerful firearm that AI enemies had only used for the first time in the recent playtest. Apparently, it was in the game for good now. As far as ranged weapons went, it had to be top tier in *GGO* when it came to maximum damage output.

The tip of the launcher's sharp, cone-shaped missile was full of contact explosives. Rocket fuel was packed into the rear for propulsion, so once lit, the projectile could reach a speed of 350 meters per second, just under the speed of sound.

The men turned to one side to stop their skates. They put down the long tubes that had just appeared over their right shoulders, quickly loaded the grenades, and steadied the weapons.

Smoke jetted behind one of them, and his grenade shot forward. It blasted out like a cannonball, then ignited its rocket and accelerated faster. It was aimed right at the train.

About two and a half seconds later, the first rocket passed a few meters in front of the speeding train.

"It's too late! Just blaze through it!" Pitohui told M.

It was even harder to stop a train than a car. If M started applying the brakes now, the train wouldn't actually come to a complete halt until they were on the bridge over the lake.

At that point, they'd be a sitting target with no place to escape.

The next moment, the second rocket came roaring toward the locomotive's left side as it approached the start of the bridge. It struck the engine room in the train's rear, causing a shudder to run through the entire structure.

"Whoa!" "Hyaaa!" "Eeg!" "Dwaah!"

SHINC and T-S screamed, falling over and on top of each other on the narrow catwalk. It was a miracle that none of them fell off.

Perhaps the attack had damaged the engine, because the train's speed noticeably dipped.

A third rocket came right on the second's heels and blasted the coupler at the front of the cab. It tore loose one of the thick metal arms.

The fourth hit the roof over the control car, but luckily only grazed it without exploding and traveled onward into the sky before vanishing.

"Get outside, Fuka. M, keep us moving even if it kills you!"

"Got it," answered M with a firm nod.

Fukaziroh and Pitohui rushed out of the control car onto the catwalk on the train's right side. Thankfully, it was still safe there. The massive engine was now between them and the enemy, and even a rocket's explosion couldn't make it through all that metal.

The moment the two made it outside, the fifth rocket struck the left side of the train cab.

The explosive was designed to blast through tank armor; the control car's wall might as well have been paper by comparison. A screeching roar of splintering iron echoed through the locomotive's interior. Windows blew out from the inside, and half of the roof was torn upward.

"Oof..."

However, M was okay because he'd kept his head low on the

right side of the cab. If the rocket had struck the other side of the car, he would have died instantly.

The sound and shock of the explosion were considerable, however, and they thrashed his head. M's vision went awry, and he lost his sense of balance. Even still, he kept the master controller pushed up to ensure the blast didn't jar it loose.

The engine was still moving, but the train was slowing every second.

Next came the sixth rocket. It was met with a gust from the northeast. RPGs had fins that caused them to drift upward on the wind, something that made them distinct from bullets.

The timely breeze caused the rocket-propelled grenade to shift toward the rear of the train instead.

"Hyaaa!" shrieked Tanya from the back of the locomotive. It passed behind her, close enough that she could have reached out and touched it on the way. The rocket continued on and collided with the ruins of a building to the right of the tracks. The structure quickly began to burn.

Down on the lake, each member of PORL had shot one rocket.

"Ooh, that's fun!"

They materialized new rockets and loaded them into the RPG-7 launchers. They weren't single-use antitank weapons, so as long as you had more ammunition, you could keep using them.

They had stopped skating to shoot, so the squad was still four hundred meters from their quarry. When it came to accuracy with an RPG-7, closer was better. However, when one considered the enemy's grenade launcher, this was the best distance for PORL to be at.

For one thing, their target was a giant mass of metal seventy-two feet long. It was also approaching a stop right as it reached the bridge. Once still, it was a sitting duck.

The six men formed a horizontal line so that their rockets' ignition gas didn't knock anyone over. As each one was ready to fire again, he bent his knees to crouch.

They aimed their scopes, aligned their bullet circles over the train—and fired the second wave.

"Fuka! What happened?! Fuka!" Llenn repeated, but her friend was apparently too busy to reply.

"I can see it!" called Clarence, who was up in the turret with her binoculars. She described the action to the other two. "Uh-oh, they're getting blasted! Something just flew up from the left—it's a rocket! They're bombarding the train while it's crossing the bridge!"

"Wha…?" Llenn was stunned.

"Oh wow! They hit it again! I'm amazed that the engine's still going. There's smoke coming out of the left side! It looks like a steam engine now!"

You don't have to sound so entertained, Llenn grumbled to herself.

Even Llenn could see that the locomotive was slowing down. Through the windshield, she could see the shape ahead was getting larger, a plume of black smoke rising from it. Beneath the engine's roar and the whistling of the wind, she could hear the echoing of explosions.

"Wh-where's the attack coming from?"

"To the left… Can't see where, but probably from the lake!"

"Shirley! Take us down to the lakeside!"

"Why? Pitohui's right ahead of us!"

"That's not going to matter if she dies ten seconds from now! Besides, don't you want to run somebody over?"

"Y'know, you make a good argument." Shirley grinned fiercely and yanked the Humvee to the left.

At the edge of the city was a road that ran along the lakeside. The Humvee roared down it, then veered off toward the bank. Once they were down onto the mixture of gravel and sand, their visibility improved considerably.

The frozen lake was like a white desert: vast, colorless, and flat. The shore was about a hundred feet across. They stopped the Humvee there.

As Shirley stomped on the brakes, she asked hesitantly, "Are you sure we can drive this out there?"

Llenn was not aware that Shirley lived in Hokkaido. She had plenty of experience with frozen lakes, but that also meant she knew how dangerous they could be.

Using snowshoes or skates was one thing. Driving a heavy vehicle on frozen water was another. Depending on the location, you might be able to do that in Hokkaido, but only if you were sure how thick the ice was.

"It's fine! Boss said so! They drove on one of these out to the middle of the ice with that alliance!"

"But not from this spot, right? What if it's thinner here and we break through? You realize we'll die, right?" Shirley asked. Her concerns made sense, but now was not the time to be timid.

There were trails of smoke rising from the RPG-7s a few hundred meters away out on the lake. It was too far to see the people, but the backblasts of the rockets were quite clear.

There was no way to win the Squad Jam without beating those guys.

Thus Llenn decided that she needed to convince their driver, Shirley, in the most persuasive manner possible.

She pointed the P90 at the other girl, put her finger on the trigger to produce a bullet line, and said, "Then get off! I'll drive it from here!"

It was a hijack.

"Ha," Shirley chuckled. Then she stomped on the gas pedal.

"Dwaa!"

Llenn toppled over and lost her aim. Shirley took the Humvee forward down the slope and onto the ice, which held up firmly under the heavy wheels.

"I like your spirit! Just for today, I'm going along with your crazy schemes!"

"Thanks, Shirley! That's being a true teammate!"

"We'll see about that!"

"Clarence! Light 'em up when we get close enough!"

"You bet! Wait, I don't know how much ammo we have left."

"It's fine! Just go ahead! Don't hold back! This is your day, Clarence!"

"Okay, then!" said Clarence, taking the handles of the Minigun with a smile, just as a rocket hit it.

The jet surge of the explosion went through the armor plating, ripped the Minigun out of the turret space, and took with it Clarence's left arm, which flew well over ten meters away.

"*Dgyaaaa!*" Clarence screamed, falling back into the Humvee once again. Llenn saw the Minigun clatter impotently onto the ice and that Clarence's body was now missing a limb.

"Aaaah..."

Clarence had just used a med kit, so her hit points were recovering, but the rocket had nearly brought her down to zero.

A second RPG passed to the right of the vehicle. It missed by two meters.

"Ah!"

Still, the proximity caused Shirley to jam the wheel left, veering away from their enemy.

If she hadn't done that, the third rocket would have hit the Humvee. It sped past, running perpendicular to the vehicle's tail end.

The Humvee raced to the east. Llenn could see a big, fat, red bullet line coming for them through the bulletproof glass.

Oh, so that's what a line looks like for a rocket, she marveled as the fourth RPG shot toward them from the right.

"Help, God of *Gun Gale*," she prayed for the second time that day.

Thanks to Shirley's violent steering, they passed to the side of the line and avoided the incoming projectile.

It flew just centimeters from the driver's seat.

As the Humvee raced away from the launchers at full speed, there was no fifth projectile.

"Ugh, this sucks." Clarence had only a tiny sliver of health left. "Give me back my Minigun..."

It wasn't yours in the first place, Llenn thought. Turning to Shirley, she asked, "S-so...what now?"

"What now? Nothing! We can't get any closer! They'll destroy my car!"

It wasn't yours in the first place, Llenn thought again. It seemed like they were out of options.

However, Shirley hadn't given up. "I'll put some distance between us, like seven hundred yards, then stop and snipe them. They make an easy target!"

"Ooh! Nice! That sounds good!"

Then a bullet flew into the Humvee.

Or to be more accurate, photons.

"Yeep!"

An orange light passed through the bulletproof glass right before Llenn's eyes and burst in her face.

"Ugh!" Green light did the same right against Shirley's head.

"They're shooting us with optical guns!" Llenn yelled. There was no mistaking that effect.

Llenn hadn't realized that optical guns could pierce the reinforced glass. That would be one of the advantages of optical guns in *GGO*, then. It made sense, kind of—light could pass through translucent surfaces.

If it weren't for the optical defense fields that every player wore, Llenn and Shirley would probably be dead. The luminous beams were coming at them head-on. It was like they were getting a very flashy light shower.

There could be only one source of all those colored shafts.

"It's Team RGB! They snuck up on us!"

RGB had been one minute behind the others because they were on foot, not skates.

"Dammit! We're trapped! No sniping, then! Gotta go!" exclaimed Shirley, who braked hard. It was probably the right choice. There was no time to expose herself and snipe. The

RPG-7s were behind them, and optical guns that shot through the windshield were ahead.

Escape was the only option.

However, that would mean they wouldn't be inflicting any damage on the enemy. Pitohui's group would continue to be sitting ducks for those RPG-7s.

"But—!" Llenn protested.

"But what? You have a better plan?"

"......No."

"If you want to die, I can let you off here."

"......"

Clarence stepped in to fill Llenn's silence.

"That's a good idea."

The train was going slower and slower.

The speedometer was busted, so M couldn't know for sure, but it felt like it was going under twenty miles per hour now.

The attacks stopped for a little while but resumed less than a minute later.

Yet another RPG-7 hit the train as it continued on its way over the bridge—there was nowhere else to go.

"Aaaaah!"

The railing could no longer withstand the weight, and the member of T-S who wore the number 005 fell from the locomotive. The concrete bridge was narrow and slight, with only the tracks atop it and no handrails.

"Nooooo!" he screamed, and he plunged a few dozen feet to the ice, landing on his head.

No armor was going to save him from that impact. He died instantly, and a tag appeared over his body.

"......"

Ervin, the rest of his teammates, and the others could only watch him go.

There were eleven people on the train—three from LPFM, four

from SHINC, and four from T-S—and they were like passengers on a sinking ship.

It was 2:20.

The scan commenced, but none of the people on the outside of the train could watch it. If they didn't hold on for dear life with both hands, they would be the next to plummet.

The locomotive was getting slower with every second, now down to twelve miles per hour. At that speed, you could jump off without dying, but on top of a bridge like this, your fate was almost certain to be the same as poor 005's.

"Heaven, why hast thou forsaken us?" Fukaziroh lamented. She'd made the most of her tiny size by sitting on the catwalk and dangling her legs, taking in the stunning view of the frozen lake below.

"We won't give up! Once we stop, we'll fan out on the bridge and shoot back!" Boss roared, speaking for SHINC.

Of course, they all knew that they'd just be targets for the RPG-7s and other firearms. They didn't stand a chance.

"I guess this is it… They did really well," said one of the spectators in the bar. The crowd was rapt with attention, determined to see the train escape through to the end.

Until then, however, they were immensely enjoying the rocket attacks, treating the explosions like a fireworks show for their viewing amusement.

"Llenn's not on that, right?"

"I saw her on the Humvee earlier."

"They got the Minigun blown off, and now they're on the run. There's no way to win when that many players surround you."

The results of the Satellite Scan came up on the subscreens.

ZEMAL was among the craters, and MMTM sat at the airport. Nothing new there…

However, LPFM's leader, Llenn, was currently in a northeast escape over the lake. SHINC and T-S were on the bridge. V2HG was doing its best to chase on foot but was still stuck in the city.

PORL was to the east of the bridge, firing RPG-7s nonstop. Less than a mile east of them was RGB, who had run up on their own.

Lastly, smack in the middle of the lake, where they had been for so long, were WEEI and SATOH. One of them had to be the leader of this alliance.

Thoughts abounded during the Satellite Scan.

In the bar…

"Even the toughest team can lose when they're cornered. I feel like this Squad Jam was meant to teach us that lesson."

"Don't try to turn this into a moral exercise! This isn't some after-school special!"

On the frozen lake…

"Give them all you've got! Don't hold back; it's all returning in another ten minutes!"

PORL spared none of their RPGs, knowing they could abuse the unique rules of SJ4.

"We won this fight pretty easily."

"Yeah. We're the very model of artillery."

"I wasn't sure if we should do this team-up thing, but it always feels good to be on the winning side."

"Agreed. Once we're done with these guys, let's keep up the momentum and slaughter Fire's team next."

Right between PORL and RGB, where the Humvee had first made its escape, a single woman now lay flat on the ice.

She was covered in a white poncho, blending in with the frozen water. The one-armed woman waved her hand to tinker with her inventory.

Motes of light gathered and took form right beside her, merging into a large green backpack.

"Time to kick some ass!" Clarence said with a smile, and she pulled the string extending from the backpack.

CHAPTER 18
ZEMAL

CHAPTER 18
ZEMAL

Llenn saw the giant explosion in the rearview mirror of the Humvee, but not as much as she felt it.

The mirror was busted and cracked because of all the times Shirley had crashed, but enough of it remained for her to see the huge white shock wave orb appear and disappear, followed by a crimson surge of light and flames.

The seismic force rocked the Humvee when it hit and knocked loose the dying rear mirror.

Llenn looked forward and saw the *X* next to her teammate's name on the list in the upper left.

"Clarence..."

Just moments earlier.

"If you want to die, I can let you off here."

"......"

Clarence stepped in to fill Llenn's silence.

"That's a good idea."

She used her remaining hand to access her inventory, selected a pure-white poncho meant to offer snowy camouflage, and equipped it.

"Wh-what are you doing?"

"Preparing to get out!" Clarence responded. She hit the ACCEPT button hanging in the air, which whisked away the backpack of explosives they'd won from Team DOOM into her inventory.

"All ready. Wait, just kidding. One more thing."

Lastly, Clarence dumped all her many ammo magazines onto the floor of the Humvee. They were for her AR-57—and also a P90.

"You should use them again, Llenn! My magazines seem to bring you luck! Take them and win it all once more! Shirley, get revenge for me! I'll be cheering you on from the afterlife! On the other hand, maybe you'll stand a chance of winning if you actually work with Pitohui the tiniest bit, hmm?"

"..."

Llenn understood what Clarence was going to do but couldn't find the words to say anything. She hadn't actually won SJ2 after borrowing Clarence's ammo, but she wasn't going to correct her on that point.

"Are you going to die? You're going to die, right?" Shirley asked.

"I guess," admitted Clarence.

"Dammit! You're not allowed to die without my say-so, partner."

"But if I don't bite it here, everyone else will."

"......Dammit! I wanted you to bear witness to my killing Pitohui!"

"Look, I can hang out with you whenever you want. Now stop the car!"

"......"

Shirley said nothing more but granted Clarence's request.

"Don't worry so much, Shirley! You gotta take it easy and enjoy your life... Your gaming life, I mean!" Those were Clarence's last words before she opened the Humvee's left rear door. She slid out onto the ice and lay flat on her stomach.

Less than a minute later, she blew herself up.

The force of the explosion raced across the lake as a ripple of air pressure, throwing off the aim of one of the men about to shoot his RPG-7. It fired, but the grenade dipped and bounced uselessly off the ice many times.

The shock wave also hit RGB, forcing them to stop shooting briefly. The swelling crimson fireball climbing up into the sky as a mushroom cloud completely overwhelmed them.

It was a tremendous discharge, to be sure, but they had no idea why it had happened, and it was distant enough that none of the twelve of them suffered any damage.

"What the hell was that?"

"Dunno."

Similar exchanges were happening all over.

Pitohui was made aware of the explosion when the sound reached the train.

Just to check, she asked Llenn, "Who blew themselves up? Was it Clare? Or Shirley? Or both?"

Llenn didn't have the focus to answer that question.

"Oh crap oh crap oh crap, hurry hurry hurry!"

"That idiot! Was she trying to kill *us*, too?"

The two women in the Humvee were in a terrified panic. Llenn clambered up to the top of the turret to look behind them.

"Aaaaaaaah, it's gaining on us!"

The source of her manic anxiety was a deep crack that was getting closer.

The whole thing was quite the spectacle for the audience in the bar.

The events being relayed—or re-created, technically—on their screens were displayed from a very high angle, offering a clear view of the vast, darkened hollow the explosion had created. The heat of the blast had instantly melted the surrounding ice and left scorch marks on the parts that had managed to stay solid.

And that created a series of black fissures that extended outward like bolts of lightning.

"It's breaking!"

"That makes sense… I mean, when you hit the ice with that much power…"

While it might have supported heavy cars, the frozen water was not as firm as a thick concrete bridge.

And once the tense, frozen sheet had cracks in it, the change was irreversible.

Like on a glass window smashed with a rock, the fractures spread farther and farther.

"Why was that explosion so huge…?"

"What item was it? Where do you buy that?"

"Good thing it was so far away…"

"They're driving off in the Humvee. Should we get 'em?"

RGB was stunned at the seemingly boneheaded maneuver.

"Dammit! I wasted a rocket!"

"Holy crap, that was powerful…"

"What kind of bomb was that?"

"Who cares? We're all fine. It was way too far from us."

"What the hell was the point of that?"

The members of PORL exchanged similar statements. The cracks in the ice were approaching both groups faster than the speed of a car.

By the time they heard the terrifying crunching sounds, it was all too late. Of course, even if they had taken off on foot after hearing the blast, they wouldn't have gotten to shore in time.

The fissures grew and expanded like a living creature, snatching the solid ice from under the feet of all twelve of them at once.

"Gyack!" "Huh?" "What the—?" "Aaah!" "Bwf!" "Aiee!" "Why?" "Hnn?"

They toppled and screamed as they were plunged into the black waters beneath the ice.

Some of them were dragged down by their heavy weaponry,

disappearing into the inky depths. Others desperately struggled to stay afloat but found themselves trapped by the chunks of ice. One or two used their guns as props over the holes in the ice before they ultimately fell in, too. Naturally, a few players from PORL tried to skate away, only to discover their feet were on separate pieces of frozen water. They collapsed into painful splits.

"First skating, now diving?! I didn't think this was the Olympics!" someone shouted shortly before he disappeared from SJ4.

"Noooo! Crap, crap, crap! Hurry, hurry! Gaaaaas!"

Just behind the racing Humvee, the ice that had so faithfully served as a road was fracturing.

Llenn looked forward again and saw that she and Shirley were almost back to the shore. It was a distance of maybe a hundred yards.

We'll make it!

Sadly, her hopes were dashed. A monstrous crack reached forward and snagged their rear tire. The left rear part of the Humvee was stuck in a crevice, coming to a lurching halt.

"Aaah!"

Llenn was up leaning over the turret, so the laws of inertia threw her forward. She would have hit the Minigun had it still been there. Instead, her tiny body slipped through the armor around the gunner stand and dropped out in front of the Humvee.

"Aaaaa— *Ow!*"

She did a somersault in the air and landed bottom-first on the ice, then slid forward with momentum, bouncing several times before she stopped. "Guh-guh-guh-guh!"

Her butt stung, but fortunately, she suffered no actual damage. She hopped to her feet at once.

"Huh?" Immediately, she learned that she was on safe ground. There was gravel under her feet. She'd been hurled so violently off the Humvee that the momentum had carried her across the ice like a curling stone to the lakeshore.

Relieved that she was safe, Llenn turned around to look out at the water…and saw the Humvee stuck in a fissure.

"Oh no…"

About fifty yards away, the Humvee had both wheels below the ice level, with just the front two trying to pull it forward. All they could do was spin in the air above the surface of the ice.

Through the bullet-pocked windshield, she could see Shirley struggling in the driver's seat.

"Get out of the car and run!" Llenn screamed, but Shirley didn't have her comm on and couldn't hear her.

She looked to be panicking. Her mind was locked into jamming on the accelerator, not realizing that the sinking back end was pulling the wheels up into the air.

At least the Humvee was still on the ice; either the cracking was not as intense near the shore or the force of the fracturing itself was slowing.

I— I've gotta save her!

Llenn considered rushing over to tell Shirley what to do, or perhaps pull her to safety.

Oh, but…

Llenn's little devil appeared. A tiny Llenn wearing black with pointed wings and tail poofed into existence over her head.

"It's okay; forget her. You'll be better off if Shirley dies right here, don't you think?" it whispered to Llenn.

"But—!"

"Listen, she's still after Pitohui. Who knows what she'll do next? Do you really want that anxiety hanging over you at every moment? It'll grind you down to the bone."

"But—!"

"And what if you go out there to help and end up falling in, too? You're gonna die. You're so gonna die."

"Aw…"

"Should I start playing the 'Wedding March' again? We could do Wagner's 'Here Comes the Bride.' One, two… Dah, dah, da-dah, dah, dah, da-dah!"

"Awwww... Yeah, there's a good reason I can't let myself die... And I shouldn't take risks that might endanger me...and Shirley's still thinking about assassinating Pito... Awwwwww-wwwrrrgh!"

Llenn's heart was just about to fall to the dark side when she heard a voice.

"Llenn, you don't need a reason to save people!"

"P-chan!"

Llenn felt like the P90 slung over her shoulder was speaking to her.

"Yes, she's got some problems, but Shirley's an important member of the squad! Do it for the team!"

"That's right! You gotta save your teammates!"

"Exactly! Plus..."

"Plus?"

"You'll still have chances to shoot Shirley dead after this. And I'll be right here when that time arrives!"

"Er, wait a minute."

"Why aren't we moving?!"

Shirley pumped the gas harder and harder, yet the car stayed put.

"Dammit! Move! Move!"

It was a common mistake among rookie drivers.

If Shirley had eased up, it might have improved the tires' grip. As a resident of Hokkaido, a snowy region of Japan, she actually already knew that, but when she started to panic, logic went out the window.

The crack in the ice widened, dipping the Humvee's back end farther down. The rear wheels were in the water now, the front ones in the air, though Shirley couldn't see that from the driver's seat. All she could see was the sky.

The next moment, the driver-side door was flung open.

"Give it up and run!" shouted a tiny pink person.

"Ah!"

Shirley came back to her senses. She grabbed the R93 Tactical 2 resting between the front seats and jumped out of the Humvee.

Once her combat boots were resting on ice, she ran for her life—sprinting, stumbling, sprinting again.

"Aaahh!" At last she reached the gravel on the shore. Her legs gave way, and she fell back onto her butt. "*Huff*... Shit... *Huff*... Shit... *Huff*..."

Once she collected herself a little bit, Shirley looked for Llenn.

No one to the right.

No one to the left.

All she could see was wide-open lake and shoreline.

"Ah!"

She spun around and saw the front grill of the Humvee, just barely visible above the floe. The fissure extended all the way toward the shore, the waters beneath appearing black and menacing.

"Oh no..."

"Get off. You're heavy," mumbled Llenn, her voice coming from under Shirley's butt.

* * *

"Well, hello again, Llenn. Good to see you!"

It was 2:25.

Llenn and Shirley made it up to the train that was stopped on the bridge. They'd had to run the entire way. The bridge was only as wide as the train itself, so they were careful to go right down the middle of the tracks so they didn't fall off the sides.

When they arrived at last, they were greeted by Pitohui and Fukaziroh, who exclaimed, "Llenn! It's so good to see you alive, my child!"

Behind them were the smiling faces of Boss and the rest of SHINC. T-S was up on top of the locomotive.

Llenn managed to pry Fukaziroh off her and went to talk with Boss.

"I'm so glad… I'm so glad…"

"It's been a really rough Squad Jam. But it's not over yet!"

"Yeah!"

"Let's beat Fire and finish our duel!"

"You bet! You're on!"

Llenn and Boss were enjoying a passionate moment of friendship and rivalry. Meanwhile, Pitohui called to Shirley, "Hey there, nice to see you! I'm surprised you're still alive!"

She still had the KTR-09 with the safety off hanging on her chest, though, so if she needed to shoot her sworn enemy, she was ready.

"Same to you. Circumstances conspired to make us work together again, but you'll never see my attack coming. Just a warning," Shirley snarled, her features as deadly as a naked blade.

Pitohui grinned back at her and replied, "Warning taken. Thanks for saving us from that disaster at the airport, by the way!"

"Huh? How do you know about that?" Shirley inquired, her face now as pale as crabmeat pulled from the shell.

Again, Pitohui smirked and answered, "Well, it really couldn't have been anyone else. You sniped from the control tower, didn't you? That was a serious long-distance shot."

"The next one's got your name on it."

"Sure, sure. Well, all aboard! No one's checking tickets!"

"Um…can it still go?" Llenn asked as she followed Fukaziroh onto the locomotive. She'd seen it get buffeted by rockets earlier, and it certainly wasn't moving now.

"Dunno."

"'Dunno'…?"

They had climbed onto the catwalk on the left side of the engine. It was dented and burned from all the RPGs, but the walkway had mostly been spared.

Even so, there was only the handrail. If you slipped and lost your footing, there was a hungry lake waiting below. Llenn watched her step very carefully.

M and a member of T-S were a little past the midway point of the train. They'd opened up a vast hatch and were peering inside.

There were four T-S survivors. Ervin was 002, plus 001, 004, and 006. Three of them were on the roof, keeping an eye on the area. The one talking to M was 006.

Llenn reasoned that they'd put numbers on themselves because, otherwise, there would be no way for them to tell one another apart. Up close, she could hear 006 talking.

"It's a good thing the trucks didn't take any hits. That's the wheels-and-axles part of the train. If the engine's still working, and it's not moving, then it must be the electrical system that's damaged. There's a good chance we can switch it to a backup line and get it running again."

M looked surprised at this. "You can tell?"

006 turned to face M, although his face was hidden behind his helmet. "In another world and another time, I was just your average railway engineer."

"Good to have you around."

* * *

At just after 2:26, the audience in the bar watched as the train chugged ahead on a bridge overlooking the lake—its surface a mosaic of white chunks of ice separated by black water.

Despite its tattered exterior and the holes and charred metal where it had been blasted, the locomotive continued onward, carrying thirteen players.

It reached the shore and beyond, as the bridge continued aloft over the highway that ran from east to west. This was probably the highest elevation point of the bridge.

The view was very good here—which also meant that the train was at the spot most visible from a distance.

* * *

"I've found them, Goddess!"

"Shinohara. I keep telling you not to call me that. I told you my name, remember?"

"Yes! Forgive me, my queen."

"Ugh… So what's the situation?"

"They're on a train. It's pretty packed, from the look of things. I can see at least six. The Amazons, the pink shrimp, and the space soldiers."

"That's good news. You've identified three different teams. I assume Pitohui is their leader."

"You can tell?"

"I guess. What would you call it, gamer's intuition? There's only one place they want to go. We're going to set up a net. Execute my earlier instructions."

"Yes, my goddess!"

"You've been through hell, missy. I'm glad to see you alive."

"Yeah, I guess."

Fukaziroh and Llenn sat side by side, enjoying the breeze on the train.

Now that they had equal use of both catwalks, it wasn't nearly as packed as it had been earlier. They were sitting on the right side at the moment.

With 006's help, the train had regained power and was cruising at forty-five miles per hour. Not its maximum speed, but good enough.

Once over the highway, the tracks began to descend toward the ground again. On the right was a landscape riddled with craters like the surface of the moon, while on the left were low houses, then a diamond-shaped domed stadium, and behind them all, the gigantic shopping mall.

Pitohui popped her head out of the cab and called out, "Everybody over to the left side!"

The train promptly began to slow. Llenn and Fukaziroh did as

Pitohui had commanded and made their way leisurely toward the rear of the locomotive. Through the comm, Llenn asked, "Are we stopping? We're not going to the forest?"

As a matter of fact, she'd never heard what the train's destination was. All she'd done was celebrate her reunion with the group.

Her initial assumption was that they'd travel into the forest, protected by the bridges, and fight there with the trees at their backs. It was a more passive approach, but with the damage they'd suffered, safety was best.

"Nope," Pitohui replied over the comms, just as Llenn and Fukaziroh reached the back of the engine.

Immediately, a hail of bullets bore down on the train.

It happened without warning.

The projectiles were like a rainstorm that began without any clouds in the sky.

Kakakakakakakakakakakakakakakan, kakakakan, kan, kakakan!

Bullets met the train's right side and beat against it as though it were a metal drum.

"Gahk!"

In what could only be described as a terrible stroke of luck, one of them split the throat of Tohma, who was on the catwalk. She lost her balance, slipped, and fell from the narrow metal platform.

"Ah!" 001 of T-S grabbed her hand. The bullets hit him, too, but they all deflected off his armor. He pulled Tohma up with both hands and dragged her to the rear deck.

"Tohma!" Boss called, leaping over from the right side and passing Llenn and Fukaziroh.

The last thing Tohma said was "Boss…sorry! Drag… Use… Give M gun…back…" Her head lolled back, and a DEAD tag rose over her body.

Boss took the Dragunov sniper rifle off Tohma's back. "Thank you. Drop her," she said to 001.

"…Got it," he replied, understanding her meaning. To prevent it from getting in the way of the living players on the narrow catwalk, he carefully, gently threw Tohma's body off the train.

Slowing or not, the train was still moving. Tohma's body bounced off the rails once, then tumbled away and out of sight as the locomotive continued onward.

"Aw, there goes another teammate..."

The train's passengers now totaled twelve. Another group of red bullet lines appeared, followed by the shots that had created them.

There were nearly thirty every second—more than one gun could produce. At least three people were firing simultaneously.

"Tsk! I didn't expect them to try this!" Pitohui snapped, staring to the southwest through binoculars as the bullets clanged off the roof of the cab over her head.

Everyone knew what squad was shooting.

It was the firepower fanatics of the Squad Jams. Every member was equipped with a machine gun: the All-Japan Machine-Gun Lovers, known as ZEMAL, for Zen-Nippon Machine-Gun Lovers.

However, they were nowhere to be seen.

It was nothing but brown wasteland with no cover for several hundred yards to the right of the tracks. Shots from a machine gun would have produced a visible muzzle flare.

"Long-distance machine-gun high-angle suppressing fire... That's the best possible tactic," said M from the driver's seat, crouching low.

Suppressing fire, of course, was shooting to block the enemy from moving. Jake's attack at the airport had been an example of such, but this was a more direct case of the concept. ZEMAL had chosen high-angle shots—launching their bullets into the air like artillery so they would fall down on their target—from a distance far enough away that they were out of sight.

It was much like using a grenade launcher, though this was more extreme.

They were firing from hundreds of meters away, possibly even as much as a kilometer. That meant they probably weren't shooting by hand and were instead using tripods for stability down in the bottoms of the craters.

When an automatic weapon was fixed on a stand, the legs absorbed all of the recoil, significantly increasing precision and stability, allowing the gunner to concentrate on a very narrow range.

Naturally, if the group on the train couldn't see ZEMAL, the opposite was likely true as well. This raised the question of how exactly ZEMAL was aiming and timing their shots.

The solution was a spotter. Someone was watching from a different location and telling the shooters when to pull the trigger. That would produce bullet lines, which the spotter used in turn to guide the gunners toward their target. In *GGO*, you didn't even have to shoot a bullet first.

Over an hour had passed since ZEMAL stood supreme in the crater area. That was plenty of time for them to set up and test their plan. Perhaps that was why they'd never left the place to begin with.

They had set up a net, a trap that would hurtle a rain of bullets from incredible range down on any enemy that approached. Naturally, as the train tracks were the widest artery into that area, ZEMAL made sure they could cover that spot. And the train had traveled right into their snare.

It was the perfect tactic for ZEMAL, making the most of their three 7.62 mm machine guns.

"They're too good at this. What the hell happened to them? Did they eat something expired?" wondered M. It was a mystery to him how the muscle-brained idiots on that squad could execute such a cunning plan.

"Aw, they got me. I guess they must have had someone with a little brains. They got me!" Pitohui lamented, grimacing happily.

She'd glanced at the scan earlier and seen that ZEMAL was smack in the middle of the crater zone, as though they'd grown roots and settled in permanently. There hadn't been time for them to come to the edge.

It was probably a classic leader-position trap, leaving one

member at the center of the area to draw attention while the rest set up elsewhere. Still, ZEMAL was the last team you'd expect to try that.

Over and over, Pitohui's strategies in SJ4 were backfiring. "Guess today just isn't my day," she said, shrugging. It didn't seem to bother her that much. "Well, it happens sometimes."

"I only ask this for clarification," M prompted, his big, ugly face looming closer, "but you didn't do this on purpose to force Llenn to marry Fire, did you?"

M trusted Pitohui. He worshipped her. So this was a very daring suggestion on his part. She shook her head and her hands in protest.

"No, no. Definitely not. I mean…"

"You mean what?"

"*I'm* the one who's going to marry her!"

"……"

M said nothing.

The train would be stopping soon. They had passed beyond the bridge onto flat land, with roads on either side of the tracks. On the right was cratered wasteland, while on the left were low-lying residential homes.

Pitohui exited onto the left catwalk and called out, "Once we stop, get off at once and run as fast as you can to the east! Keep an eye out for bullet lines until you've reached the nearest home for cover! And be wary of ambushes!"

Run in a straight line at maximum speed, while watching for lines and bullets coming from the rear *and* possible ambushes from the houses they were moving toward? It was an impossible order to obey.

"Why are we getting off here, Pito? Shouldn't we be riding into the forest?" Llenn asked.

"We'll be even worse off in the woods! We need to run to the place that offers us the best chance of winning!"

"Where is that?"

"Obviously, it's the ma—," Pitohui began, but only the first sound of the word was audible.

There was a huge rattling of gunfire and sparkling bullet lines as a new wave of lead flew closer. These did not come from overhead, but the nearest home, just eighty meters to the east.

What had started as a sprinkling of rain from overhead was now a fire hose blasting from one side.

The projectiles' density was intense, choked closely enough together that every person present suffered at least one hit. It all happened in the blink of an eye.

Llenn took a shot to the outer part of her left thigh right as she started running, causing her to tumble spectacularly. Fortunately, her tumbling to the ground kept her from suffering anything further.

Fukaziroh took one bullet to her side and another to the helmet. That happened after she'd already hit the ground, then she started crawling across the dirt like a particular despised insect whose name began with the letter R. One more shot hit her on the sole of her foot before she found shelter behind a train wheel.

Pitohui was lifting her KTR-09 to counterattack when she was shot through the right hand. Though she dropped the gun, she managed to land on the ground and curl up to minimize the target she created. One bullet hit her back and bounced off her armor.

As M left the train cab, bullets passed through the thin door and hit his back and legs, causing him to topple over. It dropped him to the floor of the shrapnel-filled cab, where he cut his face on the metal scraps, but the next wave of projectiles passed over his head.

One bullet grazed Shirley's left flank, but another hit her right ankle. As she fell, she fired the R93 Tactical 2 once at Pitohui, but her desperation shot only exploded uselessly on the ground. As she attempted a second, a bullet hit the plastic body of her gun and ripped it out of her hands.

Tanya was the unluckiest of the group. As usual, she was running ahead and took the most fire from the closest range, riddling her with holes. The sixth shot was enough to label her DEAD, but ZEMAL didn't stop there. Her soaking up more rounds than required to kill her actually helped the people in the back.

Rosa was lifting her PKM machine gun to fight back when she was struck. No bullet actually *hit* her; they only grazed her shoulder. Still, several of them burrowed into the machine gun's ammo box, doing enough damage to the part to obliterate it into virtual pieces. It tore loose the belt that was supposed to ferry bullets into the gun.

A shot went clean through Boss's right knee. She buckled forward on the spot, and another projectile hit her considerably sized bottom.

"Eeeek!" she shrieked, given the sensitive nature of the spot.

Only the four members of T-S made it through the triple-machine-gun onslaught unscathed—saved by their high defenses.

That didn't mean they could just keep taking hits indefinitely, however.

"Hyaii!"

Ervin and the others had to scurry around behind the train for safety. Their armor spat sparks with each bullet they took. It was the right decision; if they had stayed put and tried to return fire, their weapons would have been blasted to pieces in their hands.

All told, it was five seconds of shooting, but it was enough to ensure that not a single person remained standing near the train.

Amid this execution atmosphere, Llenn glanced at her 40 percent health and the HP bars of her teammates and tried desperately to think of a plan that might get them out of this.

Oh crap, oh crap, crap, crap…

It was about fifteen feet from where she'd fallen to the train.

If she could get up, run, and hide under the wheels—but a single shot the moment she rose would be the end of her.

What if she burst forward into enemy territory? She might be able to dodge one or two people shooting at her, but three was asking too much.

They weren't shooting now, but not because they were exchanging ammo belts. ZEMAL used their own belt-reloading system that allowed them to fire continuously. They must have stopped on purpose.

After a second of silence, Llenn had mostly given up. She'd been through a lot of perilous situations in the Squad Jams, but nothing had ever felt as urgent as this.

From her spot on the ground, she could see the wheels of the train, as well as Fukaziroh huddled between them and T-S running away.

Her racing mind caused everything to move in slow motion.

T-S could handle a few hits just fine, but rather than fighting back or supporting their companions, they were sprinting for their lives toward the right side of the tracks.

Well, I guess that's all right, thought Llenn, who couldn't muster the strength to get angry.

If they had fought back, the next round of attacks would have inevitably destroyed them. At least this way, if they fled from the scene of this slaughter, they might have a chance for revenge against ZEMAL later.

They'd shot Llenn's team from behind in SJ2, but this time they'd helped out, to a point. If the squad's fate was to die here, at least T-S would survive a little longer.

However, no sooner had Llenn mused as much than those hard, armored sci-fi soldiers all perished in an enormous blue surge.

It was a trap…

ZEMAL had set up a booby trap on the right side of the train tracks. A plasma grenade buried in the dirt exploded like a land mine, tearing up T-S's powerful armor. The four men lost their lower halves almost entirely, and DEAD tags appeared on their airborne bodies, signaling the team's elimination from SJ4.

Five seconds passed without gunfire.

Instead, there was the sound of approaching footsteps.

Llenn turned her head and saw a woman standing about fifty yards away.

* * *

She had never seen this person before.

Not up close—and not on any video.

It was a female avatar who looked about twenty years old. She had delicate features and smooth skin. Her gray eyes were piercing beneath wine-red short hair and a navy-blue beanie on top.

She was small and delicate, though not as much so as Llenn. Her combat fatigues had a green tiger-stripe pattern.

Dangling over her front was a short and unfamiliar machine gun with a drum magazine that looked like a cookie tin attached.

Um, who is that?

It was undeniable that their opponents were ZEMAL, but had they always had this woman on their squad? Probably not. She wasn't one of the usual guys in drag, either.

The bigger mystery was why she'd chosen to walk into the open and expose herself so brazenly.

Her teammates were surely keeping their aim behind her. But did she not consider the possibility that someone might recover from the pain and shoot her first? These questions and more flooded Llenn's confused mind.

A full ten seconds after the shooting stopped, the woman said, "So would you do us the favor of resigning?"

Everyone was so taken aback that they forgot about counter-attacking.

Not that anyone in LPFM or SHINC was in a position to strike back at the moment. If they had tried, they doubtlessly would've been shot by the two men behind the woman. So the group had no choice but to hear her out.

"We could be ruthless and wipe you out, of course, but which would you prefer? I'd feel better about it if you chose to surrender instead. A nice, clean resignation, like in chess. Or would you favor dragging this into a checkmate? "

Llenn was stunned. Situations like this were why the phrase

mouth agape existed. In a game about virtual killing, who demanded the other side surrender before the fun part?

She noticed that the numbness in her legs was starting to fade. Once she was able to move better, she could at least get to the woman. If she could grapple her, the two men behind her wouldn't shoot. And once Llenn had sliced the woman up good, she would probably bite it herself.

It was at that moment that someone behind Llenn called out, "All right! As the leader, I accept your offer!"

It was Fukaziroh.

Pardon?

Llenn spun to find Fukaziroh emerging from beside one of the large locomotive wheels. She had no weapons in her hands as she approached.

When did she become the leader? Llenn wanted to ask, but she was patient enough to wait. Things became clearer when Fukaziroh turned her head in Llenn's direction and, in a voice only the comm would pick up, muttered, "Run."

Fukaziroh quickened her walking pace toward the space between Llenn and ZEMAL. If Llenn started sprinting as soon as Fukaziroh got in front, her friend would be shot to pieces like a rag doll, but Llenn might be able to get behind the cover of the wheels.

Whatever would happen after that was anyone's guess, but Llenn, the one person who really couldn't afford to die here, was appreciative of her friend's sacrifice.

"Fuka…," Llenn mumbled.

"Fuka?" repeated the woman from ZEMAL, who heard her.

Fukaziroh answered, "That's right! I am the leader of Team LPFM, the charismatic and talented Fukaziroh! In case you were curious, our team name is short for Lovely Pretty Fukaziroh the Monstrosity!"

You could have picked a better word. I mean, Marvelous *and* Magnificent *are sitting right there*, Llenn thought as she prepared to make a break for it. Fukaziroh would soon pass by her. The numbness in her leg had faded to a negligible amount.

The first and final chance.

Then the machine-gun woman asked, "Wait, Fukaziroh? The Zweihänder Sylph?"

Fukaziroh came to an abrupt stop six feet in front of Llenn.

I can't run away if you stop there!

However, at the same time, Llenn was intrigued by the woman's question. It seemed like she knew who Fukaziroh was.

"Ohhh...hoh-hoh-hoh... So you too...have been reincarnated... from the world of fairies? You've spoken an epithet that was never meant to be said here," replied Fukaziroh, looking truly wicked.

She let her right hand slink closer to the M&P holster on her side, just like a gunman in a Western, despite the fact that there was no way she'd land an accurate shot with it.

"I knew it! I'd heard you hadn't shown up much in *ALO* recently, and now it makes sense. You were here in *GGO*! Your fairy was a real bombshell, but in this world, you're just a little cutie-patootie!" the woman exclaimed, looking delighted for some reason. She lifted her hands, but rather than fire her machine gun, she spread them apart to offer a better view of herself.

"How are you doing? It's me! Ah, well, I suppose you don't recognize me. I *do* look completely different here, after all!" the woman continued, speaking like this was a reunion between old friends. Actually, that's probably what it was.

"Oh? Ohhh yeah! Hang on; I'll guess! You must be someone I met in *ALO*!" Fukaziroh said. She was entirely out of battle mode now. "Are you Mabel? Sorry about knocking you off the top of the fortress that one time. I didn't think you had so much trouble flying!"

"*Bzzzt!* Wrong."

"Then you're Exure! I feel bad about splitting your head in two that one time. But that's just what happens if you run past me when I've got my sword."

"Nope, wrong."

"Villares! My bad for kicking you into the flames that one time. I know how chilly you can get, so I wanted to warm you up."

"Um, no. Not me."

"Maybe Elaine! Sorry for luring all those monsters toward you that one time. I thought you loved animals. Also, that was the most peaceful way to get you to die."

"Close! Just kidding; you're way off."

Fuka, how many people have you killed? Llenn wondered. She kept her mouth shut, however, not interested in getting into this conversation.

"Okay, maybe this is harder to guess than I figured. The correct answer is Vivi," the woman admitted at last.

"Ohhh! Vivi!" Fukaziroh said with a beaming smile. Then she erupted into a furious roar. "Youuu! You crushed me with a giant stone pestle! You sliced off my wings in midair! You grilled me to a well-done crisp at the mouth of that volcano! You shot me in the head with an arrow! You let me sink into the bottomless swaaaamp!"

Fuka, how many times have you been killed? Llenn wondered. She kept her mouth shut, however, not interested in getting into this conversation.

"Fuka, do you know her?" asked Pitohui. Llenn craned her neck and saw her teammate standing beside the tracks, gleaming damage light on her empty hand.

"You bet! This is Vivi. She killed me tons of times in *ALO*. She's a salamander, sworn enemy of the sylphs—a fire fairy! She wore this goofy red vest, though. Looked like a bodybuilder!"

"I see. Well, since you know each other, can I ask you to talk to Vivi and make her see reason?"

"Sure thing. I'll send her head spinning so fast that she'll become our henchman!"

"Can you ask her to let us go, this one time?"

Huh?

Llenn was stunned, and she could sense in the atmosphere that everyone else—Shirley, M, the two SHINC survivors—was equally taken aback.

Who would have guessed that Pitohui, of all people, would make such a request?

Even Fukaziroh seemed stunned by the appeal. "Sure! Wait… what? Are you serious, Pito?"

"Dead serious. If they're just going to shoot us anyway, why not gamble on the tiniest chance of survival?"

"Um, well, I guess…"

"Just ask. What's the harm?" Pitohui insisted quietly.

"F-fine…," answered Fukaziroh, giving in to the pressure. She turned to Vivi. "Um…"

She wasn't quite sure how to proceed.

"Sure, that's all right," Vivi acquiesced, answering before Fukaziroh had even gotten the words out.

CHAPTER 19
Handguns Only

SECT.19

CHAPTER 19
Handguns Only

"Huh? You sure? What?"

Fukaziroh's surprise spoke for the rest of the group.

Llenn thought that Pitohui's statement was the most unexpected thing she'd heard all day, but Vivi's answer was a close second.

"Yes, it's fine. We'll let all of you go—on one condition," Vivi appended.

Ha. I should have known, Llenn thought. She was obviously going to follow this up with a one-liner like *You all have to diiiie!* or *We'll shoot your asses as you run!* Sure, that sounded kinda rude, but Llenn was assuming that Vivi was a typical ZEMAL member. She'd never met this person before, but if she was an old acquaintance of Fukaziroh's, then she *had* to be like that. No further explanation was necessary.

"Got something to add, Llenn?" snapped Fukaziroh suddenly.

Damn psychic, Llenn cursed silently.

"Can you guess what my term is?" Vivi asked.

Pitohui's reply was prompt. "Giving up our main guns?"

"Very sharp."

"Then that's what it'll be."

Huh? What? That's what what will be?

Llenn wasn't following at all. She glanced at Boss and Rosa; they looked just as dumbfounded.

"Ahhh, I see. So that's the ploy," said Fukaziroh, the only one who had figured it out. "Wait…what is it, exactly?"

Okay, maybe she hadn't.

"I'll explain later," Pitohui dismissed. "Everybody, drop your primary weapons on the ground over there. You've all recovered feeling by now, I trust?"

Boss's curiosity got the better of her. "Wh-what does this mean? Explain, please!"

"I'll do it while we're on the move. Just hurry! It's nearly after the twenty-ninth minute," Pitohui said.

That told Boss that it had something to do with the scan. She got to her feet without the Vintorez in her hands.

"You too, Llenn. It's time to say good-bye to P-chan for a while. Don't worry; it'll come back when this is over. Shirley, put down the rifle."

"I'm not sure what's going on…but we can keep pistols in our inventory, right?"

"Of course. Time to run!"

"Goddess…did you really mean to let them get away?" asked Peter, watching the other group leave as he stood by the train.

He was the shortest member of ZEMAL, and the piece of tape over his nose was his trademark. There was an ammo box on his back, which ran on metal rails to the Negev machine gun in his hands.

Next to him stood Max, the dark-skinned avatar with a shaved hairstyle. Like Peter, he was equipped with a loading backpack for his Minimi and carefully eyeing his surroundings.

With these two standing guard over her, Vivi watched the Satellite Scanner. Glancing at the weapons the other group had left behind, she said, "It's fine. They won't be coming back. I'd guess that all of them are going to die inside that mall."

* * *

"Huh? What just happened?"

Nobody in the pub could explain what they'd just seen.

T-S had been wiped out by a long-range machine-gun attack, a devastating ambush, and a booby trap.

Everyone had assumed that this was the end of LPFM and SHINC. But after speaking with a mystery woman, both teams' survivors had just taken off running—after leaving their primary weapons behind, no less.

Beside Tanya's dead body was a pink P90, Pitohui's KTR-09, M's M14 EBR, Shirley's R93 Tactical 2, Boss's Vintorez, the Dragunov borrowed from Tohma, and Rosa's PKM.

"Huh? What just happened...?"

The clock on the screens hit 2:30, and the next scan commenced.

"What is this situation, exactly? Oh, poor P-chan..."

Llenn was on the run, and she didn't know what was going on, either.

The others had told her to rush on, so she'd taken point ahead of them. The single-story residential homes on the east side of the tracks made for a good view, but the lack of a weapon in her hands left her feeling very uneasy.

Still, she was alive.

P-chan sacrificed itself for me, she thought.

Vivi from ZEMAL had promised, "Don't worry, we won't use the guns you dropped, nor will we destroy them." There was no choice but to trust her on that. And for now, it was most important to listen to Pitohui.

"I'm going to explain the situation while M watches the scan. I'm sure I already know what the results will be, though."

"All right."

Llenn kept her eyes peeled for booby traps and ambushes while she focused on hearing Pitohui's voice through the comm.

Far behind her, Boss, Rosa, Shirley, and Fukaziroh followed behind, presumably harboring the same feelings as Llenn. The two SHINC members were close enough that they could hear Pitohui's voice in person.

"First, we know that woman is a seriously talented, experienced player. I mean, she's killed Fuka in *ALO* all those times, so that tells you something."

"I just wasn't paying attention!"

All of those times? Llenn thought.

"She'd anticipated that someone would use the train, guessed where it would stop, and put down a triple-part trap to catch us."

"That's what I don't get! How did they know where it would come to a halt?" Boss shouted, cutting Pitohui off.

It was indeed a mystery. They could have surmised that someone would ride the locomotive, but guessing where it would stop would have been difficult.

Pitohui answered that mystery by explaining, "That spot leaves the shortest distance across the map to the mall."

"Huh? The mall?" Boss repeated.

"Yes, that's where we're headed: the giant shopping mall. I wanted us to go there, so I stopped directly west of it so we could run down the big street. Vivi saw that decision coming."

"Ohhh, got it... So that's why," replied Boss, picking up on the logic quickly.

But Llenn was not as fast on the uptake, asking, "Why the mall? Are you going shopping?"

"No! We're going to fight there!"

"Why?"

"Have you forgotten the special rules, Llenn?"

"About the monsters? Oh, you mean the ammo coming back?" she said, amending her statement after seeing the notice about ammunition restoration at two thirty.

"The other one."

"...?"

"Pito, she's completely forgotten," remarked Fukaziroh.

Llenn quickly grew frustrated. Evidently, she was the only

person not getting it. Still, she was honest enough to ask, "Um… what other one?"

"Ahhh, the mall, then…"

Kenta from MMTM was driving a trike. David, the team leader, was sitting on the back. Instead of riding along the highway to the south of the airport, they cruised along an ordinary road farther east.

The pair's destination was the massive shopping center on the southeast side of the map. This was the answer to the question posed at two fifteen, when they were just hanging out and relaxing.

"The pistol rule," said David. "That damned author set up a special condition for us to ignore weight to ensure that he could put in a spot where only pistols are allowed. The most obvious place for such a parameter is that mall. It's the most suited for a handgun fight."

"What made you think Pitohui would head there?" Kenta inquired.

"It's an easier battleground for her and the pink shrimp. Plus, it'd eliminate any threat of assault rifle shots that could kill you when your health is low. However, the main reason boils down to her psychology."

"Ooh. How so?"

"She's the kind of person who thinks, *If they set up a pistol-only area, shouldn't we enjoy it to the fullest?*"

"If they set up a pistol-only area, shouldn't we enjoy it to the fullest?" Pitohui added at the end.

"*That's* your reason?" Llenn demanded, annoyed.

They were running through the town, the dome of the stadium visible on the left. The shopping mall was directly ahead of them, the off-white structure looming beneath the cloudy sky on the opposite side of the highway. It looked like a fortress.

"Well, it does make sense," said Boss, her braids swaying as she kept pace beside Pitohui. "Building interiors make for very close-range battles, so running and hiding is easier. A pistol's power with a single shot is limited. It's much less likely that you'll die immediately from a sudden shot. That means Fire's goons will have a harder time killing Llenn. Not a bad call."

"Well reasoned, Evacchi. Hey, you wanna join my team?"

"I'll pass."

"Okay, I get the purpose now," stated Llenn, "but do you think Fire's side will play along? The longer he leaves us alone, the higher the chance that he wins without a scratch, right? Would he really get into a firefight at the mall where he's more at risk?"

M, eyes still on the scan, provided the answer to that question.

"He will. He's already on his way."

Spectators in the bar watched the scan as it revealed the locations of the surviving teams.

Excluding ZEMAL, who were still in the crater area, and V2HG, who had passed through the city, every team was converging on the mall. There were no battles underway, so the screens were showing everyone on the move.

Two members of MMTM were approaching fast from the east. They were on a trike, so they were making good time, although they were still the farthest away.

From the west, LPFM's and SHINC's survivors were running on foot, albeit from much closer to the mall.

The teams called WEEI and SATOH were traveling south toward the shopping plaza on a single truck. A man dressed in desert camo was driving the rig. They must have found it early in the game and kept it hidden until now.

With things proceeding as they were, it was obvious what would happen next.

Within minutes, five teams would gather at the mall—and rush inside from their respective directions.

* * *

"So Vivi decided that if we were going to die inside that mall, there was no reason for them to do the job directly. Instead, they'd be happy if we stayed alive to fight our mutual enemies and weaken them for ZEMAL," Llenn deduced at last. "I got it. I get it."

Llenn felt confident regarding her view of Vivi and Pitohui's assessment. She was quite curious about this Vivi character who had beaten Fukaziroh so often and had somehow reached an unspoken understanding with her. Still, for now, she had to put that feeling aside.

The opponent at hand was more important.

Llenn's group was likely to run up against MMTM, SATOH, and WEEI inside the mall—the last two being teams under Fire's control. If they were willing to get into a pistol fight, Llenn wasn't going to say no.

Even so, the pink-dressed girl wasn't without her doubts. "I haven't shot a pistol since the very first tutorial!"

She hadn't prepared one, either, so she was using Pitohui's, but Llenn wasn't familiar with it at all. Could she actually use it? In a close-quarters indoor battle, she was more than ready to fight with the combat knife she had strapped to her back.

"We can figure that out once we get to the mall. More importantly, everyone, take your medicine now, while you can!" Pitohui instructed, ordering the group to heal themselves to maximum health.

They'd suffered a lot of damage from ZEMAL's gunfire earlier. Llenn had fallen below half, so she used one of her two remaining med kits. She'd take the last one in another three minutes.

That would put her back at full health—but only after six minutes.

Llenn wasn't the toughest of characters; could she survive that long? Whatever the case, she had to outlast Fire. So long as she lived even a split second longer than he, it was her victory. If he wound up in arm's reach, she'd bite him if need be.

Fukaziroh had 60 percent left. She was out of healing items, so there was nothing she could do.

Pitohui and M had taken significant damage in the ruined city and had used up all their emergency med kits. Even now, Pitohui was under half health. M was a bit better, at 60 percent.

They would have to make that last. Thankfully, the trio possessed very high base athletic values, meaning there wasn't too much difference between them at half life and Llenn at max. Llenn would have died several times if she'd suffered as much damage as they had in SJ4.

Shirley had barely been struck at all, by comparison. She had all three med kits left, and her hit points were at 60 percent. She healed once; it would be up to her to decide what to do once she was at 90 in three minutes.

Though Llenn couldn't see their information, SHINC's two remaining members had their own troubles. Boss had seven-tenths of her HP remaining and no means of recovery. Rosa was at 80 and had two med kits, but she didn't use them.

On the opposing side, every member of Fire's group was likely at max life with all med kits ready. That pair from MMTM had been hurt a bit, but their team's health pool was undoubtedly still greater than that of Llenn's side.

Llenn and the others were at an undeniable disadvantage.

A wounded gaggle of seven against an allied, healthy team of twelve, plus two members from MMTM who weren't likely to render much aid.

Yet there was no giving up, no giving in.

Things looked grim, but it wasn't over until the fat lady sang.

This Squad Jam had been moving from one danger to the next, but Llenn was still alive.

No matter what happened, she would fight.

If her avatar had actual body temperature, it would be skyrocketing. The domed stadium was to the left and quickly passed Llenn by as she hurried on toward the shopping mall.

"I'll beat Fire!" she swore as she ran.

* * *

Eventually, the obnoxiously massive building came into view.

The off-white structure rose up into the cloudy sky like a giant wall.

What Llenn was looking at was just a part of the mammoth construct. It was the west wall of the exterior. The main building was rectangular, about eight hundred yards east to west and three hundred north to south. An entire residential sector could've fit inside that one building.

It was twice as long and over three times as wide as the luxury cruise ship from SJ3.

While Llenn couldn't tell how many floors it had, the windowless building loomed over the scene like an aquarium. On each of the four corners was an octagonal structure about 150 yards across.

When checking the map at the start of the game, M had surmised that the four corners were four major department stores. He was right; as Llenn drew nearer, she could see the signs. The letters were missing here and there, but Llenn recognized some famous international department store names. Maybe the fact that some of the letters were missing made it okay to use real-world brand names.

On the right was a JCP—NEY and on the left was a SE-RS. Llenn continued alone through the wide-open parking lot until she reached the mall entrance, where the glass doors were broken and scattered across the ground.

The structure's name adorned the space over the entranceway—Mall OF THE WORLD. A very ostentatious name. However, it might have meant that this was the largest shopping plaza in the world.

Llenn did not immediately enter; she waited carefully next to the doorway. Beyond the doors, which were partially full of jagged glass where they had broken, there was a standing map of the mall, but she did not look at it yet.

"Listen up, everybody. Once we go inside, we won't have time to sit around coming up with a plan, so I'm going to say everything now while we have time," said the distant Pitohui. "Once we go in, we'll be working as a team to an extent, but there's no saying what might happen depending on the flow of battle. We might end up fighting separately."

I hope we don't get split up, Llenn thought, but she knew that there were times when battle made it necessary.

"But at the very least, I want us to work on a buddy system. That way, everyone will have one person to watch the other direction. Turn off your comm to everyone but your partner. Use radios to talk as needed. The pairings are as follows: M and me, Eva and Rosa, Fuka and Shirley."

"I'd rather be alone!" cried Shirley.

"Nope. Two-player teams at all times. Every sniper needs a spotter, doesn't she?" Pitohui scolded. Shirley offered no further protest.

"Don't worry, sweetheart. I'll watch your cute ass," teased Fukaziroh. That was sexual harassment, of course, but it wasn't the only problem with her statement. Fukaziroh had a reputation for terrible handgun aim.

Llenn felt a bit sorry for Shirley, but the pairings left her with a question. "Pito, what about me?" She had thought for sure that she was going to be assigned a partner.

"Llenn? Isn't it obvious? You're on your own."

"Hey, that doesn't add up with what you said earlier! How come?" Llenn fumed, stomping her feet alone at the entrance to the mall.

"The reason is simple: Nobody else can keep up with you if you have to go all out. If Tanya were still around, I would've paired you up with her."

"Aw..."

That cut Llenn's tantrum short. *Oh, Tanya, why did you have to die?* she wondered, mourning the girl she'd been in a deadly battle against just an hour ago.

"Still, I don't think this puts you at a disadvantage, Llenn. Just the opposite," Pitohui stated. She sounded serious. It was an honest remark, not lip service. "This battlefield suits you! Use your advantage in speed among these tight hallways to fight to your heart's content!"

"G-got it…"

"That's a good girl. Now you can open your present."

"Present?"

Aw, I hate to admit it, but…it's cute! thought Llenn as she materialized the gift from Pitohui. She didn't want to express as much out loud, though, knowing how much Pitohui would smirk about it.

The motes of light coalesced into a backpack.

It was black, but pink-and-white vertical lines adorned the thing—presumably to match Llenn's cap.

It was about fifteen inches tall and twelve inches wide. The depth was a bit less, maybe ten inches. It was no larger than a common day pack, but with the tiny Llenn carrying it, the thing seemed comparable to M's supersize rucksack.

What's inside? I mean, aside from the pistol.

Llenn set down the backpack and opened the top zipper. She reached in and pulled out the contents.

Llenn's first thought was that it was cute.

It was a pink-painted automatic pistol that came in a black nylon holster.

The frame and slide were a rose color. The grip and added parts on the front were of a lighter shade.

It was altogether *extremely* pink, but there were black portions, too. The barrel. The trigger. The hammer. The screws that held it all together. And the dots carved under the sight for better aim.

Llenn hadn't studied handguns, so she didn't know the model, but it resembled the gun the female instructor had given Llenn during the tutorial. That one was called a Colt M1911A1—or a

Colt Government. It was a large military pistol, one of the most famous and recognizable handguns in the world.

This pink firearm was similar, but it felt smaller. Perhaps it would be considered a midsize handgun.

For one thing, the grip was shorter, but as if to make up for that, there was a little hornlike extension at the bottom of the magazine that Llenn's pinkie could rest on. It felt both spacious and snug in the girl's hand.

The gun ran shorter than a Government, too, and something was attached to the muzzle that wasn't a slide. Llenn couldn't tell what it was for.

The sides of the frame toward the front were another mystery piece that seemed to pinch the slide from below. She didn't know what that did, either.

"This part is cute...," Llenn murmured, because the flared bit of that portion had a white line through it, just like her hat.

As it happened, the streak only ran on the left side of the gun, not the right. Again, just like Llenn's hat.

"Sounds like you approve," said Pitohui, who could hear Llenn's remarks through the comm.

Llenn looked up and saw the rest of the group in the distance, making their way across the spacious parking lot. It would be at least another minute before they arrived.

"I hate to admit it, but it's adorable... I accept your gift... What's it called?" Llenn inquired.

"I'm glad you asked! That is...a custom model I created!" Pitohui declared.

"You made this?"

"Yep. You know that there's a Gunsmithing skill and mode in *GGO*, right?"

"Yeah. I used it to change my weapon's color, but that's it."

"I had a feeling we'd need handguns this time around, and that got me thinking about what would be best for you."

"And this is what you came up with...?"

"Yup. The base is a gun called the AM.45, a weapon that only

exists in *GGO*, but it's basically just a modified Detonics Combat Master with extra parts. It's fairly popular in *GGO* for being a compact but powerful backup weapon. Ever heard of it?"

"Nope."

"That's all right. It was originally black, so I painted it pink, added the white line, and set it up for you! I decided on a two-tone pink finish instead of a one-color style like P-chan. It took several days before I had it just the way I wanted."

"Um, thanks..."

It felt like Pitohui could've been doing something more productive, especially considering her busy schedule, but Llenn wasn't going to point that out now.

"And that's the result! I call it the AM.45 Version Llenn! But its nickname is the Vorpal Bunny!"

Both of those names sounded pretty long to Llenn, and she got to work thinking about what she'd call it. Llenn didn't know what *vorpal* meant, but calling the gun Bunny would be easy enough.

On the left side of the slide, the words VORPAL BUNNY were printed in small letters next to the larger AM.45.

Llenn was a pretty good English student, but she still had no idea what *vorpal* meant, even seeing it written out.

"Hey, Pito, can you define *vorpal*?" Llenn asked, giving up on interpreting it alone .

She was hoping that her friend would gleefully offer the answer, but instead, Pitohui replied, "Hmm, it's too long to explain. We don't have the time right now." So Llenn made a note to look it up on the Internet later. For now, she'd stick with her usual style and refer to it as Vor-chan.

Pitohui explained, "It's just a shortened version of the Government, so it works the same way. You remember?"

"I guess..."

Llenn checked to see that there was a magazine inserted, then pulled the firearm's slide.

It made the sound of metal sliding on metal and loaded the first bullet. In the bottom right of her vision, a gun icon appeared, indicating that she had equipped it as a weapon, along with a 6 to display the remaining rounds—six shots to a magazine.

If it was the same as a Government, then it used .45 ACP bullets. That was the most common kind of .45-caliber pistol projectile. That was quite large, giving the shots a powerful punch.

The Government series placed the safety about where the thumb would rest when one was holding the firearm by the grip. Llenn rarely put the safety of her P90 on, but she decided to use it for her new weapon. This was no time to be accidentally shooting herself. At least with this pistol, the safety was in a convenient place.

"Okay, here's the lowdown, so listen up! The added parts at the front of the gun are for close combat. The portion on the tip ensures you can still fire the gun even when it's pressed against your target. The things on the sides ensure the slide won't be affected if you press the pistol against something for increased stability."

"I see…"

Llenn brushed the pieces with her left hand. They were firmly fixed to the frame, so even if something was touching the weapon, there would be no effect on its firing.

Many pistols could be rendered inert if you managed to hold down the slide. Other issues with the slide could cause the gun to jam. Pitohui's customization was meant to overcome those weaknesses.

"So don't be shy. Get right up in your opponent's face. Make use of your small size, burst, and speed. There's nothing more beautiful than pressing a gun against your opponent's throat and shooting like you're biting into them! Remember your days PKing with the Vz. 61 Skorpion!"

Llenn thought back on that time fondly. She'd run up on people and kill them without even getting a good look at their faces. At present, however, she wished she could go back in time to apologize for having done so.

"Treat this the same as back then. Get in close, blast them with both, then run away! Good luck!"

Both? Llenn dug deeper into the backpack. *Oh my. I didn't even notice…*

There was another gun in the sack, identical to the first. Llenn had two pistols.

That led to a new question: Should she call both of them Vor-chan or just the one? She didn't have a lot of time to waste on the matter, so she decided that the two of them would both be called Vor-chan.

"Put your P90 magazine pouches in your inventory and attach the holsters I gave you. There's a right and a left—well, I'm sure you can tell the difference."

Llenn did as Pitohui instructed. The P90 ammo pouches that ringed her waist like a skirt vanished, leaving room for a sheath to wrap around each thigh.

Llenn stowed her two new firearms in their holsters, then pulled the slide for the left-hand gun to load it. The icon for her equipped weapon doubled.

"You should get some practice shots in now, at least one magazine for each. Make sure to put on your backpack first," stated Pitohui.

Llenn obeyed, storing both pistols, then shouldering the bag they'd come in. Two buckles on straps ran across Llenn's chest to hold the thing tight to her back.

Thanks to the rule that kept handguns from adding to your weight, the backpack hardly felt like anything at all. It had little more weight than an empty sack. At this level, it wouldn't affect Llenn's speed in the least. However, she'd have to be aware of its wide dimensions if she needed to squeeze through tight spaces.

Llenn reached for the thigh holsters, putting her hands into the so-called akimbo position on her hips. For this reason, dual-wielding pistols in games was often referred to as playing akimbo style.

The rest of the group was much closer now, but still a few dozen seconds away.

As instructed, Llenn drew her handguns and thumbed off their safeties. Like she had with the Skorpion, she extended her hands slightly, as though to catch something with both arms.

This was to minimize recoil with her elbows and decrease the chances of the enemy getting close enough to grab the weapons or knock them aside—both of which would be problems if she simply straightened her arms.

The pistols' slides would move automatically, so it was dangerous to hold them too close to the face. Llenn made sure both were at least ten inches away.

The guns were inclined slightly toward each other so that they diagonally framed Llenn's field of view. Not pointing them straight made for a more natural arm angle, which fostered more comfortable shooting and adjustment.

With two handguns, using the sights on one didn't make sense. Llenn placed her fingers on the triggers, producing two bullet circles. The girl in pink aimed them over a tipped trash can next to the mall's entrance, a distance of roughly twenty meters.

Dababababababababow!

The pistols blared. Llenn had gotten used to the powerful kickback of a 45-caliber weapon during the tutorial. What's more, her Strength stat had risen since then. Thus the bullets stayed true and struck the trash can.

"Ooh…"

Twelve shots, six from each pistol, turned the waste receptacle into a shattered mess of polygons.

"These seem pretty easy to use," Llenn admitted.

The Vorpal Bunny had a very light trigger, activating with only the tiniest bit of finger pressure. The two weapons fired at a comfortable pace, and the slides whipped back and forth tightly.

However, Llenn still had her concerns. The slides of the pistols stayed back, indicating that they were out of ammo. With the P90, she could grab a fresh magazine from a pouch and pop it in, but she had no pouches for the handguns.

I fired off my guns. The next big question becomes: How do I reload?

As Pitohui crossed the last fifty yards to reach the mall, she gave Llenn the answer to that haiku query.

"Drop the empty magazines. Then put your arms behind your back and stick the pistol grips into the holes at the bottom of your backpack."

"...?"

Llenn pressed the magazine catch buttons on the inner sides of the grips with her thumbs and middle fingers. The empty things silently slid free of the pistols.

Next, she swung her arms behind her back and brought them toward the bottom of the pack, where she found the apertures in question.

Click! The metal popped into place. Llenn felt the small vibration run through her hands.

"Oh?" She pulled her arms forward again and saw that there were fresh magazines in both pistols. The squat, fat bullets were visible through the ejection ports.

Llenn pushed down the top lever of each pistol's slide with her right thumb and left index finger. The retracted slides grabbed the new bullets and pushed them forward before returning into place. The ammo icons in the bottom right corner of Llenn's eye informed her that both weapons were now fully ready to go.

"Ooh..."

Pitohui rushed up to Llenn as the latter marveled at her guns. Fukaziroh and the others came shortly after. Llenn made sure to switch the safeties on and stowed the guns in their holsters.

Her benefactor patted the backpack and said, "Pretty cool, huh? It was a custom order! It's got a big stack of magazines and a gizmo inside that loads them when you stick your grips inside! It's like a giant ammo supply! There are twenty magazines on each side of the backpack! That's two hundred and forty shots!"

"I see..."

It was indeed a convenient item. With this, Llenn could shoot all she wanted and quickly reload. It solved the most significant hang-up that dual pistols caused.

Pitohui waved a hand to bring up her game window. When she was done pressing buttons, it spat out another backpack. This one was all black, and it looked much smaller on the taller woman's back.

"One for me, too."

Pitohui had XDM handguns on each leg, so she had arranged the same speedy reloading system for herself. Or more likely, she'd developed her own first, then made another for Llenn.

"There's one more trick to it, too," Pitohui appended, punching the back of Llenn's pack. It made a hard, hollow sound. "Every surface of this is lined with thin layers of the same material M's shield is made from."

"Pito, isn't that…?"

"Yep. No pistol bullet is going to break through that bag. If the enemy's going to shoot you, crouch and turn your back or run and guard your head. Got that?"

"Got it!"

At present, a single shot, even from a handgun, could slay her. Thus, having armored gear to protect her was a tremendous boon.

Weapons and gear that had been custom-tailored to suit the user. Llenn could only wonder how much it would have cost had she tried to arrange for these things herself. She thought it best not to get to the bottom of that mystery.

"Ooh, very nice. Where's mine?" Fukaziroh asked as soon as she arrived. She only had a single gun on her—the one she couldn't hit the broad side of a barn with.

"Maybe next time," Pitohui offered smoothly.

"Tch!" snapped Fukaziroh, and she drew her M&P. With her left hand, she opened her item storage. A moment later, Fukaziroh's pack full of grenades vanished, replaced by a large carrying bag for ammo magazines on her left hip.

There were still explosives packed into her vest, but Fukaziroh did not seem interested in removing them for some reason.

Boss and Rosa both had their official SHINC pistols, Strizhes, at their sides. Both took the time to make sure the weapons were loaded. They also produced a significant number of magazines in pouches that they attached to their hips and chests.

They'd returned the plasma grenades they typically carried back to their inventories. Those could explode if struck by a bullet, taking out their owners and nearby comrades as well. Plus, they were difficult weapons to use in a cramped interior. Instead, Boss and Rosa equipped themselves with standard fragmentation grenades, Russian RGD-5s.

The entire time they exchanged equipment, they made sure their backs were to each other, maximizing their vigilance. It was unlikely there would be any enemies coming this way, but they were ready to dart right into the mall, just in case.

M pulled his shield out of the backpack. He arranged two panels vertically and gripped the portable barricade with both hands. There was an HK45 on his leg, but he didn't draw it.

The plan was for M to hold the shield up as protection while Pitohui did the attacking from behind. M was a big target, so blocking was a more viable option for him than trying to run and hide.

As for Shirley, she didn't pull out anything. All she did was adjust the hat resting over her green hair while everyone else got set up for battle.

Fukaziroh noticed this and asked, "Shirley, did you drop your pistol somewhere? I'm afraid I can't lend you mine."

"No, I just haven't taken it out. I'm not showing what I've got until I have to. I'll be the only one leaving this mall alive. Then I'll go back for my R93 and do whatever is necessary to wipe out ZEMAL, no matter how long it takes."

"Holy crap, that's crazy," marveled Fukaziroh, but Llenn knew that based on Shirley's remaining HP and med kits, her sniping ability, and her exploding bullets, it wasn't that far-fetched.

The clock reached 2:38.

"We're going to watch the next scan, confirm the number of enemies, then go in. Look at this before we go," Pitohui said, beckoning the group of seven around the entrance to the building.

Through the glass, they could spy a few lights on inside. The hallway stretched straight ahead, and it looked much brighter farther in.

At the entry was the map of the mall that Llenn had ignored earlier. Now she examined it closely to memorize the layout.

The chart was large, about the size of a school blackboard. It was designed for people who were visiting for the first time. While it didn't have details on every outlet, there were general descriptions of what could be found in each section of the shopping center, all in English.

Simply put, the mall was designed like a donut.

Its enormous rectangular shape was not packed all the way through with stores; there was a large open space at the center. Based on the amount of light coming through, that section likely had a skylight.

That center area alone was six hundred yards across and one hundred yards wide—truly enormous.

Judging by the map, the courtyard area looked to house an amusement park. There were images of old-fashioned cottages and a roller coaster.

A wide path ran in a circle along the outside of the building, with storefronts flanking the trail all the way around. The structure's exterior surrounded the shops on the outer side of the path, so they had no windows to the outside. The stores on the inner side faced the courtyard and possessed balconies that leaned into the center's open area.

Escalators and staircases decorated the walkway at regular intervals. Elevators were stationed at the shopping center's corners and the centers of the corridors, totaling six altogether.

The four corners of the structure were different department stores. The walkways ran diagonally to meet their interior entrances. These larger shops had escalators in their centers and elevators along the walls.

The design was relatively simple, so Llenn had no difficulty memorizing it. Since there would be no landmarks to navigate by,

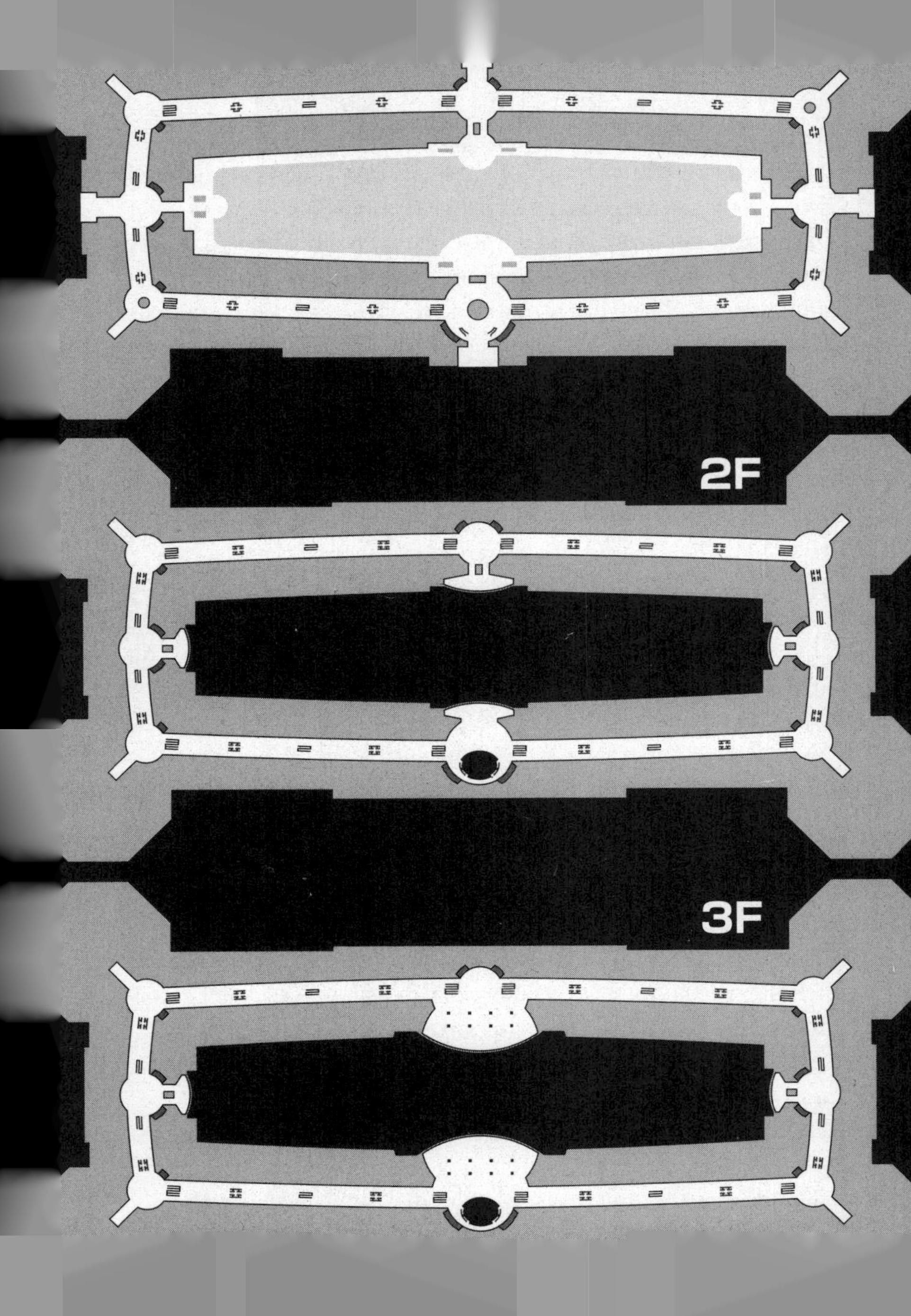

2F
3F

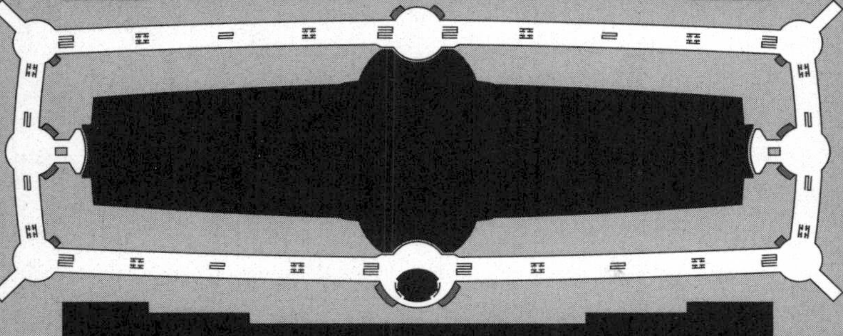

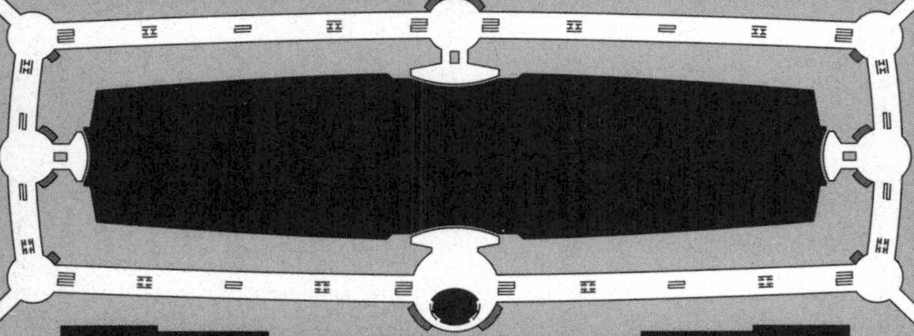

6F

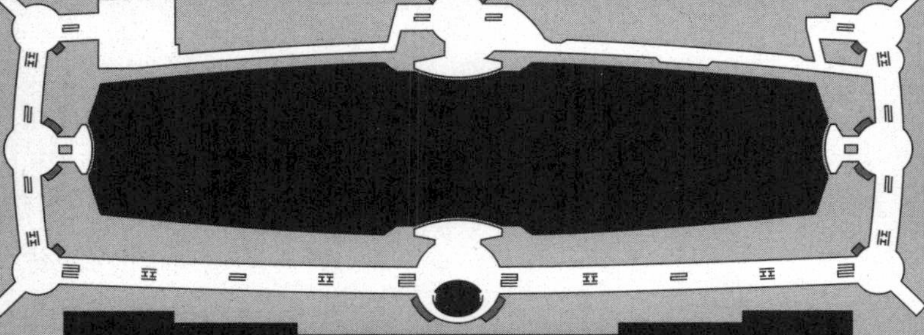

she'd have to keep an eye on the rotating compass that sat at the top of her vision to maintain her bearing.

"Do we all understand the layout?" Pitohui asked. The group nodded in reply.

"So where can I go to get some cute clothes?" Fukaziroh asked.

"There's no time for that. Although I do need something for the fall season," Llenn admitted.

"Looks like the northeast quadrant on the third floor has all the fashion stores," Pitohui stated.

"Shall we fight there, then?" Boss inquired.

"Take this seriously, dammit," snapped Shirley.

* * *

"I bet that woman's on the opposite side right now."

"You seem to be having fun, Leader. Or 'funlee' for short."

While Llenn's group was prepping at the west entrance, David and Kenta had arrived at the east side of the mall. It looked much the same as the exterior of the other side, with the mall's name displayed overhead.

The trike that had done so well for them had finally given up the ghost in the road about a third of a mile away due to lack of gasoline. They'd had to run after that.

The two quickly readied their pistols after stowing their assault rifles and backup ammo, which would be useless inside the shopping mecca.

David drew his favorite Steyr M9-A1 9 mm pistol from its holster and pulled back on the slide a bit to check that it was loaded.

The sights on the weapon differed from the standard kind. They had a unique design featuring a sizable triangular divot with a smaller three-sided sight at the front. You wouldn't find this feature on any other gun.

David always claimed that it was much easier to aim with once you got used to it, but none of his teammates agreed.

Next, David removed a different pistol from his inventory—a Beretta APX. Every member of MMTM was sporting that kind of handgun this time around. It was also a 9 mm, with a seventeen-round magazine.

The APX appeared in its carbon fiber holster, which David equipped to his stomach, right around the solar plexus. As always in *GGO*, all you had to do was navigate a menu to strap something snugly to your person.

David drew the APX, loaded it, then holstered it again. Then he produced another one and attached that to his left hip.

Kenta, too, materialized two guns he hadn't been holding earlier, and, like David, attached them to his stomach and left hip.

Lastly, the pair called up some pouches full of magazines for their APXs and stuck them where there was room on their belts and backs.

MMTM's strategy for the handgun fight in this Squad Jam was to shoot like hell.

If their primary pistols ran out of ammunition and they didn't have time to pop in a fresh magazine, they'd pull their secondary armaments off their stomachs and continue firing. If those ones were out, they'd reach for the guns on their left sides.

That would allow them to maintain pressure on the enemy instead of running for cover. MMTM's goal was to close the gap, overpower the opponent, and finish them off.

Once their triple pistols and ammo were all set up, including spare magazines on each one's back for the other to grab, they added one last detail: ordinary grenades, wherever there was room for them to hang without hitting anything else.

They were down to two at this point, but MMTM was itching to fight.

"All set, Leader. Let's do this."

"Yeah. First I'll kill Pitohui, then we slaughter every other person inside this mall!"

*　*　*

Slightly *before* Llenn and MMTM were making their preparations, a man from team SATOH was speaking with Fire's team, WEEI. He was the team leader, and the mustache and beard suited his face.

"Couldn't we attack them now, before they get into the mall?"

They were in a moving truck. Aside from the SATOH driver, the remaining eleven passengers were facing one another in the bed, beneath a canopy.

SATOH's members were dressed in the US Marine Corps' brown desert camo, and their equipment matched. They hadn't joined the alliance in the beginning like other squads, so they did not have masks and sunglasses like the others.

All of them sported the same primary weapon, the M27 IAR.

At first glance, this gun was similar to an HK416 assault rifle but with a longer, thicker barrel plus a scope and bipod that came attached by default. Its caliber was 5.56 mm.

"I suppose we could," answered someone in WEEI, not Fire. They were all wearing blue tracksuits with masks and sunglasses, so it was impossible to discern who was who among their ranks.

They were driving down the highway that ran north to south. As the scan had revealed, LPFM was most likely moving toward the mall, and this truck was as well. SATOH had spotted the vehicle just after SJ4 had started, and they'd kept it hidden until now. They were now heading down the center highway at an average driving speed.

SATOH's team leader suggested that if they picked up the pace and took a longer route, they might cut off LPFM and SHINC before reaching the west entrance.

"But that would be dangerous. They'll notice us when we approach, and in the open environment of the parking lot, it would be an even fight. They have M's shield, the sniper with the explosive rounds, and SHINC's antitank rifle. Fighting with handguns in the mall gives us a better chance," asserted the man from WEEI.

Naturally, he and the others present had no idea that all the members of Llenn's group were heavily injured, SHINC was down to two members, and all their best weapons had been taken away by ZEMAL.

The WEEI man continued, "Still, I understand your point of view. You joined our coalition, and we've kept you out of the fighting this entire time. I'm sure it's been dull. If you want to break away and attack LPFM while you can still use your rifles, we won't stop you. We'll get off along the way and head for the mall on foot. What's your call?"

"......"

SATOH's leader considered this, his bearded mouth twisting with contemplation. In the end, he smirked.

"All right, I get it. We'll stick with you and fight side by side in the mall. We've come all this way together; might as well see it through to the end that way."

"Thank you. And I have a request."

"What's that?"

"When we get to the mall, we want you to engage first. We'll hang back until your battle is over."

"So we're just the warm-up act, eh? And only when we're all dead will you finally join the skirmish?"

"That's right. You'll fight first to ensure Fire doesn't die. You are expected to *lay down your lives* for that cause."

SATOH's leader chuckled. "If I hadn't heard about the payment you promised, I would tell you to go to hell," he said, and he extended a hand to shake—not toward the WEEI man he'd been talking to, but to Fire. "I hear you loud and clear. We'll enter the mall and attack LPFM and SHINC. I intend to win, of course, but they're tremendous opponents. I'll go in under the assumption that my team will get wiped out after dealing as much damage as we can. The rest will be in your hands. Go on and seize that trophy."

Without saying a word, Fire looked him right in the eyes and clasped his hand. When he let go, the only words he spoke—with great conviction—were "I'm counting on you."

SATOH's leader replied "We've got this" and patted the holster at his waist. It contained a brown automatic pistol—a Colt M45A1 CQBP.

This, too, was a Marine Corps standard firearm, one of the latest variants of the classic Government model. CQBP stood for Close-Quarters Battle Pistol.

Every member of SATOH had one, the same as the rifles. The holsters were larger than the silhouettes of the guns because the guns were equipped with flashlights. That was a common practice in real life when fighting in darkness was expected.

In *GGO*, there were no genuinely dark environments, and pistols were not in high demand, so almost no one affixed illumination sources to their firearms. Any team that went out of their way to put flashlights on their pistols already had great respect for, and experience with, handguns.

The man from WEEI remarked, "I suppose we should get ready, then."

The squad's five players, aside from Fire, began to work on their game windows.

Soon, each of them was holding a different kind of pistol. Battle loomed, and they were preparing.

"……"

SATOH's leader swallowed hard as he watched them go about their work.

With sincerity, he admitted, "I'm glad you're not our opponents."

CHAPTER 20
Battle of the Mall I

CHAPTER 20
Battle of the Mall I

At 2:40, every player in the game, and every audience member in the bar, watched the scan results with great interest.

Those near the mall only needed a single glance at the results before they were satisfied and immediately put away their devices. Then they charged through the shattered glass into the building.

MMTM from the east.

WEEI and SATOH from the north.

LPFM and SHINC from the west.

The battle of the shopping mall had begun.

As soon as she passed through the broken doorway, Llenn saw a warning message that she'd been expecting.

You have entered the handgun area! Long guns such as rifles are locked. Only handguns, grenades, photon swords, knives, and bludgeoning weapons are allowed here!

Llenn glanced around the new battlefield as she ran. There was an entry hall about forty yards wide. It felt like a tunnel, yet the ceiling height was the same as in any other shopping center.

It was abandoned, of course, but the building structure was still firm, with less trash and rubble than she would have expected. There were fashionable brick tiles underfoot, with few cracks or potholes that might catch her as she ran.

About half of the ceiling lights were out. It was darker than outside, of course, but once Llenn's eyes got used to it, it was hardly difficult to see. Plus, lots of natural light came in through the massive skylight in the middle of the building.

The mall's interior was not so different from the style you saw in real-life Japan. The main difference was that it was about five times larger. If it wasn't for the ceiling overhead, Llenn might have thought she was just running through the shopping area of town.

"This place is huge," marveled Fukaziroh. "Llenn, don't run too far ahead and get lost."

"Same to you! We can't put out a call for you over the PA!" she shot back, right as she reached the intersection with the main thoroughfare that circled the mall.

The walkway was carpeted.

It was thick and easy on the feet. The material muffled footfalls, making a clandestine approach much more feasible.

Here, too, there was tons of space, about sixty feet from side to side. In the center of the walkway were benches and small stands, like a street during a festival.

The stairs and escalators were also located in the middle of the path, creating a narrow vertical space where the routes between floors were open.

If Llenn turned right here, she would proceed around the building on the south side. To the left was the north route. She also had the option of rushing up some nearby steps or an escalator.

From this point on, scan locations were no longer useful. Llenn could encounter hostiles at any time. Although the shopping mall was enormous, the environments were far smaller than outdoors. She'd be able to hear the sounds of battle when they erupted.

And once the fighting started, it probably wouldn't take long to finish.

"Time for the pistol battle at last…," murmured a member of the crowd as he watched LPFM and SHINC venture into the mall.

On other screens, you could see MMTM, SATOH, and WEEI in their respective locations.

MMTM was down to two members, so they had to stick together for survival. David and Kenta rushed up the stairs at the east end, hoping to gain a height advantage over their foes.

SATOH's group of six stayed close as well. They were going to fight as a team.

More surprising was WEEI. The men in the tracksuits did not show up on-screen. They'd come through the north entrance, but they hadn't yet emerged onto the main path around the mall. It was impossible to guess what they were up to.

"Pistol fights will be tough," remarked one of the spectators, slapping his holster. "You can only hit a target from so far away. If there was someone twenty yards away from me, I couldn't hit 'em with this. That was a shock to me when I started *GGO*."

It was a shameful thing to admit, but no one laughed at him.

The grim truth about pistols was that they were inaccurate.

When you were shooting, the slightest change in a muzzle's aim would only grow more pronounced over distance. And no matter how much you practiced, there was no way to aim with a handgun as reliably as with a rifle. Especially when you were on the move and trying to strike a running target.

Optimal ranges ran at about thirty meters for a stationary target and twenty for a moving one, though someone truly skilled could hit a mobile opponent at up to thirty-five meters. At such distances, the bullet circle could help, but the bullet line was virtually meaningless to the one being attacked. By the time you saw the streak, the bullet had already hit you.

Pistol rounds were individually weaker than rifle shots, and a bullet or two that didn't happen to strike a vital area wouldn't kill a target. So even if you were taking body shots, you had a few seconds to fight back with your own pistol or knife.

A chaotic, close-range handgun fight inside the mall was sure to be much fiercer than outdoor combat.

"Crap, I can't wait to watch this!"

"Me too! It's nice when you can actually see the two sides fighting on the same monitor."

This was the sort of action the audience appreciated more than any other.

"Go on, guys! Let's see some shooting!"

"Llenn, take the lead and keep your eyes peeled. Boss, your pair can go next. M and I will go in the middle. Fuka, you're on rear guard and support."

Although they hadn't discussed or planned on it, Pitohui naturally started calling the shots. Nobody was going to argue.

"Okay, but which way?"

Llenn had three options: straight ahead into the courtyard area, right to the south side, or left to the north.

Fire's group had entered on the north, so if they wanted a showdown with the archenemy, left was the answer. Llenn wondered if that was too aggressive.

"Let's see—," Pitohui began.

The rumbling of an explosion shook their feet, and a split second later, the sound of it echoed through the mall.

A distant blast hit them like a punch in the gut. That kind of deep register belonged to a grand grenade, most likely. No one spied the signature blue flames or smoke from the blast.

"From the north…?" Llenn guessed on pure instinct.

"Yep. Where Fire's group is located," Pitohui agreed, then added, "but isn't it too early for battle?"

"You don't think their alliance finally broke down, do you?" Llenn posited hopefully. *That's it, more!* she thought.

Da-dooom.

There was another tremor.

"No, that's not it," M commented in his characteristically calm manner. "The explosion's coming from the left side. They're rushing forward and blowing up the corridor behind them."

"Ahhh, I see. It's an invitation to fight them head-on," Boss concluded.

"Okay, then! We'll take the bait!" exclaimed Llenn.

"No, we'll withdraw to the south side," corrected Pitohui. "M and I will take up the rear. Everyone else goes first."

"Hrmm."

"An explosion?"

David and Kenta from MMTM were in the overlook area on the sixth floor over the courtyard interior when the first blast happened.

They had raced up the stairs as fast as possible to ensure the advantage of altitude. As a team of just two, they could not win in a straightforward fight against bigger squads, so they decided to wait for the time being in a location with good visibility. They'd settled on one of the balconies that could be found at the edge of every cardinal direction on every floor but the first.

The rounded verandas leaned over the courtyard area, with fashionably designed railings at their edges. The view from there was enough to make you forget that you were still indoors.

Up above was a glass roof supported by a pipe frame. The pipes came in different sizes, and the arrangement looked like it belonged in some kind of temple. The metal pieces were falling apart, but none of the glass was broken. The gray sky illuminated the structure's interior.

Below was the spacious courtyard area.

As shown on the map, it was about six hundred yards across the long way and a hundred the short way.

Most of the space was taken up by the amusement park, with a roller coaster that wound all around the interior, plus a Ferris wheel, a merry-go-round, a Viking ship, and even a waterslide.

Little stands dotted the ground, offering hot dogs and ice cream treats. The ground was painted kid-friendly pastel colors. It was creepy now that it had faded with time, but it was perfect for people who loved ruined environments.

Thick, black gas was billowing from the right side of the courtyard—the north end. It clearly hadn't come from a smoke grenade. The vapors were from a more commonplace source.

"A fire… The north-side teams are igniting the building," David snarled.

There was another explosion. This time, David could see the pale surge of fire. The grand grenade blast started on the first floor of the mall and took a piece of the second and third floors with it.

That explosion alone shouldn't have been enough to start a fire. Someone had to be spreading gasoline, too.

Slowly but surely, the flames and smoke began to fill the vast mall.

Llenn's group had moved down the circular path to the southern side and were now approaching the center portion from the third floor.

There was a large food court here, more spacious than was typical. Light from the courtyard flooded through, so it was very bright.

A series of wide pillars crossed the hundred-yard space. Each one was three feet across and sturdy, reinforced with steel pipes. They were placed about twenty yards apart.

Unlike elsewhere in the mall, the ceiling here was raised through to the fourth floor. The pillars went all the way up there, with three-foot chandeliers hanging between them. It was like a high-class restaurant, an unthinkable extravagance for a shopping mall food court.

The floor here was tiled for cleanliness and packed with tables and chairs. They were not simple plastic but fashioned of wood for a chic look. The tables were round, four feet in diameter, and reasonably thick. They looked suitable for deflecting pistol bullets if you tipped them over.

Along the wall of this space were the food court offerings, if they had still been operating. From famous burger chains to Chinese, Japanese, Mexican, and even fusion cuisine, all kinds of food had once been served here. However, the area was silent as death now.

As the place boasted excellent visibility, Pitohui had designated it the group's base for the time being. The only wall was to the south, so they turned their backs to it and split up to watch the points of entry.

About five hundred feet away, on the opposite side of the courtyard, black smoke rose from the ground floor and steadily filled the building.

"Not only are they blowing stuff up, but they're also committing arson! How dare they trash this place of rest and relaxation!" fumed Fukaziroh.

"Yeah!" Llenn chimed in.

"Hang on. What did you do to that cruise ship last time, again?" Fukaziroh felt compelled to quip. Llenn's past exploits included splitting a cruise ship in half.

Boss peered out at the billowing smoke from behind a table and said, "Are they trying to drive us out of here? Did they not intend to fight in the mall at all?"

The structure was so massive that it would take quite a while for the entire place to fill up with choking smoke, but they couldn't just sit back and let it happen. For one thing, their side didn't have any weapons suitable for outdoor combat.

Rosa thought of this as well. "Did that Vivi woman tell them? She could have alerted the allied team—"

"Nah, she wouldn't do that," Fukaziroh stated. There was no evidence to overturn that assertion, so SHINC said nothing more on the matter.

The explosions continued unabated on the north side, and they were a source of distraction when the enemy abruptly arrived.

"Enemies! From the east!" Boss called.

At the same time, Fukaziroh shouted, "Attack incoming from the west!"

"Whut?" chirped Llenn, who was looking north and didn't know which way to turn.

Assuming that one of them was confused about directions, Llenn decided that Boss was more trustworthy. With a silent apology to Fukaziroh, she turned to the east. Their companions were near the center of the food court, twenty meters to the south of Llenn's position.

As the gunfire started, Llenn saw her friends shooting both left and right from behind the food court's tables and chairs.

On the left, Boss and Rosa were hiding behind a pillar and reaching out around it to fire their Strizh pistols toward the east.

On the right, Fukaziroh was concealing her head behind a table and blasting away with her M&P, while M held up his shield nearby so Pitohui could fire her XDM over it. They were all facing west.

It was about three seconds later that an electric cart rushed toward Boss and Fukaziroh.

The mall provided electric carts for the elderly, children, and others who could use assistance to traverse all over the building's prodigious span.

Despite the cute name, the vehicles were nearly five feet wide and close to ten feet long. They were practically miniature automobiles. They'd be a significant impediment in any walkway smaller than those found in this shopping center.

The brilliant blue of the car had faded over time. Rust had consumed much of its exterior, making for a hideous sight. Behind the driver's seat were two rows of sideways seats, four each. Eight passengers could sit in the cart in total. No framework enclosed them.

Before the driver's seat was a large basket like the type found on shopping carts. A table had been shoved into it. It resembled the ones Llenn and the others were using for cover. There must be another food court on the other side of the building.

The table blocked the 9 mm and .40-caliber bullets Boss and Pitohui were shooting.

Aha! So that's it!

It took Llenn only an instant to put everything together in her mind.

SATOH had split up, three members each into two carts, placed tables on the fronts in place of bulletproof armor, and come racing down the walkway—from the east *and* the west.

At top speed, the carts could move faster than a person could run. They hurtled pell-mell toward their prey.

All of those explosions had been a mere diversion from the assault. The vibrations and smoke were meant to cover the carts' sounds and draw attention to the courtyard area. The enemy must have seen that Llenn and the others were setting up here on this floor.

There was one other thing that could be gleaned from this, too.

This level of preparation was only possible because they had come to the mall long before this point. In previous scans, they must have left their leader outside to hide that fact.

By the time Llenn arrived, they had probably already been in the shopping center for a while and had closely inspected the place. They would have known that they could use the carts and stack the tables on them for protection.

When Boss spotted the cart, it was still eighty meters away.

Because it was heading straight for her, she was briefly freaked out by the sight of a table rushing in her direction, but it didn't take long for her to realize that it was being pushed by a cart with adversaries driving it.

"Enemies! From the east!" she warned her companions, and she pointed her Strizh out from the side of the pillar.

When the bullet circle was over the table, she fired. Rosa began to shoot the same way.

The projectiles struck the table and sprayed wood chips but did not penetrate through to the other side.

"No good!"

The exact same thing happened to Fukaziroh on the other side of the food court.

She spotted the cart, warned her friends, and started to shoot—except that not a single shot hit the target. The 9 mm bullets tore up carpet, punched holes in the glass windows of stores behind them, and burrowed into the stairs' handrail.

However, when Pitohui started shooting from behind Fukaziroh, she put new marks on the table.

"Tsk!"

Llenn watched as the electric carts charged forward from either side, crunching and smashing tables and chairs out of their way.

She wondered if the vehicles meant to carry passengers through the mall were really supposed to be going as swiftly as they were. It was actually just a different driving mode for moving the carts quickly through large parking lots, or after hours when there were no pedestrians around.

The enemy was using the high-power mode to burst into the food court at top speed.

The carts gouged through the lines of tables and chairs in the food court before coming to a stop after a few dozen meters of progress.

Then a trio of men in brown combat fatigues jumped out and began firing their pistols.

Immediately, things descended into chaos.

There were seven friendlies and six hostiles in a space measuring no more than a hundred meters to a side. The battle was a mess of confusion.

An incredible number of events happened within the span of just a few seconds.

*   *   *

After Fukaziroh wasted an entire seventeen-round magazine and her gun was empty, the cart plunged toward her. Chairs sent flying by the vehicle nearly struck Fukaziroh's head.

A man got off the cart just ten meters away and pointed an M45A1 at her.

"Oh crap."

She ducked, and the first shot passed over her head.

"Aieee!"

By falling on the ground, she ensured that the next bullet deflected off the table.

When she lifted her head, the man's face was a mere three meters away, smirking with the certainty of victory.

As Boss changed out a spent magazine for her Strizh, she told Rosa, "Split off!" and jumped out from the right side of the pillar.

Rosa took the left side. But a table deflected by the cart struck her leg and caused her to take a spectacular tumble.

"Haugh!"

Boss had a good angle to aim at the left side of the electric cart. Unfortunately, that meant she was in the enemy's sights as well.

It was nine meters away. Boss saw the man through her bullet circle. He was training on her chest.

"Haah!" She pushed off the ground with her feet, hard. Her large body collapsed to the floor, back-first. A fat .45-caliber bullet passed through her arms and whizzed past her face.

The moment Boss hit the ground, she fired her Strizh—and the bullet struck the man's M45A1, breaking his finger and yanking the weapon out of his hand.

"Dammit."

Rosa tumbled until she wound up resting belly-down atop a table, where bullet lines quickly trained on her. They were coming from the driver and right rear passenger of the cart.

The merciless .45-caliber bullets penetrated Rosa's thigh and side.

"Urhgh!"

The shock forced her body to roll over.

One of the SATOH members continued to fire, pushing in closer all the while. Standing with a column in front of him, the rear member was protected from enemy shots while the lead member attacked. Once the one in front was out of bullets, the pair would instantly swap places. This switch tactic was common in VR games.

As the hail of bullets mercilessly riddled Rosa's body, she pulled the pin from a grenade on her waist.

"Take this!"

Pitohui saw the electric cart stop twenty meters away from her and M. Two men disembarked and wasted no time aiming their weapons at them.

M quickly stepped forward and raised his shield with both hands. The bullets clattered against it, creating quite a racket.

He withstood the pounding to protect Pitohui from harm. Then he began to charge forward against the flow.

"Yaaaaah!"

Tables and chairs bounced away as they collided with the barricade in his powerful arms. It resembled what the carts had done only a few moments ago.

"There we go!"

Pitohui dropped the magazine out of the XDM she'd been firing and stuck the gun into her backpack. With her other hand, she drew another gun.

Then she hurried through the opening M had cleared like a snowplow and ordered, "Duck!"

M obeyed, leaving his shield up. Pitohui ran onto his shoulders and then off them.

She soared over the metal plates with an XDM in each hand. As she glided through the air, Pitohui let fly a storm of lead down upon the men.

* * *

Llenn aimed with one arm, holding up one of her new Vorpal Bunnies.

As soon as the carts began crashing through the food court, she had rushed for her companions, gun in each hand, but she would not arrive in time. The man shooting at Fukaziroh had his sights trained right on her where she'd fallen.

There was still twenty meters of distance.

Llenn had no confidence that she could hit an opponent at that range, but if she didn't do something, Fukaziroh was going to die.

She stuck out her right arm, took aim over the sight—no time to wait for the bullet circle—and pulled the trigger.

Please work!

At the same time, the grenade on Rosa's belt exploded, showering the entire area with shrapnel and bits of wood from the tables and chairs.

Yet again, several things happened in the few seconds that followed.

As the burst blew past her, Fukaziroh saw the head of the man who was about to finish her off pop into pieces, like a watermelon dropped onto the floor.

Out of sheer momentum, the headless body took a few steps forward, then toppled over toward her.

"Whoa!"

Fukaziroh lifted her feet upward to catch the falling man's chest.

"I know you like me, but the rules say no touching."

Boss rolled backward and used her spine as a spring to flip up onto her feet, her boots on carpet once more.

The blast caused her to wobble to the right, but she did not stop charging at the man whose gun she'd shot loose.

"Raaaahh!"

She fired her Strizh like mad. He took several bullets but kept his fists raised like a boxer. Boss jumped.

A powerful kick to the face was the end of his story.

She looked just like a ballerina.

The grenade explosion left Rosa with only half a body, and she was out of SJ4 for good.

Her final act of resistance had embedded shrapnel in the face of the man before her, taking him down with her.

However, the enemy behind was virtually unharmed, and he turned his attention and M45A1 to his left.

When he saw the gorilla-woman with pigtails ram the tip of her boot into his teammate's face, he pulled the trigger on instinct.

Pitohui landed between the men she'd been shooting at.

"I'll start with you," she said, pointing her right XDM at the enemy on the right and putting a bullet through his eye.

Then she gave the foe on the left a powerful elbow. The bearded man had already taken several bullets, so he was unable to evade in time. Pitohui's arm met his neck hard, tossing him onto his back.

"There!"

Pitohui's left foot came down on his head. Between the kick and the impact with the ground, the man bounced and shrieked. "Aaagh!"

"M! Grab him!"

"Got it."

M's considerable mass came diving onto the helpless man, shield and all.

"Huh?"

Llenn could not understand why the man who'd been aiming at Fukaziroh suddenly lost his head.

She hadn't fired her Vorpal Bunny. Her target's skull had simply exploded before she could shoot at him.

Then the gust of air from Rosa's grenade to the left rustled the ears of Llenn's cap.

"Huh?"

It was Boss who kept fighting the longest.

When she kicked her adversary to death and landed back on the ground, she was greeted by a pain in her left shoulder.

It was only because Boss evaded the next bullet so quickly that she managed to stay in the game. Immediately, she raised her Strizh in the direction the projectile had come from.

She spotted the man who'd tried to take her life standing beyond the electric cart. He narrowed his eyes at her, glee apparent in his expression. The muzzle of the large pistol he was carrying was pointed squarely at her.

"Take this!" Boss shouted back happily, and she fired.

Bullets flew over the cart from both directions.

From the arrival of the carts to Boss's last bullet passing through the man's head, the battle of the food court lasted less than twenty seconds.

It was pandemonium that began and ended very abruptly.

In that time, five members of SATOH died, and M caught one.

Rosa died, and Boss dropped to 30 percent health.

Llenn rushed over to M and his captive.

The bearded man was in brown combat fatigues, sitting cross-legged on the ground. He'd been relieved of all weapons. His body was covered in glowing bullet-wound effects.

"You got us… I can see why you're champs and high rankers. You folks are really tough. I thought this plan had an excellent chance of working. We got beat by a team of only seven, and we only killed one. That's pathetic. Carrying the shield in your hands like that was a good move. Mind if I borrow that tactic?" he asked, gracious and forthright in defeat.

I guess that's what it's like when a man comes clean and admits he's lost, Llenn thought. She was dead wrong.

Bang.

Pitohui shot the man right through the knee.

"Aaah! Owww!"

"Eep! Pito, what are you doing?"

It was just a game, so this didn't count as torturing prisoners, but blasting at an opponent who had already surrendered was extremely poor form. Not that this was a surprise coming from the same player who had committed similar atrocities in SJ2. In fact, Llenn had done something very similar under the dome.

"All right, no passing along information anymore!" Pitohui snapped at the man. Llenn suddenly realized how naïve she'd been.

The man's comm was still live to Fire's team, and he had just passed along enemy tactics to his allies, as well as the fact that Llenn's group totaled only six now.

In that case—! Llenn thought. There was something she wanted to ask about Fire, too.

She walked over to the bearded man, Vorpal Bunny in each hand. She kept her right-hand gun aimed directly at him.

"So...you're with Fire, huh?"

The bearded man looked up at her and laughed. "With him? I suppose. We're on different teams, but we decided to team up this once. You must be Llenn, eh? I've seen you on the previous Squad Jam videos. You're fast. Pretty tough, too."

"Thank you."

Fukaziroh, Pitohui, M, and Boss—after offering a quick prayer for Rosa—all listened to the conversation. Shirley had been absent during the fight but had reappeared and was watching the exchange as well. Of course, they were all watchful of their perimeter.

"You tell Fire that we've taken out a number of your coconspirators."

"I don't like the word *conspirator*. It has negative connotations. But sure. You've done really well and eliminated a number of our teammates. Very impressive."

"And only your team is left."

"That's right. Only Fire's team is left."

"And we're going to go beat him now, no matter what."

"Hmmm. No matter what, you say? Well, I like your spirit. I'm sure he's happy to hear that, too. It wouldn't be worth it any other way."

Llenn bobbed her head, then pointed the Vorpal Bunny right at the man's face. Her finger touched the trigger, putting a bullet circle on his forehead.

"One last thing: a personal question to you."

The man looked at the bullet line, the Vorpal Bunny, and then Llenn.

"What is it?"

"How much did that guy give you for partaking in this collusion? How many credits does it take for you to serve him so faithfully? Why would you give up on your chance in Squad Jam, when your team could have won on its own?" Llenn demanded.

"Bfft!" the bearded man suddenly chuckled. "Ah-ha-ha-ha-ha! Ah-ha-ha-ha, ah-ha-ha-ha! Ah-ha-ha-ha-ha-ha!"

The outburst of mirth caused Llenn's brow to furrow. "Did I say something funny?"

"Ah-ha-ha-ha-ha! You sure did! Here, I'll let you in on a little secret… You don't understand a thing!"

"I don't care about that. I'm asking how much money Fire gave you."

"Ah-ha-ha-ha. I can't answer that question."

"……"

Llenn glanced at Pitohui. The other woman gave her a permissive smile, so she pulled the trigger.

A man watched the little girl in pink execute his teammate with a pink pistol through the lens of his binoculars. "They've done their job. Let's do ours. I'll make the first attack. You all do whatever after me."

"Got it. Good luck, Beralto."

The man in the tracksuit known as Beralto lifted his head, mask and sunglasses still on, and picked up his "pistol."

"Get down, Llenn!" Shirley cried. Llenn complied immediately.

She practically left an afterimage with her tremendous agility as she squatted. No sooner had she done so than a shot raced overhead.

"Urgh!"

It rammed into M's stomach; he'd been standing next to Llenn.

M fell off his feet, losing hit points. He crumbled to the ground next to Llenn, shaking the floor.

"Sniper! Keep your head down!" Shirley shouted again.

If it hadn't been for the first warning, Llenn would have died. It hit M because she dodged it, but that was merely poor luck.

M's hit points went from 60 percent to 50. The bulletproof armor around his midriff had done its job, but 10 percent of *his* health from a shot that didn't even penetrate his skin was some serious power.

"From where? Why? How?" Llenn wondered. Or, to elaborate into proper questions, *How could such a powerful bullet be here, and from where? In an area where only pistols are legal? And there aren't any enemies in range, are there?*

Without getting up, M replied, "Sniper. Rifle round."

"That's crazy!"

You weren't supposed to be able to fire a rifle inside the mall. Which meant…

"From outside? The roof?" Boss wondered.

Llenn thought that if you could get up onto the roof, then break the glass, it might be possible.

However, Shirley ruled all of that out. "No. The enemy's on the other side of the courtyard. About two hundred yards that way!"

"There's no pistol that can shoot that far," Boss argued.

"There is! You haven't been studying enough! I'll show you!" Shirley replied, and she held up her gun.

The pub's audience marveled as a member of the tracksuit gang placed his pistol against a table in the food court for support.

It was a weapon nearly eighteen inches long, over twice the length of a typical handgun.

"Whoa! A Remington XP-100!" shouted one spectator, who *had* been studying.

If Remington's XP-100 could be described in a phrase, it would be *A pistol made by chopping both ends off a rifle.*

Remington was famous for its bolt-action rifles and shotguns. The XP-100 had resulted from its attempt to create a handgun with a long range that could shoot rifle rounds.

The weapon had been intended for hunting. There was a benefit to a powerful, long-range gun being comparatively compact and light. Eighteen inches was quite large—but tiny compared to a nearly three-foot rifle—and it could be stashed in a backpack.

The firing mechanism used the same bolt-action power as a rifle. Because it was a single-shot gun, the bolt had to be used after each bullet was loosed. It was a simple, reliable mechanism.

Since it was a pistol, it had no stock, of course, so it could only be held and steadied by the grip below the middle of the body.

It was also adorned with a pistol scope with long eye relief—the distance between the lens and the eye.

Wouldn't that just make it a customized rifle that had been cut down?

You might think so, but given that the XP-100 was always labeled and sold as a pistol by its manufacturer, it fell into the Handgun category in *GGO.*

In real life, it was a minor gun that only aficionados would know about. In *GGO*, it was something of a hidden oddity that most people didn't even know existed.

Its range and accuracy were low for a rifle, while as a pistol, it was too big and hard to aim. The weapon could have its uses in hunting, but its master-of-none design made it a poor choice in battle.

Any battle except this one.

Beralto's XP-100 had a rifle bipod attached to it, which he used to steady it against the tabletop. He peered through the scope, aimed at the little pink target, and fired.

If it hadn't been for Shirley's keen eye picking up faint, distant movement beyond the thin screen of smoke through her scope, Llenn would almost certainly have died.

Beralto saw the bullet hit M, pulled back the bolt, and expelled the empty cartridge. The large piece of metal flew out of the gun, hit the floor, and vanished. He took another .308 Winchester rifle round out of his vest pocket, stuck it into the gun, and pushed the bolt closed.

Once again, he aimed at the target two hundred meters away.

"Hmm?"

Then he saw the green-haired woman pointing her gun at him.

"Ha-ha!" he chuckled, and he quickly withdrew.

A bullet passed through the spot where he'd been just a moment before.

The gunshot drew Llenn's attention to its source.

About ten meters to the south, next to one of the food court pillars, Shirley was holding a large gun, the likes of which she'd never seen before.

Shirley pulled the bolt back, then loaded a sizable bullet from a pouch on her waist.

"I see. An XP-100, huh? Good thinking," muttered M.

* * *

So Shirley had wound up packing the same gun as the enemy. But that didn't mean she knew all about the weapon.

For one thing, she was a rifles-only kind of girl, with no knowledge of any sort of firearm outside of what she might use to hunt.

When she went shopping with Clarence, who knew more about pistols, her eagle-eyed partner had spotted the odd duck and picked it out for her.

The XP-100 came in several calibers, but naturally, Shirley had chosen the .308-caliber model, which was the same size as her R93 Tactical 2. That meant she could use her homemade explosive bullets in this gun, too.

Shirley did not attach a bipod to it. She wanted the weapon as light as possible.

She couldn't balance it against her shoulder as she could a rifle, so she had to prop it up on something else or press it against some surface as she fired.

After practicing, Shirley was able to hit a human-sized target with perfect accuracy at four hundred meters. That was without showing a bullet line, of course.

In the category of pistols, where hitting a target at fifty meters was considered a colossal jackpot, Shirley was able to transform into a handgun sniper with a range eight times as large.

Naturally, it was Shirley who'd killed the man aiming at Fukaziroh earlier.

Beralto reported to the other WEEI members through his comm.

"This is hilarious. Someone else had the exact same idea I did. The green-haired sniper woman. She's shooting explosive rounds," he explained while crawling slowly on all fours.

Once his comrades had responded, he held up his reloaded XP-100 and kicked over a nearby table.

"I'll pin them down here. You handle the rest… This should be a fun one."

Shirley fired. Although she'd pressed the left side of her XP-100 against a pillar, the gun still bounced up from recoil.

The shot passed through the merry-go-round in the courtyard and exploded against the table that Beralto had just kicked over. Typically, a bullet would cut a hole less than an inch in diameter through the wood, but this one blasted a chunk the size of a human head out of it.

"Whoo! Yikes, man! Guns are scary," Beralto remarked leisurely. He stood up in the open and took his time aiming.

One thing that made an XP-100 different from a rifle was the long loading time.

You pulled the bolt to expel the empty. Then took a new bullet out of a pocket or vest loop, inserted it in front of the retracted bolt, and pushed it forward to close.

Doing all of these steps quickly required both hands. It was nearly impossible to do them while maintaining sight of the target through the gun's scope.

Beralto deliberately generated a bullet line to shine on Shirley as she rushed to reload, letting her know that he had her dead to rights.

"Shit!"

Shirley pulled back, but no bullet flew toward her.

"Ahhh..."

As a fellow sniper herself, Shirley realized what the other man was doing as she kissed the food court's tile floor.

To her teammates—temporary though they were—she said, "Get away from here!"

"Huh?" said Llenn.

"The enemy sniper's trying to keep us locked in this area! If you don't move now, we'll be surrounded soon!"

"Ack!"

That was very bad. Even Llenn could understand that this location was dangerous. Nobody wanted another fight in the food court.

First of all, it was visible to the enemy sniper. Even with Shirley giving him trouble, it was possible Llenn or the others could get taken out when they popped out of cover. Getting hit with a rifle bullet was instant death at this point.

Additionally, other enemy players were undoubtedly on the way, and Llenn's group was open on both sides, allowing an approach in a pincer formation.

Pitohui understood as much and drolly stated, "Okay, people, listen up, I got an announcement. We're gonna leave this one up to our girl Shirley and skedaddle, got it?"

She sounded like a meddling auntie at an arranged-marriage meeting, making an excuse to get up and let the potential couple get to know each other.

"Whaddabout me, Pito?" asked Fukaziroh.

Shirley snapped, "Don't need you! Go!"

"Hey, don't be like that! We're buddies! Guess I'll be off, then!"

"Did you want to stay or not?" Llenn muttered.

"Okay, Evacchi and Fuka are new buddies! This time, M and I will take the lead. Llenn, you get the rear. Let's go searching and kill us some baddies!" Pitohui said, as though they were about to embark on a picnic.

"Yeah! Let's go!" Llenn agreed heartily. She wanted to get into a good fight with Fire's team and send them to their virtual demises with her Vorpal Bunnies. "I'll turn this mall into their graveyard!"

"That's my Llenn."

"Excuse me? I'm not *yours*, Pito."

LPFM was running high on morale.

But had they forgotten about somebody?

Go east, to the right, or west, to the left? There would unquestionably be enemies in either direction.

"Right, then," decided Pitohui, and the team was off.

The opposing sniper had eyes on the food court, so they snuck beneath tables until it was safe to stand up again.

M took the lead down the broad walkway, holding his shield in front of himself to catch any shots from foes they might encounter. Next came Pitohui. Then Boss and Fukaziroh, and lastly Llenn.

"Do your best, Shirley!" Llenn called out to their other member, who was behind one of the food court's pillars.

"Like I need your encouragement to do that."

Bakoom. Shirley fired her huge pistol, the noise resounding through the entire structure.

Though the enemy couldn't possibly hear her, she shouted anyway.

"C'mon, shoot me! I'm your opponent here!"

The bullet flew toward the pillar where Beralto was hiding and exploded there, gouging out a massive chunk of concrete. It caused quite a lot of damage. Another ten shots in the same spot might topple the entire pillar.

"Damn, that thing packs a punch. Don't destroy the whole mall."

Beralto lifted the XP-100, rested the bipod on a table, and aimed over Shirley's head as she ducked down to reload her gun.

It roared.

The bullet speed was lower than that of a rifle because of the short barrel—but it still moved far faster than any pistol bullet, striking a spot seven meters from Shirley.

"What? Where is he shooting?" Shirley asked mockingly. She looked up with her gun loaded again, right as a chandelier collapsed onto her back.

"Aaagh!"

The thing landed directly on Shirley's head, back and shoulders, slamming her body down onto the tile floor.

"Gaah...aaah..."

Her avatar glowed all over with damage indicators, and her hit points dropped quickly. The damage the center part of the chandelier did to her head was particularly bad. In the span of four seconds, her 90 percent health dropped down to less than 40.

"Shit..."

Under the weight of the chandelier, she moved her left arm to take out an emergency med kit and use it. The slow healing process began.

Then she tried to push back against the chandelier, which weighed dozens of pounds. Unfortunately, it wouldn't budge.

"Rrgh..."

Her back and shoulders were numb to simulate the sensation of pain and wouldn't let her summon enough muscle strength to move the heavy object.

Pew! A bullet split the air over her head. It hit the chandelier and shattered the glass.

"How can...he aim at me...?"

The enemy sniper was on the same floor as Shirley. No matter how high he stretched, there was no way he could get an angle on her when she was flat against the floor.

Pew! A second bullet grazed Shirley's boot.

"Can't hit her. Not in this position," said Beralto, who was attempting some extreme acrobatics in the attempt to hit the spot where the chandelier had fallen.

He had retrieved a ten-foot rope from his inventory and tied it around the pillar, and he was holding the end in both hands, then pressing his feet against the surface. By maintaining tension on the rope with the weight of his body, he yanked it upward with him as he climbed the side with nothing but the strength of his legs.

Like a monkey, he scaled about twenty feet, nearly to the ceiling, then wrapped the end of the rope around his left hand to maintain position and shot the gun with his right hand. Once he had fired, he rested the gun on top of his tilted belly and used his free hand to move the bolt, put a new bullet in, then aim again and fire.

This one actually hit the chandelier, but there was still no DEAD tag over it to indicate that he had bested his quarry.

"Rrrgh..."

This time, Shirley felt confident that she was going to die.

The projectile passed through the chandelier and hit her butt, numbing her right leg. Her hit points dropped down to 10 percent. She was down in the red zone.

Yet, by budging her body, bit by bit, Shirley was slowly freeing herself from the light-fixture prison.

Inch by inch, she crawled forward.

"Ugh..."

Shirley refused to give up. She wanted to live. She wanted to kill Pitohui.

Then a red line landed on her face.

This time, it was aligned perfectly to hit her in the head.

"Dammit!"

She opened her mouth wide, allowing the line to intersect with the back of her throat, intending to catch the bullet in her teeth out of sheer determination.

Then Shirley's field of vision went light blue.

Gank!

Her ears caught a metallic crunching sound.

"Huh?"

Just inches in front of her face was an electric cart.

And sitting in the driver's seat was Fukaziroh.

"Yo, buddy! Need a hand?" she said, and she hopped down. Then she grabbed the center shaft of the chandelier that had Shirley pinned and, using all the strength she'd earned in *ALO*, roared, "Get the hell outta here! Yeet!" and hurled it over to the other side of the cart.

"......"

Liberated but stunned, Shirley had enough presence of mind to grab her XP-100 and get up.

"That's it! Let's move!" said Fukaziroh, who ran a few steps in the other direction, but Shirley did not follow her. "Huh? Hey, c'mon!"

Using the electric cart's rear seats as cover, Shirley rested the XP-100 on top of one and peered through the scope. She found the man at the top of the pillar, looking very much like a power company technician, finishing his reload, and took aim.

He aimed her way as well.

"I like your spirit!"

Shirley did not back away. She pulled the trigger.

As the lens bounced with recoil, she saw the muzzle of her opponent's gun flash.

CHAPTER 21
Battle of the Mall II

CHAPTER 21
Battle of the Mall II

An enormous ball of fire exploded in Shirley's face.

Brilliant orange flooded her eyes, and heat pounded her skin.

"Aaaah!" She pulled back in a panic.

Human beings have an instinctual fear of fire, so flames were frightening even in a virtual setting. Although it might vary by individual, most people in *GGO* found fire much scarier than a knife or gun attack.

The flames had come from the side of the electric cart. They were growing in strength by the moment, threatening to engulf their fuel source.

The pillar of fire was soon ten feet tall, looming like some ghastly Christmas tree. There was a deep, bass roar, like someone blowing into a conch shell.

The rifle round had hit the vehicle's battery and set it on fire. Ironically, that had saved Shirley's life. If not for the battery, it would have passed through the cart's body and struck her.

She backed away from the vehicle, pushing tables aside, and reloaded the XP-100.

"Wait, you aren't going to run?" asked Fukaziroh, who was already sixty feet away at this point.

"Not until I'm sure he's dead!" Shirley pressed the XP-100 against a pillar and looked through her scope. She could no longer find anyone across the courtyard.

Then she looked lower and saw a floating tag reading DEAD near a bunch of tables and chairs.

"Yeah! Eat it!"

As a matter of fact, Shirley's desperation shot had not actually hit Beralto.

It had struck the pillar, and the explosion had snapped the rope he was holding to keep himself steady. Since he'd just fired his own weapon, he naturally fell toward the ground back-first.

"Whoo-hoo-hoo!" he shrieked happily, and he kicked off the pillar with both feet, shifting his movement vector from straight down to diagonal. That helped him avoid landing directly with full force. Instead, he crashed through some of the tables and chairs on the way down.

The plummet took 30 percent of his HP, but it was better than dying. He could still fight. What's more, he had all three med kits, too.

"Hoh-hoh! I'm not dead yet!" Beralto smirked, staring up at the ceiling.

"That's right. And that's why I have to kill you," came a man's voice. A knife plunged into the sniper's sunglasses.

David killed the masked man with a stab of his combat knife, then stayed crouched behind the tables for cover.

Moments later, Kenta said, "All clear, Leader. They both went for the north side," and David stood up. LPFM's sniper and the blond shrimp were no longer in the open on the mall's far side.

David quickly wove his way through the tables toward the north edge of the food court where Kenta was. The two reunited in front of a burrito shop.

"So far, so good," David remarked.

As a two-man team, MMTM had a strategy code-named (by David) Operation Sneaky Sneakers.

Because they were just a duo, going toe to toe with the surviving teams, which totaled up to a possible eighteen combatants, would be suicide. Thus their plan was to sneak and hide as best they could while looking for chances to pick off one or two opponents at a time.

Taking out a man busy sniping while also avoiding being spotted by Shirley was as good a result as they could have hoped for.

"What next?" asked Kenta, who was keeping an eye out with an APX in hand.

David replied, "Go down to the right and sneak up behind that battle. Let's be dirty as hell."

In the distance, the mall echoed with the clatter of gunfire.

"Why did you come back?" asked Shirley as Fukaziroh's tiny figure up ahead hurried east down the hallway.

Fukaziroh glanced over her shoulder, holding the pistol she couldn't hit a single target with, and answered, "I ran away because I was going to die."

"Oh. Okay." Shirley figured that she was lying as a way to avoid admitting that she was concerned about her teammate.

But then the sound of a fierce firefight filled their ears, and Fukaziroh fumed, "They're still at it!"

"Oh, you were telling the truth," Shirley said.

* * *

Moments earlier, the LPFM group had made their way down a passage leading from the south side's food court on the third floor, expecting to run into enemies along the way.

If hostiles were approaching them from both east and west, it was better to strike out in one direction to meet them directly—so they chose to run to the east.

And on the southeast curve of the mall's thoroughfare, when they were halfway around the angle, M called out, "Enemy! Straight ahead!" and crouched in the middle of the open avenue. His shield covered his body from exposure to gunfire.

Instantly, things descended into an explosion of shooting.

Prrrrraaaaaaaaaaaaaaaa!

It was continuous, full-auto fire, with no audible pauses between the shots to make it percussive, just like a submachine gun.

Kshaaaaaaaaaaaaakkkk!

Just as fast as the shots themselves, the sound of bullets hitting M's shield was a ceaseless stream of noise. There was no way for the human ear to distinguish individual sounds in that flow.

Pitohui slid down behind M's shield and snapped an order to Llenn and Boss as they approached from the rear: "Get off this floor! You'll only be collateral!"

"Got it!" replied Boss. She stopped at once and rushed over to the stationary escalator nearby, leaping over the handrail to get on.

Llenn followed her a beat later. *Pito, M, stay safe!*

She wished she could stay to support her friends, but Pitohui was right. If they tried to get any closer to help, they'd just get shot. Going the other way would only expose their backs to incoming bullets, too. The best choice was to rush to a different floor.

The sound of automatic gunfire prompted Llenn to ask Boss as they ran, "Is that legal?"

"It is if it belongs in the Handgun category! I'm sure some handguns are fully automatic."

"Damn, that's not fair!"

"If there's ever another one of these, we'll have to study up. Where's Fukaziroh?"

"Huh?"

Llenn turned back, nearly to the fourth floor by now, but saw no one behind her. So she answered the question as honestly as she could.

"She ran."

The bullets smashed against M's shield without rest.

These were no fools, so they did not *only* focus on the shield.

By shifting aim to the sides and top of the barrier, they could ensure that Pitohui had no time to pop up and shoot back.

Bullet lines glimmered around the shield, then vanished as the bullets came.

Pitohui had an XDM in either hand but found herself without a chance to use them. The enemy never gave her a turn. Their continuous fire was incredible.

"What is that? How many are there?"

"I only spotted two. Just one is firing," M replied. He could tell it was a single player based on the incoming projectiles. If there were two, the lines would be coming from different directions, but the stream of bullets had only a single mouth.

"Guess I gotta use it," Pitohui stated, resigned. She went into her inventory and produced the mirror she used to peer around corners.

A corner mirror was a common tool in *GGO*. She pulled out the extendable rod with the reflective bit on the end and poked it around the shield, hoping for a glimpse of the enemy—only to lose the mirror in that very instant. Even the extendable rod turned into light particles and vanished.

"Ugh, this is why I didn't want to use that stupid thing. Enemy confirmed: a man in heavy protective armor in the middle of the hall. Probably has Glock 18Cs in each hand. Behind him is his dedicated reloader," Pitohui detailed, having deciphered the enemy's strength from a single glance.

The man shooting at M from about twenty meters away was nearly as large as his target.

He was tall and broad, and he looked absolutely terrible in his blue tracksuit. He was wearing a vest with room for armored plates over his chest and stomach and padded guards over his thighs, knees, and shins, like a baseball catcher. These were designed for combat, however.

A sturdy helmet protected his head. A thick face shield was attached to the headgear, going over the usual mask and sunglasses. This was a protector that police special forces around the world used, and it would deflect any pistol bullet.

Just as Pitohui had surmised from her brief glimpse, he was using Glock 18Cs. The Glock 17 was a famous automatic pistol, and the 18C was its fully automatic special version. It was *technically* in the Handgun category.

The selector on the side of the slide allowed for switching between semi-auto and full auto. The latter had a speed of 1,200 shots per minute—twenty per second.

There was a thirty-three-round magazine sticking far out of the bottom of the grip, but that would only take 1.7 seconds to empty.

The man had one Glock in each hand and was firing them on full auto, one at a time. His Strength stat alone was keeping the tremendous recoil in check. He was a monster. Once he had fired all the bullets from his right gun, he started firing the left. Once that was over, he fired from the right again.

The secret of this seemingly endless stream of bullets, as Pitohui had guessed, was a dedicated reloader standing behind him—another man in a blue tracksuit.

He was short and skinny. He wore nothing over his tracksuit and had only a single holster attached sideways to his lower back above the waist.

After the large man shot one gun until it was out of bullets, the magazine dropped from the bottom of the Glock 18C, and he pulled that arm behind his back. Then the small man in waiting stuck a new magazine in its place.

There was a bag on the large man's back that was stuffed with munitions. So their battle style was to combine two people into one ultra-efficient, high-speed shooting machine.

The strategy had M and Pitohui wholly pinned.

"Penebia here. I've got the shield man and the ponytail woman trapped on the third-floor walkway, southeast corner. I'm with Ron," said the man shooting the Glock 18Cs.

Penebia took a heavy step forward. The small player named Ron followed, sticking in the next ammo mag.

Shoot, shoot, shoot, then step. Rinse and repeat.

Slowly but surely, they got closer and closer to M and Pitohui.

While he was firing the Glocks, Penebia spoke into his comm. "The pink girl and gorilla-woman ran to the fourth floor. Can we leave them to someone else and have fun with these two?" he asked.

Three seconds later, he got his answer.

"Roger that. Then we'll enjoy things here. Squad Jam heroes should make for some fun opponents."

Prrrraaaaaaaaa!

Kshaaaaaakkkk!

The combination of gunshots and bullets bouncing off metal made for an unearthly din. What had once been a place for peaceful, relaxing shopping was now a battlefield of flying lead.

Through the clattering against the shield, Pitohui said, "Ugh, this is annoying. The day's going to be over by the time we're done dealing with these two."

M replied, "I know."

"Then I'll leave him to you."

"………Got it."

Pitohui promptly swung her right arm outward. She was holding the magazine catch on the XDM, so it sent the magazine flying away to the right. The bullets immediately targeted it, hitting the pack in midair.

At the same time, Pitohui darted left and used her other gun to shoot at Penebia, the large man, while crossing the hallway toward the nearest store.

His left Glock 18C spat full auto bullets at Pitohui, getting close to her back—but just before he struck her backpack, she dived into the store and was out of sight.

"I'm your opponent here."

M picked up the shield and started to sprint forward.

Penebia shot with his reloaded right-hand gun, but the projectiles bounced off the metal barrier and did nothing to stop M's advance.

"Heh! Very well." Penebia grinned beneath his mask. "Ron! You get the woman! Enjoy the indoor battle you've always wanted!" he exclaimed to the small man behind him.

"Just what I've been waiting for!" answered the reloader, smiling so broadly that it moved his mask. As he leaped out into the open, Ron grunted under his breath, "For Fire."

"For Fire," Penebia echoed.

The audience in the bar saw the two giants clash in the middle of the mall thoroughfare.

One was M. The other was in a blue tracksuit.

Once the man shooting Glock 18Cs at M was out of ammo, he simply tossed his weapons aside. As M rushed closer, shield up for a body blow, his opponent held out his arms in preparation for the impact.

The little man slipped away to the right and hurried past M, who surely saw it happen but did nothing.

"Little one went your way. Have fun," M informed Pitohui. He continued his charge, his thick, heavy legs thudding on the floor, pushing off the carpet.

Now that he knew the other man wasn't shooting, he pulled apart his shields a crack so he could see ahead. When he spotted his opponent with arms spread in waiting, he chuckled.

"Haah!"

The big tracksuit man had bulletproof armor, a helmet, and a thick defensive visor over his face.

M chose *not* to use his HK45 pistol. Instead, he lifted his arms, still holding the halves of the shield, and pointed the halves at his opponent. He was going to bash the enemy with them like cudgels.

Naturally, the other man narrowed his arms slightly, preparing to block.

The two giants collided.

The moment Penebia caught the heavy pieces of metal with his hands, M released them. While his opponent was still gripping the things, M lowered his left shoulder for a charge, making full use of the momentum he'd built up running over.

He made contact with Penebia's defensive helmet and armor and pushed with all his leg power.

"Mrgh!"

The force of the impact caused Penebia to buckle. He let the shields fall to the carpet below.

With his arms free, Penebia grabbed M low around the waist to gain control of his center of gravity. It was like sumo wrestling.

M did not pull back. "Nrrrrh!" he growled, pushing and pushing, until—

"Guh!" Penebia could not hold his ground and tottered backward, taking step after step until he met a glass window thirty feet away and smashed through it. The two men had picked the most dynamic possible way to enter the store.

Then they fell.

"Oh?"

"Huh?"

Penebia and M plummeted downward.

It was so dark that they hadn't seen that there was no floor beneath them. There was no floor beyond the storefront's window. Entangled, the two men dropped around twelve feet, from the third floor to the second.

"Gaah!"

"Guhh!"

Penebia suffered more damage in the fall, having landed directly on his back. Because of the human cushion, M got away with only light bruises.

The shock and bounce of the impact threw the two apart. Both scrambled to their feet.

"They're falling!"

The crowd in the pub watched on the screen as two large avatars smashed through a pane and dropped through the empty space beyond.

And they landed on…an airport.

The two men fell into the middle of a runway, warping its straight lines.

"Huh?"

"What the—?"

For a moment, the spectators thought there had been a bug.

Had the two combatants somehow warped to the airfield in the northeast section of the map while at the same time becoming giants?

Obviously, that wasn't the case.

The room they had crashed into was large—one hundred feet to a side, with another square, sixty-five feet to a side, situated in the center.

"Oh, I get it. It's a miniature of the city!"

The room was not a store, but an exhibition. The smaller area in the center of the chamber was a miniaturized display of the map they were fighting on—before it had fallen into disrepair, of course.

The model city had to be one five-hundredth the size of the real one. The details were so intricately re-created that looking down on it felt like watching from an aerial drone.

The camera angle dipped down until the second-story entrance to the room was visible.

There were signs in English explaining that this room held a miniature re-creation of the area, that entry and photography were free, that visitors should move clockwise around the model, and that it had taken locals several years to put it all together.

The miniatures were indeed laboriously meticulous. Someone

had cut out tiny pieces of translucent plastic for each window on the airport terminal one by one. Colorful planes in one-five-hundredth scale lined up at the gates, and the twenty-inch control tower still had vibrant paint color.

It took all of a second for one of four burly legs stomping around to flatten the terminal.

At well over six feet tall, M and Penebia loomed over the tiny world as three-thousand-foot monsters.

M's right foot crushed the airport's passenger terminal with one stray step, leaving a gigantic footprint on the runway. Penebia stomped forward, the impact traveling through the ground and bouncing the little planes up into the air like popcorn on a frying pan.

"It's like a *kaiju* movie."

"Even *kaiju* aren't *that* big, though."

The audience had an aerial view of the two giants struggling.

Penebia threw a right hook at M. His opponent took a half step back for distance, grabbed Penebia's outstretched arm, and twisted it left, going for a takedown. Penebia jumped in that direction, bending his body around the axle of that arm into a flip and flattening the highway with both feet as he stood firm.

As soon as the other man started to rotate, M let go. He retreated slightly, putting a few meters between them. In the process, his foot kicked the control tower into pieces.

"Ooh. Can that tracksuit do MMA?"

"This seems like a tough fight."

M drew his HK45 pistol. Even if the bullets were going to be deflected, it was a means to keep the opposing player at a distance.

However, the moment he pointed the muzzle at the enemy, Penebia's large right foot kicked M's hand with a long-distance roundhouse. Naturally, that was not an in-game skill in *GGO*.

It knocked the HK45 loose, sending it flying over the freeway junction in the center of the map and into the town, where it smashed tiny houses.

Penebia jumped, going high in the air with his knee outstretched. The pointed end smashed against the left side of M's face from above.

"Urgh!"

M's hefty body lurched to the right while another kick from Penebia pounded his side. This one was a clean blow to M's side, like something a kickboxer would do.

The tip of Penebia's boot jammed into unguarded flesh. M toppled onto the highway, demolishing it instantly.

And then he was on his feet again.

"You're a pretty good fighter," praised Penebia, pausing his assault. If he had persisted without talking, he might have gotten knocked back by M when he bounced back up.

Penebia's eyes darted away for a split second, looking up to the left.

He was on the airport, while M was standing on the other side of the east-west highway. That put the model of the mall, where they were *actually* located right now, just behind M's foot.

"Your name is M, right? I saw you on the Squad Jam replays," Penebia continued, waving his left hand. It brought up his window, which he used to remove his armor. The heavy helmet and guards vanished, leaving him light and nimble in his tracksuit.

He was clearly ready and willing to finish this fight in hand-to-hand combat—if not face-to-face; his mask and sunglasses were still on.

"……"

M spread his feet in a stance and warily shed his backpack. It fell onto the model of the mall and squashed it, along with several other buildings in the vicinity.

With evident excitement, Penebia stated, "You're used to getting hit, I can tell. Very good at deflecting the force of each blow."

M maintained his silence.

"I've been practicing fighting my whole life in the real world. I was expecting to take you easily."

For the first time, M spoke. "I'm sorry to have disappointed you."

"No, not at all! It's more fun when I can't win the easy way!"

"Glad to hear it. You're pretty tough, too. Fire hired the right mercenaries."

"Mercenaries…? Ah, I see. Good point. In the sense that we're fighting for his wishes, I suppose that word is appropriate," Penebia muttered, briefly confused.

"…?"

So was M.

*   *   *

But roughly two minutes before M stood amid the model city with a confused expression, Pitohui had leaped into a men's clothing store.

The 130-foot store interior was packed with suits. There was nothing fancy about the display; they were just lines of ensembles on hangers. Now and then, just for good measure, there was a full-length mirror and a mannequin, but for the most part, it was so austere that it might as well have been a factory.

Would anyone actually want *to buy a suit in a place like this?* Pitohui glanced at the tags; the suits were all the same size and color. Every outfit was a men's medium in navy blue.

It was obvious that when designing the assets for this store, the artists had cut corners and copied and pasted the same suit and mannequin over and over to fill it out. By *GGO*'s usual intensely detailed standards, this was a hack job.

"Little one went your way. Have fun," M's voice informed her over the comm. Pitohui pointed her reloaded XDMs back toward the entrance.

Ron, the small man in the tracksuit, pulled his pistol out before rushing into the store after Pitohui.

His weapon was a Sturm, Ruger & Co. MK III pistol from the United States with a fused silencer attached. With Japanese pronunciation, it sounded the same as the famous German Luger, but this was a different armament.

The MK III had a thin barrel that shot .22-caliber Long Rifle bullets, which were no larger than beans. However, the gun possessed excellent accuracy, and the efficiency of the built-in silencer made it an ideal weapon for assassins.

Ron rushed into the store, black gun in hand, and promptly leaped into the air. His quick jump carried him over a line of suits, as well as the bullets that Pitohui shot in his direction.

"What are you, an acrobat?" she snapped as she ducked and hid amid the forest of fabric.

Ron landed on the shoulders of a dummy and jumped even higher from there. With his Acrobat skill at an extremely high level, it was like he didn't weigh anything at all. According to players who built their skills out this way, it felt like gravity didn't exist.

He dangled by one arm from the lighting hanging from the ceiling, then started to fire the MK III in the direction he thought the enemy had shot from.

The .22-caliber bullets might be small, but they were deadly projectiles nonetheless. A suit offered no protection from them. Three rounds caught Pitohui's body, certainly by coincidence, and left small glowing marks on her. She lost about 10 percent of her hit points, which brought her down to 40.

"Tch! Damn street performer!" Pitohui swore, and she operated her inventory while she tumbled away, a rather impressive bit of dexterity on her own part. She came to a stop and grabbed what had appeared before her.

Ron let go of the light and landed silently amid the rows of outfits.

An object came over a few rows toward him. He did a back handspring using only his open left hand to distance himself from the thing, moving as quickly and precisely as a gymnast.

It was a grenade that had been lobbed at him, though not an explosive one. Gray clouds began to fill the large store. Since there was no wind inside, nothing pushed the fog in any direction.

"Haah!" Once Ron had given himself plenty of distance, he opened his menu with his free hand. He had a plasma grenade stored, which he quickly called up and hurled into the sea of gray vapor.

The surge and blast of the explosive instantly cleared the smoke cover.

Ron jumped again. Bounding like a flea, he went from row to row over the suits, looking for Pitohui from above.

"Hmm?"

She wasn't there.

All he saw were clothes and hangers that had been toppled by the grenade, some hangers that were still upright, and well-dressed mannequins.

By the time he noticed that one of the mannequins was pointing a gun at him, it was just a bit too late.

The bullet struck Ron right in the forehead as he landed, just before he could jump again. Yet his hit points didn't reach zero until after his feet left the floor once more, and he became a corpse in midjump.

Ron fell into the fabric with his DEAD tag. Pitohui, dressed in one of the suits, looked at him with satisfaction and said to M, "I got it done. How about you?"

M was getting kicked and could not respond.

"Hya!" Penebia howled, and he reached to grab him.

M used his palm to block the other man's hand.

Two massive men were grappling in a contest of strength atop the highway. Despite their incredible investment in the Strength stat, they had reached a stalemate. Their thick arms paused, frozen, trembling with effort.

"Aaaah!" Penebia exhaled happily.

"Hrrgh!" M grunted, summoning more force. But it was Penebia who was gaining the upper hand.

M's arms were getting closer and closer to his chest. His back began to arch. Then it buckled, and Penebia was leaning over M, leaving his stomach vulnerable to a sudden kick.

M was trying a judo throw called a *tomoe nage*, rolling onto his back with his foot against the opponent, but Penebia saw it all coming. He lifted his knee to block M's foot and slammed him to the ground.

The half-destroyed mall was now completely flattened under M's back. Penebia was straddling his stomach. He reared back and threw a ferocious punch at M's exposed face.

Crunch!

It was a nasty sound. M's face began to glow with a damage indication light.

Another punch came swinging down before M could grab Penebia's arm, and his face glowed even brighter.

"Gah! Guh!"

Then a third.

M might have been good at shrugging off blows, but there was nothing he could do about punches from directly overhead. With each hammer blow, M's body crunched farther down through the wreckage of the model mall. The fourth one caused his hands to go limp, and he collapsed against the ground.

"Hmm. Was hoping you'd hold out a bit more," Penebia grunted before lifting his fist for the final blow. Down it went.

However, the strike only caught a mass of green nylon.

M had grabbed his backpack to protect himself. It was still holding the shield plates, and it absorbed all of the blow.

"Hng!" Penebia grunted again, surprised at the sudden deflection of his blow. "So what?"

Whud.

He continued punching, deciding to smash M through the backpack. If he persisted, the metal plates would eventually slam against M's face and squash it.

Whud.

After the sixth punch, as Penebia raised his fist for another, he caught sight of M's left hand.

It was clenching something, right in front of the backpack. A round metal object…

"Wha—?!"

It exploded the instant he realized it was a shrapnel grenade.

The grenade blew while still in M's grip—completely obliterating his upper arm.

It tore a hole in the nylon backpack but did not pass through a single layer of the special shield.

Almost all the shrapnel burrowed into Penebia's upper half, and the force of the blast blew him backward.

"You got me! Ha-ha-ha-ha-ha!"

Penebia died laughing, his entire torso glowing red.

"Oh! M's almost dead!"

Llenn was alarmed to see her teammate's HP dwindling to nearly nothing. Even she could finish him off with a punch at this point.

"That doesn't matter! Focus here!"

"Yeah, I know, but—!"

Boss and Llenn were fleeing. They were rushing down the mall hallway on the fourth floor, running to the west from the southeast corner. As it happened, that was where they'd come from, but circumstances had forced them to double back.

There'd been no other option.

A small explosion roared behind them. It didn't cause them any damage, but the force of the blast shook Llenn and Boss. Bits of debris struck their backs and heads.

"Yeep!" Llenn shrieked.

"What is that thing?!" Boss demanded, but no one volunteered an answer.

* * *

Llenn's speed was her strength, and Boss was quite nimble, too, for her size, but the man in the blue tracksuit behind them was keeping pace fifty meters behind.

Over his clothes, he wore a vest packed with small pouches. And in his right hand was a black pistol.

From the shape of the gun and the grip's angle, it looked like a revolver, but it didn't have that iconic rotating chamber, and the barrel looked abnormally wide.

The man stopped running, took aim at Llenn and Boss, and fired.

His weapon loosed a silver shell that was 68 mm across and over 250 mm long.

It was the spitting image of a shell with wings, but it was much too small to be something like that.

The object raced down the corridor, struck a pillar, and exploded.

"Shit!"

Boss managed to avoid the blast and shrapnel by hiding behind a bench. With her Strizh in hand, she returned fire.

That said, her target was fifty meters away. Just because he was visible didn't mean Boss could reliably hit him. Still, she got off a few rounds, hoping for a lucky hit. Unfortunately, the man watched for her bullet lines, dodging and dropping to the floor. All of Boss's shots went to waste.

Llenn pointed both Vorpal Bunnies at her pursuer and opened fire, covering for Boss as she exchanged her gun's magazine. The heavy .45-caliber shots echoed off the exterior of shop fronts displaying mugs and frying pans. Her volley was as successful as Boss's.

If only I had P-chan right now…

Llenn swiped her hands behind her back to reload. If she had access to her usual armaments, the enemy would assuredly have a rifle or a 40 mm grenade launcher. It was because of the pistol restriction that the pink-dressed girl was still alive.

The slides clicked back into place.

I need to master using these...

"That's right! You have to help us shine in the spotlight!"

"Close combat is where handguns are the star! C'mon, get us closer!"

Llenn could have sworn she heard her Vor-chans talking to her but chose to believe that hadn't been the case.

While stray bullets whizzed past the man in the tracksuit, he bent his gun in half.

It was a folding-type weapon. The front half of the gun collapsed forward like it was bowing, exposing the thicker rear part of the pistol. A fat golden cartridge popped up and fell to the floor.

Then the man extracted a golden tube from a pouch and stuck it in. He pulled the bent gun back into place, took aim, and fired again.

"A grenade launcher? That's no fair!" fumed Llenn, ducking away from the blast. Despite her protests, the thing was a handgun.

The tracksuit man was wielding a Walther Kampfpistole. It was a small grenade-launching pistol used by the German army in World War II. Initially, it was meant to fire 65 mm flares. But over time, it had been improved to launch grenades, which was the source of its eventual name, which translated to "combat pistol."

It was probably the world's smallest grenade launcher, and like so many other strange weapons, it was classified as a handgun in *GGO.*

Since his appearance, the man had kept Llenn and Boss on the run. The Kampfpistole had a range of over fifty meters, and when the projectile finished its ballistic flight, it exploded upon contact. The shrapnel had a splash radius of about two meters.

It was a single-shot gun that took time to reload, so Llenn and Boss might have stood a chance if they'd found time to rush their opponent. However, with the way he was shooting off grenades at them, it was too dangerous to approach.

The pair considered hiding in the stores on either side of the hall, but if the tracksuit man continued launching explosives into the interiors, they'd only get blown up without a fair chance to fight back. Since they were now hiding behind a pillar, he couldn't risk drawing too near. It seemed he planned to maintain a certain distance, keep Llenn and Boss in his sights, and steadily track them down. He was a nasty opponent—a real piece of work.

"Dammit, why are all of Fire's henchmen so tough? And they're packing the perfect weapons for a pistol fight!" Boss swore.

Then she realized something and gasped, "Wait...maybe these people were chosen *because* they would fight here, with this gear... Perhaps the fact that they never used any long guns outside was because they weren't packing any in the first place..."

WEEI had prepared for the pistol battle better than anyone else. They'd selected specialized weapons and split up their team to fight individually. LPFM had been led into this situation by none other than...

"Hey, Llenn, do you think—?"

"Not now! Just focus on trying to beat him!" Llenn snapped back.

"Fine. Got it. You're right."

This was no time to get distracted, especially by thoughts about how Pitohui had skillfully led the group through a series of events that ended with them in the mall.

Doubts wouldn't stop the enemy's bombardment.

A thick bullet line curved downward right in their vicinity, so Llenn leaped away. She ran diagonally down the hall and had just reached the edge of the stairs when she felt the blast on her back. Black smoke filled the space where she had just been standing.

"Yo! You seem to be having trouble!" came a loud voice from the bottom of the stairs.

Llenn turned on pure reflex and pointed both Vorpal Bunnies at the newcomer.

"Eep! Don't shoot!" yelped Fukaziroh.

"Fuka! You're all right?"

"Somehow. Beat the sniper on Fire's team," said Fukaziroh, hopping up the steps. And she wasn't alone.

"Shirley! Please help! There's a tough enemy up here! Shoot him!" she said, calling upon her handgun sniper of a teammate.

"Who is it? I'll mop the floor with him."

Shirley could pick off a target at over three hundred meters. A guy wandering around less than seventy meters away was a sitting duck to her.

Watchful for bullet lines, Llenn beckoned Shirley up the stairs. Once she was just a few steps away from the fourth floor, Llenn popped her head up to see into the walkway and said, "There!"

The grenade pistoleer was standing smack in the middle of the mall, like a bronze statue.

Shirley was hiding right beside Llenn at the top of the stairs. She placed the XP-100 on the carpet to keep it steady and looked through the scope.

"Can you get him?" Llenn asked.

"Easily. Just a standing target," said Shirley. She took steady aim and put her finger against the trigger. There was a loud gunshot.

"Gaah!"

A bright-red bullet effect formed on Shirley's back.

"Huh?"

Someone pushed Llenn up the stairs and back to the fourth floor. When she turned around, she saw them, two men firing pistols up from the third-floor hallway below.

She recognized the angular green camo, as well as their sharp, mean faces.

"MMTM!"

The two who had survived the airport had finally come back to haunt them.

Shirley's HP had been recovering but was now going down again after that hit in the back. She had less than 20 percent remaining. Llenn was struck twice as well, only surviving thanks to her armored backpack.

Even so, the impact pushed light little Llenn off the stairs. That ensured that the next shots did not hit her.

"Shit…"

Shirley stayed prone on the steps and focused again on aiming her XP-100 at the man in the tracksuit. Normally, she would have stood up and made a break for safety. Her legs were still fine, after all.

Curiously, that was not what Shirley chose to do.

The instant she caught the tracksuit player in her crosshairs, she pulled the trigger. The XP-100 roared, and a lethal explosive bullet lanced forth.

A moment later, more 9 mm bullets met Shirley's back, dropping her to zero HP.

That's weird. Why didn't I run away? she wondered as she died, but there would be no answer for her in Squad Jam 4.

The 7.62 mm explosive round Shirley had fired for her team's sake found purchase in the man wearing a blue tracksuit.

He just so happened to have his left arm placed in front of his stomach at the moment. He had been reaching across his body for a new grenade on his right hip.

Shirley's bullet struck his arm and exploded.

"Hng!"

Instantly, his left arm from the elbow downward exploded into polygonal pieces, but that ensured that he stayed alive.

"Dammit!" Llenn swore, watching the DEAD tag gleam over Shirley's body.

She lay flat on the ground in front of the stairs, sticking just the Vorpal Bunnies over the top step to fire downward. She didn't care about the probability of landing those shots. She just needed to make sure the enemy couldn't climb up.

After a dozen rounds, she stuck her hands into her backpack for a reload and popped her face up just a bit. David had managed to find a favorable angle for cover at the bottom of the stairs and was poking one eye and his gun out. He fired up at Llenn.

"Eek!"

She pulled her head back, and the projectile sped through where her skull had been a second earlier.

The shooting stopped there. Llenn prepared herself for an enemy assault, but he wasn't charging up the steps for the moment.

"One MMTM on the floor below!" Llenn called to her remaining teammates over the comms.

From behind her, Boss replied, "Got it! The grenadier's still alive!"

"All right. Where's Fuka?"

"I'm here. Look up."

Llenn did just that and spied her friend on the stairs leading from the fourth level to the fifth. The angle kept her safe from both the grenadier and MMTM.

"So they got Shirley... Everyone, come up here for now. There's no shame in running for your life, ya know?"

It hurts to lose sight of the enemy, but I guess it's our only choice, Llenn thought, and then she heard fierce fighting erupt on the floor above.

"Hyee! Oohoop!" Fukaziroh gurgled mysteriously, and she slid down the stairs on her butt.

Dakoom! There was a heavy gunshot, and a bullet cracked against the metal of the handrail on the stairs, bending it in half. That had to be the most powerful pistol bullet class there was.

Fukaziroh flopped down beside Llenn and said, "Never mind, there's a tracksuit up there, too! He saw me! If you pop out, you'll get shot!"

"Argh! Is it Fire?" Llenn asked. If he was there, she had a mind to jump up and try to take him out with her.

"No, it wasn't a tall, skinny guy. He had a huge freakin' gun on him."

Behind a pillar, at a store about twenty meters to the east of the stairs on the fifth-floor hall, stood a man in a blue tracksuit. He had been sneaking nearer and was the one who'd fired when he'd spotted Fukaziroh climbing the stairs.

From behind the pillar outside a highly regarded pillow store, he extended a large black automatic pistol: the Desert Eagle.

That name had become synonymous with any automatic pistol that could fire Magnum rounds, like .357 and .44 Magnums. It was large, simple, and powerful, qualities that gave it great popularity.

This member of WEEI carried a model that launched the most potent and largest-caliber bullet of them all, the .50 Action Express (AE). When shot at close range, those projectiles delivered as much kinetic energy as an AK-47 rifle round. Since the Desert Eagle was a pistol, it couldn't aim long distances, and the bullet itself was large and heavy and had poor air resistance, which hurt its range.

However, in a mall, the weapon might as well have been the Grim Reaper.

"Let's go west then, Fuka!"

"Okay!"

The east side of the hallway was a no go. Death awaited on the stairs going up *and* down. So the only option was to run west on this floor. Llenn decided to roll the dice on the one possibility to turn the situation around.

"Aiee!"

But then Fukaziroh got shot again, right before Llenn's eyes.

Running down in a zigzag pattern from the far side of the corridor was the other MMTM member, Kenta.

As the quickest member of his squad, he had run back across the third-floor hall, then darted up an escalator so he could surprise them from the fourth floor in a pincer attack from the west.

His APX bullet caught Fukaziroh's right leg as she got up to run.

"Bwehf!" She toppled to the floor on the spot. Her hit points were down to 50 percent. "You filthy bastard!" she swore, taking aim from the carpet with her M&P and firing. If you could call it "taking aim."

She was just shooting at random, not expecting to hit him, necessarily. The spread of random projectiles was actually more difficult to dodge than accurately aimed bullets.

Kenta gave up on getting closer and leaped toward a fancy women's lingerie store to their left—his right—on the south side of the corridor. He was about thirty-five meters from Llenn and Fukaziroh.

He thrust a mirror on a stick past a mannequin wearing a pink brassiere to get a look at the rest of the hall. Then he passed on the information he found to the only surviving teammate he had, David.

"I'm on the west side of the fourth floor! The sniper woman's dead. Only Pink, Blondie, and Gorilla left. Enemies somewhere on the fifth level and the east side of the fourth, one each!"

"Got it! No M and poisonous bird, eh…? No use being aggressive here, then. Let the enemies do the heavy lifting. If they run your way, ice 'em!"

The gunshots ceased, and a period of silence settled in.

"There's no…escape…," Llenn muttered.

She was on the floor in the fourth-floor hall. Right near the stairs.

Fifty meters to the east was an enemy with a grenade pistol.

David waited at the bottom of the steps.

Above the stairs was an enemy with a powerful pistol.

Thirty meters to Llenn's west was Kenta, hiding inside a shop.

Whichever way she went, she was going to get shot.

Whichever way she attacked, she was going to get hit from behind.

"It's no good…"

"Llenn! Don't give up!" shouted Boss, who was in cover behind a pillar ten meters away.

She popped off a few shots with her Strizh, but the one-armed grenade pistoleer nimbly dodged her bullets. Thankfully, having one hand made it much harder to reload, so he wasn't shooting back nearly as often. It seemed more like he was content to keep a watchful eye for now.

Llenn glanced at her team's health bars. M was nearly dead. Pitohui had about 40 percent left. Fukaziroh was at 50. Her own healing had finished, putting her at max life.

"Ugh! But…"

Despite Boss's reprimand, Llenn couldn't conjure up a solution to her predicament.

Then she heard an airy, aloof voice say, "Oh, good grief. Is this where the cool, cute one steps in?"

"Fuka?"

"I've lost Rightony and Leftania. But I've still got plasma grenades to spare. All the pouches over my vest are filled with them."

"And?" Llenn pressed, not getting the picture.

From somewhere else in the mall, Pitohui's voice rang in her ear. "Sounds good! Then let's go with that in ten seconds!"

"Pito?"

"Got it! Hey, Eva! You know what to do! We need your pistol skill. Not the forehead this time!" Fukaziroh replied.

"You bet!" answered Boss, spinning around from behind the pillar with a smile.

"Okay! I'll leave what I borrowed from you on the floor!"

Huh? Llenn still had no clue what was happening.

"Five, four, three," Pitohui began to count, "two, one, go!"

Before Llenn had time to ponder further, the final battle commenced.

CHAPTER 22
Light a Fire in Your Heart

CHAPTER 22
Light a Fire in Your Heart

"Here we go!"

Fukaziroh got to her feet and started running to the west from the fourth-floor stairs. On the floor behind her, she left a Degtyaryov antitank rifle.

"What?!" Llenn's eyes went wide with disbelief.

She was headed for Kenta. It was practically suicide. No, scratch that. It *was* suicide.

Fukaziroh waved the M&P around, firing erratically, closing thirty-five meters of distance and preventing Kenta from popping his head out.

"Do it!"

She spun around on the spot when she was out of bullets and began to run backward—right in front of the lingerie store.

"Hey!"

Naturally, Kenta saw Fukaziroh approaching and aimed his APX at her.

Kenta and Boss fired at the same moment.

Kenta's bullet went into Fukaziroh's head.

A moment later, Boss's bullet hit the grenade pouch on Fukaziroh's vest, right over her stomach.

"Yesss!" Fukaziroh cheered as a blue explosion engulfed her body.

*   *   *

That one blast quickly grew into a chain that spanned twenty meters.

The fourth-floor hallway was demolished, a huge hole punched in both floor and ceiling. Stores caught in the explosion were eradicated.

"Run, Leader!"

Kenta's body was blasted through the store behind him and blown into pieces, covered by bras and panties.

The discharge rattled through the third and fifth levels as well.

David felt the wind batter him as it came rushing down the stairs.

"Gah!"

He'd stood up at Kenta's warning, and the force of the explosion tossed him twenty meters to the west. His head struck a bench in the process, taking damage, but a huge chunk of rubble landed where he'd been standing, so if not for that, he would have died.

The surge of air similarly buffeted Llenn.

"Rrgh!"

Only when Fukaziroh had turned around did Llenn at last understand what the plan was, and she spun to hide behind the pillar. Debris flew like shrapnel in her direction.

While the rest of the building shook as though suffering an earthquake, Llenn noticed that Fukaziroh's HP gauge now read empty.

At the same time Fukaziroh sacrificed herself, a large shape was charging along the fifth floor's east side.

It was M, one-armed, stomping down the center of the carpeted walkway.

"Hng!"

The player with the Desert Eagle noticed him and took aim from forty meters.

"...?"

However, something about the way M was running straight for the man elicited confusion. Nevertheless, he trained his weapon on the approaching enemy. When the bullet circle was at its smallest, fitting perfectly within M's silhouette, he pulled the trigger.

Immediately after he fired, the shock wave from Fukaziroh's explosion hit him on the fifth floor. So the .50 AE bullet plunged straight on course toward M.

It struck him in the face, removing the few hit points he had left. His large body toppled forward.

Then a dark shadow leaped over his back.

"What?!"

As Fukaziroh's blast rocked the entire mall, pushing the track-suited man forward, he spied a woman dressed in black, charging right for him.

A photon sword glowed blue in her hand—a Muramasa F9.

"Hi-yaaaah!"

The rippling blast winds made it impossible for the player in the tracksuit to aim, allowing Pitohui to rush forward. Blue light glinted eerily off of the crazed woman's wild grin.

However, she was still thirty-five meters away.

Once the gales settled, the man tried to aim the huge muzzle at Pitohui.

"Dammit!"

Pitohui hurled something with her free hand. The man couldn't tell if it was a normal grenade or a plasma one, but he could tell that it was rolling toward him.

"Ah!"

He turned his Desert Eagle on a display window instead, blasting the glass open with a few shots before jumping inside.

The man in the blue tracksuit landed flat on his stomach, covered his ears, and opened his mouth, but there was no explosion.

"It was a trap!"

Instead of a grenade explosion, he heard the woman's quick steps growing louder and the sizzling of the air as her photon sword approached.

He hurried to his feet and scampered off, grabbing one of the store's displayed products as he went.

"Where's the little boys and girls who want to diiiiie?!" Pitohui growled, like a monster meant to scare children, a photon sword in one hand. With the other, she picked up the grenade she had just rolled, and she pulled the pin out with her mouth before tossing it into the store.

This time, the shrapnel grenade *did* explode.

However, the store interior was spacious enough that only a small part of it blew up. Pitohui hadn't expected to eliminate her target with the bomb anyway. Instead, she extinguished her photon sword and rolled nimbly into the smoking aftermath.

Then she ignited the pale blade of light again, just as a large object came flying toward her.

"Hya!" she cried, recognizing it was too big to be a grand grenade, and she slashed through it. It was a perfect, quick, straight cut, made possible by Pitohui's VR swordfighting experience going back to the beta test of *SAO*. The flying object was cleaved into two halves—which then exploded.

The force tossed Pitohui backward and knocked the photon sword from her hand. The blade even severed its owner's limb from the elbow down before it hit the floor. Pitohui's black-clothed left arm fell with a thud.

"Rgh!"

Was that a lucky or an unfortunate turn of events? If the sword had fallen a bit farther out, her arm would've been perfectly fine. Yet, if it had dropped any closer to her body, she would have died instantly.

The explosion hadn't come from a grenade. As proof of that, it wasn't black smoke that filled the air, but white water vapor.

"A steam explosion…?" Pitohui muttered, her hit points down

to 20 percent. Instantly, the interior of the shop was as foggy as an outdoor hot spring in the winter. Through the haze, she heard her enemy say, "Welcome to the water shop. I thought you might be thirsty."

Near Pitohui was a shelf that had toppled over from her grenade earlier. Lying on their sides were three- and four-gallon plastic bottles of water.

Some of them still held liquid, while others had burst from the shrapnel, spilling water onto the ground. The man had hurled one of the full four-gallon containers at Pitohui.

She had split it in two with her photon sword, also cutting through the water kept inside in the process.

"You haven't practiced enough with your lightsword if you don't even know what happens when it touches water," the unseen man in the blue tracksuit said.

Pitohui's brow wrinkled. "What do you mean? What about the Leidenfrost effect? And for that matter, what about the human body, which is mostly made of water?"

A steam explosion happened when a heated object made contact with water, instantly evaporating—and thus expanding—it with such force that it caused an explosion.

The Leidenfrost effect Pitohui had mentioned was a phenomenon by which water vapor covered the space between water and the heated object, preventing that heat from reaching the entirety of the liquid. It's the reason water dripped onto a hot frying pan doesn't immediately evaporate but maintains its shape.

Pitohui had assumed that a quick slice through water wouldn't cause a blast of steam. And all the human bodies she'd cut through with a photon sword had technically been full of water, too.

Her questions were perfectly reasonable, but the man avoided them. "Look, I don't know about all of that," he admitted. "You can ask the developers if you ever meet them. I hear they log in now and then to hear player opinions."

"I'll kill them before I ask."

"You'll have to leave SJ4 first, then," the man stated as he hurled another bottle that had to weigh at least thirty pounds at Pitohui's face.

"Don't mess with me!" she snarled—and punched it.

If she couldn't cut it, a good fist would do the job. A single right punch slammed the heavy projectile away, and she bolted in the direction it had come from.

There was a shelf in the way, several bottles resting on it. Pitohui smashed to one side using her thighs and hips, like a bull knocking over a matador who'd failed to dodge.

Through the steam, she finally spotted a player in a blue tracksuit trying to ready a Desert Eagle.

"Too late!"

"Ugh!"

The man fired. The Magnum bullet boomed across the store—but Pitohui was already between his gun and his face.

She was so close that she was practically hugging him. Pitohui pressed on his left toes with her foot and used one hand to push his face. He fell backward and landed flat on the floor.

"Gah!"

"Raaah!"

Pitohui stomped on the wrist connected to the hand clutching the Desert Eagle, then dropped into a quick crouch and slammed her other knee into his solar plexus.

"Gburfh!"

"Don't die yet," she instructed, reaching out with one arm to pull a toppled four-gallon bottle closer and popping the lid off with her thumb. Then she lifted the lip of the bottle over the man's mouth.

"'I thought you might be thirsty,'" she parroted. The mouth of the bottle stuck into his face through the fabric of his mask, sending water gushing out onto him.

"*Gobblubbublrble!*" he gasped, attempting to say something. She ignored it.

"Go on, drink up," Pitohui said, pushing the bottle down as hard as she could.

"Urbl! Gluk! Hagk!"

Gablunk, gablunk, gablunk, went the air bubbles sucked into the spout as its contents emptied into the man's mouth.

"Goblbobl! Gabluburbgublah!"

"Yes, yes! Of course! I understand you!"

"Gurhklkgurblurukgkbl!"

"On the weekend, too? Sounds like a very strict workplace."

"Gaggagaggagagl!"

"What? Chicken curry's your favorite?"

"Gulk..."

He went silent, falling into suffocation mode. For the following twenty seconds, until a DEAD tag appeared over his body, the man was unable to do anything but twitch under Pitohui's hands and feet.

All the while, Pitohui sang one of Franz Schubert's famous lullabies in a soft and perfect pitch. *"Schlafe, schlafe, holder, süßer Knabe, leise wiegt dich deiner Mutter Hand..."*

* * *

Moments before, just after Fukaziroh's tremendous explosion took out Kenta...

A large blast could cause retraction when it consumed all the air at its epicenter. In response, the surrounding gas rushed back inward to fill the void. This phenomenon was even more violent indoors, where air movement was limited.

The surge of retracted air coursed through the mall, buffeting tiny Llenn from her place behind a pillar.

"Aieee!"

"Uh-oh!" The heavier and stronger Boss grabbed Llenn to keep her steady. Though Boss's braids whipped in the wind, her body stood firm.

"Boss!"

"We've got to make use of the opportunity Fukaziroh gave us!"

"Yeah!"

The gale died down. Boss released Llenn and grabbed what Fukaziroh had left on the floor before she'd run off: the PTRD-41 Degtyaryov antitank rifle.

"What will you do with that?" asked Llenn, knowing the weapon was inert inside the mall. Boss answered with action. She rushed over to an electric cart that had been abandoned at the side of the hallway and jammed the gun's long barrel through the gap in the steering wheel.

The member of Fire's squad with the Kampfpistole was rocked by the explosion like everyone else, but his missing arm prevented him from keeping his balance, and he doubled over before falling to the floor.

"Dammit!" he spat. The air in the hallway was expelled from front to back, then surged from back to front. Only when it had calmed did he raise his head.

"Hnn!"

And that was when he saw an electric cart zooming straight toward him.

Without getting up, he used his one arm to aim the Kampfpistole—and promptly realized the vehicle coming his way had no passengers.

"What the…?"

In place of any people, there was a PTRD-41 antitank rifle thrust vertically into the driver's seat at the front of the cart.

Instantly and intuitively, the man understood that the long, heavy metal rod was jammed there to keep the steering wheel and accelerator in place.

The hallway was perfectly straight, so the unmanned cart came racing right at the man. Even so, avoiding such a thing was simple. The vehicle could only move straight forward. All the man with the Kampfpistole had to do was roll two meters to one side, and he'd be safe.

However, he remained where he was, even in the face of a cart advancing toward him at twenty-five miles per hour. The man couldn't see the girl in pink or the big woman with braids, but he knew they had to be behind the vehicle—assuming they hadn't just run away.

As long as he stayed put, they couldn't attack him. The cart was a shield protecting him from the enemy.

Once the vehicle was twenty meters away, the man had to roll to avoid being hit. He could have gone in either direction, but he chose to go right since he had no left arm. Naturally, as this was a game, the stump of his limb didn't hurt, but his instincts told him not to risk pressing his wound against the floor as he tumbled.

And that was precisely what Llenn had been counting on.

"Gotcha!" she cried in midair, pointing her Vorpal Bunnies at the man and firing.

"What?!" the man screamed, taking on shots as he continued to roll. If he stopped, he was dead. He had to keep going, keep moving until he reached a store on the right side of the hallway.

Amid his wildly rotating vision, he spied a small pink figure in the air. She was excitedly unloading her weapons on him.

Only ten meters separated the two. It was close enough that any pistol could hit its target.

How had she gotten so close?

Suddenly, the man in the tracksuit understood. The hint was the electric cart, which was trundling straight through the place where he had been standing previously, thanks to the PTRD-41 stuck into the driver's seat like a spear.

The little girl in pink had been running right behind the cart, going at full speed to match the vehicle's velocity. She was short enough that he couldn't see her with the thing in the way.

While he'd been distracted, she'd jumped high in the air for a better shooting angle.

"Ha! Not bad!" the man howled with delight. He slammed against the double doors of a storefront and roll-roll-rolled his way right into the place.

Llenn landed on her feet, barely seven meters from the open

doorway. She had loosed twelve rounds, so she stuck the grips of her pistols into her backpack for a reload.

It took only three seconds to do so, but that was enough time for the man to roll his way out of sight.

You're not getting away! Llenn couldn't allow him to escape and regain his other arm. She didn't have time to wait here for Boss to catch up.

Llenn held up the Vorpal Bunnies and charged through the entrance.

Above the doorway was a sign reading BASEBALL SHOP.

Indeed, what Llenn found inside was a business selling baseball supplies. The spacious and bright interior was full of neatly arranged shelves and wall racks full of gloves of different colors, finely stitched baseballs, large buckets for holding ice water, replica uniforms from famous big leaguers, colorful spiked cleats, and a long wooden bat being swung by a man with one arm.

"Eeesh!"

If Llenn hadn't pulled back with the maximum possible speed, she would never have heard the bat slicing through the air—because it would have split her skull first.

She'd been expecting gunshots. A blunt, close-range weapon had been the last thing on her mind. But now that she'd dodged it, the time was ripe for a counterattack.

Eat this, Llenn thought, aiming her .45-caliber pistols at the enemy player wearing a tracksuit.

She popped off three rounds with each gun so she didn't need to reload immediately. That was more than enough for an opponent this close.

How about that? she thought, certain of her victory. There was no way she could miss a target two meters away, but her confidence was quickly shattered by a bat that lanced into her stomach.

"Gerf!" was the sound the air made shooting out of Llenn's lungs.

Like a fencer, the man jutted his right side forward and jabbed at Llenn's chest with the end of the bat. Llenn was so light that the blow shoved her three meters back and right out of the store. It did enough damage that the game declared her ribs broken, and she immediately lost 30 percent of her HP. It was only her sheer tenacity that kept the Vorpal Bunnies in her hands.

Llenn fell onto her back, her pack propping her torso up.

"Why you—!"

Llenn fired her remaining six shots, nearly all of which struck the man. His body glowed with bullet effects. Even one of the cheeks beneath his mask shone a brilliant red.

Unfortunately, he still wasn't dead.

About four meters ahead of Llenn, the man slowly brought the bat up to rest on his shoulder.

"Whew... Both out of bullets, I assume," he said, staring at the Vorpal Bunnies in Llenn's hands; their slides were retracted.

"You're...so...*tough*!" she gasped.

While only armed with handguns, Llenn had still put several rounds into her opponent's body and at least one into his face. Yet he was still alive. What was going on with his HP? He had to be even hardier than M and Pitohui.

"Oh, I've barely got anything left. You could probably kill me with a forehead flick," he admitted, his mask stretching and twisting as he spoke. With the sunglasses, his face was completely hidden, but Llenn got the sense that he was smiling.

"My whole body is numb, and it's hard to move. It's like getting a really intense acupuncture session. But I can still do enough to split your head in half. I mean, the whole reason we're in this Squad Jam is to kill you, after all."

Peh! Llenn thought. She let her disdain carry over into a spoken insult as well. "That's right! As a hired gun, you won't get Fire's money unless you win!"

But the man reacted in a way she hadn't been expecting at all.

"Money...? Shut up!" he yelled. "Shut up! I don't need that! I'm fighting for the company president! I'm fighting for his romance! We all are! We're battling for his future!"

There was real anger in his voice. Given that he called Fire "the company president," he seemed to have revealed that he was an employee who worked for the man.

His reason for participating wasn't cash; he had entered the Squad Jam for the sake of Fire Nishiyamada.

Llenn paused, taken aback, and the man did not miss his chance.

Rather than charging, he simply sauntered toward her. It was so relaxed that she briefly failed to realize he was doing it.

"Crap!" Llenn yelped, reaching behind her back to reload. However, the moment she'd wasted could not be made up. *I won't be ready in time!*

The tracksuit player picked up speed, and he swung the wooden bat with his one hand.

The Vorpal Bunnies finished reloading, and Llenn quickly pulled them free, pushing down the slide stops. Sadly, she had done so just in time to see that the end of the wooden bludgeon was coming straight for her skull.

Oh, I'm dead. Dead, deader, deadest.

Surprisingly, the bat vanished.

The man brought his arm down with an empty hand. His fist nearly grazed Llenn's face as it flew by.

"Huh?"

The two locked eyes, though one pair was behind a set of sunglasses.

Llenn brought up her .45-caliber weapons. "Sorry!" Then fired them both into the man's face. Two shots to the brain *were* at last enough to kill the man. The DEAD tag appeared immediately.

He fell limply to the ground. As she backed away, Llenn said, "Thanks for saving me, Boss..."

Twenty meters away, to Llenn's left, her friend was in firing position with a Strizh pistol. She'd hit the bat and knocked it out of the enemy's hands while he was swinging. That was some serious aim.

"No problem. That was pretty sloppy of you, though. What were you talking about?" asked Boss.

Llenn couldn't bring herself to explain.

"Gotcha!"

David, having been saved by Kenta's last words, dashed forward while firing an M9-A1 pistol. The 9 mm bullets whizzed down the open mall walkway, struck Boss's ankle, and knocked her to the ground.

"Rrgh!"

David sent a few more shots in Boss's direction, then changed his focus to Llenn, twenty meters farther away.

"Yeep!" The lines gleamed around Llenn. She shrank away and ducked down, allowing the armor plates in her backpack to guard her from the projectiles.

David hugged a pillar five meters away from Boss, ignoring the large, prone woman. He was after Llenn now.

"Eek! Eek!" With each round that hit her back, Llenn shook a little. She shrank as small as she possibly could for maximum protection.

"Tsk! That damn backpack!" David cursed, even though Boss was collapsed on the ground just five meters away, groaning and nearly dead.

He pressed himself against a pillar for steadiness, aiming carefully at Llenn's tiny target twenty-five meters away and firing one shot at a time.

"Hya! Hyaii!" Each one hit Llenn's back, eliciting a terrified response. Her Vorpal Bunnies were still loaded, but exposing herself by turning around to return fire seemed ill-advised. If she tried to stand up and run, he'd hit her.

David continued shooting from his place of cover. He was determined to finish Llenn off while he had the chance. He didn't want her getting away.

At last, one bullet grazed the backpack and hit Llenn's foot, creating a glowing damage mark on her boot.

"Eep!" She trembled, giving David the opening to strike her shoulder.

Llenn's hit points were down below a third now. She screamed, "Aaaah! Someone help!"

"You got it!"

"Huh?"

David had emptied his M9-A1, so he tossed it aside and drew a Beretta APX from his midriff.

He leaped out from behind the pillar, intending to close the gap with Llenn and finish her off in one bold stroke.

Then Pitohui dropped in front of him.

David was so taken aback that he thought an elevator had suddenly materialized out of nowhere.

Pitohui landed with a thud on the fourth floor, riding on a round piece of flooring, right before David's eyes as he ran.

"Perfect!" she screamed, and she thrust the photon sword with her remaining arm.

At this range, the power of the photon sword was absolute. One or two 9 mm bullets wouldn't kill his opponent, and there was no way to stop her from running him through and killing him.

Instead, David attempted to use the greatest firepower he owned.

"You've got nothing!"

It all happened in the span of a few seconds. David released the APX in his left hand but kept his index finger inside the trigger guard, where it pressed against the trigger and pushed the gun forward with his right hand.

That dragged his index finger against the trigger, firing the gun. The recoil was more powerful than the force of his arm, pushing it backward. In doing so, it returned the trigger to neutral, resetting the weapon so it could be used again.

Because his right hand was holding the gun forward, the pressure on the trigger from his finger returned immediately, firing it again, causing the recoil to jump the gun backward—and this repetition resulted in ultra-fast shooting.

This technique was known as bump-firing, the fastest method of using a semiautomatic weapon. It was much swifter than pulling the trigger regularly, allowing you to fire quickly and wildly like with a fully automatic gun.

Pitohui's lightsword pierced through to the back of David's chest right as his shots struck hers.

"Gahk!" "Aaah!"

They exhaled together and went still, almost as though locked in an embrace.

"You've gotten so much tougher," Pitohui murmured as she died.

"It's all thanks to a certain…someone," replied David as he perished.

Pitohui grinned. "If I knew you were going to get this strong…I might have actually fallen in love with you…Daviiid…" She toppled backward.

David crumpled to his knees and muttered, "That's nice to hear…"

They were going to meet their end together.

"Oh, I'm joking, of course. Don't take it seriously," Pitohui appended.

"Why, you bi—"

He never got to finish that sentence.

"Oh…"

When the shooting stopped, Llenn hesitantly turned around and took in the aftermath.

Just thirty feet away, lying dead and faceup on the ground, were Pitohui and David.

There was a circular chunk of floor between them, and up above, a hole in the ceiling gave a tiny view of the fifth level.

Pitohui had cut a hole for herself and fallen through it down onto the fourth floor, right in front of David. Then they had fought and killed each other.

The photon sword rolled out of Pitohui's hand. It was still ignited. Where it touched the floor, it burned away the carpet and melted through the material underneath, sinking like a hot knife through butter.

Lower and lower it sank until it had cut through the ground and disappeared. It would probably continue to descend into the earth until it ran out of power.

"Aw…Pito…"

There were five *X* marks next to the names of Llenn's squadmates on the list in the upper left corner of her vision.

Clarence, Shirley, Fukaziroh, M, Pitohui—everybody was dead. Only Llenn remained now—a miracle considering her HP was only at 30 percent.

"I need to apologize to Pitohui," said Boss.

She slowly pushed herself upright on numbed legs. She was glowing here and there because of David, but she was alive. Her natural defense was no joke.

Boss gazed at Pitohui with wonder and remarked, "So she wasn't actually doing this for Fire at all… She wouldn't have come to your rescue otherwise…"

Boss was right. Pitohui had been up on the fifth floor because she'd been battling some other blue-tracksuited player up there, no doubt.

"True… I should say sorry for suspecting her, too," replied Llenn, standing up and walking over to Boss. "What's your HP situation?"

"Barely ten percent. I only survived because a few of his shots hit my magazine pouch."

"Great! You're a lucky girl!" said Llenn, reaching out.

"Not as lucky as you," remarked Boss, taking the offered hand. She started to rise but ended up dragging Llenn down and flopping backward.

"Gyack!"

"Oops, sorry."

"You're so heavy! God, you're huge!"

"My bad, shrimp."

The pair broke out into spontaneous laughter.

"Pfft! Ah-ha-ha-ha-ha-ha-ha! Ah-ha-ha-ha!"

"Bwa-ha-ha-ha-ha-ha-ha-ha-ha-ha!"

For a good thirty seconds, they sat there, roaring with laughter, one's laugh deep and one's high-pitched, shot full of holes, in the middle of a shopping mall littered with dead bodies.

Once they'd had their fill of giggles, Llenn popped up to her feet. "Okay! Time for us to fight, I think!"

"I'm grateful for the offer—but if you lose, what happens to your deal with Fire?" Boss asked, lifting herself now that the feeling in her legs had returned. She reloaded her Strizh, checking for enemies, but they were alone.

Secretly grateful that Boss was still concerned for her well-being, Llenn smirked and answered, "I don't have to worry about that if I win! But if it comes to that, I'll just pretend I have no idea what he's talking about!"

"Ooh, you're bad… Well, in that case…"

"Let's do this! Where should we go, and how should we do it?" Llenn asked, demonstrating that she was ready to go, whatever the situation.

Boss grinned back at her. In a frightening way. "Right here. Right now."

"Okay!"

They were standing two meters apart.

Boss clicked the Strizh into the holster on her hip.

Llenn refreshed the ammo in the Vorpal Bunnies, then placed them in her thigh holsters without switching on the safeties.

Making full use of the spacious hall, Boss stepped backward until they were at a comfortable distance. Ten meters felt appropriate for a shootout.

"Let's do this duel style, then. I saw this once in the BoB prelims, and I've always wanted to try it out."

Boss took a spare magazine out of her ammo pouch.

"I'll throw this up in the air, and when it hits the ground, we draw. Deal?"

"Deal. Just like in a Western. One shot will seal our fate."

"Yeah."

Llenn had 30 percent of her hit points remaining, and Boss had 10. But their respective levels of physical stamina were vastly different. If anything, Llenn probably had less survivability in terms of how much damage she could take. However, neither of them expected to live past the first hit.

One might think Llenn had the advantage, being so small and fast, but Boss was not slow in the least, either, and she was more comfortable with a pistol. Today was the first time Llenn had ever used handguns in a serious fight.

Llenn thought that put them on an equal footing, and she understood why Boss had suggested this as a way of having their contest. There was no reason for her to decline.

She set her backpack on the ground. Not to make herself lighter, but because having bulletproof armor on her back would be unfair.

That meant she couldn't reload anymore, so she would only have six bullets in each Vorpal Bunny. If she couldn't finish the fight within twelve shots, she would be dead.

Llenn dropped her center of gravity and smacked the sides of her thigh holsters. There were no straps keeping the guns snug. She just had to pull them out.

Her hands waited, right next to the holsters, almost touching the grips.

"Ready whenever you are."

Boss kept her right hand next to its holster, too.

"Here we go."

She chucked the magazine underhand with her other hand, high into the air.

Boss's physical coordination from being on the gymnastics team was no joke; the magazine rose until it nearly touched the ceiling, then began to fall perfectly placed between the two combatants.

Gleefully, Llenn stared at Boss.

Gleefully, Boss stared at Llenn.

The magazine began to fall, slowly rotating…

Thud!

It landed with a muffled sound on the carpet.

Boss whipped the Strizh out of its holster with tremendous speed, just as Llenn leaped into the air.

Llenn's jump rotated her to the right, during which time she drew the Vorpal Bunnies. Amid her turn, when her body was sideways and offering the smallest possible target, Boss's 9 mm bullet passed in front of her chest.

And before her spin had finished, Llenn opened fire with both hands.

The two bullets flew straight, one of them passing over Boss's shoulder.

"Gah!"

The second struck her in the forehead and lodged itself in her brain.

"Nice…ly…done…"

With those last words, Boss toppled backward, lifeless. Her large body fell to the floor of the mall thoroughfare, thudding heavily.

"…Ahhh!" Llenn gasped, landing with her pistols at the ready. "It…worked…"

Llenn had gambled on a long shot.

She'd assumed that Boss would draw and fire first. So she'd considered how to dodge—or at least, what gave her the best chance of evading: a rotating jump.

If she chose the usual crouch or sideways lean, Boss would react accordingly. However, when faced with a high-speed rotation, she would pull the trigger the moment she saw what was happening.

It was entirely possible that Boss's bullet could have hit Llenn anyway. This had been a pure coin toss with no room for a third possibility. One of them was going to win, and the other had to lose.

And Llenn had come out on top.

"You did it! Way to go, Llenn!" cheered one of the Vor-chans.

"Even though she was this close to her target, one of our shots still missed!" chided the other.

Llenn stuck them back in their holsters.

"Mrph!" "Mrph!"

Then she picked up the backpack and put it back on, fastening the straps.

"No point letting your guard down after a victory. Not that I'm victorious yet… First, I have to find Fire…," Llenn muttered to herself, alone in the hallway.

Until a man's voice replied, *"No, you've won this. You and your friends."*

"Ah!"

Llenn spun around, drawing her guns, pointing them in the direction from which she'd heard the voice. It was lightning fast.

"Wha…?"

The only thing she saw was the body of the man in the blue tracksuit.

"I'm talking on the wireless," informed the voice. It was coming from the comm on the dead body. She realized that it was Fire's voice.

"Fire! Have you been listening to all of this?!"

It clicked into place. There was a communication device with a speaker attached at the dead man's side, transmitting his voice and status to Fire at all times. Now it was relaying Fire's words the other way.

That meant that he must have heard the conversation where she asked how much money Fire's lackeys were getting paid, and her insistence that she'd just pretend she had no idea about the deal.

The eavesdropping freak! Llenn fumed. But maybe declaring that she wouldn't honor the deal had been worse than what he'd done in this case.

"Fire! You're the only one left! And I'm the only one here! Where are you?! I'm going to rush over there and beat you senseless!" Llenn shouted at the wireless device. She was thinking, *But what if Fire's set up a trap wherever he says to go?*

Llenn had absolutely no idea what kind of weapon he had or how he would fight.

Fire had to be an amateur when it came to combat, but given how his teammates were decked out with fancy pistols, he must have armed himself to the teeth, too. He'd probably spent tons of actual money to buy himself all the handguns and armor he'd need.

Llenn had no idea if she could beat him on just 30 percent of her hit points, but it didn't matter; she was going.

She had to for the sake of her teammates who had fought and died to protect her.

"I'm in the courtyard. Right in front of the merry-go-round. Can you come down?"

"I'll be there in three seconds!"

That may have been an overly optimistic appraisal.

*　　*　　*

Even at Llenn's fastest, it took thirty seconds to descend from the fourth floor to the mall's inner area.

She raced into the open area only to find it occupied by a theme park so sizable that Llenn didn't feel like she was indoors anymore. All around were rides and attractions that sat silent and still.

Eventually, Llenn came upon the merry-go-round.

The paint was chipped and peeling, but what was there was brightly colored. The horses ran in concentric circles around the center underneath a fancy, cake-like canopy. Poles were stuck straight as ramrods through their torsos.

Standing in front of the ride, leaning against the handrail, was a tall, thin man.

"Fire!"

There didn't seem to be any traps around, and Fire wasn't armed, but Llenn was cautious all the same. She rushed over, stopping about thirty-five meters away, and pointed both of her pistols at her long-sought enemy.

"Here I am! Let's fight!" she said happily, giving him a huge smile.

Fire's handsome face did not twist into anger or break into a grin of its own. He simply stated, "What did I just say to you? You won. Your side wins."

Is this a ploy? Llenn wondered. She couldn't sense anyone else around. The only thing occupying the space between him and her was tile flooring. There was no place any grenades could have been set up to explode.

Still, Llenn remained on alert, ready for anything. Her eyes scanned all around her as she paced slowly closer to Fire. Once she was ten meters away, where there was no way she could miss, she said, "You're still here! Why won't you fight? Why aren't you trying to get me?"

Fire extended his long arms, opening them before him. "I have no way to do so. I don't have any weapons."

Even Llenn was surprised at that. "Um…what?"

"I hate tools meant for causing harm, like guns and knives. Even here in the game, I would never choose to carry them. So I trusted my team and waited. They fought very hard for me. But they weren't quite up to the task."

"……"

Llenn was speechless.

She'd prepared herself for Fire to be the last boss, for him to pull out some wild, outlandish, and powerful weapon. But he had nothing.

"If you could kill someone with surprise, I'd be dead right now," she admitted.

She prepared herself to shoot him. She took aim, touched the triggers, and fit the bullet circles over Fire's body when they appeared.

"But there is one thing I'd like to say now, while I have the chance," Fire added, staring at the bullet lines coming from Llenn's weapons.

"Your last wish? I'm listening." Llenn did not pull the triggers yet.

"I'm sorry for making fun of full-dive VR games and *GGO*. I take those words back. Go on and mock those statements as the words of a person ignorant of what these games are."

If surprise could kill, Llenn would have died twice now.

Eyes wide, she said, "Okay…I accept your apology."

"I'm glad. I feel better getting that off my chest. If there was anything I wanted to avoid, it was perishing without having said that. Well, go on and shoot me. You've won our bet."

"……"

For three seconds, Llenn considered what to say, whether to cuss Fire out or laud him for his effort in the fight.

But she couldn't think of anything.

So in the end, she decided to have an actual conversation with Fire. There was no worry of being overheard here.

After Fire's apology, there was one thing Llenn wanted to say to him. It was likely to be the last time they ever met, so she might as well have it out here.

She stared Fire in the eye and opened her mouth.

"So, um…"

A horse appeared behind Fire and opened its mouth wide.

A monster! You idiot, this is because you waited here for too long!

Foolishly, Fire had been holed up by the carousel longer than five minutes. And as a result, an equine monster had spawned. For a moment, Llenn almost thought one of the merry-go-round animals had started moving, but that was not the case—the game had simply created a similar-looking, if distasteful, enemy.

"Shit!" Llenn swore, and she fired.

Two bullets hit the horse's face, blasting it into smithereens. Fire hadn't noticed it, and he looked somewhat confused.

Naturally, this called down more monsters.

Shlurp...

A rustling sound in the previously silent center of the mall drew her attention. There were living things nearby.

Many of them.

"Ugh!"

The creatures were oozing up out of the tiles around them.

They had human fingers that came out in bunches, then joined together at the base to form hands, extending into arms, and eventually, a face.

Gross!

Zombies, creatures in human form, wearing human clothes, but with disfigured, ashen-gray skin, milky-white eyes, and unsteady legs that wobbled in a way that suggested no working core muscles.

Presumably, the game was spitting out humanoid enemies because this was a shopping mall where people had once gathered.

"Gross! What terrible taste! Whoever came up with this idea, show yourself!"

Llenn felt genuine disgust at the line of thinking that had led to this. It had to have been that shitty writer.

Bang!

Before the rotting hand coming up from the ground could grab Llenn's leg, she shot it. Each monster died from a single pistol bullet; the problem was their numbers.

"What's this? What a sight," remarked Fire, watching the dead rising from the ground where he stood at the merry-go-round.

"What are you doing?! Run!" Llenn yelled at him.

"Oh, the contest is already over. You're the one who should be running."

"Dammit!"

Llenn's guns blazed. She popped a few shots into the head of a zombie that appeared between her and Fire. When the Vorpal Bunnies ran out of ammo, she reached behind her back and chunked new magazines in, then resumed shooting.

Damn it aaaall! What am I doing?! Llenn thought, moving closer to Fire as she shot the monsters. The Vor-chans spoke to her, urging her on.

"C'mon, what's wrong with this? You wanted more action; let's give them some."

"You've still got plenty of bullets. Let us roar!"

Llenn snapped back, "I know! I am! You bastaaards!"

The gleam in her eyes was turning dangerous.

"I'll kill every last one of you!"

Llenn's right-hand shot blew off half the rotting face of a young zombie. Her left went through the throat of a middle-aged monster and struck the chest of a young woman behind it. When that female monster wobbled, Llenn broke into a run, weaving between the creatures and handily finishing the job with another shot.

"Whew!"

However, there was no time to rest, as Llenn was immediately surrounded by a wealthy family who had come to the mall to shop—the grandpa, grandma, dad, mom, middle-school daughter, all zombies.

"Yaaaah!"

The first thing she did was shoot the bearded grandpa with two bullets to the face, one from each gun. Then she ducked, crossed her hands, and blasted the hearts out of the grandma and daughter.

When the father came rushing straight toward her, she kicked him in the chest with both feet, using the recoil to spin toward the mother and smashing her face with the side of a Vorpal Bunny. The woman's rotting jaw flew off her skull as a mass of flesh.

"*Urgargargargar!*" she grunted through her mangled mouth, not vanquished yet.

"You shut up."

Llenn jammed her left Vorpal Bunny into the empty space where the jaw had been and pulled the trigger. It blew off the back of the head, which slumped over the front part of her gun.

Then she rotated on her heel and blasted the brains out of the risen father.

Dammit! There are too many!

Zombies were weak enemies, but dealing with the same amount as the entire team had earlier was a huge challenge.

Thankfully, the Vor-chans were rooting her on. *"Get 'em! Get 'em! Shoot!"*

"That's our Llenn!"

"Thanks!" their owner answered. She could keep going.

Her right pistol ran out of bullets, so she reloaded it while blasting away with her left. Then that one ran empty and needed to be refilled. Llenn kicked over a few zombies, but then a horse monster approached.

"Tch!"

Llenn jumped sideways, taking herself out of the path of the wild stallion so she could pump a few bullets into the easy target that was its hefty rear as it rushed by.

Now there were more typical monsters among the zombies. A leopard-like creature snuck through the undead and pounced at Llenn, swiping with its front claws.

"Gah!" It caught Llenn's backpack and threw her spinning to the ground. Thankfully, it wasn't rough enough to cause actual damage. Less fortunate was that the side of the backpack was torn, and the magazines stacked inside came spilling out.

"Shit!" Llenn's wonderful reloading apparatus was destroyed. She spun around and blasted the leopard's face. "Take that!"

Then she told her empty left Vorpal Bunny, *"Sorry, it has to be one of you!"* and threw it aside.

"No faaaaair!" it screamed.

She yanked off the torn backpack, decided to make camp

where the magazines had spilled across the tiles, and blasted at the approaching zombies with just the one remaining handgun.

She fired straight ahead, she fired right, she fired behind, and she fired left.

The one saving grace of this experience was that they were the good old-fashioned "slow zombies." They shuffled and plodded toward her, faces exposed.

"Yah! Hey! Bam! Daa!"

Blam, blam, blam, blam.

The .45-caliber lead bullets burst through their targets. When Llenn ran out of ammunition, she just crouched, grabbed a mag off the ground, and loaded it into the gun manually.

Then she glanced over at Fire. He was still lounging in front of the merry-go-round.

The zombies weren't attacking him at all. He was like a telephone pole, an inert part of the background, and they just walked right past him.

Why? Oh! Because he doesn't have a weapon, Llenn realized quickly.

As long as you defeated the scout without shooting it, more wouldn't spawn. And the monsters would not attack any player who wasn't holding a weapon.

Whoever had designed the system had probably meant it to be a lifesaving measure for a character who had lost their weapons in battle. They wouldn't have foreseen that any player would enter the event without one in the first place.

In other words, the monsters would keep attacking Llenn and only Llenn, and if she died, she would lose.

This is fun! she decided, suddenly surging with energy.

Fire's declaration that the competition was over had felt anticlimactic, so Llenn made this her new contest.

If she could beat all the spawning monsters, she would win.

That was it. She had issued her judgment.

Ba-ba-blam!

She took out a series of zombies standing side by side with three quick shots and flashed Fire a sharp grin.

She fought for what had to be around a minute and a half.

Time lost meaning as a concept, and nearly all the magazines at her feet were gone when the horde of zombies slowed down to a trickle. While spawns were large, they had limits. The few enemies left had to be the last ones.

"Rrrah!"

Blam! Llenn sent a tourist zombie with an SLR camera around its neck to Hell.

"Uryaa!"

Blam! Llenn shot a little girl in a dress right through the teddy bear she was holding.

Then she was out of ammo.

"Hey, reload me. If you don't, I'm just a pink paperweight," said Vor-chan.

"There're none left!" Llenn exclaimed, holding an empty magazine. The next one she tried was also vacant. There wasn't a single golden glint of bullets anywhere around her.

Troublingly, there *were* eight groaning zombies left, shambling toward her. From a distance of four meters, they encircled her. There was no escape.

Police!

However, Llenn spotted a familiar navy-blue uniform on one of the zombies. There was a police belt around its waist with cuffs and a baton—and a holster.

"Yah!"

She threw Vor-chan at the zombie.

"Aaah, what was that for?!"

The Vorpal Bunny struck the police zombie in the face, knocking it back. Llenn leaped at the creature, reaching for the holster on its right hip.

She pulled out the friend of the American police officer, a Glock 17.

Any gun found in *GGO* could be used. Llenn pulled back,

switching the gun to her dominant hand, then pointing it at the police officer's stomach and pulling the trigger.

Click.

It only made a tiny sound and did not fire. The primer was too old to ignite.

"Dahh! You don't have to be *that* realistic!" Llenn groaned before hurling the worthless weapon at its owner's face.

Now Llenn had no firearms. The zombies continued to advance, step after step. Escape seemed unlikely.

"Heh!" she chuckled. There was one more weapon tucked under her backpack and behind her waist; she reached for it. The familiar texture of the grip met her fingertips.

"Here we go, Kni-chan Number Two!" Llenn exclaimed, pulling out the combat knife.

"Ready and raring to go! Ahhh, Miss Llenn, I feared that I might not have the chance to see combat today!"

Fire watched the action all the while, still leaning against the carousel.

Llenn advanced on the police officer zombie first, slicing open its windpipe. Before the monster even disappeared, Llenn was faced with a boy zombie holding a bag of popcorn. No sooner had she sped past it than its little head toppled to the ground.

A middle-aged zombie came lunging at her with both hands, but Llenn grunted and moved like lightning, leaving an afterimage.

The monster's hand fell to the ground, followed by an arm. However, the woman still had teeth for biting, so Llenn turned the knife sideways and stabbed the creature's heart through the ribs.

"Five to go!"

A zombie dressed in a fast-food uniform kicked something. The object slid cleanly over the tile floor and tapped Fire's boot—*clunk.*

It was a pink pistol with the slide extended.

"......"

He crouched and reached for it.

* * *

"Three more!" she cried after slicing open the stomach of the fast-food zombie. Then she paused for a second. "Huh?"

Two of the remaining zombies—a woman in a sexy red dress and a fat man in a slobby T-shirt, like guests at a party of some kind—were walking toward Fire.

"Why?!"

Without missing its chance, the third zombie fell over on top of Llenn. "Ah!"

The undead man in a suit squashed her against the tile floor, opened its mouth wide, and tried to bite her.

"Ooogh..."

"Hey!" Llenn shouted, and she stuck the tip of the knife into the monster's neck. Then she extended her arm into a full swing, bisecting the zombie's face.

Llenn fell back to the floor and saw, upside down, two zombies not three meters away from Fire.

He was utterly still, as though waiting for them to kill him. In his hand was one of the Vorpal Bunnies Llenn had tossed aside.

Loaded or not, a gun was a gun. Pink or not, a gun was a gun. The monsters had reacted the moment Fire had picked it up, and they'd locked on to their new target.

"That idiot!" Llenn snapped, and she sprang to her feet, rushing for the zombies. They were five meters away.

The woman zombie was slightly faster than the other and reached out for Fire, leaning forward. Though Llenn couldn't see for certain from her angle, she was sure the creature had its mouth open.

Realizing that there wasn't enough time to rush over, Llenn said, "Ugh, fine! Take this!" and flipped the knife into a traditional grip before throwing it.

It stuck into the spine of the lady zombie, which fell to the ground right before Fire. But that did nothing to stop the other one, the fat older man.

"Raaaah!"

Llenn jumped forward. She had no weapons, but that didn't matter.

She could still fight. She would keep going until she was dead.

It was how she'd beaten Pitohui in SJ2.

She took a few quick strides and pounced, latching herself on to the body of the big zombie and sinking her teeth into its neck.

"Arrrrgh!"

Shrnk! Llenn's mouth filled with the texture of throat skin, and a dull pain ran through her left eye.

The old zombie's thick thumb tried to fight back against the little pink combatant in its own way, lodging itself in Llenn's eye. It pushed harder, working its way into her skull.

Crap! Aware of how much of her HP was being taken away, Llenn bit down even more fiercely, until—*crunch.*

She bit through the zombie's carotid artery.

The old man turned into glowing particles and vanished, body and thumb and all.

Llenn fell to the ground on her back. "Bwegh!"

She stared up at Fire, who stood tall over her. Her hit points kept dropping. The damage was severe enough that it was clear the zombie had not hurt just her eye, but the brain behind it as well.

She was already under 10 percent, and when it became clear that death was unavoidable, she said, "Fire, I—"

But she could not finish that final thought of hers.

Her one working eye remained open to the last moment—but all she saw was the cold, quiet figure of Fire holding the Vorpal Bunny before everything vanished.

Two screens presented the action to the audience in the bar.

On one they saw Llenn dying, right next to a tall man in a tracksuit operating a game window. Then he fell limp on the spot. A tag reading RESIGNED appeared over his character.

On the other screen, three men wearing armor and masks were running desperately down the highway while a storm of bullets assailed them.

They were from V2HG, coming all the way around the broken lake to rescue Fire, but they died without ever reaching the shopping mall.

CONGRATULATIONS!! WINNER: ZEMAL!!

The huge, shining message appeared in the sky with a bit of musical fanfare.

Five men with machine guns connected to their backpacks by metal rails—and one woman—stood on the highway.

The men were standing in the middle of the road, guns blazing, while Vivi called out, "Congratulations! We won it all!"

They lowered their weapons, smoke rising from the barrels, and slowly turned around to face her.

To Vivi's surprise, however, her squadmates didn't look pleased.

Tomtom, the man in the bandana, looked nearly ready to cry. "Um, Goddess, if you'll forgive me for speaking frankly…"

"What?"

"Is this the end of the game?"

"Of course!"

"Then…that makes us very sad."

"Why? Even though you won?"

"That's true, but if we're honest, we really wanted to shoot some more… We wanted to shoot like crazy…"

"Huh? So you didn't want to win?"

"Er, well, surviving as long as possible allowed us to fire for the longest amount of time, so that part's good, but…"

Vivi looked at the mournful Tomtom and the rest of the group, then murmured, "Hmm, maybe I picked the wrong strategy…"

Time of game: two hours and fifty-eight minutes.

Fourth Squad Jam: complete.

Winning team: ZEMAL.

Total shots fired: 234,901.

CHAPTER 23
The Melancholy of Karen

CHAPTER 23
The Melancholy of Karen

Saturday, August 29th, 2026.

Mai Kirishima was on her way to work.

She left her apartment at eight thirty in the morning and enjoyed a drive flanked by greenery and watched from above by blue skies.

Her job as a nature guide did not have "weekends." That was especially true during summer vacation.

Of course, here on the great northern island of Hokkaido, the short summer holiday had already ended. But many on the main island of Japan still had time off and visited Hokkaido.

Mai was a twenty-four-year-old Japanese woman in real life and looked nothing at all like Shirley, her *GGO* avatar.

For one thing, she was short: about five foot one. Her *GGO* character was taller than the average Japanese height, but that was not a surprise at all. Karen and Miyu were exceptions to the rule.

Unsurprisingly, her hair was black and long enough to drape down her shoulders. It was currently tied into a ponytail. Her facial features resembled Shirley's. They gave her an air that did not mesh with cute clothes. Depending on how complimentary you wanted to be, she was either bold or feral.

For clothes, she wore a famous brand of outdoor jeans and a red flannel shirt under a bright-orange vest with plenty of pockets. On her head rested a waterproof nylon baseball cap.

Mai always wore the same thing when working as a summer nature guide; it was practically a uniform for her. The vest was worn out and starting to fray, so she'd been considering purchasing a new one.

Three days had passed since the fourth Squad Jam.

Shirley had gone through quite an adventure that day, but in the end, she had failed to take down Pitohui.

That was frustrating all on its own, but after reflecting upon her battle, she felt that she had enjoyed a fair amount of action and killed a satisfactory number of enemies over those three hours.

She'd had fun. That was nothing to be upset about.

Mai remembered what Clarence had said during the game: "Don't worry so much, Shirley! You gotta take it easy and enjoy your life… Your gaming life, I mean!"

Then, because she had her hands on the wheel, she recalled all the crazy driving she'd done in the Humvee and chuckled. "Hee-hee!"

She took the next curve with more confidence than she would have three days ago. Still within the realm of safe driving, of course.

Smiling serenely, she said to herself, "I'll still have plenty of chances to kill her."

Thankfully, there were no police officers around to hear her.

Mai hadn't spoken a word to Clarence since then.

When she returned from SJ4, the other girl had already logged out. So the next time she saw her in *GGO*, she had something to say. "We can meet in person, if you want."

When August ended, Mai would get a late summer vacation of her own. She was willing to pay a visit to Clarence, no matter where in Japan she lived—even if it was the distant islands of Okinawa—and do a little sightseeing there as well.

Mai wanted to tell her, "I'm taking it easy and enjoying the game."

As she pondered the idea, Mai arrived at her workplace for the day, a local farm open to tourists. It was time to clock in.

The time wasn't quite nine o'clock yet. She parked her car and went to say hello at the office.

Today, her job was to help get a visitor from Tokyo onto a horse, then lead the way on horseback as they enjoyed a gentle walk through the great outdoors.

She got tasks like this frequently during the summer holiday, although the patrons were usually entire families, so this was a bit different.

A married couple ran the farm. The wife was in her forties. She explained the visitor's situation to Mai.

Today's guest, arriving around ten o'clock, was a girl from Tokyo in her third year of middle school, although she was not currently attending. She'd never been comfortable in classes, and by fourth grade, she was unable to go anymore. Since then, she'd been homeschooled. Worried that she would withdraw from her social life, her parents had convinced her to come to the farm.

Therefore, the woman explained that Mai would have to be very careful with how she acted around the girl to ensure her sensitive feelings weren't hurt. It sounded difficult.

Mai had never refused to go to school. To her, it was a great place where she was able to see the friends and teachers she liked every day. She couldn't relate at all.

Perhaps that showed on Mai's face, as the woman reassured her, "You should be fine just being yourself. You're very gentle, Mai."

"Huh? I am?"

"Of course. Haven't I said that before? Especially lately. All the rough edges have been sanded off. Why is that? Is it because of that *Gun Gale Online*–something game everyone plays? Are you nice in the game, too?"

Because she didn't play, the woman did not know that in *GGO*, Shirley was more of a hellish demon. She shot and killed people and ran over them with big cars.

"Um, I don't know...," Mai replied, trying not to answer. She wondered if feeling satisfied from the game made her more relaxed in real life. "Oh, and by the way, you got all the words of the title right."

* * *

By ten o'clock, Mai had prepared the horses and supplies, and a rental car drove up carrying a woman and a girl about Mai's height.

The girl's black hair ran down to the center of her back, her skin was pale to a medically troubling degree, and she had gaunt and unhealthy features—er, scratch that. She was "as cute as a doll," as they say. She wore a flower-pattern dress.

While the woman running the farm greeted the two warmly, Mai watched the child. Their eyes met, and the girl looked away promptly.

Hmmm, can we even hold a conversation? It's kind of hard to do this if she doesn't say a word...

Still, work was work. As always, Mai took the visitors to the office first.

To Mai's surprise, the fifteen-year-old girl, named Ai Onoda, had no trouble speaking.

While Mai was taking the reins in helping her change into riding overalls and practice getting on the horse, the girl only said three words: *yes*, *no*, and *okay*.

However, once they got out into the pasture, she commented on things just like every other kid who came to the ranch.

"It's really beautiful out here."

"This is my first time riding on a horse. I was scared at first, but it's pretty fun."

"I'm happy I got this chance. I always wanted to try it."

Ai spoke very carefully and politely. The overall impression Mai got was that she was a smart young lady who had been raised well.

She heeded all the directions about riding a horse and kept to them strictly. If she was this good her first time riding, she could develop into a master rider if given the chance—even better than Mai, perhaps.

They wore riding helmets in case of a fall, as well as airbag vests that would deploy to protect them. But the horses were calm and slow enough that it wasn't likely to happen.

"Good. Very good," Mai murmured, deciding to pick up the pace a little.

Their horses were an indigenous Hokkaido breed known as Dosanko. They were smaller and squatter than the famous Thoroughbred and alternated opposite front and rear legs at the same time, leading to a very stable walk.

The two horses and their escort, the office's large mutt, George, passed through the pasture's gentle hills, taking a narrow trail through the woods and down across the valley.

"This really is fun. I'm glad I came to Hokkaido," said Ai, her pale face smiling.

"I'm glad to hear it! It always makes my day when a visitor says that." Mai beamed back.

After the forest, they proceeded through fallow farmland and flat plains. George led the way, the two horses following side by side.

Ai began to talk about herself unprompted. "I don't go to school because I hate it. But everything else is fun. I think you should give everything a try. Except for school."

If she had mentioned that she hated school twice within seconds, it must run pretty deep. Mai pushed her own fond memories out of her mind and replied, "Well, I suppose it might be irresponsible of me to say 'Then you don't have to go there,' so I won't. What other places do you like?"

Ai was right beside her at this point, offering a clear view of her face as she said, "Outside of the time that I have to study, I like listening to music, cooking for myself and my family, reading books on the Internet, and watching movies. I also play full-dive VR games. I like all of those things."

"Ohhh," murmured Mai. She thought about mentioning that she played full-dive games, too, but decided to keep quiet about that.

If she mentioned what game she played, the girl would probably ask what her avatar's name was. And she did not want anyone but her friends to know about the vicious infamy of Shirley.

"I won't say what game it is I usually play," said Ai, who was very smart to keep that private, "but I love how I can be a different person in the game. I'm not a weak and cowardly girl; I'm a tough, cool lady."

"Yeah, yeah, I—"

Mai started to say *I get that*, but she changed her mind and finished, "I think that's interesting."

Yikes, that was close, Mai thought, looking up. *You don't see sky this blue in* GGO.

"The thing I've learned most from playing games...," Ai continued. She clearly wanted to talk, so Mai let her go. If the girl wanted to speak, then that reduced the amount of thinking Mai had to do.

"...is that everyone is dirty. Including me."

"Pardon?"

"Um, let me try to explain. In an online game, all kinds of people play characters in the game world, but since it's not real life, you can do anything. You can act good, or you can act dirty."

"That's true. That makes sense. And?" Mai asked, getting sucked into the conversation despite herself.

"Well, I assume you wouldn't know this, but in a full-dive game, you can't have an avatar of the opposite sex."

"Ohhh," Mai responded, pretending she hadn't known that.

"Since I have a female avatar, I get all kinds of comments from different guys. Most of them are nasty."

No surprise, Mai nearly remarked aloud. Plenty of men had made glib comments to Shirley that they would never make in real life, just because it was a game and they could get away with it. They still did it.

Ai had probably endured the same unpleasant experiences. She might play a sexy grown woman as an avatar, but it was still a fifteen-year-old girl on the inside. It was appalling that anyone would say such things to a child—but they had no way of knowing, of course. That was one of the downsides of an online game where you couldn't see the real player.

From her spot atop the horse's back, Ai continued, "But I'm just as dirty as them."

"What?"

Mai looked over and saw the girl's pale face staring right at her. She was calm and collected, but it seemed like there was a faint smile playing over her features.

"I know the dirty thoughts those men harbor, and I've decided to make use of it. I have no problem doing nasty things with my avatar, because it's not the real me. It has nothing to do with me. If anything, it's fun to get to do things I can't do in real life."

Ummm...

Mai wasn't sure how to react to this. She did not want to promote this behavior, but she couldn't deny that the most fun part of playing Shirley was the pleasure of all those activities she couldn't normally do.

"What do you do?"

"I got my avatar dressed really sexy—you can't get naked in the game, so it's just underwear—and showed it to a teammate of mine, then used that to blackmail him. I used a recording item to capture a really embarrassing and pathetic sound clip of him and told him I'd upload it to the Net. So I forced him to be on my squad and got him to pay me in-game money and items. He did things for me that I could never ask for in real life. It made my character supertough really fast."

Yikes!

Mai was freaked out. This was quite an admission.

A girl in her third year of junior high engaging in honeypot behavior in an online game? Very sketchy.

But then again...

Mai considered that she probably lacked the caution that an

older person would have because she was so young. Mentally, she was still basically a child.

And Mai knew from going through junior high herself that girls were more mature than boys at that age.

If she hung out at home on the Internet all the time, she'd end up as a precocious young lady, absorbing information from beyond her generation because she wasn't around her peers all the time at school. At that age, the brain was like a sponge.

Mai thought back on how she'd spent her younger days running around outside all the time. With all due respect to Ai, Mai was very glad that she'd chosen to be a horse girl instead.

She tried to find a way to wrap up the topic. "Ah, I see. So you can do that in a game, huh? Well, it might not be the most moral behavior, but it's not like it's illegal or anything, as long as it's all part of the game and not spilling over into real life."

"Oh, definitely. I don't want to make things any worse for my mom and dad."

"That's good. I'm relieved to hear that. Have you told anyone else about this?"

"No."

"Then I'm the first and the last. I won't tell anyone, and the horses and George are good boys. They'll keep your secret."

"You won't scold me?" asked Ai.

"Do you want me to?"

"I don't know."

"Then I won't. See, I'm not such a perfectly mature person that I can tell anyone else how to live their life. The only thing I can teach you how to do here is horse riding."

"Then let me ask you. Do you think I should keep doing this? Or should I force myself to be like everyone else, suck it up and deal with the school that I hate, and live like a normal person, starting tomorrow?"

Mai understood that this was the question Ai had wanted to ask her most of all. She had told the riding instructor all these things about herself so that she could make this urgent inquiry.

"Let's see. Here's what I can say to you," Mai began, obliging her. "Don't worry so much. You gotta take it easy and enjoy your life!"

They were still talking when they reached a river. It was a shallow, small stream, running where the plain dipped a little. George happily splashed his way across it, followed by the two horses, Mai taking the lead at a gentle pace.

"Upstream from here, there's a place right by the river that has a natural spring. Sometimes my friends and I go in," Mai said, changing the subject.

Ai's eyes lit up. "That sounds amazing! I want to try that!"

"Exactly! That's what I thought the first time I heard about it! But it's way up in the middle of the mountains, so it takes over three hours to get there, even on a horse. And you have to do three deep-river crossings. Only college students with riding experience can go there, with a guide."

"So it won't be for a long time…"

"And until then, you just enjoy other things, okay? Enjoy studying; enjoy your game. The hot spring isn't going anywhere."

"Will you still be a nature guide by the time I'm old enough, Mai?"

"I'm not really cut out for any other kind of work."

"That's good. I'm relieved. I'll try to figure out how not to worry about things so much. The next time I visit, I want you to teach me more about riding horses."

"You got it."

It was after noon, and the horse ride that had lasted much longer than anticipated was over. Slightly sunburned, Ai returned to her relieved mother, and they drove away.

However, before Ai got into the car, she turned back and gave Mai a very deep bow.

Next to Mai, the woman from the farm waved, beaming, until the car passed behind the windbreak at the property's edge. Then the woman turned to Mai and gasped, "Whew! You wouldn't believe all the questions and worries that rich mother had while we were waiting! She must have asked 'Is she okay? Is my daughter causing trouble?' at least thirty-two times!"

Mai stopped waving her hat and set it back on her head. "She'll be fine. Like I said earlier, she's a good kid."

"What did you talk about with her, Mai? Were you able to have a decent conversation?"

"Of course. She loved the scenery, and I made a promise to teach her more about horse riding the next time she comes."

"Oh my. So she'll be an annual visitor? A big spender?" The woman grinned. She was nothing if not a good businessperson.

"Perhaps she will be." Mai sincerely hoped as much anyway.

"If she does show up, you'll be her exclusive guide, Mai!" the woman declared, unaware of what Mai was thinking.

"That's fine. Will you give me a raise for it?"

"Hmm, we'll have to talk about that! For now, how about a late lunch?"

* * *

It was two thirty PM on Saturday, August 29th, 2026.

Karen was at the entrance to a shopping mall in Tokyo.

She was dressed in reasonably fashionable clothes, plus the necklace she'd gotten from Saki and the girls.

For a date with Fire.

Three days earlier, her time in SJ4 had ended when she died from getting her eye crushed by a zombie, sending her back to the waiting area. But the event itself concluded before Llenn had time to chat with her defeated teammates. ZEMAL had won.

P-chan was at her feet again, and then she was back in the bar.

They'd started in a private room, so the original four were back in the same place. Shirley had been in the waiting area, but she'd gotten sent to a different location and was nowhere to be seen.

The next thing Llenn heard was the bustle of the audience in the bar. The crowd was cheering for ZEMAL over their victory. Llenn cracked the door a bit to listen.

"Way to go, you guys!"

"You're the besssst!"

"Congrats on winning!"

"If I buy a machine gun, let me join your squadron!"

"Will you go on a date with me, lady?"

"I believe in you! I knew you'd win one day! I always knew you had it, from the very first Squad Jam!"

"That is definitely a lie."

The crowd was in rare form, yelling whatever they felt like. The men of ZEMAL looked slightly guilty, standing amid so much adulation.

Thane, the player who did his own commentary, said, "Let's have an interview with the winning team! We'll start with the lady over there who gave such brilliant tactical orders! What was the main ingredient in your victory, would you say? Was it your strategy?"

He thrust a tiny microphone into Vivi's face. She smoothly replied, "What? It's because they all played so well. I was only able to lead the team as effectively as I did because they shut up and followed my commands."

Everyone was so focused on this little scene, hanging on Vivi's every word, that nobody seemed to have any interest in the fourth-place team.

That was fortunate because it allowed Llenn's group to don robes and sneak out of their private room and then the building.

As they walked down the dimly lit alley, Pitohui said, "Okay, shall we have an after-party where we talk about how we got our asses kicked? Let's go get drinks! It's on M!"

However, Llenn declined. "Sorry, Pito. I've been in this dive for too long—I'm tired. I'll log off."

"Oh, that's too bad. Well, thanks for playing! It was fun! You can keep the pistols!"

"See ya next time, Llenn!"

"You did well today."

"Thanks, everyone. I'll find a way to thank you properly later!" Llenn said as she went into the window to log off.

Pitohui asked, "Oh yeah! What are you gonna do about the date with him?"

As she vanished, Llenn said, "I keep my word."

She didn't have time at the end of the Squad Jam to ask for Fire Nishiyamada's contact information—but she didn't need to ask her father for that.

A simple search of his distinctive name on the Internet turned up a hit for his company right away. There were also interviews with him on business news sites. More than a few, in fact.

Karen went to his company website and saw a picture of Nishiyamada, surrounded by many of his employees. It was the kind of photo that graduating students took with their teacher.

Over a hundred employees, all of them extremely happy, smiling as though their fat little company president was their pride and joy.

Karen sent an e-mail to the company address and received a response in two minutes.

At Nishiyamada's suggestion, their first date was at a shopping mall in the middle of Tokyo.

The weather had been expected to be poor on Saturday, and the forecast was spot-on. It was raining like crazy outside. A date at the mall, where everything could happen indoors, was very welcome.

Karen was able to take the subway straight from her apartment building to the mall without setting foot outside. And this was a place with a movie theater, aquarium, and restaurants to spare.

Nishiyamada's careful, precise message had suggested that the afternoon get-together would only last two hours.

And the date ended up being nothing more than drinking tea at an open café along the spacious thoroughfare.

Karen had no experience or knowledge of how to date. Still, she found this a very casual and low-stakes invitation, compared to rushing into a romance, seeing a movie, or having dinner at a fancy restaurant.

Karen had already reported the news to Miyu over the phone.

"Okay, that sounds good, right? It's a public place, so he won't like, push you up against a wall or hug you or try to drag you somewhere. Anyway, good luck. I'm worried, so I wish I could be there at the next table over to keep an eye out. If only I didn't have sudden plans on that day…"

"It's fine! Don't come all the way to Tokyo just for that! When it's over…I'll let you know how it went."

"All right. Anyway, this date is just a tea party. Don't get all nervous just because it's your first time, okay? I go in humming casually, every single time. I ask whatever I want, whenever I feel like it, and if the guy sucks, I'll tell him."

"Ohhh, I get it… So that's why…"

"Hmm? Why what?"

"Never mind. Also, just to be doubly double sure…"

"What's with all the doubles? Go on."

"Don't tell Elza and Goushi, all right?"

"Sure thing! I won't tell them! I'll only write it to them in text form."

"That's not what I said."

"Well, I doubt they have that much free time anyway. They're not going to go spy on you if they find out!"

It turned out they had plenty of free time.

Spectators were watching from a different restaurant on the

other side of the mall thoroughfare at a table all the way in the back.

They were Miyu Shinohara, fresh off a morning flight from Hokkaido, Goushi Asougi, and Elza Kanzaki. Each of them was in disguise, however, so they didn't look like their usual selves.

Miyu was wearing a long blond wig, flashy glasses, and a colorful outfit.

Goushi was in his usual suit, but he had a thick beard and was also wearing a wig. The wig was salt-and-pepper, so he looked like he was in his forties. The addition of sports sunglasses was bizarre and did not look good.

Elza Kanzaki wore a hat pulled low plus a face mask: the classic method of going incognito. They hadn't dressed up like this before coming, of course; each had snuck to the bathroom to change.

Plates covered their table, emptied of the food they'd carried. The group had been here for over an hour already.

It was 2:40. Nishiyamada, dressed in a suit, had taken a seat at the café twenty minutes ahead of schedule.

"So...what will become of Kohi and her boy toy? Oh, that rhymed," Miyu babbled.

She spied Karen arriving eighteen minutes ahead of schedule.

The waiter guided her to the table, where she sat at a right angle to her partner.

"I'm sorry for being late," Goushi suddenly murmured.

Miyu spun around in surprise. "Hwuh?"

"No...I just got here, too," Goushi continued, so Elza explained.

"He can read lips. He can't see that closely from here, of course, so we put a tiny camera inside the planter earlier. He's watching the footage on his glasses lens."

"Holy crap! How can he do that? Why does he have spy skills?" Miyu asked, twice shocked.

"They're stalker techniques and gadgets."

"Ugh! What the hell!" Miyu exclaimed, doubly disgusted. "I *really* think you should reconsider your relationships, ma'am."

"Perhaps you're right."

"I mean, this is crazy. The police could show up right now and arrest him."

"Maybe they will."

But Goushi ignored the degrading commentary from his companions and continued to read Nishiyamada's and Karen's lips. "'Thanks for coming today.' 'Well, we made a deal.' 'That's right—thank you.'"

"On the other hand, this is great. Makes it so much easier for me to send messages!" said Miyu, who had her smartphone under the table, where she was blasting out a text to someone with rapid taps.

The message currently read: THEY'RE STARTING! FIRST UP, NICE CASUAL GRIEVING! THAT'S SUPPOSED TO BE GREETINGS! AUTOCORRECT!

"Messages? To whom?"

"Boss and the girls. They spent so much time helping us, I couldn't say no when they wanted to hear how it was going. I bet they're all together at one of their houses, hanging on my every word!"

Tall, thin Karen and short, squat Nishiyamada.

The odd couple naturally attracted a certain amount of attention. The other guests at the café glanced their way, and virtually everyone walking past their table in the mall itself looked at them.

However, Karen did not pay them any mind. Right now, her job was to have a proper conversation with this man.

The gentle herb tea she'd ordered arrived at the table. Karen picked up the dainty teacup and took a tiny sip.

"Mmmm."

Nishiyamada, meanwhile, did not drink at all.

He was wearing an uncharacteristically stern expression, though Karen had only met him once before, so she wasn't sure. The man was thinking something over.

Or perhaps he was extremely nervous.

Maybe she was the one who was feeling more relaxed here, Karen mused. She decided to say what she'd meant to tell him if they ever met again. She'd gotten the idea two days ago, thinking that none of this meant anything if she didn't say this first.

She turned to her right to look at him and stated, "Mr. Nishiyamada…I mean, Fire. I think it might be easier for me to say it, if you don't mind."

Goushi relayed the dialogue.

"Whoa, whoa, Kohi, already on a first-name basis? That's kinda cute! You're gonna get a guy interested!" Miyu said, worked up.

Elza remarked, "Maybe that's what she's after. Very crafty, Karen."

"What? No way. Holy crap, Kohi's turning into one of those bewitching vixens!"

"That's just fine. I don't mind at all, Karen," replied Nishiyamada, who didn't seem as confident as before. Still, he gave her a stiff smile, and she bobbed her head.

"I came here to have a proper talk with you," she began, "but I want to say something first. It's what I wanted to say at the end of the game."

"Wh-what is she launching into…?" Miyu wondered, leaning back in her chair. She was worried.

"Is she going to say she loves him first?" posited Elza excitedly, leaning forward.

Goushi quoted, "'All of the teammates that you had on your alliance fought very hard for your sake. So I want to say sorry for being rude to you.'"

"Whut?"

Nishiyamada just stared at Karen in silence, allowing her to continue.

"Please offer my apology to all of them. From the start of the event, I thought they were just mercenaries, people you hired to fight...but I was completely wrong. They were your employees, your friends, your companions...and it wasn't until the very, very end that I finally realized they were working for you out of friendship, not for money. And you got them all together with a simple word. I felt ashamed of myself. I have a new respect for you."

"......"

It was a while before Nishiyamada actually spoke again.

"'All right. I'll tell them. I promise. I'm sure they'll all be thrilled to hear that.'"

"What is she talking about...?" Miyu asked, aghast.

"This is just like Karen, though." Elza grinned, presumably. She was still wearing the mask.

"Thank you. I'm relieved that I was able to get that off of my chest," Karen admitted. She lifted her cup and took a quiet sip of herbal tea.

She'd done what she needed to do. And now...

They could see Karen turn her chair to face Nishiyamada directly.

"Oh crap! Kohi's totally in 'love-acceptance mode'! That's the expression of a woman who wants to say yes!" wailed Miyu, making a face like the man from Munch's *The Scream*.

"Very astute of you, Miyu. You understand how it goes."

"Exactly. How many times do you think I've been in that position? I just never expected to see Kohi like this..."

"'Karen, I just have one question for you,'" Goushi said, repeating Nishiyamada's words.

"Yes?"

Karen straightened her spine, waiting for what would come next.

She was prepared for whatever it might be. Ready to answer.

However, what Nishiyamada asked took her slightly aback.

"The Karen that's here now...and Llenn in *GGO*... Which is the real you?"

It wasn't an inquiry she'd been expecting, but the answer came to her immediately. There was no doubt in Karen's heart—she had only one response. It had been true since the day she'd cut her hair. Or perhaps since the day she'd beaten Boss? Either one worked.

She put a hand to her chest and answered, "Both are me."

"Um...I'm really sorry... I think... Er, excuse me. Please hear me out...," Nishiyamada stammered, suddenly much less sure of himself.

"Huh?"

Karen's mouth hung open in a rather unflattering way. In other words, agape.

"'Um...I'm really sorry... I think... Er, excuse me. Please hear me out...,'" Goushi said, suddenly more polite.

"Hwa?"

Miyu's mouth hung open in a rather unflattering way. Basically, agape.

"Um, well, you see... Gosh, this is very hard to say..."

"Huh? Go ahead..."

"Um, I'm afraid you'll have to excuse me..."

"Huh?"

Nishiyamada stood up. Even when he was standing, his face was only level with Karen's while she was seated. There were huge beads of sweat on his face.

"Um, are you feeling unwell?" Karen questioned.

"I'm sorry!" Nishiyamada stated. He promptly gave a quick bow and bolted away from the table. Though extremely flustered, he still had the presence of mind to take the bill with him to the register to pay.

When he was finished, he left without a backward glance.

"What…?"

Karen could only watch him go.

What happened to Fire? Does he have an upset stomach? Was the drink he just had no good? Or is he feeling unwell because he spent so much time in the unfamiliar environment of a VR game?

Karen was left alone to ponder the answer. She had experienced poor health as a result of too much VR, too.

At this point, she could easily go four or five hours at a time, but at first, if she was online for even two, she would suffer terrible headaches and mild dizziness from the time she logged off until the next day. Miyu had told her it was muscle pain for her brain, but she didn't know if that was what it truly was.

Karen considered the possibilities.

Was nearly three hours of constant battle in SJ4 way too much stimulation for someone who had never played VR games before? If so, it was possible that the full aftereffects hadn't hit Nishiyamada until just now.

If he had rushed off for medical help, should she have gone with him? Karen suddenly realized that was the right choice, and she hurriedly got up to leave—but then her smartphone went off in her purse.

She stopped to look at the screen, thinking that the message might be from him. Sure enough, the name Nishiyamada, which she'd registered the other day, was there on the screen, but it was a text, not a call.

"Is that from Fire? What does it say?" she heard Miyu say.

"Hang on. I'll open it right now."

"Okay."

Karen tapped the screen to call up the message. Before she read it, she suddenly looked up.

"Uh?"

Karen then uttered the funniest sound she'd ever made in her life. *"Obloo!"*

Three very fishy-looking people were standing nearby.

And on closer examination, she recognized all of them.

The trio slipped into the empty seats at the table. Elza, her face hidden behind a mask, had dragged the waiter with them so she could order "Three of the same."

The way he silently nodded, removed Nishiyamada's cup, and left spoke to his professionalism.

Karen's mouth trembled and chattered. "Wha—?! Wha-wha-wha-wha-wha-wha-wha-wha—?"

Miyu reached out and squashed Karen's cheeks between her hands.

"Wmurp."

"C'mon, you can save your surprise for later. Let's get to that juicy message, yeah?"

Miyu let go, and Karen gave her a dazzling smile.

"Miyu, I'm going to destroy you later."

"Yeah, yeah, later. I mean, no, you don't have to do that at all. Just read the message, yeah? There might be something incredible in there."

"Incredible?"

"Yeah… Like, 'I left all of a sudden because I have a surprise present! I bought out an entire flower shop just for you!' or 'Let's go on a vacation overseas! We'll fly first class!'"

"Um, what?"

"Or maybe it's something simpler, like 'Sorry, this is really embarrassing, but I got so nervous that my stomach cramped up. But it's all because I love you so much…' You know?"

"…Um, I doubt it has anything to do with love…"

"Look, just read the dang thing. Nothing's going to happen unless you read it."

"Grr…"

She hated to do what Miyu was telling her, but Karen acquiesced and looked down at the screen.

She read the text.

It said…

* * *

"Miyu's messages have stopped…," Saki stated with dread.

The rest of SHINC—Kana, Shiori, Moe, Risa, Milana—were there in her room with her, dressed in their high school uniforms.

It wasn't a very big room, so the girls were all seated in a circle on the floor. The population density was quite high.

Saki was gazing at her smartphone with the other five around her, waiting on every update. Miyu had been delivering messages on the status of Karen's date, but the last one had been about three minutes ago.

What was happening to Karen?

Had Nishiyamada cleverly tricked her with honeyed words, taking her to the kind of place that good high school girls should never go?

What if he found out Miyu was there, too, and took them both with him?! To a place where good high school girls should never go! Just to take a "rest"!

Saki's imagination was running away with her when the object in her hands finally buzzed.

"Here we go!"

"What does it say?!" all five other members of SHINC demanded in unison. The gym team was very coordinated.

"Wait, young ladies…wait… I'll read it now," placated Saki, slowly and carefully examining the screen. Then she repeated the words verbatim.

"'Bring everyone here.'"

"Huh?" all five of them asked.

Saki said, "Hang on, there's a link here," and hesitantly reached a slender finger to tap it. "You don't think it's…the 'rest' area…?"

What popped up on her screen hardly cleared up the confusion. It was the glitzy home page of a karaoke place at a big train station three stops away.

* * *

Fifteen minutes later, the bare minimum of time necessary to complete their travel, Saki and her friends were at the karaoke place, still dressed in their uniforms.

At the counter, they announced they were with the Shinohara party and were guided to the building's top floor. Along the way, the girls argued about what could have happened, but there was no consensus.

"Pardon us…," they said as they opened the door to the private room.

Dun, daka-dun!

Sitting there, dramatically strumming an acoustic guitar, was a short woman wearing a white mask and a large hat that hid her features.

"……"

Next to her, back painfully straight, was a handsome young man in a suit, tapping a tambourine to the beat.

"Huff…huff…"

Karen stood with a mic in her hand, breathing heavily.

"Yo, gang! You made it! That was quick!" called Miyu, who smiled and beckoned the girls inside.

The song had just finished, the last note fading out. The fishy-looking woman playing the guitar gave the chord a final flourish.

There was no next song cued up, so the karaoke room went quiet.

"Um…what's going on…?" Saki inquired. It was a bit awkward, so they didn't walk through the door.

"Oh, it's okay—just come in. C'mon, gang, pack in," urged Miyu, pushing the guitarist and the handsome man together so that there was space for the teens to sit down. It was a reasonably spacious area, but ten occupants was creeping up on maximum occupancy.

"In that case, pardon us…"

Saki went first, and the six girls in their summer uniforms filed bashfully in and sat on the sofa.

The karaoke room was pretty eerie.

You had this ominous woman whose eyes were only visible through a strip between her mask and hat. Her gaze was all but beaming at the members of SHINC. The handsome man sat extremely straight and did not say a word.

They had no idea who these people were or why they were here. It was kind of scary.

"Oh, you guys are here… Welcome…," said Karen, greeting them lifelessly with dead-fish eyes. Now things were getting into horror movie territory.

Out of all of them, only Miyu seemed to be acting normally. "Oh, you girls will want some drinks, right? It's an open tab, so order whatever beverages you want! The adults are paying today, so don't feel bad about it!"

"Th-thanks, we appreciate it…"

SHINC used the special terminal for ordering to get drinks for the group. The beverages were delivered to the room right away. Perhaps this booth was right next to the kitchen?

The employee was utterly unfazed by the chaotic sight of a bunch of high school girls mingling with the four creepy adults.

The staffer merely stated "Enjoy your time!" before leaving with a smile.

"Um…Karen, Miyu…can we ask…what happened…?" Saki questioned, very unsure if it was, in fact, okay to ask.

The silent, handsome man and the masked woman with the smiling eyes were scary, but the girls chose not to look at them.

"Well, here's the thing… Kohi, you mind if I borrow your phone? It's probably quickest to show them, y'know?" said Miyu, prodding Karen as the tall girl slurped some iced tea.

"Mm," grunted Karen, straw in her mouth. She handed over the phone.

Miyu took it, moved over next to the high schoolers, and tried to show the text to them, when—*dun-dun-dundunnn!*

"Eek!"

The gymnasts flinched when the masked woman abruptly riffed on the guitar.

"Hey, Sis! Don't tease the young'uns!" Miyu scolded. That just raised more questions.

Was she Miyu's older sister? They'd never heard about her having one. Or was she Karen's older sister, the one who lived in the same apartment building? Was the handsome man her husband?

Mysteries abounded in the karaoke room, but the two strangers' identities were not the most important one.

"This is the message that Fire Nishiyamada sent to Karen earlier…," Miya explained.

Saki and the others huddled together to look at the phone screen.

This was the message they saw:

IF KAREN AND LLENN ARE THE SAME PERSON, THEN I THINK I'M AFRAID OF YOU.

I DON'T THINK I CAN BE WITH YOU.

I'M REALLY SORRY.

PLEASE, JUST FORGET ABOUT ME.

I'M REALLY SORRY.

"Huh?" "Hweh?" "Hoy?" "Augh?" "What?" "Why?"

Saki, Kana, Shiori, Risa, Milana, and Moe all expressed their feelings at once.

They were in perfect synchronization, but each one uttered a different sound.

"Whaaaaaaat?! What is that supposed to mean?!" Saki exploded, her pigtails swinging.

"Well, basically, as you know, Kohi kept her word and went on this date, but before it even got to the point of giving a yes-or-no answer to his question, he completely dumped her and left her hanging," Miyu explained unceremoniously.

Of course, to Miyu, dumping or being dumped was as natural and familiar as breathing, so it was no big deal to her.

"B-but…"

Saki had watched the replay, so she knew what Llenn had done after their one-on-one duel. Even so, refusing to be with Karen over something like that?

Just because of that…? Only that…? Okay, to be fair, it was pretty freaky.

Saki had no words. Fortunately, Miyu was there to freshen things up.

"Well, what's done is done! And that's why we're holding this fancy event: the Comforting the Rejected Woman Karaoke Special! And now that you know what's going on, you have to participate, too!"

"I-in that case, we'd be happy to! We're on your side, Karen! Hang in there!" Saki shouted. The rest of the gymnastics team added their own words of encouragement.

"We're here with you! Don't feel down!"

"Let us sing with you, Karen!"

"We're here for you!"

"Yeah, totally!"

"I'll do whatever I can to help!"

Despite the teenagers' sympathy and comfort, Karen was totally dead eyed. "Ha-ha-ha… Yeah…um…thanks…"

The necklace she'd received as a present dangled around her neck.

"Well, now that we're all here…"

Daka-daka-dun!

"Let's sing a song to get you pumped up!" shouted the masked woman with the guitar.

"Um…I hate to be rude, but," Saki began, finally summoning the courage to ask what she so desperately wanted to know. "Who are those two…?"

The rest of the team sent silent gazes that all but spoke *Way to go, Captain! Thanks for asking!*

The mystery woman replied, "Members of SHINC! Greetings! I am the woman known in that distant world by the name of Pitohui! Next to me is M! Nice to meet you!"

"Whaaaat? Is that t-true, Miyu?" Saki gasped. The others

looked just as shocked. None of them seemed to believe what they had heard.

"Yup, it's true. I've known her in real life for a little while now, actually," Miyu admitted casually, and it didn't sound like a joke for once. If she had looked dead serious and tried to be convincing, *then* the teens would have assumed it was a fib.

"Allow me to introduce you. This is Pito's player, and the handsome guy next to her is M's player."

Goushi rose to his feet. "It's a pleasure, everyone. We owe you quite a lot for all the experiences we've had during the various Squad Jams. I'm very pleased to have the chance to meet you in person," he said, bowing politely. The girls bowed back automatically.

"Oh my gosh…um, hello. What can I say…?"

"You're fine! We know what you want to say already!" shouted the strange woman in the hat, although the girls did not know what *she* was going to say. "I can tell you apart! I already knew from the conversation that you were SHINC, but I can tell who's who! From the left, it's Boss, Sophie, Rosa, Tanya, Tohma, and Anna."

"Oh my!" SHINC exclaimed, each member wide-eyed.

"How can you tell?" Miyu asked the woman.

"By the vibe. Their appearances might be different in the real world, but the subtle movements each of them makes comes through. It's just the way they carry themselves."

"Wow. That's amazing," Miyu praised. Then she went ahead and introduced Saki and the team by their real names. In true athletic fashion, they bolted to their feet one by one as their names were called, and each bowed vigorously.

Once Moe had finished and sat down, Milana asked, "That guitar of yours is the Elza Kanzaki model, isn't it?"

Elza Kanzaki's famous acoustic guitar had special stickers on the frets that looked like a white cat walking along the fretboard and leaving footprints behind.

The other team members nodded along, indicating that they had noticed this as well.

"That's right! You have an excellent eye!"

"Heh-heh! We all love Elza Kanzaki!" Milana stated proudly.

"Aw, that's so sweet! But you might not after today," responded the woman.

Milana took that to be a joke and smiled innocently. "Why? Of course I will!"

Saki snorted and said, "We're just as big fans of Elza Kanzaki as Karen and Miyu are! Believe it! Our dream is to go see an Elza Kanzaki concert together one day!"

"That sounds wonderful!"

Da-da-da-dun, the masked woman strummed.

Behind her, Karen finished drinking her iced tea and inputted a new song on the karaoke machine. There were no other tracks queued in the list, so the title immediately popped up on the big screen.

Karen had chosen Elza Kanzaki's "Independence."

"Ooh!" exclaimed the girls, leaning forward and clenching their fists. They all knew how to sing this one.

"Karen! We'll do the harmonies before the chorus!"

Da-da-da-dun.

"Then I'll play the guitar!" said the masked woman, and she ripped off her disguise.

"Huh?"

The six gymnasts stared dumbfounded as the intro melody began playing, the same as the one during the chorus.

Elza started playing her instrument along with the song—and yes, it was undoubtedly Elza Kanzaki herself.

"Eeeek!" the teens screamed, nearly loud enough to break the glass window of the door. They completely ignored the man jangling the tambourine next to Elza.

The shocking revelation that Pitohui was Elza Kanzaki was like a series of chain explosions in their brains. The song continued unabated during their freak-out.

As the intro from the speakers and acoustic guitar got louder, the six-foot-tall girl with the microphone got to her feet and said, "It's time for a song from Karen Kohiruimaki, the loser in romance!"

After all of my anguish
What am I, some tragic princess?
No way, that's not me

Karen's voice filled the room.

This was one of Elza Kanzaki's most energized rock tunes, but Karen was up to the task. She was belting out the lyrics like each line needed two exclamation points after it. It was aggressive and intense.

And her singing was good. Not as good as Elza's, of course, but quite passable for an amateur. The girls had not heard her sing before. They shared a look, then raised their hands and cheered, "Whoooo!"

Shiori and Risa grabbed the maracas and joined the rhythm section with Goushi's tambourine. Elza was banging away on the guitar, of course, but now she had a bit more sound behind it.

I had blind faith until I could see
Ideals, ideas, it's all fluid
But I know what I am, cogito ergo sum

She rocketed through the lyrics, and the song reached the part where the backup harmony came in before the chorus.

Accompanied by guitar courtesy of the singer herself, Saki and the gymnastics team added their voices.

(Of all the hundreds of choices)

Their coordination was perfect, adding a tremendous new depth to the performance.

Karen continued with her lyrics, determined not to fall short.

* * *

I think I'm losing sight

(There's only one decision)
Of the outline of life
(Of all the thousands of pressures)
The only thing that can feel it
(There's just one blow of resistance)
Is these fingers

The back-and-forth verse construction shared by the gymnastics team and Karen ended—and the soulful chorus began.

Karen knew all the words, so she didn't need to look at the screen. She closed her eyes, tears welling, and clenched the mic.

Rest in peace, Miyu thought, willing her friend's dead romance to the afterlife.

Don't discard it, I will keep it
The devil can't buy this
Independence I've won
It's meant to be, this breath, this pulse
Will stop one day, but when that is
I will never let fate decide for me

After the second chorus, the end of the melody played on the speakers, and Elza matched it on her guitar.

Karen had sung her heart out, face covered in sweat. Miyu patted her on the back.

"Nice singing, Karen! Listen…every night ends with the dawn."

"Awww…"

Karen really wanted to offer some retort to that, but she remained tough and swallowed her words.

"It's all right, Karen! You don't need a man to be happy!" exclaimed Elza, handing her precious guitar to Goushi and squirming past Miyu to get closer. "If you want, I can spend the night with you…"

That could be taken for an unwanted sexual advance—it certainly was—but Karen blocked the other woman's approach. All it took was her hand on Elza's face to keep her at bay.

"Mrgh!"

Elza struggled and writhed, much to the shock and consternation of the teenage girls.

"I'm going to keep living in *GGO*!" Karen yelled.

The mic was still in her hand, so the booming declaration resounded through the room.

The End

AFTERWORD
Gun Gale Diary: Part 9

Hello, everyone. I'm Keiichi Sigsawa, the author of this book.

It's been four months since the release of Volume 8. Has anything changed in your life?

Sword Art Online Alternative Gun Gale Online (hereafter "the series") has reached its ninth volume! I'm so happy.

And that means this Afterword *Gun Gale* Diary, where the author can write whatever he feels like, has also reached its ninth installment.

In the first eight installments of this segment, I mentioned how to dance when your back feels itchy, my favorite bullets, the fact that my ring finger is longer than my index finger, my recipe for turning thick sushi rolls into tempura, the easiest way to get to the moon in a rental car, and the fact that I had my first-ever three-part miniseries. We've covered a wide range of topics, beloved by all. And this time, the subject of choice is "the turbulent year of 2018."

If you are buying this book on the very day it comes out in Japan, it's early December.

2018 is coming to an end. In Japanese, the traditional name for this month is *Shiwasu*. It means "the teacher is running." This is because at the end of the year, even calm and mild-mannered instructors are bustling about, busy with their tasks.

I am writing this afterword in October, so I can only speak for the first ten months, but I want to make something very clear: 2018 has been the most turbulent year in the life of Keiichi Sigsawa!

I have never known a crazier time. I cannot recall one.

I completed an astonishing amount of work in 2018.

The reason, as I mentioned in the previous volume, was the *GGO* anime.

I had perfect attendance on recording and overdub sessions. I went to every single one.

To my surprise, I also was tasked with writing a script, so I did my best and made my animation screenwriter debut with episode 5.5!

I also penned a special story that came packed with the sixth DVD/Blu-ray!

I worked very hard on promoting the original airing in April, and then the re-airing in July. My Twitter account really came in handy for that. If I didn't have one, I'd just be yelling through a loudspeaker outside my local train station. I guess that'd make me no different from any other weirdo.

Among all of this, I received news that made me just as happy as the anime series itself.

Tokyo Marui, Japan's most famous air gun manufacturer, put out official *GGO* merchandise…the pink electric air gun P90 Version Llenn!

I can't believe that my story has its own real-life air gun made by an official manufacturer…

I'm so happy. This is the feeling of true fulfillment. I got to hug P-chan. It did not speak to me. It must be because I'm not Llenn.

I got to write a bonus short story packed in with that product, too. You better believe I was pumped up for that one!

But of course the thing I worked on the hardest was the book in your hands at this very moment, *GGO* 9.

SJ4 has ended at last, I wonder how it went?

This book's a thick one, isn't it? I needed all those pages to get the entire plot written out. *GGO* 3 was very hefty, too, but this one just barely surpasses it in length.

There was so much writing and so little time that we nearly ended up having Volume 7 (Part One), then Volume 8 (Part Two), followed by 9 (Part Three, First Half) and 10 (Part Three, Second Half). But I kept it together and got it done—barely.

And now, I'd like to talk about the pistols Llenn is shooting on the cover of this book. (Incidentally, this is the very first *GGO* cover that features Llenn actually firing a gun.)

To explain without spoiling anything, the weapons are of custom design, modified versions of an existing handgun called the Detonics.

I had their design done by Kouji Akimoto, who also worked on the Flute, a fictional modular semi-auto rifle that Kino uses in *Kino's Journey*, as well as the gun illustrations that appeared at the end of *GGO* 3.

Akimoto's job with Tokyo Marui is designing fictional firearms that aren't based on real ones. He showed me pictures of a gun that he had announced at a previous event.

It was so cool that my blood pressure rose to a dangerous level. I requested permission to have Llenn use it in my book and received it.

Akimoto, Tokyo Marui, thank you so much for this!

I asked him if he could paint it pink because Llenn would be using it in the story, and at my request, he also added a white line on the "ear" of the gun to match Llenn's hat.

While writing SJ4, I was continually asking myself *What would be the right sort of pistol for Llenn to use?* because I wasn't sure of the answer. I'm delighted with the final gun. Or, uh, guns.

Look forward to more pistol action!

But while my year was hyper-charged with *GGO*, let's go back to early July, when I was invited to attend Anime Expo, the largest anime convention in the United States.

For the first time in my life, I went to Los Angeles!

The previous year, I went to Crunchyroll Expo in San Francisco for the *Kino's Journey* anime. For the second year in a row, I was overseas during the summer.

And let me tell you, Los Angeles was *hot*…

California is hot in general, but I happened to be visiting during a record-breaking heat wave. Even the locals were sick of it.

I got to experience something you'll never feel in Japan: According to my heat sensor, it reached 109 degrees Fahrenheit. (Of course, in Japan, we have our own swampy sort of heat…)

After the event, I got a full day to go sightseeing, so I took the opportunity to visit a firing range for the first time in a while. I got to use lots of guns for the first time. It was very interesting.

Doing research is crucial. I'll have to set up another visit to Guam, I think. This Sigsawa guy sure loves his research.

Let's not mention that I kept buying more ammunition to fire while I had my attending staff waiting in the heat.

And that was how my 2018 was hyper-charged with *GGO*.

Admittedly, at the same time, I went through some very big events in my private life. I mentioned this on Twitter, but I'll detail a little of it here, too.

At the end of 2017, my mother went into a coma after a long battle with an illness. She was hospitalized for two months before passing away.

My mother would always read my books. As soon as I got my

samples back, she would read them—probably the very first reader in the entire world of each of my works. And now she's gone. It hurts.

Perhaps some of you are aware, but when you get the box holding someone's cremated remains, it's still warm.

The warmth of my mother's skin while she was unconscious in the hospital. The coldness after she died. The warmth of the box when I held it.

I'll never forget 2018.

As for my mother, I'm sure she's making a name for herself after being reincarnated in another world. If you hear any rumors about her adventures, let me know.

I started with something sad, but there were many enjoyable things in my life this year, too.

While I was busy with work and visiting the hospital, I've got nothing but gratitude for the friends who joined me for dinners and traveling.

I hope we'll continue to enjoy things in 2019.

Around the time all the meetings started for the *Kino's Journey* anime (January 2017), I'd been leaving the house and eating out more often, as well as getting less exercise. Inevitably, I gained a lot of weight. I'm not in very good shape right now.

At my medical checkup, my doctor told me to slim down. At the time of writing this, I'm in the midst of a weight-loss regimen.

I wonder what the results will be by the time this book comes out. It's a contest against myself. Don't give up, me. Hang in there, me. You've got me on your side.

With that, it's time at last to conclude this column all about 2018.

I don't know what will be happening in the next volume

yet—but I'd really like to put out a short story collection for *GGO* sometime.

Shining the spotlight on minor characters, pursuing some unsolved mysteries, showing off Llenn from before SJ1, revealing how Karen and Miyu met in high school, and so on.

I've made it through many trials, and now I'm ready to charge into 2019. It's the end of the Heisei era, and a new imperial age is beginning.

That's all for now. Let's meet again in the next volume!

By the way, my next idea for this little column is "Using your computer monitor as a cutting board so you can see your food preparation and the recipe steps at the same time; isn't that convenient?" Look forward to that.

Keiichi Sigsawa

At some point, Llenn started experimenting with flower-pattern elbow and knee guards. She continues to pursue her own sense of fashion in GGO.
Sorry for making up design elements on my own...